THE CRITICS PRAISE
Robert Silverberg and

TOM O'BEDLAM

"Silverberg is our best . . . time and again he has expanded the parameters of science fiction."

—*Fantasy & Science Fiction*

"No matter if Silverberg is dealing with material that is practically straight fiction, or going way into the future . . . his is the hand of a master of his craft and imagination."

—*Los Angeles Times*

"Silverberg deftly develops and intermingles his characters . . . he writes fluently, even lyrically, of ecstatic experience. . . . He is a master painter of altered states tableau . . . a master, too, at describing alien life forms. . . . *Tom O'Bedlam* is good reading." —*Fantasy Review*

"Brilliantly imagined . . . one of the finest writers ever to work in science fiction." —*Philadelphia Inquirer*

more . . .

Winner of two Hugo Awards and four Nebula Awards, Robert Silverberg has long been acknowledged as one of the master writers of the science fiction field. The author of such contemporary science fiction classics as *Lord Valentine's Castle, Majipoor Chronicles* and *Valentine Pontifex*, and reteller of such archetypal tales as *Gilgamesh the King*, Mr. Silverberg is a well-respected editor and anthologist, a past president of the Science Fiction Writers of America, and a frequent guest at major science fiction conventions. Currently, he resides in Oakland, California.

ALSO BY ROBERT SILVERBERG

A Time of Changes*
Hawksbill Station
To Live Again*

Published by
WARNER BOOKS   *forthcoming

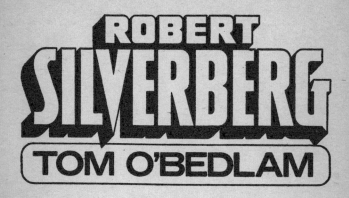

ROBERT SILVERBERG

TOM O'BEDLAM

WARNER BOOKS

A Warner Communications Company

This one's for Don

To consider the Earth the only populated world in infinite space is as absurd as to assert that in an entire field sown with millet only one grain will grow.

—Metrodoros the Epicurean
c. 300 b.c.

One

From the hag and hungry goblin
  That into rags would rend ye,
And the spirit that stands by the naked man
  In the book of moons, defend ye.
That of your five sound senses
  You never be forsaken
Nor wander from yourselves with Tom
  Abroad to beg your bacon.

While I do sing, "Any food, any feeding,
  Feeding, drink, or clothing?
    Come, dame or maid,
    Be not afraid.
Poor Tom will injure nothing."

—Tom O'Bedlam's Song

THIS time something had told Tom to try going westward. West was a good direction, he figured. You head for the sunset, maybe you can walk right off the edge into the stars.

Late on a July afternoon he came struggling up the slope of a steep dry wash and paused in a parched field to catch his breath and look around. This was about a hundred, hundred-fifty miles east of Sacramento, on the thirsty side of the mountains, in the third year of the new century. They said this was the century in which all the miseries were supposed finally to end. Maybe they really would, Tom thought. But you couldn't count on it.

Just up ahead he saw seven or eight men in ragged clothes, gathered around an old ground-effect van with jagged red-and-yellow lightning bolts painted on its rusting flanks. It was hard to tell whether they were repairing the van or stealing it, or both. Two of them were underneath, with their heads and shoulders poking into the propeller gearbox, and one was fiddling with the air intake filter. The rest were leaning against the van's rear gate in a cozy proprietary way. All of them were armed. No one paid any attention to Tom at all.

"Poor Tom," he said tentatively, testing the situation. "Hungry Tom." There didn't seem to be any danger, though out here in the wild country you could never be sure. He rocked back and forth on the balls of his feet, hoping one of them would notice him. He was a tall, lean, sinewy man with dark, tangled hair, somewhere around thirty-three, thirty-five years old: he gave various answers when he was asked, which wasn't often. "Anything for Tom?" he ventured. "Tom's hungry."

Still no one as much as glanced toward him. He might as well have been invisible. He shrugged and took his finger-piano from his pack, and began to strum the little metal keys. Quietly he sang:

> *Time and the bell have buried the day,*
> *The black cloud carries the sun away—*

They went on ignoring him. That was all right with Tom. It was a lot better than being beaten up. They could see he was harmless, and most likely they'd help him out, sooner or later, if only to get rid of him. People generally did, even the really wild ones, the killer bandidos: not even they would want to hurt a poor crazy simpleton. Sooner or later, he figured, they'd let him have a bit of bread and a gulp or two of beer, and he'd thank them and move onward, westward, toward San Francisco or Mendocino or one of those places. But five minutes more went by, and they continued not to acknowledge his presence. It was almost like a game they were playing with him.

Just then a hot, biting wind rose up suddenly out of the east. They paid attention to that. "Here comes the bad news breeze," muttered a short thick-featured red-haired man, and they all nodded and swore. "God damn, just what we need, a wind full of hard garbage," the red-haired man said. Scowling, glaring, he hunched himself down into his shoulders as if that would protect him from whatever radio-activity the wind might be carrying.

"Turn on the props, Charley," said one with blue eyes and rough, pitted skin. "Let's blow the stuff back into Nevada where it came from, hey?"

"Yeah. Sure," one of the others said, a little sour-faced Latino. "That's what we oughta do. Sure. Christ, blow it right back there."

Tom shivered. The wind was a mean one. The east wind always was. But it felt clean to him. He could usually tell when radiation was sailing on the wind that blew out of the dusted places. It set up a tingling sensation inside his skull, from an area just above his left ear to the edge of his eyebrow ridge. He didn't feel that now.

He felt something else, though, something that was get-ting to be very familiar. It was a sound deep in his brain, the roaring rush of sound that told him that one of his visions was starting to stir in him. And then cascades of green light began to sweep through his mind.

He wasn't surprised that it was happening here, now, in this place, at this hour, among these men. An east wind could do it to him, sometimes. Or a particular kind of light late in the day, or the coming of cold, clear air after a rainstorm. Or when he was with strangers who didn't seem to like him. It didn't take much. It didn't take anything at all, a lot of the time. His mind was always on the edge of some sort of vision. They were boiling inside him, ready to seize control when the moment came. Strange images and textures forever churned in his head. He never fought them any longer. At first he had, because he thought they meant he was going crazy. But by now he didn't care whether he was crazy or not, and he knew that fighting the visions would give him a headache at best, or if he struggled really hard he might get knocked to his knees, but in any case there was nothing he could do to keep the visions from coming on. It was impossible to hold them back, only to bang and jangle them around a little, and when he tried that he was the one who got most of the banging and jangling. Besides, the visions were the best thing that had ever happened to him. By now he loved his visions.

One was happening now, all right. Yeah. Yeah. Coming on now, for sure. The green world again. Tom smiled. He relaxed and yielded himself to it.

Hello, green world! Coming for to carry me home?

Golden-green sunlight glimmered on smooth alien hills. He heard the surging and crashing of a distant turquoise sea. The heavy air was thick as velvet, sweet as wine. Shining elegant crystalline forms, still indistinct but rapidly coming into sharp focus, were beginning to glide across the screen of Tom's soul: tall fragile figures that seemed to be fashioned of iridescent glass of many colors. They moved with astonishing grace. Their bodies were long and slender, with mirror-bright limbs sharp as spears. Their faceted eyes, glittering with wisdom, were set in rows of three on each of the four sides of their tapering diamond-shaped heads. It wasn't the first time Tom had seen them. He knew who they were: the aristocrats, the princes and dukes and countesses and such, of that lovely green place.

Through the vision he could still dimly make out the seven or eight scruffy men clustered around the ground-effect van. He had to tell them what he was seeing. He always did, whenever he was with other people when a vision struck. "It's the green world," he said. "You see the light? Can you? Can you? It's like a flood of emeralds pouring down from the sky." He stood with his legs braced far apart, his head thrown back, his shoulders curving around as if they were trying to meet behind him. Words spilled from his lips. "Look, there are seven crystallines walking toward the Summer Palace. Three females, two males, two of the other kind. Jesus, how beautiful! Like diamonds all up and down their skins. And their eyes, their eyes! Oh, God, have you ever seen anything so beautiful?"

"Hey, what kind of nut do we have here?" someone asked.

Tom barely heard. These ragged strangers hardly seemed real to him now. What was real was the lords and ladies of the green world, strolling in splendor through glades and mists. He gestured toward them. "That's the Misilyne Triad, d'ye see? The three in the center, the tallest. And that's Vuruun, who was ambassador to the Nine Suns under the old dynasty. And that one—oh, look there, toward the east! It's the green aurora starting! Jesus, it's like the sky's on fire burning green, isn't it? They see it too. They're all pointing, staring—you see how excited they are? I've never seen them excited before. But something like this—"

"A nut, all right. A real case. You could tell, right away, first thing when he walked up."

"Some of these crazies, they can get damn ugly when the fit's on them. I heard stories. They bust loose, you can't even tie them down, they're so strong."

"You think he's that bad?"

"Who knows? You ever see anybody this crazy?"

"Hey, crazy man! Hey, you hear me?"

"Let him be, Stidge."

"Hey, crazy man! Hey, nutso!"

Voices. Faint, far-off, blurred. Ghost-voices, buzzing and droning about him. What they were saying didn't matter. Tom's eyes were glowing. The green aurora whirled and blazed in the eastern sky. Lord Vuruun was worshipping it, holding his four translucent arms outstretched. The Triad was embracing. Music was coming from somewhere, now, a heavenly music resonating from world to world. The voices were only a tiny scratching sound lost somewhere within that great mantle of music.

Then someone hit him hard in the stomach, and he doubled over, gagging and gasping and coughing. The green world whirled wildly around him and the image began to break up. Stunned, Tom rocked back and forth, not knowing where he was.

"Stidge! Let him be!"

Another punch, even harder. It dizzied him. Tom dropped to his knees and stared with unfocused eyes at brown wisps of withered grass. A thin stream erupted from him. It felt like his guts ripping loose and spewing out of his mouth. It was a mistake to have let himself fall down, he knew. They were going to start kicking him now. Something like this had happened to him last year up in Idaho, and his ribs had been six weeks healing.

"Dumb—crazy—*nut*—"

"Stidge! Damn you, Stidge!"

Three kicks. Tom huddled low, fighting the pain. In some corner of his mind one last fragment of the vision remained, a sleek and gleaming crystalline shape, unrecognizable, vanishing. Then he heard shouts, curses, threats. He was aware that a fight was going on around him. He kept his eyes closed and drew his breath carefully, listening for the inner scrape of bone on bone. But nothing appeared to be broken.

"Can you stand up?" a quiet voice asked, a little while later. "Come on. Nobody's going to hurt you now. Look at me. Hey, guy, *look* at me."

Hesitantly Tom opened his eyes. A man whose face he did not know, a man with a short-cropped dense black beard and deep dark rings under his eyes—one of those who had been working inside the gearbox before, most likely—was crouching beside him. He looked just about as mean and rough as the others, but somehow there seemed to be something gentler about him. Tom nodded, and the man put his hands to Tom's elbows and delicately lifted him.

"Are you all right?"

"I think so. Just shook, some. More than some."

Tom glanced around. The red-haired man was slumped down by the side of the van, spitting up blood and glaring. The others were standing back in a loose semicircle, frowning uneasily.

"Who are you?" the black-bearded man asked.

"He's just a fucking nut!" the red-haired one said.

"Shut up, Stidge." To Tom the man said again, "What's your name?"

"Tom."

"Just Tom?"

Tom shrugged. "Just Tom, yeah."

"Tom from where?"

"Idaho, last. Heading for California."

"You're in California," the black-bearded man said. "You going toward San Francisco?"

"Maybe. I'm not sure. Doesn't matter a whole lot, does it?"

"Get him out of here," Stidge said. He was on his feet again. "God damn you, Charley, get that nut out of here before I—"

The black-bearded man turned. "Christ, Stidge, you're asking for a whole lot of trouble." He brought his right arm up across his chest and cocked it. There was a laser bracelet on his wrist, with the yellow "ready" light glowing. Stidge looked at it in astonishment.

"Jesus, Charley!"

"Just sit back down over there, man."

"Jesus, he's only a nut!"

"Well, he's *my* nut now. Anybody hurt him, he's gonna get hard light through his belly. Okay, Stidge?"

The red-haired man was silent.

Charley said to Tom, "You hungry?"

"You bet."

"We'll give you something. You can stay with us a few days, if you like. We'll be going toward Frisco if we can ever get this van moving." His dark-ringed eyes scanned Tom closely. "You carrying anything?"

Tom patted his backpack uncertainly. "Carrying?"

"Weapons. Knife, gun, spike, bracelet, anything?"

"No. Nothing."

"Walking around unarmed out here? Stidge is right. You *got* to be crazy." Charley flicked a finger toward the blue-eyed pitted-faced man. "Hey, Buffalo, lend Tom a spike or something, you hear? He needs to be carrying something."

Buffalo held out a thin shining metal strip with a handle at one end and a teardrop-shaped point at the other. "You know how to use a spike?" he asked. Tom simply stared at it. "Go on," Buffalo said. "Take it."

"I don't want it," Tom said. "Someone wants to hurt me, I figure that's his problem, not mine. Poor Tom doesn't hurt people. Poor Tom doesn't want any spike. But thanks. Thanks anyway."

Charley studied him a long moment. "You sure?"

"I'm sure."

"Okay," Charley told him, shaking his head. "Okay. Whatever you say."

"They don't come no crazier, do they?" the little Latino asked. "We give him a spike, he smiles and says no thanks. Out of his head crazy. Out of his head."

"There's crazy and crazy," said Charley. "Maybe he knows what he's doing. You carry a spike, you likely to annoy somebody who's got a bigger spike. You don't carry any, maybe they let you pass. You see?" Charley grinned. He clapped his hand down on Tom's bony shoulder, hard, and squeezed. "You're my man, Tom. You and me, we going to learn a lot from each other, I bet. Anyone here touches you, you let me know. I'll make him sorry."

Buffalo said, "You want to finish on the van now, Charley?"

"To hell with it. Be too dark to work, another couple hours. Let's get us some jackasses for dinner and we can do the van in the morning. You know how to build a fire, Tom?"

"Sure."

"All right, build one. Don't start no conflagration, though. We don't want to call attention to ourselves."

Charley began pointing, sending his men off in different directions. Plainly they were *his* men. Stidge was the last to go, limping off sullenly, pausing to glower at Tom as though telling him that the only thing keeping him alive was Charley's protection, but that Charley wouldn't always be there to protect him. Tom took no notice. The world was full of men like Stidge; so far Tom had managed to cope with them well enough.

He found a bare place in the dry grass that looked good for making a fire and began to arrange twigs and other bits of kindling. He had been working for about ten minutes, and the fire was going nicely, when he became aware that Charley had returned and was standing behind him, watching.

"Tom?"

"Yeah, Charley?"

The black-bearded man hunkered down next to him and tossed a narrow log on the fire. "Good job," he said. "I like a neat fire, everything lined up straight like this." He moved a little closer to Tom and peered around this way and that as if making sure no one else was nearby. "I heard what you were saying when you were in that fit," Charley went on. His voice was low, barely more than a whisper. "About the green world. About the crystal people. Their shining skins. Their eyes, like diamonds. How did you say the eyes were arranged?"

"In rows of three, on each side of their heads."

"Four sides to the head?"

"Four, yes."

Charley was silent a while, poking at the fire. Then he said, in an even quieter voice, "I dreamed of a place just like that, about six nights ago. And then again night before last. Green sky, crystal people, eyes like diamonds, four rows of three around their heads. I saw it like I was seeing it in a show. And now you come along talking about the same place, shouting it out like you're possessed, and it's just the same place I saw. How in hell is that possible, that we could both have the same crazy dream? You tell me: How in hell is that possible?"

2

THE sun was still half an hour on the far side of the Sierra Nevada when Elszabet awoke and stepped out on the porch of her cabin, naked, just the way she had slept. The coolness of the summer morning enfolded her. A soft blanket of fog lingered on out of the night, shrouding the tops of the redwoods and drifting more thinly down to ground level.

Beautiful, she thought. From all sides came the quiet plunking sounds of condensation, clear cool droplets falling from the lofty branches and hitting the soft carpet of deep brown duff. The hundreds of sword-ferns on the hillside in front of her cabin glistened as though they had been polished. Beautiful. Beautiful. Even the bluejays, shrieking as they started their day's work, seemed beautiful.

An altogether gorgeous morning. There was no other kind here, winter or summer. You had to like to be an early riser, here at the Nepenthe Center, because all the useful mindpick work necessarily was done before breakfast. But that was all right. Elszabet couldn't imagine not liking to awaken at dawn, when the dawn was a dawn like this. And there was no reason not to go to sleep early. What was there to do in the evenings, out here in the boonies hundreds of miles north of San Francisco?

She touched the face of her watch and the morning's schedule came scrolling up in clear glowing letters:

> 0600   Father Christie, A Cabin
>   Ed Ferguson, B Cabin
>   Alleluia, C Cabin
> 0630   Nick Double Rainbow, B Cabin
>   Tomás Menendez, C Cabin
> 0700—

A quick delicious shower, using the outdoor rig behind her cabin, first. Then she slipped into shorts and halter and made a fast breakfast of cider and cheese. No sense bothering to go all the way up to the staff mess hall this early in the morning. By five of six Elszabet was on her way up the steps of A Cabin, taking them two at a time. Father Christie was there already, slouched in the mindpick chair while Teddy Lansford bustled around him getting the pick set up.

Father Christie didn't look good. He rarely did, this hour of the morning. This morning he seemed even farther off center than usual: pale, sweaty-jowled, yellowish around the eyeballs, almost a little dazed-looking. He was a short plump man, forty-five or so, with a great mass of curling grayish hair and a soft pleading face. Today he was wearing his clerical outfit, which never managed to look as though it fit him. The collar was soiled, the black jacket was rumpled and askew as if he had buttoned it incorrectly.

But he brightened as she entered: phony brightness, stage cheer. "Good morning, Elszabet. What a lovely sight you are!"

"Am I?" She smiled. He was always full of little compliments. Always trying for little peeks at her thighs and breasts, too, whenever he thought she wouldn't notice. "You sleep well, Father?"

"I've had better nights."

"Also worse ones?"

"Worse also, I suppose." His hands were trembling. If she hadn't known better, she would have guessed he'd been drinking. But of course that was impossible. You didn't drink any more, not even on the sly, once you had had a conscience chip implanted in your esophagus.

Lansford called out from the control console, "Blood sugar okay, respiration, iodine uptake, everything checks. Delta waves present and fully secured. Everything looks fine. I'm popping the Father's pick module into the slot now. Elszabet?"

"Hold it a second. What reading do you get on mood?"

"The usual mild depression, and—hey, no, not depression, it's agitation, actually. What the hell, Father, you're supposed to be depressed this time of morning!"

"I'm sorry," said Father Christie meekly. The corners of his lips were twitching. "Does that upset your programming for me?"

The technician laughed. "This machine, it can compensate for anything. It's already done it. We're all set if you are. You ready for the pick, Father?"

"Any time," he said, not sounding as if he meant it.

"Elszabet? Okay?"

"No, wait," Elszabet said to Lansford. "Look at the lines there. Screen two. He's past threshold on anxiety. I want to talk to him first."

"Should I stay?" the technician asked without much show of concern.

"You go over to B and set up for Mr. Ferguson, okay? Give me a couple of minutes alone with the Father."

"Sure thing," Lansford said, and went out.

The priest peered up at Elszabet, blinking like an uncomfortable schoolboy about to be lectured by a truant officer. "I'm all right," he said. "I'm fine. Really, I am."

"I don't quite think so."

"No. No, I'm not."

Gently she said, "What is it then, Father?"

"It's hard to explain."

"Are you frightened of the pick?"

"No. Why should I be? I've gone under the pick plenty of times before, haven't I?" He looked at her in sudden uncertainty. "Haven't I?"

"Over a hundred times. You've been here four months."

"That's what I thought. April, May, June, July. The pick's nothing new for me. Why should I be scared of it?"

"No reason at all. The pick's an instrument of healing. You know that."

"Yes."

"But your lines are all over the screen. Something's got you up in a turmoil this morning, and it must have been something that happened in the night, yes? Because your readings were fine yesterday. What was it, Father? A dream?"

He fidgeted. He was looking worse and worse by the moment.

"Can we go outside, Elszabet? I think some fresh air would do me good."

"Of course. I was thinking the same thing."

Elszabet led him out to the back porch of the little wooden building and made him stand still beside her, inhaling deeply. She towered over him, almost a head and a half taller; but then, she towered over many men. All the same, the difference in height made him seem even more like a bewildered boy, though he was ten years older than she was. She could sense the physical need in him, the inarticulate urge to touch her and the powerful fear of doing it. After a moment she took his hand in hers. It was within the rules of the Center to offer the patients some physical comfort.

"Elszabet," he said. "What a beautiful name. And strange. Almost Elizabeth, but not quite."

"Almost Hungarian," she said. "But not quite. There was an actress, Hungarian, very big in the lasers in the mid-twenty-first century, Erzsebet Szabo. My mother was her biggest fan. Named me for her. Spelled it wrong." Elszabet chuckled. "My mother was never much on spelling." She had told Father Christie about her name at least thirty times before. But of course he forgot everything every morning, when the mindpick flushed him clean of short-term recollections and an unpredictable quantity of the long-term ones. After a bit she said, "What frightened you last night, Father?"

"Nothing."

"But you're ambivalent about undergoing pick today?"

"Yes."

"Why is that?"

"You promise you won't put this in my records?"

"I don't know," she said. "I'm not sure I can promise that."

"Then I might not tell you."

"Is it that embarrassing?"

"It might be, if it got back to the archdiocese."

"Church stuff? Well, I can be discreet about that. Your bishop doesn't have access to Center records, you know."

"Is that true?"

"You know it is."

He nodded. A little color came into his face. "What it is, Elszabet, is that I had a vision last night, and I'm not sure I want to surrender my memory of it to the pick."

"A vision?"

"A very powerful vision. A wonderful and surprising vision."

"The pick might take it from you," she said. "Very probably will."

"Yes."

"But if you want to be healed, Father, you have to give yourself up totally to the pick. Yielding the good stuff along with the bad. Later on, you'll integrate your spirit and you'll be free of the pick. But for now—"

"I understand. Even so—"

"Do you want to tell me about the vision?"

He reddened and squirmed.

"You don't have to. But it might help to tell me."

"All right. All right."

He was silent, working at it. Then in a desperate rush he blurted, "What it was, I saw God in His heavens, Elszabet!"

She smiled, trying to keep it sincere and unpatronizing. Gently she said, "How wonderful that must have been, Father."

"More than you can imagine. More than anyone can." He was trembling again. He was beginning to weep, and long wet tracks gleamed on his face. "Don't you see, Elszabet, I have no faith. *I have no faith.* If I ever did, it went away from me long ago. Isn't that pathetic? Isn't it a joke? That classic clown, the priest who doesn't believe. The Church is just my job, don't you see? And I'm not even very good at that, but I do my diocesan duties, I make my calls, I practice my profession the way a lawyer or an accountant does, I—" He caught himself. "Anyway, for God to come to me—not to the pope, not to the cardinal, but to me, me without faith—!"

"What was it like, the vision? Can you say?"

"Oh, yes. Yes, I can tell you. It was the most vivid thing possible. There was purple light in the sky, like a veil, a luminous veil hanging across the sky, and nine suns were shining at once, like jewels. An orange one, a blue one, a yellow one like ours, all kinds of colors crossing and mixing. The shadows were fantastic. Nine suns! And then He came into view. I saw Him on his throne, Elszabet. Gigantic. Majestic. Lord of Lords, who else could that have been, with nine suns for His footstools! His brow—His forehead—light streamed from it, grace, love. More than that: holiness, sanctity, the divine force. That's what came from Him. A sense that I was seeing a being of the highest wisdom and power, a mighty and terrible god. I tell you, it was overwhelming. The sweat was pouring off me. I was sobbing, I was wailing, I thought I'd have a heart attack, it was so wondrous.'' The priest paused and squinted at her quickly, a furtive worried glance. Then, without looking at her, he said in a low anguished voice full of shame, ''Just one thing, though. You know, they say we're made in His image? It isn't so. He isn't anything like us. I know that what I saw was God: I am as convinced of that as I am that Jesus is my Savior. But He doesn't look anything like us.''

''What does he look like, then?''

''I can't begin to say. That's the part I don't dare share, not even with you. But He looked—not—human. Splendid, magnificent, but—not—human.''

Elszabet had no idea how to respond to that. Again she gave him her professional smile, warm, encouraging.

He said, ''I need to keep that vision, Elszabet. It's the thing I've prayed for all my life. The presence of the divine, illuminating my spirit. How can I give that up now that I've experienced it?''

''You need to give yourself over to the pick, Father. The pick will heal you. You know that.''

''I know that, yes. But the vision—those nine suns—''

''Perhaps it'll stay with you even after the pick.''

"And if not?" His brow darkened. "I think I want to withdraw from treatment."

"You know that's not possible."

"The vision—"

"If you lose it, surely it'll be granted you again. If God has revealed Himself to you this night, do you think He'll abandon you afterward? Do you? He will return. What opened for you in this night just past will open for you again. The nine suns—the Father on His throne—"

"Oh, do you think so, Elszabet?"

"I'm sure of it."

"I hope you're right."

"Trust me," she said. "Trust God, Father."

"Yes."

"Come on, now. Shall we go back inside?"

The priest looked transfigured. "Yes. Certainly."

"And I'll send Lansford over to you?"

"Of course." Tears were cascading down his cheeks. She had never seen him as animated as this, as vigorous, as alive.

Over in B Cabin, Lansford had the pick set up for Ed Ferguson, who seemed annoyed by the delay. "You go across to the Father," Elszabet told Lansford. "I'll take care of Mr. Ferguson." The technician nodded. Ferguson, a chilly-faced man of about fifty who had been convicted of some vast and preposterous real-estate swindle before being sent to Nepenthe Center, began telling her about a trip to Mendocino that he wanted to take this weekend to meet a woman who'd be podding up from San Francisco to see him, but Elszabet listened with only half an ear. Her mind was full of Father Christie's vision. How radiant the poor bedraggled incompetent priest had become while telling the tale. No wonder he feared going under the pick this morning. Losing the one bit of divine grace, weird and garbled though it might be, that had ever been vouchsafed him.

When Elszabet was done with Ferguson and had looked

in on the third cabin, where Alleluia, the synthetic woman, was being treated, she hurried back to A Cabin. Father Christie was sitting up, smiling in the amiable muddled way characteristic of someone who has just had his mind swept clean of a host of memories. Donna, the morning recovery nurse, was with him, running him through his basic recall routines—making sure he still knew his own name, the year, where he was and why. The pick was supposed to remove just the short-term memories, but it could abrade more deeply, sometimes a lot more deeply. Elszabet nodded to the younger woman. "It's okay," she said. "I'll take over, thanks." She was surprised how hard her heart was pounding. When Donna had gone, Elszabet sat down beside the priest and put her hand lightly on his wrist. "Well, how's the Father now?" she asked. "You look nice and relaxed."

"Oh, yes, Elizabeth. Very relaxed."

"Elszabet," she reminded him gently.

"Ah. Of course."

She leaned close. He was trying to stare down the front of her halter. Good for him, she thought. "Tell me," she said. "Have you ever had a dream in which you saw nine suns in the sky all at once?"

"Nine suns?" he said blankly. "Nine suns all at once?"

3

JASPIN was late leaving his apartment in San Diego that morning. That wasn't unusual for him. When he finally got himself into gear he hurried down the freeway to the Chula Vista turnoff, swung inland, took the Otay Valley shunt toward the unmonitored county roads. Twenty minutes later he came to the roadblock set up by the tumbondé people as he was crossing a dry hot plateau.

They had the road completely closed, which was flat-out illegal, but no one in San Diego County was likely to try to tell the tumbondé folks what to do. An energy wall ran across the highway from shoulder to shoulder, and six or seven somber-looking bronze-skinned men with wide cheekbony faces were standing behind it, arms folded. They wore tumbondé costumes: silver jackets, tight black leggings with red piping, wide black sombreros, crescent-moon pendants dangling on their chests. They appeared to be wearing masks, too, but they weren't; those were simply their faces, aloof, impassive. None of them seemed the least bit interested in the pale gringo in the old battered car. But Jaspin knew the routine. He leaned out and said, "Chungirá-He-Will-Come, he will come."

"Maguali-ga, Maguali-ga," replied one of the tumbondé men.

"Senhor Papamacer teaches. Senhora Aglaibahi is our mother. Rei Ceupassear rules."

"Maguali-ga. Maguali-ga."

He was doing all right so far. "Chungirá-He-Will-Come, he will come," Jaspin said a second time.

"The parking is two kilometer," said one of the tumbondé men indifferently. "Then you walk five hundred meter. Better you run: is already starting, the procession."

"Maguali-ga, Maguali-ga," Jaspin said, as the barrier winked out. He drove past the unsmiling guards and down the dusty potholed road until he saw small boys waving him toward the parking lot. There were at least a thousand cars there, most of them even older than his own. He found a nook under a huge old oak tree, left the car there, set out at a trot down the road. Though it was not yet noon, the heat was intense. It felt like Arizona heat, no moisture in it at all, a pure furnace. He tried to imagine what it was like to stand around in black pants and a black sombrero under midday sunlight in that heat.

In a few minutes he caught sight of the congregation, milling chaotically on a high knoll just off the road. There were thousands of them, some dressed in full tumbondé gear but most, like him, in ordinary street clothes. They were carrying banners, placards, little images of the great ones. From unseen loudspeakers came a deep, unhurried, relentless drumming. The ground shook. They probably had it wired, Jaspin thought. Electrostatic nodes all over the place, and synchronized pulsation chips. Tumbondé might be primitive and elemental but it didn't seem to scorn technology.

He found a place at the edge of the crowd. Far ahead, halfway up the hillside, he saw the colossal papier-mâché statues of the divinities being carried on poles by sweating brawny men. Jaspin recognized each one: that was Prete Noir the Negus, that one was the thunder-serpent Narbail, that was O Minotauro the bull, that was Rei Ceupassear. And those two, the biggest of all, were the true great ones, Chungirá-He-Will-Come and Maguali-ga, the gods from deepest space. Jaspin shivered in the heat. Crazy as this stuff was, it had undeniable power.

A slender young woman jammed up behind him twisted around to face him and said, "Pardon me. You're Dr. Jaspin, aren't you? From UCLA?"

He looked at her as if she had bitten his arm. She was twenty-three, twenty-four, stringy blonde hair, white blouse open to the waist. Her eyes looked a little glazed. The marks of Maguali-ga were painted across her very minimal breasts in purple and orange. Jaspin didn't recognize her, but that didn't mean anything. He had forgotten a lot of people in the last few years.

Gruffly he said, "Sorry. Wrong guy."

"I was sure you were him. I audited his course in ninety-nine. I thought it was really profound."

"Don't know what you're talking about," he told her, smiling vacantly, and moved away, elbowing through. She made the sign of Rei Ceupassear at him, as a kind of benediction. Forgiveness. Screw you and your forgiveness, Jaspin thought. Then he was instantly sorry. But he drilled forward, burrowing into the crowd.

This was a low time in Jaspin's life. Somehow things had begun falling apart for him right about the year that the blonde girl said she had sat in on his classes, and he had not yet figured out why. He was thirty-four. There were days when he felt three times as old as that: heavy leaden days, ass-dragging days, sometimes a month of them in a row. The university had dismissed him, for cause, early in '02. He hadn't quite managed to begin his dissertation then—the doctorate that the blonde girl had conferred on him existed only in her imagination. What he had been was an assistant professor in the anthropology department, and he hadn't realized what a rare privilege it was in those times to have a cushy job in one of the few remaining universities. He realized it now. But what he was now was nothing at all.

"Maguali-ga! Maguali-ga!" they were yelling on all sides. Jaspin took up the cry. "Maguali-ga!" He started to move, letting himself be swept onward, up toward the vast swaying statues shimmering in the heat.

He had been coming to the tumbondé processions for five months now; this was his eighth one. He wasn't entirely sure why he came. Part of it, he knew, was professional curiosity. He still thought of himself on some level as an anthropologist, and here was anthropology raw and wild, on

the hoof, this apocalyptic messianic cult of star-god worshippers that had sprung up in the drab wastelands east of
San Diego. Jaspin's specialty had been contemporary irra-
tionality; he had hoped to write a massive book that would
explain the modern world to itself and make some sense out
of the madhouse that the good people of the late twenty-first
century had handed on to their descendants. Tumbondé was
the craziest thing going; Jaspin had been drawn irresistibly
toward it, as if by infiltrating it and analyzing it and
reporting on it he might somehow be able to rehabilitate his
broken academic career. But there was more to his being
here than that. He admitted to himself that he felt some kind
of hunger, some emptiness of the spirit that he dreamed he
might satisfy here. God only knew how, though.

"Chungirá-He-Will-Come!" Jaspin shouted, and forced
his way through the crowds.

The excitement all around him was contagious. He could
feel his pulse rising and his throat going dry. People were
dancing in place, feet rooted, shoulders wriggling, arms
flung this way and that. He saw the blonde girl again a
dozen meters away, lost in some kind of trance. Maguali-ga
the god of the gateway had come to collect her spirit.

There were very few Anglos in the crowd. Tumbondé had
emerged out of the Latino-African refugee community that
had come crowding into the San Diego area after the Dust
War, and most of these people were dark-skinned or outright
black. The cult was an international stew, a mix of Brazilian
and Guinean stuff with an underlay of something Haitian,
and of course it had taken on a Mexican tinge too; you
couldn't have any kind of apocalyptic cult operating this
close to the border without very quickly having it acquire a
subtle Aztec coloration. But it was more ecstatic in nature
than the usual Mexican variety—less death, more transfigur-
ation.

"Maguali-ga!" a tremendous voice roared. "Take me, Maguali-ga!"

To Jaspin's astonishment he realized the voice was his own.

All right. All right. Just go with it, he told himself. He felt suddenly cold despite the horrific heat. Just go with it. Nice Jewish boy from Brentwood, sure, jumping around with the pagan *shvartzers* on a sizzling hillside in the middle of July—well, why the hell not? Go with it, kid.

He was close enough now to see the leaders of the procession, rising awesomely above all the rest in their stiltlike platform shoes: there was Senhor Papamacer, there was Senhora Aglaibahi beside him, and surrounding them were the eleven members of the Inner Host. A kind of golden nimbus of sunlight flickered around all thirteen of them. Jaspin wondered how they worked that trick; for trick it surely must be. Their own explanation was simply that they were magnets for cosmic energy.

"The force it comes from the seven galaxies," Senhor Papamacer had told the *Times* reporter. "It is the great light that bears the power of salvation. Once it shined on Egypt, and then on Tibet, and then on the place of the gods in Yucatan; and it has been on Jerusalem and in the sacred shrine of the Andes, and now it is here, which is the sixth of the Seven Places. Soon it will move to the Seventh Place, which is the North Pole, when Maguali-ga will open the gateway and Chungirá-He-Will-Come will break through to our world, bringing the wealth of the stars for those who love him. And that will be the time of the ending, which will be the new beginning." That time, Senhor Papamacer had said, was not far off.

Jaspin heard the bleating of tethered goats over all the other sounds. He heard the low mournful voice of the sacrificial white bull that he knew was in the hut at the top of the hill.

Now he saw the masked dancers, cutting through the
mob, seven of them representing the seven benevolent
galaxies. Their faces were hidden by glittering metallic
shields and their bodies, which were bare, bore ornaments
in the shape of suns and moons and planets. On their heads
were red metal domes bright as mirrors, from which blind-
ing shafts of reflected sunlight bounced like spears. They
carried guard rattles and castanets, and they were chanting
fiercely:

> *Venha Maguali-ga*
> *Maguali-ga, venha!*

An invocation. He fell in behind them, chanting, flinging
his arms around. To his left, a plump woman in green robes
was saying over and over in Spanish, "Forgive our sins,
forgive our sins," and on the other side of him a leathery-
looking black man bare to the waist was muttering in thick
French, "The sun rises in the east, the sun sets in Guinea.
The sun rises in the east, the sun sets in Guinea." The
drums were louder and faster, now. Up the hill. Up. Animals were screeching in terror and pain somewhere: the
sacrifices were beginning.

Jaspin found himself standing on the lip of a huge ditch.
It was full almost to the brim with the most amazing
assortment of things: jewelry, coins, dolls, entertainment
cubes, family photographs, clothing, toys, electronic gad-
gets, weapons, tools, packages of food. He knew what to
do. This was the Well of Sacrifice: you had to rid yourself
of something that was precious to you, by way of recogniz-
ing that you would not need such things once the gods came
from the stars bringing incalculable wealth to all the suffering people of Earth. You must make a gift to the Earth, said
Senhor Papamacer, if you wish the Earth to draw gifts from
the stars. It didn't matter if what you threw into the ditch

wasn't generally considered precious; it had to be precious to you. Jaspin had an offering ready—his wristwatch, probably the last valuable thing except for his books that he had not yet pawned, a sleek IBM job with nine function nodes. It was worth at least a thousand.

This is lunacy, he thought.

"To Chungirá-He-Will-Come," he said, and hurled the shining watch far out into the cluttered ditch.

Then he was swept on, upward, to the place of communion. The blood of goats and sheep was flowing there; they had not yet sacrificed the bull. Jaspin, trembling and shivering, found himself face to face with Senhora Aglaibahi, the virgin mother, the goddess on Earth. She seemed about three meters tall; her black hair was dusted with mirror-dust, her eyes were outlined in fiery scarlet, her bare heavy dark-tipped breasts glistened with the markings of Maguali-ga. She touched her fingertip to his arm and he felt a little sting, as though she had stuck him with a needle or tapped him with a shocker. He lurched on past her, past the even more gigantic form of Senhor Papamacer, past the papier-mâché figures of the gods Narbail and Prete Noir and O Minotauro and the star-rover Rei Ceupassear, and onward around a bare charred place that was sacred to Chungirá-He-Will-Come and Maguali-ga.

Somewhere on the far side of that he felt himself growing dizzy and beginning to lose consciousness. The heat, he thought, the excitement, the mobs, the hysteria. He tottered, nearly fell, struggled to stay upright, fearing that he would be trampled if he let himself go down. He found a tree at the summit of the hill and clung to it as wave after wave of astounding vertigo came over him. It seemed to him that he was breaking free of the land, that he was being hurled by some enormous centrifugal power into the far reaches of the universe.

As he soared through space he saw Chungirá-He-Will-Come.

The god of the gateway was a great bizarre golden figure with curving ram's-horns, the strangest being that Jaspin had ever seen, rising out of a block of pure shining alabaster that covered it—him—to the waist. Over its—his—left shoulder was an immense sun, dark red, filling half the purplish sky; it seemed to be swelling and pulsing, blowing up like an enormous balloon. There was a second sun over the god's right shoulder, a blue one, fluctuating in sudden violent bursts of light. Between the two suns streamed a bridge of brilliantly glowing matter, like a fiery arch in the heavens.

"My time is soon," said Chungirá-He-Will-Come. "You will enter into my embrace, child. And all will be well."

Then the figure vanished. The red star and the blue one could no longer be seen. Jaspin clutched at the air but he was unable to bring back what he had just beheld. The wondrous moment was over.

He began to shake. He had never experienced anything remotely like this before. It stunned him; it was devastating; he could not move, he could not breathe. For an instant he had been touched by a god. There was no explanation for it and he would not seek one. Just this once he had broken through into something that passed all his understanding, something that was so very much bigger than Barry Jaspin that he could lose himself utterly in it. Good Christ, he thought, can it really be that there are titanic space-beings out there, that the tumbondé people have a pipeline across half the universe to God knows where, that these creatures are watching over our world from a jillion light years away, that they are coming to us to govern us and change our lives? It has to be just a hallucination—doesn't it? The heat, the crowds, maybe a drug the Senhora slipped into me?

He opened his eyes. He was lying under a tree, and the thin blonde girl was bending over him. Her blouse was still open, but the Maguali-ga markings on her breasts were smeared and blurred, and her skin was shining with sweat.

"I saw you pass out," she said. "I was afraid you'd get hurt. Can I help you up? You look so strange, Dr. Jaspin!"

He didn't bother to deny that he was Jaspin. In a voice strangled with awe he said, "I can't believe it. I absolutely can't believe it. I saw him. I could have reached out and put my hand on him. Not that I would have dared."

"Saw whom, Dr. Jaspin?"

"You didn't? See him?"

"You mean Senhor Papamacer?"

"I mean Chungirá-He-Will-Come," said Jaspin. "Looking at me from a planet of some other galaxy. Christ Almighty, it was the real thing! I never doubted it." He felt shrouded in a numinous aura; he felt himself exalted by the divine touch. Some part of him, he knew, *was* Chungirá-He-Will-Come, and always would be. But in another moment it all started to flee and fade; and a moment after that he was no one but miserable screwed-up Barry Jaspin again, lying sweaty and exhausted on a torrid hillside with thousands of people shouting and chanting and passing out all around him, and frightened animals bleating, and drums shaking the ground like nine-point-five Richter. He sat up and looked at the blonde girl and saw the awe and wonder reflected in her face. It was as if she too had seen Chungirá-He-Will-Come in his eyes, for that little moment before the ecstasy faded. And without warning the most terrible sadness he had ever known came over him, and he began to cry, dry racking tears and uncontrollable sobs.

4

WHEN they were finished working him over down in B Cabin, Ferguson made his way slowly up the hill to the dorm, feeling lightheaded and seasick. It was the same old *afterwards* feeling that he had every morning at this time. He knew it was the same every morning because the molecular recorder he carried illicitly under his signet ring told him so. It remembered things for him. He tapped the ring twice and the recorder told him, "You feel crappy and disoriented right now because they just picked your mind. Don't worry about it. These shits can't grind you down, boy." He had that message programmed right at the top: the recorder gave it to him first thing after pick, every morning.

Wisps of fog drifted through the trees. Everything looked damp and shining. Holy Jesus, and this is July, he thought. Feels like February. He could never get used to Northern California. He missed the Los Angeles heat, the dryness, even the smog. That was the one thing the scientists were never going to get rid of, he thought, the smog. They had it in L.A. when there was nobody but Indians living there. Maybe even when just dinosaurs. They were going to have it forever.

Ferguson thumbed the ring again and his voice said, "Lacy's coming up from San Francisco this weekend. She'll be staying in Mendo and she hopes you can get leave to visit her Saturday and Sunday. Give her a call right after breakfast. The number is—"

He frowned and hit the ring twice more, digging into deeper memory. "Request Lacy," he said.

The recorder said, "Lacy Meyers lives in San Francisco, red hair, high cheekbones, thirty-one years old, single, you met her in January oh-two, worked with you on the Betelgeuse Five deal. She can only come when she's on top. Birthday is March tenth. Home address and phone—"

"Thanks," he said. Living with pick, it was like writing your autobiography on water. But he didn't plan on living this way forever.

He went into the dorm, down the long brightly lit hall

into the third room on the left, which, according to the
orderly who had done recall routine with him today, he
shared with two roommates, an Indian who called himself
Nick Double Rainbow and a Chic named Tomás Menendez.
Neither one seemed to be around at the moment: probably
out getting picked, second shift. Ferguson stood wavering in
the middle of the room, not sure which corner was his. One
bed had a bunch of cubes on it; he picked one up and
pressed it and it said something to him in Spanish. Okay.
That was easy. The bed opposite it was covered with a
bright red blanket marked with crisscross patterns. Indian
stuff, he figured. By elimination that leaves this one over
here, must be mine.

God, I hate this shit, he thought. Starting every day like a
newborn baby.

The one thing he hadn't forgotten was why he was here.
It was either this or Rehab Two, and they were a lot rougher
with you at Rehab Two. When you got out of there you
were somebody else, meek and mild, fit only for pruning
roses. They had intended to send him there after his conviction on the space scam, but he had flipped out, or had
pretended to—he wasn't sure which any more—and his
lawyer had gotten him a year at Nepenthe instead. "This
man is no criminal," the lawyer had said. "He is as much a
victim as anyone." True? Ferguson didn't know any more.
Maybe he genuinely did have that mental thing, that Gelbard's
syndrome, or maybe it had only been one more scam.
Whatever it was, they were curing him of it here. Sure.

He flopped out of his bed and pushed his thumb down on
the phone's print-plate. "Outside line," he said.

The computer voice replied, "I have one message for
you. Do you want it first, Mr. Ferguson?"

"Yeah. Sure."

"It's from your wife. In regard to her visit, scheduled for

next Tuesday. She will arrive this morning instead, ten-thirty hours."

"Holy suffering Jesus," Ferguson said. "You're kidding. Today? What day is today?"

"Friday, July 21, 2103."

"And how long is she planning to stay?"

"Until 1500 hours Sunday."

There went the weekend with Lacy, for sure. Son of a bitch. Even here in this place he worked hard to keep everything lined up the way he wanted it, but it was too hard, goddamned near impossible when you could never remember anything from one day to the next, and nothing ever seemed to stay in position. Son of a bitch. Coming for her conjugal four days early! Furiously he said, "You sure? Dr. Lewis authorized the change of date? This has to be a mix-up."

"The authorization number is—"

"Never mind. Listen, there's a bad mix-up here. I'm due for external leave on Saturday. You've got something down there about my applying for an external leave for this weekend, don't you?"

"I'm sorry, Mr. Ferguson, there's nothing of that—"

"Check again."

"There's no record of any application for external leave."

"It's got to be there. There's been some mistake." Try arguing with a computer, Ferguson thought, despondent. "I know I applied. You keep searching. And listen, get me Elszabet Lewis right away. She knows I applied, too."

"Dr. Lewis is with a client, Mr. Ferguson."

"Tell her I want to talk with her, then. Pronto, soon as she's done." He slapped the disconnect and put both his hands over his face and pressed hard. He managed to take two or three deep breaths. Then the phone bleeped: the computer was talking to him again.

"Do you still want that outside line, Mr. Ferguson?"

"No. Yes. Yeah, sure." When he got the tone he keyed in Lacy's number in San Francisco. Seven-fifteen in the morning; would she be up yet? Four rings. Slept somewhere else last night, kid? I wouldn't be surprised. Then he wondered why he suspected that. For all he could remember, she lived like a nun. Maybe the pick isn't as thorough as you think, he told himself.

On the fifth ring she answered, sounding furry and vague.

"Yeah?"

"It's Ed, baby."

"Ed? *Ed!*" Awake in a flash. "Oh, sweet, how are you doing? I've been thinking about you so much—"

"Listen, there's trouble."

"Trouble?"

"About the weekend."

"Yes?" Suddenly very cool, very remote.

"They won't give me leave. They say I've had a setback, that I have to go in the tank for an extra rinsing."

"I've got everything booked, honey! It's all set up!"

"Next weekend?"

She was quiet a little while. "I'm not sure I can, next weekend."

"Oh."

'Even if you can't get leave, couldn't I come over there? You said there's a house for conjugal visits, didn't you? And—"

"You aren't conjugal, Lacy."

It was the wrong thing to say. He could feel the subzero chill coming up out of the telephone speaker.

He said, "Anyway, that isn't the point. I'm going to be in the tank all weekend. By the time they get done with me, I won't know my ass from my elbow. And I can't have visitors."

"I'm sorry, Ed."

"So am I. You don't know how sorry I am."

Another silence. Then: "How are you doing, anyway?"

"I'm okay. I'm not letting these bastards get to me."

"You still remember me?"

"You know I do, baby. I can see that red hair shining. I can see you sitting there high up above me going for a big one."

"Oh, honey—"

"I love you, Lacy."

"I love you too. You miss me, Ed? Really?"

"You know how much."

"It's really shitty, about this weekend. You and me walking along the beach in Mendo—"

"Don't make it any harder," he said. "You know I would if I could."

"I had so much to tell you, too."

"Like what?"

"There's a funny thing. About our space project—you remember?"

"Sure I remember," he said.

But there must have been a perceptible jiggle in his voice, because she said, "I mean, the one when we were trying to sell mind-trips to Betelgeuse Five, that one. I had a dream the other day that I took one. A mind-trip. That I really went to some other star, you know?"

He said, "You can't start believing your own scams, baby."

"It was the realest thing. There was a red sun in the sky and a blue one. And I saw a big golden thing with horns standing on a block of white stone, some kind of space monster, and it reached out to me, it seemed to be beckoning to me. It was like a giant. It was almost like a god. And in the sky—"

"Listen, baby, this call is costing me a fortune."

"Just let me tell you. It wasn't any ordinary dream. It was like *real*, Ed. I saw the trees of this planet, I saw the bugs, even, and they weren't like our trees or bugs, and—but the funny thing was, it was just the sort of gig we were trying to sell people, the one they sent you up for, and—"

"Lacy, hey. They're calling me to go down to the therapy session."

"Yeah. Okay."

"Will I see you next weekend? I can hear all the rest of it then."

"I'm not sure, next weekend. I told you, it doesn't look good."

"Try for it, Lacy. I miss you so damn much."

"Yeah, Ed. Me too."

It didn't sound convincing, how much she missed him. The bitch, he thought. Anger surged in him. If she had been within reach he would have slapped her around. And then he realized that none of this was her fault, that she had been primed to come tomorrow, that it was his wife who had scrambled things up. He couldn't expect Lacy to keep herself on ice indefinitely, week after week. Quickly he went through one of the anger exercises Dr. Lewis had shown him.

He said as tenderly as he knew how, "I love you, Lacy. I wish I could see you tomorrow. You know that."

He signed off. Then he touched his ring. "Request wife," Ferguson said.

His recorded voice replied, "Wife: Mariela Johnston. Birthday August seventh. She'll be thirty-three this summer. You married her in Honolulu on July fourth, 2098. She's hot stuff but you can't stand her any more. Your lawyer is checking to see if you've got grounds for an annulment."

Fine, he thought. But obviously nothing's happened about that yet. And here she comes for her conjugal, wiping out Lacy's weekend. Shit. Shit. Hanging in there for the community property, I bet that's what she's doing. The good little wife, coming for the conjugal.

There was a tap at the door.

"Who?" Ferguson called.

"Alleluia," said the most musical female voice he had ever heard.

Something stirred in his muddled and mutilated memory bank, but he was unable to get hold of it. He touched his ring and said, "Request Alleluia."

"Fellow patient at Nepenthe Center. Synthetic woman, terrific body, very fucked-up personality. You've been screwing her on and off all summer."

He stared at the ring in disbelief. Screwing a synthetic? You must have been awfully hard up, kiddo. But if the recorder says so, it must be so.

"Come on in," he said.

When he saw her, he started believing what the ring had told him. Synthetic or not, he could easily imagine himself going to bed with her. She had presence. She could pass for real. She was beautiful beyond all plausibility, too, the way synthetics usually were. Laser-star looks, long legs, creamy skin, tumbling black hair, perfect face. She wore something thin and shimmering, with nipples showing through. With the light from the hallway behind her, he saw the black pubic triangle plainly too. He had never really understood why they bothered putting pubic hair on the imitation people, unless it was to keep them from getting recognized too easily for what they were; but you recognized them anyway because they were better looking than any natural person could ever hope to be.

She glided into the room and said, "Are you okay?"

"Why? Don't I look okay?"

"Extremely tense. Jumpy, edgy, irritated. Maybe this is the way you always look, but you don't look relaxed."

"Irritated? Shit, yes, I'm irritated. There've been complications," he said. "The wrong person in the wrong place at the wrong time, and I don't like it. It's messed me up very bad." He shook his head. "Hell, this is no way to start a conversation, is it? Try again. Hello there, you. Alleluia. Allie."

She smiled. "I'm sorry. Hello. You're Ed Ferguson, aren't you?"

"You bet your pretty ass I am."

"I had a note under my pillow that said I ought to go introduce myself to you first thing after pick. I think I do this every morning, don't I?"

"Yes," he said, although he had no more memory of it than she did. He rose and went to her, and pulled her to him and they kissed, and he ran his hands up over her breasts. They felt the way he imagined a fourteen-year-old's breasts would feel, hard as plastic but warmer. "We do this every morning, yes. We get acquainted again. Alleluia, Ed. Ed, Alleluia. Very pleased to make your acquaintance. See? That's the system."

"It's almost worth having to do pick," she said. "To get acquainted again. Each time is like the first time, isn't it?" She laughed and snuggled against his chest. "Let's go take a walk in the woods this afternoon, okay? Your roommates will be getting back here soon."

"I can't go this afternoon, Allie."

"Can't?"

"The irritating complication I was speaking of. Got a visitor at ten-thirty. My wife. She's coming on a conjugal."

She moved back from him, looking pained. "I didn't know you had a wife, Ed."

"Neither did I, till the communications computer reminded me. She was supposed to come Tuesday, but somehow she's arriving today instead. So the woods are out, sweetheart."

"We still have three hours."

"Conjugal is supposed to be conjugal," Ferguson said. "You understand? If I could I would, you know that, but today I'm just not free. All right? She'll be gone Sunday afternoon and then we can play. Is that all right?''

He saw the anger in her eyes, and it scared him. Women's anger always did; but Alleluia's anger was special even as women's anger went, because she was special. If she wanted to, he knew, she could pull his arms and legs off the way you'd pull the wings off a fly. Synthetic people were amazingly strong. And this one was an emotionally disturbed synthetic person, and she was standing between him and the door. He flicked a glance at the phone, wondering if he could thumb the plate fast enough to call for help before she pounced.

But she didn't pounce. She went through some internal exercise—he saw the muscles moving in her cheeks—and calmed herself. "All right," she said. "After she goes. Your wife."

"You know I'd rather be off playing with you."

The artificial woman nodded abstractly. She seemed to be drifting off into some distant realm before his eyes.

"Are *you* okay?" he asked.

Quietly she said, "I'm not sure. There's something been bothering me, and it happened again last night."

"Tell me."

"Don't laugh. I've been having funny dreams, Ed."

"Dreams?"

She hesitated. "I think I'm seeing other worlds. One's all green, with a green sky and green clouds, and the people look like they're made out of glass. Do you ever have dreams like that?"

"I don't remember any of my dreams," he said quietly. "They pick them out of me, first thing in the morning. You dreamed of another world, did you? How come you remember that, if you've been picked this morning?"

"A couple of them. The green world was one. My dreams seem to stay with me, you know? I suppose because I'm a synthetic. Maybe the pick doesn't always work right on me. There's another world I've seen once or twice, with two suns in the sky."

Ferguson caught his breath sharply.

She said, "One's red, and the other one—"

"—is blue?"

"Blue, yes!" she said. "You've seen it too?"

He felt the chills starting to run down his back. This is crazy, he thought. "And there was a big golden thing with horns, standing on a block of white stone?"

"You *have* seen it! You have!"

"Jesus suffering Christ," Ferguson said.

5

IT was the third day since Charley had managed to get the ground-effect van started up. They were down out of the foothills now, into the sweltering eastern side of the San Joaquin Valley. So far, so good, Tom thought. Maybe they'd let him travel with them all the way to San Francisco.

"Look at this godforsaken crappy place," Charley said. "My grandfather came from around here. He was a god-damned rich man, my grandfather. Cotton, wheat, corn, I don't know what. He had eighty men working for him, you know?"

It was hard to believe that this had been farming country only thirty or forty years back. For sure, nobody was farming much here any more. The land was starting to go back to desert, the way it had been four hundred years ago, before the irrigation canals. Under the summer heat everything was brown and twisted and dead.

"What's that town off there?" Buffalo asked.

"I don't think anybody remembers," Charley said.

"It's Fresno," said the man named Tamale, who was full of information, all of it wrong.

"Shit," Charley said. "Fresno's way down in the south, don't you know that? And don't tell me Sacramento, neither. Sacto's out thisaway. Anyhow, those are cities. This thing's just a town, and nobody remembers its name, I bet."

Buffalo said, "They got towns in Egypt ten thousand years old, everybody remembers their name. This place, you leave it alone thirty years, who the hell knows anything?"

"Let's go over there," Charley said. "Maybe there's something useful still lying around. Let's go scratch some."

"Scratch scratch," said the little Latino one they called Mujer, and all of them laughed.

Tom had traveled with scratchers before. He preferred that to traveling with bandidos. It was safer in a lot of ways. Sooner or later bandidos did something so dumb that they wound up getting wiped out. Scratchers were better at looking after their own skins. On the average they weren't as wild as bandidos, and maybe a little smarter. What scratchers did was a mix of scavenging and banditry, whatever worked, whatever they had to do to stay alive as they moved around the outskirts of the cities. Sometimes they killed, but only when they had to, never just for the fun of it. Tom felt easy falling in with this bunch. He hoped he could stay with them at least as far as San Francisco. If not, well, that was okay too. Whatever happened was okay. There was no other way to live, was there, but to accept whatever happened? But he preferred to keep on traveling with Charley and his scratchers. They would look after him.

This was rough country out here. It was rough country everywhere, but this was rougher than most.

And he figured he was safe with them. He had become a sort of mascot for them, a good-luck charm.

It wasn't the first time he had played that role. Tom knew that to a certain kind of person, someone like him was desirable to have around. They regarded him as crazy but not particularly dangerous or unpleasant—crazy in a nice way—and somebody like that had some appeal for men of that sort. You needed all the luck you could get, and a crazy like Tom had to be lucky to have lived as long as he had, wandering around on the edge of the world. So now he was their pet. They all liked him, Buffalo and Tamale and Mujer, Rupe and Choke and Nicholas, and especially Charley, of course. All but Stidge. Stidge still hated him, probably always would, because he had gotten beaten up on Tom's account. But Stidge didn't dare lay a hand on him, out of fear of Charley, or maybe just because he thought it would bring bad luck. Whatever. Tom didn't care what reason, so long as Stidge kept away from him.

"Look at that place," Charley kept saying. "*Look* at it!"

It was dismal, all right. Broken streets, slabs of asphalt rising at steep tilts everywhere, the shells of houses, dry grass poking up through shattered pavement. Sand creeping in from the fields. A couple of dead cars lying on their sides, everything stripped.

"They must have had one mean war here," Mujer said.

"Not here," said Choke, the skeleton-looking one with the crisscross scars on his forehead. "Weren't no war here. The war was back east of here, dummy—Kansas, Nebraska, Iowa, where they dropped the dust."

"Anyhow," said Buffalo, "dust don't smash a town up like this. Dust just garbages it all with hard stuff, so you burn when you touch anything."

"So what did this?" Mujer wanted to know.

"The people moving away, that's what did it," Charley said in a very quiet voice. "You think these towns repair themselves? The people left because there wasn't any more farming here, maybe too much dust in the air bringing hard stuff from the dead states, or maybe it was because the canal broke somewhere up north and nobody knew how to fix it. I don't know. But they move on, off to Frisco or down south, and then the pipes rust and you get an earthquake or two and nobody's here to fix anything and it all gets worse and worse, and then the scratchers move in to grab what's left. You don't need no bombs to destroy a place. You don't need anything. Let it be, and it just falls apart. They didn't build these places to last, like they built Egypt, hey, Buffalo? They built them for thirty, forty years, and the thirty-forty years, they used up."

"Shit," Mujer said. "What a world we got!"

"We'll go to San Francisco," said Charley. "It's not so bad there. Spend the summer. At least it's cool there, the fog, the breeze."

"What a screwed-up world," said Mujer.

Tom, standing a little way apart from them, said, "For the indignation of the Lord is upon all the nations, and His fury upon all their armies: He hath utterly destroyed them, He hath delivered them to the slaughter."

"What's the looney saying now?" Stidge asked.

"It's the Bible," said Buffalo. "Don't you know the Bible?"

"And thorns shall come up in her palaces, nettles and brambles in the fortresses thereof: and it shall be an habitation of dragons, and a court for owls."

Charley said, "You know it all by heart?"

"A lot of it," said Tom. "I was a preacher for a time."

"Whereabouts was that?"

"Up there," Tom said, jerking his thumb over his right shoulder. "Idaho. Washington State, some."

"You've been around."

"Some."

"You ever been really east?"

Tom looked at him. "You mean, New York, Chicago, like that?"

"Like that, yeah."

"How?" Tom said. "Fly?"

"Yeah," said Mujer, laughing. "Fly! On a broomstick!"

"They once did," Tamale said. "Coast to coast. You get on a plane in San Francisco, it take you to New York, three hours. My father told me that."

"Three hours," said Stidge. "Shit. That's just shit."

"Three hours," Tamale repeated. "Who you calling shit?" He had his knife out. "You calling my father shit? Go on, call it again. Call my mother something too, Stidge. Go on. Go on."

"Quit it," Charley said. "We came here to scratch. Let's do some scratching. Stidge, you're a pain in the ass."

"You think I'm gonna believe that? Three hours and you're in New York?"

"My father said it," Tamale muttered.

"A different world then," said Charley. "Before the Dust War it was all different. Maybe it was five hours, huh, Tamale?"

"Three."

Tom felt all this talk pressing on his skull like a brain tumor. Three hours, five, what did it matter? That world was gone. He walked away from them.

He sensed that a vision was coming on.

Good. Good. Let it come. Let them bicker, let them cut themselves up if that was what they wanted. He dwelled in other, finer worlds. He walked up a little way, around the raw jagged upended block of pavement, past a mass of rusty iron gridwork, and sat down on the curb of a sand-choked street with his back against an enormous palm tree that

looked as though it meant still to be here when California
and everything man had built in California had been swept
away by time.

The vision came rushing on, and it was a big one, it was
the entire deal all at once.

Sometimes he got it all, not just one alien world but the
great stupendous multitude of them coming one on top of
another. At times like that he felt himself to be the focus of
the cosmos. Whole galactic empires surged through his
soul. He had the full vision of the myriad realms beyond
realms that lay out there beyond mankind's comprehension.

Come to me! Ah, yes, come, come!

Before his astounded bugging eyes came the grandest
procession he had ever seen, a sequence of worlds upon
worlds. It was like a torrent, a wild flood. The green world
and the empire of the Nine Suns and the Double Kingdom
first, and then the Poro worlds and the worlds of the
Zygerone who were the masters of the Poro, and rising
above them the figure of a Kusereen overlord from the race
that ruled who knew how many galaxies, including those of
the Zygerone and the Poro. He saw quivering transparent
life-forms too strange to be nightmares. He saw whirling
disks of light stretching to the core of the universe. Through
him raced libraries of data, the lists of emperors and kings,
gods and demons, the texts of bibles sacred to unknown
religions, the music of an opera that took eleven galactic
years to perform. He held on the palm of his hand a
jewelled sphere no larger than a speck of dust in which were
recorded the names and histories of the million monarchs of
the nine thousand dynasties of Sapiil. He saw black towers
taller than mountains rising in an unbroken row to the
horizon. He had full perception in all directions in time as
well as space. He saw the fifty demigods of the Theluvara
Age that had been three billion years ago when even the
Kusereen were young, and he saw the Eye People of the

Great Starcloud yet to come, and the ones who called themselves the Last, though he knew they were not. My God, he thought, my God, my God, I am as nothing and You have brought all this wonder upon me. I Tom your servant. If I could only tell them the things You show me. If I could only. How can I serve You who created all this, and so much more besides? What need do You have of me? Is it to tell them? Then I will tell them. I will *show* them. I will make Thy wonders manifest in their eyes. My God, my God, my God! And still the vision went on, and on and on, worlds without end.

Then it was gone, winking out with a snap, and he lay sprawled in a ruined street in a deserted town, stupefied, gasping for breath. His clothing was drenched with sweat. Charley's worried face hovered before him.

"Tom? Tom? Can you talk, Tom?"

"Yeah. Sure."

"We thought you had a stroke."

"It was the big one," he said. "I saw it all. I saw the power and the glory. Oh, poor Tom, poor poor Tom! It was the big one, and never will it come again!"

"Let me help you up," Charley said. "We're ready to move on. Can you stand? There. There. Easy. You had another vision, huh? You see the green world?"

Tom nodded. "I saw it, yeah. I saw everything," he said. *"Everything."*

Two

Of thirty bare years have I
  Twice twenty been enraged
And of forty been three times fifteen
  In durance sadly caged.
On the lordly lofts of Bedlam
  With stubble soft and dainty
Brave bracelets strong, sweet whips, ding-dong
  With wholesome hunger plenty.

And now I do sing, "Any food, any feeding,
  Feeding, drink, or clothing?
    Come, dame or maid,
    Be not afraid,
Poor Tom will injure nothing."

—Tom O'Bedlam's Song

THERE was unexpected trouble with Nick Double Rainbow that morning, something close to a three-alarm psychotic break coming out of nowhere and more than a little violent acting-out, ugly stuff and difficult to deal with. Which was why Elszabet was late getting to the monthly staff meeting. All the others were there already —the psychiatrists, Bill Waldstein and Dan Robinson; Dante Corelli, the head of physical therapy; and Naresh Patel, the neurolinguistics man, deployed around the big redwood-burl conference table in their various relaxation modes—when she finally entered the room a little past eleven.

Dante was staring into the pumping whorls of golden light coming from a little Patternmaster in her hand. Bill Waldstein was leaning back contemplating the flask of wine sitting in front of him. Patel looked to be lost in meditation. Dan Robinson was fingering his pocket keyboard, jamming inaudible music into the recorder circuit for playback later.

They all straightened up as Elszabet took her place at the head of the table.

"Finally!" Dante said stagily, overplaying it as if Elszabet were two years late for the meeting, minimum.

"Elszabet's just been showing us that she knows how to be passive-aggressive too," said Bill Waldstein.

"Screw you," Elszabet told him casually. "Thirteen big minutes late."

"Twenty," said Patel, without appearing to break his deep trance.

"Twenty. So shoot me. You want to pass some of that wine over here, please, Dr. Waldstein?"

"Before lunch, Dr. Lewis?"

"It hasn't been a wonderful morning," she said. "I will thank all of you to recalibrate for a lower bullshit quotient, okay? Thank you. I love you all." She took the wine from Waldstein, but drank only the tiniest sip. It tasted sharp, full of little needles. Her jaw was aching. She wondered if her face was going to swell. "We've got Double Rainbow cooled out on fifty milligrams of pax," Elszabet said tiredly. "Bill, will you check in on him after lunch and consult with me afterward? He decided he was Sitting Bull on the warpath. Smashed up I don't know how many hundreds of dollars of equipment and took a swing at Teddy Lansford that knocked him halfway across the room, and I think he would have made a lot more trouble than that if Alleluia hadn't miraculously come floating into the cabin and corraled him. She's amazingly strong, you know. Thank God *she* wasn't the one who psychoed out."

Waldstein leaned toward her, hunching over a little. He was a tall, thin man, about forty, whose dark hair was just starting to go. When he hunched his shoulders like that, Elszabet knew, it was a gesture of concern, protectiveness, even overprotectiveness. She didn't care much for that, coming from him. Quietly Waldstein said, "The noble redman hit you too, didn't he, Elszabet?"

She shrugged. "I got an elbow in the mouth, more or less incidentally. Nothing detached, nothing even bent. I'm not planning to file charges."

Scowling, Waldstein said, "The crazy bastard. He must have been out of his mind, hitting *you*. Poke Lansford, I can understand, but hitting *you*? When you're the one who sits up half the night listening to him sob on and on and on about his martyred ancestors?"

"I beg to remind," said Dante. "*All* these people here are crazy. That's why they're here. We can't expect them to behave rationally, right? Anyway, Double Rainbow doesn't remember how nice Elszabet's been to him. That stuff's been picked."

"No excuse," Waldstein said sourly. "We all have martyred ancestors. Fuck him and his martyred ancestors: I don't even think he's the Sioux he says he is." Elszabet looked at Waldstein in dismay. He liked to think of himself as genial and mellow, even playful; but he had an astonishing capacity for irrelevant indignation. Once he got worked up he could go on quite a while. "I think he's a phony," Waldstein said. "A con man, like sweet Eddie Ferguson. Nick Double Rainbow! I bet his name is Joe Smith. Maybe he isn't even crazy. This is a nice rest home, isn't it, out here in the redwoods? He might just—"

"Bill," Elszabet said.

"He hit you, didn't he?"

"All right. All right. We're running late, Bill." She wanted to rub her throbbing jaw, but she was afraid it would touch off another volley of outrage from him. It might have been simpler, she thought, if she hadn't turned Waldstein down when he'd made that sudden but not altogether unpredictable play for her a year or three back. She hadn't let him get anywhere. If she had, maybe at least she wouldn't have to endure his ponderous chivalry all the time now. But then she thought, no, it wouldn't have made anything any simpler if she had done that. Then or ever.

Switching on the little recorder in front of her, Elszabet said, "Let's get started, people, shall we? Monthly staff meeting for Thursday, July 27, 2103, Elszabet Lewis presiding, Drs. Waldstein and Robinson and Patel and Ms. Corelli in attendance, 1121 hours. Okay? Instead of starting with the regular progress reports, I'd like to open with a discussion of the unusual problem that's cropped up in the past six days. I'm referring to the recurrent and overlapping dreams of a—well, fantastic nature that our patients seem to be experiencing, and I've asked Dr. Robinson to prepare a general rundown for us. Dan?"

Robinson flashed a brilliant smile, leaned back, crossed his legs. He was the senior psychiatrist at the Center, a slender, long-legged man with light coffee-colored skin, very capable, always wondrously relaxed: truly the mellow man that Bill Waldstein imagined himself to be. He was also probably the most reliable member of Elszabet's staff.

He put his hand on the mnemone capsule in front of him, hit the glossy red activator stud, and waited a moment to receive the data-burst. Then he pushed the little device aside and said, "Okay. The space dreams, we're starting to call them. What we are finding, either by direct report from the patients or as we go through the daily pick data to see what it is that we're combing out of their minds, is a pattern of vivid visionary dreams, very spacy stuff indeed. The first of these came from the synthetic woman Alleluia CX1133, who on the night of July seventeenth experienced a glimpse of a planet—she identified it as a planet in her consultation the following morning with me—with a dense green sky, a thick green atmosphere, and inhabitants of an alien form, glassy in texture and extremely elongated in bodily structure. Then, on the night of July nineteenth, Father James

Christie experienced a view of a different and far more elaborate cosmological set-up, a group of suns of various colors simultaneously visible in the sky, and an imposing figure of apparent extraterrestrial nature visible in the foreground. Because of his clerical background, Father Christie interpreted his dream as a vision of divinity, regarding the alien being as God, and I gather he underwent considerable emotional distress as a result. He reported his experience the following morning to Dr. Lewis—rather reluctantly, I gather. I've termed Father Christie's dream the Nine Suns dream, and Alleluia's the Green World dream."

Robinson paused, looking around. The room was very still.

"Okay. Now on the night of July nineteenth Alleluia had a second space dream. This one involved a double-star system, a large red sun and a smaller blue one that seems to be what astronomers call a variable star because it has a pulsating kind of energy output. This dream too was associated with an impressive extraterrestrial figure of great size—a horned being standing on a monolithic slab of white stone. I call this dream the Double Star dream. It's possible that Alleluia has had this dream several times; she's become a little evasive on the whole subject of space dreams." Robinson paused again. "Where this gets interesting," he went on, "is that on the night of July twentieth, Tomás Menendez experienced the Double Star dream also."

"The *same dream*?" Bill Waldstein asked.

"It checked in every detail. We have the pick data for both of them: of course there aren't any visuals, but we have exactly the same adrenal-output curves, the same REM fluctuations, the same alpha boost, isomorphic all the way. I think it's generally agreed that these things correlate very closely with dream activity, and I'd like to postulate that identical dreams will generate identical response curves."

He glanced questioningly at Waldstein.

"I would buy identical curves meaning identical dreams," Waldstein said, "if I could buy identical dreams. But who has identical dreams? Is there any record anywhere in the literature of such a thing?"

"In visionary experience, yes," Naresh Patel said softly. "There are any number of examples of cases where the same vision was received by a host of—"

"I don't mean out of the Upanishad or Revelations," said Waldstein. "I mean documented by western observers, contemporary clinical work, twentieth century or later."

Patel sighed, smiled, turned up the palms of his hands.

"Hold on," Dan Robinson said. "There's more. We have a fourth dream that I call the Sphere of Light dream, where the sky is a globe of total radiance and no astronomical features are evident at all because of the high level of illumination. Against this background extremely complex extraterrestrial figures are seen, what appear to be some unusually intricate life-forms with a great many limbs and appendages, so complicated that our patients are having trouble describing them in detail. So far the Sphere of Light dream has been experienced by these patients: Nick Double Rainbow on July twenty-second, Tomás Menendez July twenty-third, April Cranshaw July twenty-fourth. Father Christie experienced the Double Star dream on July twenty-fourth; once again he interpreted it as a divine manifestation, God in yet another guise—the horned being, I mean. That makes three of our people who have had that dream so far. The Green World dream was reported by Philippa Bruce on the twenty-fifth. Last night it reached Martin Clare. That's three Green Worlds here too."

"Four," Elszabet said. "Nick Double Rainbow last night, too."

Robinson said, "That's not the full list. There's an epidemic of overlapping space dreams. They're being reported all over the Center. Except, I think, from Ed Ferguson. I believe he's the only patient who hasn't said a word about them to any therapist."

"Isn't he the man who got convicted for selling real estate on other planets?" Dante asked.

"Planets of other stars, no less," Bill Waldstein said.

"Ironic that he's the only one who doesn't get to visit other worlds when he's asleep, then," Dante said.

"Unless he's concealing the dreams," Dan Robinson suggested. "That's always a possibility with him. Ferguson monkeys around with his data something fierce."

"I suspect he's got a recorder of some kind, too," Waldstein said. "Somehow he doesn't seem to pick clean— there's always a continuity that shouldn't be there—"

"Please," Elszabet said. "We're getting a little off the track. Dan, you say there are other space dreams on your list?"

"A couple. At the moment the reports are just fragmentary on those, and I'd prefer to skip them for now. But I think I've made the basic point."

"All right," said Elszabet. "We have a mystery here. A phenomenon. How do we deal with it?"

"Obviously they're telling each other their dreams," Bill Waldstein said.

"You think so?" Dan Robinson asked, startled.

"Obviously that's it. They're trying to screw us over. They all see us in an adversary position, anyway. So they're in cahoots, passing their dreams around, coaching each other—"

"We pick them," Naresh Patel said. "Then the dreams are gone. Do they meet at dawn before pick time to rehearse?"

"Alleluia doesn't always seem to lose her dreams to the pick," Dan Robinson said.

Patel nodded. "We know that is a problem, the synthetic woman's dream retention. But the others? We suspect Ferguson of making recordings, but he doesn't report dreams. Surely Father Christie is not engaged in any sort of deception, and—"

"Naresh's right about Father Christie," Elszabet said. "His dreams are real. I'd stake anything on that."

"Telepathy?" Dante said.

"Not a shred of evidence, ever," said Bill Waldstein.

"Maybe we're getting the evidence now," Dan Robinson said. "Some kind of communion going on among them— maybe it's even a pick phenomenon, an unsuspected artifact of the process—"

"Balls, Dan. What kind of wild speculation is that?" Waldstein asked.

"A speculative one," Robinson replied mildly. "We're just fishing around, aren't we? Who knows what the hell's going on here? But if we try all sorts of ideas—"

"I'm not yet convinced it *is* going on," Waldstein retorted. "We need to run reliable crosschecks to eliminate the possibility of patient collusion. After that you can talk to me about overlapping dreams, okay?"

"Absolutely," Robinson said. "No quarrel there."

"We need more data," said Patel. "We must find out all there is to know about this matter. Yes, Dr. Waldstein?"

Waldstein nodded uncertainly. "If it's really happening, yes, we need to explain it. If it's a fraud, we need to get control of it. Yes. More data. Yes."

"Fine," Elszabet said. "We're starting to reach some understanding here. Does anyone else want to say anything about this space-dream business now?"

Apparently no one did. She looked around the table twice, and there was silence on all sides. The meeting moved on to more mundane Center business. But afterward, when everyone was beginning to leave, Naresh Patel remained in his seat. The dapper neurolinguistics expert, small and fine-boned, ordinarily serene to the point of impassivity, looked oddly troubled.

"You want to see me, Naresh?" Elszabet asked.

"Yes. Please. Just for a moment."

"Go ahead." She rubbed her jaw. It was definitely beginning to puff up where Nick Double Rainbow had belted her.

Patel said in the softest possible voice, "This is a thing I did not want to say during the general meeting, though perhaps it would have been useful. This is a thing I am not yet ready to share with all my colleagues, and especially not with Dr. Waldstein in his present frame of mind. But with your permission I would like to share it with you, and only with you."

She had never seen him this disturbed. Gently she said, "You can count on my discretion, Naresh."

The little man smiled faintly. "Very well. It is this only, Dr. Lewis. I too have had what Dr. Robinson calls the Green World dream. Two nights ago. A sky like a heavy green curtain. Crystalline beings of extreme grace and beauty." He gave her a rueful look. "I am not part of the conspiracy that Dr. Waldstein insists is taking place. May we accept the truth of that declaration? I am not in league with the patients to upset the equilibrium of the Center. Please believe me, Dr. Lewis. Please. But nevertheless I tell you this, that I have had the Green World dream. Indeed. I have had the Green World dream."

2

"IT isn't much," Jaspin said. "Don't expect much. It just isn't much at all."

"That's all right," the blonde girl told him. "You don't expect much, do you, times like these?"

Her name was Jill. Her last name hadn't stuck, one of those bland nice American names, Clark, Walters, Hancock, something like that. He'd find some way of getting her to say it again. Somehow she had stayed with him after the tumbondé ceremony, holding his head against her skinny chest while he was having those weird hysterics, helping him down from the hillside when he was so shaky in that scorching heat. And now somehow they were standing outside his little place in University Heights. Apparently they were going to spend the night together, or at least the evening. What the hell, it had been a long time. But part of him wished he had managed to shake her off back there in the countryside. That was the part that still was resonating to the drums of the tumbondé folk; that was the part that still saw the titanic form of Chungirá-He-Will-Come, absolutely and unquestionably real on his throne of alabaster on the planet of some far star. Having this girl around was only a distraction, a sort of a buzz, when there were things like that throbbing in his soul. Still, he had not done much by way of getting free of her after the ceremony. What the hell.

He put his thumb on the doorplate and the door asked him who he was, and he said, "It's your lord and master. Open the hell up, fast!"

She laughed. "You've got a very individual style, Dr. Jaspin."

"Barry. Please. Barry, okay? I don't even *have* a doctorate, hard as it is for you to accept that fact." The door, having scanned his vocal contour and found it acceptable, slid back. He gestured grandly. "Entrez-vous!" They stepped inside.

He hadn't deceived her any. It wasn't much. Two rooms, fold-out kitchenette, a little terrace facing south. The building was a decent one, Spanish style, whitewashed walls, red tile roof, lush California plants crawling all over everything—purple bougainvillea, red and white hibiscus, great spiky clumps of aloes, some agaves, sago palms, all that subtropical whatnot. Probably the place had been a nice luxury condo development before the war. But now it was divided into a million tiny apartments, and of course there was no maintenance being done any more, so the property was running down very seriously. What the hell: it was home. He had wandered into it at random his first day in San Diego after he had decided he ought to get out of Los Angeles, and he was starting to feel almost comfortable in it by now, fourteen months later.

"You live in San Diego?" he asked.

She managed not to answer that. He had asked it before, when they were going to the parking lot, and she had managed not to answer it then, either. Now she was drifting around the place, agog at his library: a considerable data resource, he had to admit, cubes and tapes and chip-clusters and disks and even books, good old ancient-but-not-yet-obsolete *books*.

"Look!" she cried. "You've got Kroeber! And Mead! And Levi-Strauss, and Haverford, and Schapiro, and *everybody*. I've never seen anything like this except in a library! Do you mind?" She was pulling things off the shelves, caressing them, fondling them, the books, the tapes, the cubes. Then she turned to him. Her eyes were bright and glowing.

Jaspin had seen that look of rapture before, from girls in his classes, in the days when he had had classes. It was pure love, abstract love. It had nothing particularly to do with him, the real him; they adored him because he was the fount of learning, because he walked daily with Aristotle and Plato. And also because he was older than they were and could, if he cared to, open the gates of wisdom for them with the merest gesture of his finger. Jaspin had used his finger on a number of them, and not just his finger, either, and he suspected that some of them had actually come away the wiser for it, though perhaps not in the way they had been expecting. He figured he was past all that stuff now.

"Look, Jill," he wanted to say into that adoring gaze, "it's a real mistake to romanticize me like this. Whatever you may think I might have to offer, it just isn't there. Honestly." But he couldn't bring himself to say it.

Instead he went toward her as if he meant to sweep her into his arms; but at the last moment he simply took the book she was holding from her and fondled it as she had been doing. A true rarity, Cordry on Mexican masks, a hundred thirty years old and the color plates still bright. He was gradually selling off his library to a professor at the La Jolla campus to pay for food and rent, the same way he had acquired most of this stuff ten and fifteen years ago when he was the one with money and somebody else had been down and out.

"It's one of my great treasures," Jaspin said. "Look at these masks!" He flipped the pages. Diabolical horned faces, nightmare creatures. *Chungirá-He-Will-Come? Magualiga?* He heard the drums beginning to beat in his head again.

"And this. And this. And this." She was going into ecstasy. "Such a wonderful library! What an amazing person you must be, to have gathered all this knowledge, Dr. Jaspin!"

"Barry."

"Barry."

She went out on the terrace, reached into the hibiscus, pulled off a bright red flower to stick into her hair. Just a waif, he thought, a stray. Probably a little older than he had first guessed—twenty-seven, maybe. "You live in a very nice place," she said. "For times like these. We're lucky, aren't we, being in coastal California? It's not so good inland, is it?"

"They say it's pretty rough in there. And the farther from

the coast you get, the worse it is. Of course the worst is the states on the edge of the dusted zone. I hear that's an absolute jungle, bandidos everywhere and nobody gives a damn, everyone dying of radiation sickness anyway.'' He shook his head. It sickened him to think of it, the mess that the Dust War had made. No bombs, not a single bomb dropped, you couldn't use bombs without touching off the ultimate holocaust that everybody agreed would mean mutual annihilation, so they just used the controlled radiation clouds instead, taking out the agricultural states, wiping out the whole heartland, breaking the country in half, in thirds, even. As we did to them, only worse. And now thirty years later we crawl around in the remains of western civilization, pruning our bougainvilleas and playing our music cubes and going to anthropology class and pretending that we have rebuilt the world out here in the sunshine of California while for all we know people have turned into cannibals five hundred miles east of here. He said aloud, ''That's what I was going to write about. The modern world from an anthropological view: almost sociology, sort of. The world as high-tech jungle. Of course I won't do that now.''

''You won't?''

''I doubt it. I'm not with the university any longer. I have no sponsorship. Sponsorship's important.''

''You could do it on your own, Barry. I know you could.''

''That's very kind,'' he said. ''Listen, are you hungry? I've got a little stuff here, and the prickly pears growing on that cactus in the courtyard are actually edible, so we could—''

''Do you mind if I just take a shower? I feel real sticky, and there's this paint all over me, the Maguali-ga markings—''

''Sure,'' he said. ''What day is it? Friday? Sure, we have shower water on Fridays.''

She was out of her clothing in a moment. No shame. No

breasts, either, no hips, buttocks flat as a boy's. What the hell. She was female, anyway. He was pretty sure of that, although you couldn't always tell for certain, the way they did transplants and implants and such nowadays. He showed her into the shower cubicle and found a towel for her. Then—what the hell—he stripped off and went in with her. "We don't have much of a water quota," he said. "We'd better double up."

She turned to him when they were under the spray and wrapped her legs around him, and he backed her up against the tiled wall, holding her with his hands under her buttocks. His eyes were closed most of the time, but once he opened them and he saw that hers were open and that she still had that adoring glowing rapturous look. Like he was putting fifty encyclopedias into her with each thrust.

It was all very fast, but very satisfying, too. There was no getting away from that, the satisfaction of it. But afterward came the sadness, the guilt, the shame, and there was no getting away from that, either. Making love, somebody had called it, long ago. What love, where? Two pathetic strangers, jamming parts of their bodies together for a few minutes: love?

Jaspin thought, I have to try to be honest with this girl. It would have been nicer if I had tried to be honest before we did it, but then maybe we wouldn't have done it, and I guess I wanted to do it too much. That's honest too, isn't it? Isn't it?

Leaning calm and dejected on the edge of the sink, he said, looking at her little pink-tipped breasts, her boyish hips, her damp stringy hair, "I've got to tell you this flat out. You think I'm some sort of noble romantic intellectual figure, don't you? Well, I'm not, okay? I'm nobody. I'm a phony. I'm a failure, Jill."

"So am I," she said.

He looked at her, startled. It was the first authentic thing he had heard out of her mouth since he had met her.

He said, "I used to be somebody. Bright kid, rich L.A. family, lots of promise. Going to be one of the great anthropologists, but somewhere along the way I became *farblondjet*." A mystified look. "You don't know it? Yiddish word. Means confused, bewildered, totally mixed up. The cafard of the soul, the great early-twenty-second-century disease, what I think they're calling Gelbard's syndrome now. I fell apart, is what I did. And I didn't even know why. It became too much trouble to get up in the morning. It became much too much trouble to go to classes. I wasn't exactly depressed, you understand—Gelbard's syndrome is something a little different from clinical depression, they tell me, it's deeper, it's a response to the whole human mess, a sort of cultural exhaustion, a burnout phenomenon—but I was *farblondjet*. Still am. I have no career. I have no future. I am not the heroic demigod of culture that you probably imagine me to be."

"I sat in on your course. You were very profound."

"Repeating the stuff I had found in these books. What's profound about a glib tongue? What's profound about a good memory? I sounded profound to you because you didn't know any better. What was your major at UCLA, anyway?"

"I didn't have one. I just audited courses."

"No degree?"

A shrug. "I wanted to learn everything. But there was so much, I didn't know where to start. So I guess I never started. But now I'll have a second chance, won't I?"

"What do you mean?"

There was a strange bright edge on her voice, like thin copper wires scraping together. "To learn. From you. I'll do the cleaning, the shopping, whatever, all the jobs. And we'll study together. That's all right, isn't it? I'll help you with your book. I don't actually have a place to live right now, you know. But I don't take up a lot of room, and I'm very neat, and—''

It surprised him that he had not seen it coming. He felt his forehead beginning to throb. He imagined that Chungirá-He-Will-Come had reached out with one enormous paw and had closed it around his entire head, and was squeezing, squeezing, squeezing—

''I'm not going to write the book,'' Jaspin said. ''And I'm not going to stay here in San Diego.''

''You're not?''

''No. I won't be here much longer at all.''

He was startled beyond measure by what he had just said. That came as news to him, that he was leaving San Diego.

''Where will you go?'' she asked.

He waited a beat for his mouth to supply the answer, and then he heard himself say, ''I'm going to go wherever Senhor Papamacer goes. To the Seventh Place, I guess. Following the tumbondé people to the North Pole if I have to.''

''Do you mean that?''

''I suppose I do,'' Jaspin said. ''I have to do it.''

''To study them?''

''No. To wait for Chungirá-He-Will-Come.''

''You believe in Him, then.'' He could hear the capital *H*.

''I do now. Since today, on that hillside. I saw something, Jill. And it changed me. I felt literally knocked to my knees, the true conversion experience. Maybe conversion's too pretentious a word, but—'' This is preposterous, he thought, a couple of naked people who don't even know each other, sitting in a tiny bathroom talking nonsense like this. ''I've never been a religious man,'' he said. ''Jewish, at least my parents were, but that was just a cultural thing, nobody actually went to synagogue, you understand. But this is different. What I felt today—I want to feel it again. I want to go wherever I stand a chance of feeling it again. It's the times, Jill, the era, the *Zeitgeist*, you know? In times of total despair, revelatory religion has always held the answer. And now it's happened even to me, cynical urban you-name-it Barry Jaspin. I'm going to follow Senhor Papamacer and wait for Maguali-ga to open the gateway for Chungirá-He-Will-Come.'' There was fire pumping through his veins. Do I really mean all this, he wondered? Yes. Yes. I actually do. Amazing, he thought. I actually mean what I'm telling her.

"Can I come with you?'' she asked timidly, reverently.

3

CHARLEY said, "Now tell me about the one you saw yesterday, the one where the starlight lights up the sky like day.''

"The world of the Eye People, that's what you mean?'' Tom asked.

"Is that it?''

"The Eye People, yes. Of the Great Starcloud.''

"Tell me,'' Charley said. "I love to listen to you when you're seeing this stuff. I think you're a real prophet, man, you're something straight out of the Bible.''

"You think I'm crazy, don't you?'' Tom said.

Softly Charley said, "I wish you'd stop saying that. Do I tell you that I think you're crazy?''

"I *am* crazy, Charley. Poor Tom. Poor crazy Tom. Ran away from one madhouse right into another one.''

"A madhouse? Really? An honest-to-Christ nuthatch?"

"Pocatello," Tom said. "You know where that is? They had me locked up a year and a half."

Charley smiled. "Plenty of sane men locked up like that, plenty of crazy ones outside. Don't mean a thing. I try to tell you, I respect you, I admire you. I think you're phenomenal. And you sit here saying I think you're crazy. Come on. Tell me about the Eye People, man!"

Charley seemed sincere. He isn't just making fun of me, Tom thought. It's because he's seen the green world himself. I hope he gets to see some of the other ones. He really wants to see. He really wants to know about these worlds. He's a scratcher, maybe even used to be a bandido, I bet he's killed twenty people, and yet he wants to know, he's curious, he's almost gentle, in his way. I'm lucky to be traveling with him, Tom told himself.

"The Eye People don't exist yet," he said. "They're maybe a million, maybe three million years from now, or maybe it's a billion, that's very hard to know. I get confused when these past and future things come in. You understand, all the thought impulses, they float around the universe back and forth, and the speed of thought is much faster than the speed of light, so the visions overtake the light, they pass it right by, you can get a vision out of a place that doesn't even exist yet, and maybe a million or a billion years from now the light of that sun will finally get to Earth. You follow what I'm saying?"

"Sure," Charley said doubtfully.

"The Eye People live—or will live—on a planet that has maybe ten thousand stars right close around it, or a hundred thousand, who can even count them, one next to another all jammed together so that from this planet they look like one single wall of light that fills the whole sky. You go out any time of day or night, what you see is this tremendous light

blazing away from all sides. You don't see any one star, just
a lot of light. All white, like the sky is white-hot."

Mujer came over. "Charley?"

"Be with you five minutes."

"Can you talk to me now, Charley?"

Charley looked up, annoyed. "Okay, go ahead."

The scratchers were camped a little way east of Sacramento,
toward the coastal side of the Valley. There still were some
working farms around there, and most of them were very
well defended. The scratching was lousy here; Charley and
his men were getting hungry; he had sent a bunch of them
out scouting that afternoon.

Mujer said, "Stidge and Tamale just came back. They
say they found a farm down in the river fork that they think
can be taken, and they want to go in as soon as it gets
dark."

"Why you the one telling me, then, and not Stidge?"

"Buffalo said you'd gone off with Tom and didn't want to
be bothered, and Stidge decided not to bother you."

"But you did?"

Mujer said, "I wanted to talk to you before Stidge and
Tamale did. You know, Tamale's always wrong about everything. And that Stidge, he's a wild man. I don't trust them a
lot."

"You think I do?"

"When Stidge says a place can be taken, and Tamale says
it too, then I don't know, Charley, I think maybe we ought
to keep away. That's all. I wanted to tell you before Stidge
got to you."

"Okay, man. I understand what you're saying."

"I wouldn't have bothered you otherwise," Mujer said.

"Sure. But we need to eat, Mujer. I think what I'll do,
I'll take a look at this place of Stidge and Tamale's. Maybe
they're right for once and we can take it, and if I think so,
we will. And if I don't think so, we won't. Okay, Mujer?"

"Okay. Sorry I bothered you."

"Nothing, man." Charley waved Mujer away. Turning to Tom again, he said, "Okay. The Eye People."

Charley doesn't have much trouble, Tom thought, shifting gears like that. One minute he's talking about raiding somebody's farm, the next he wants to be told about worlds in the stars. He didn't seem like a killer. His eyes were deep and somber, and there was something close to kind and almost poetic about him sometimes. And other times not. He really was a killer, Tom knew. Underneath the kind, underneath the poetic. But what was underneath that?

Tom said, "They live in a world of light that never goes dark and it's so thick and dense that they can't see the rest of the universe. In fact, they can't really see anything at all, because the light of the Great Starcloud is so bright that there's no contrast, there's no way to pick out one thing against another. It like blinds you, there's so much of it. You overdose on light. Instead of seeing, they *sense*, and every part of their body picks up images. All over their skins. That's why they're called the Eye People, because they're like one big eye all over. You understand, they don't exist yet. But they will. They're one of the coming races. There are a thousand four hundred coming races listed in the Book of Moons, but naturally that's just the ones in the Book of Moons. In fact there are billions and billions of coming races, but the universe is so big that even the Zygerone and the Kusereen don't know a thousandth of it. But there they are, the Eye People, and their minds are so sensitive that they can reach out and *feel* the rest of the universe. They know about suns and stars and planets and galaxies and all that, but it's by guess and feel and intuition, the way a blind man knows about red and blue and green. Their minds are in contact with the other worlds of the Sacred Imperium, past and future. They learn about the outside universe, and in return they show other people the

Great Starcloud, which is holy because its light is so powerful, so complete. It's like the light of the Buddha, you know? It fills the whole void. And so the Eye People—"

"Charley? They said you were through talking to him." Stidge.

"I'm not quite," Charley said. Then he stood up. "Shit. All right. We'll finish some other time. What is it, Stidge?"

"Farmhouse. Seven hundred meters down, in the fork. Man, woman, three sons. They got screens up but the electronics is lousy. We can go right in."

"You sure of that?"

"Absolutely. Tamale saw it too."

"Yeah," Charley said. "Tamale's got terrific judgment."

"I'm telling you, Charley—"

"Okay. Okay, Stidge. Let's go down and have a look at this place, you and me? Okay?"

"Sure," Stidge said.

Tom stayed where he was, under a big plane tree at the side of a little mostly dried-up stream that probably flowed only in winter. He watched Charley and Stidge go off into the late afternoon shadows; and then after a while they came back and spoke with the others, and then all eight of them went off together. Tom wondered about that, what was going to happen down at the farm in the river fork. After a while he found himself wandering over that way to find out.

The farmhouse came into view in just a few minutes. It was a small white wooden building that looked about a hundred fifty years old, with dark green shingles and a huge fat-trunked palm tree out front overshadowing the porch. The red glow of a protective screen surrounded the house. Just as Tom got there the screen winked out, and then he heard shouts and screams and one very loud scream above all the rest of the noise. After that it was quiet for a moment; then there were shouts again, angry ones. Tom went to the door, thinking, Be strong and of a good courage, be not afraid, neither be thou dismayed: for the Lord thy God is with thee, whithersoever thou goest.

He looked in. Two people, a man and a woman, were sprawled on the floor in that peculiar twisted herky-jerk way that indicated they had been killed with a spike. A third person—boy, rather, maybe sixteen, seventeen—was pressed up against the wall, white-faced, bug-eyed, and Stidge had his spike against his throat.

"Stidge!" Charley yelled, just as Tom entered. "Stidge, you crazy son of a bitch!"

"I got him," Mujer said, coming up behind Stidge and smoothly grabbing the red-haired man's wrist with one hand while locking his other arm around Stidge's throat. Stidge growled in surprise. Mujer, who seemed incredibly strong for the wiry little guy he was, bent Stidge's arm outward until the spike in Stidge's hand was practically touching Stidge's right ear. "Let me kill him this time," Mujer begged. "He's no good, Charley. He's a wild man. Look what he just did, the farmer and his wife."

"Hey, no, Charley," Stidge cried in a strangled voice thick with terror. "Hey, make him let go!"

"You didn't need to do that, Stidge," Charley said. His face looked bleak and stormy. "Now we got two deads on our hands and two of the sons got loose, and what for? What for?"

"Should I do him, Charley?" Mujer asked eagerly.

Charley seemed to be considering it. Tom stepped forward. No one had noticed him come in; now they all looked at him in amazement, all but Stidge, whose face was to the wall. Tom touched Mujer's arm. His eyes felt strange. He was having trouble seeing straight: everything looked glazed and blurred, as if it were coated with ice.

"No," Tom said. "Let him be. Vengeance is mine, saith the Lord. Not yours, Mujer. Avenge not yourselves, but rather give place unto wrath. Let him be." Tom took firm hold of Mujer's arm and pulled it back until the spike was well away from Stidge's face.

"What . . . ?" Mujer was astonished. "The lunatic?" He whirled, ripping the spike from Stidge's hand and bringing it around as if he meant to jab it into Tom's chest.

"The Lord my God is with me, whithersoever I go," said Tom mildly. His eyes were still out of focus. He saw two Mujers and just a red-topped blob instead of Stidge.

"Jesus," said Mujer. "Jesus, what do we have here?"

"All right," Charley said, irritated. "Enough of this goddamn stuff. Mujer, give Stidge back his spike."

"But—"

"*Give it back*." To Stidge, Charley said, "You're lucky Tom walked in here when he did. I had a half a mind to let Mujer do you. You're a liability to us, Stidge."

"I'm the one turned the screen off, didn't I?" Stidge shot back. "I'm the one got us in here!"

"Yeah," Charley said. "But we could have gotten in and out without killing. Now we got two deads lying here and two missing. Stidge, you got to keep control of those weapons of yours. You don't let yourself get out of hand again, you hear? Next time we're gonna do you, you run wild. Hear?" Charley waved his hand at the others. "All right, start packing up anything we can use. Food, weapons, whatever. We can't hang around."

"I don't believe it," Mujer muttered, staring at Tom. "He hates you, you know? Stidge. I'm about to do him, and you come over and grab my arm. I don't believe it."

"Come out, come out, thou bloody man, thou son of Belial," Tom said.

"The Bible again," said Mujer disgustedly. "Damn looney."

Tom smiled. They were all staring at him. Let them stare. He could not have countenanced killing in cold blood. Even Stidge. Tom glanced toward him. There was a cold baleful glare on Stidge's face. He hates me even more now, Tom realized. Now that he knows he owes his life to me. But I am not afraid. Love your enemies, that's what He taught us, do good to them that hate you, bless them that curse you. He realized that he was seeing straight again, calming down some. "Thank you," Tom said to Charley. "For sparing him."

"Yeah," Charley grunted. "Jesus, Tom. You had no business. That was crazy, what you did. Walking in like that. Mujer, he might have put the spike right through you and Stidge both. You know that?"

"I would not let another life be taken. The Lord is the only judge."

"You had no call messing in. It wasn't your place to decide things here. It was crazy, Tom. Doing what you did just then. Okay? That's what I call it, crazy. It wasn't your place at all. Now get the hell out of here until we're finished. Go on, get out."

"Okay," Tom said. He went out. But he looked back through the window, just long enough to see Charley lift the laser bracelet on his wrist and aim a shaft of fiery light at the terrified farmboy cowering against the wall. The boy fell, most likely dead before he hit the ground. Tom winced and muttered a prayer. A little while later Charley came out of the house. "I saw that," Tom said. "How could you do that? I don't make sense out of it. You got angry when Stidge killed the man and the woman. And then you yourself—"

Charley spat. "Once there's killing, there got to be more killing. Kill the parents, you better kill the son too, or he'll track you down no matter where you go. The other two boys got away, and I hope to hell they didn't see our faces." Then, shaking his head, he said, "What's the matter? I told you not to stick around. You had to look, didn't you? Well, so you saw. You think I'm a goddamn saint, Tom?" He laughed. "This ain't no time for being a saint. Come on," now. Come on. Tell me some more about the Eye People. You really *see* all this shit, don't you? Like it's really real to you. You're amazing, you crazy son of a bitch. Tell me. Tell me what you see."

4

FERGUSON said to April Cranshaw, "You're honest to God not making all this up? The sky full of light? The flying jellyfish beings? Hey, hey, do me a favor and own up to it. It's all just a big joke, right? Right?"

"Ed," she said reproachfully, as if he had just peed on her party dress. "Stop trying to do that to me, Ed. I'm going to walk away from you if you keep messing with my head. Be nice, Ed."

"Yeah," he said. "I'll be nice."

The bastards were all in a sweat over this stuff. Talked of almost nothing else. First thing in the morning when you went in for your pick, they wanted to know about your dreams. Then they had meetings all afternoon. People being summoned for special testing, questioning, whatnot.

Not him. Never him. He didn't get the dreams, not ever. That puzzled them. Puzzled him, too. Made him wonder why he was singled out, the only one. Made him wonder if the dreams were happening at all. Bastards, the bunch of them. Trying to cut him out, trying to fool him all the time.

"Just give me a straight answer," he said. "You aren't making this up? You really do have dreams like that?"

"Every night," she said. "I swear."

He studied her face like it was a prospectus for an oceanfront development scheme. She looked like a pudding, bland and jiggly. She looked sincere as hell. Sweet wide smile, gentle blue-green eyes. Ferguson didn't see how she could be capable of lying. Not this one. The others, sure, but not this one.

"Sometimes even during the day," she went on. "I close my eyes a minute, still awake, and I get pictures under my eyelids."

"You do? Daytimes?"

"This very day. The jellyfish people, middle of the morning."

"After you were picked, then."

"That's right. It's still fresh."

"Go on. Tell me what you saw."

"You know we aren't supposed to tell each other—"

"Tell me," he said.

He wondered if he had ever slept with her. Probably not: she was eighty, a hundred pounds overweight, not his type at all. His recorder didn't have any information on the subject, but that didn't mean it hadn't happened, only that he hadn't bothered to feed the data about it into the recorder, and now it was too late to know. He could have *shtupped* her ten times last month and neither of them would have any way of knowing it now. Things came and went. That time last month when Mariela had visited—she had been like a stranger to him, he didn't really know her at all. Or want to. His own wife. If he hadn't put it on the recorder he wouldn't even know she'd been here.

Uncomfortably April said, "Dr. Lewis told me I must absolutely not reveal my dream content except during the interrogatory sessions, that it would contaminate the data."

"You always do whatever you're told?"

"I'm here to be healed, Ed."

"You give me a pain, April. You and that sea wind that blows all the time."

"Let's walk a little," she said.

They were at the edge of the woods, going along the trail through the redwood forest just east of the Center. It was the free-time part of the afternoon. The wind, cool and strong, was coming in off the ocean like a fist, the way it always did this time of day. Every afternoon they gave you an hour or two of free time. No therapy in the afternoon; they wanted you to go out and stroll in the forest, or play skill games in the rec room, or just futz around with your fellow inmates.

Ferguson would rather have been with Alleluia right now. But he didn't know where she was, and somehow April had found him. She had a way of doing that, somehow, during free-time.

"You're really obsessed with the space dreams, aren't you?" she asked.

"Isn't everybody?"

"But you keep asking all the time, what are they like, what are they like."

"It's because I don't get them myself."

"You will," she said softly. "It just isn't your turn, yet. But your turn will come."

Yeah, he thought. When? This had been going on, what, two weeks now? Three? Hard to keep track of time in this place. After you had had a little picking, each day started to flow seamlessly into the one before, the one after. But the dreams, everyone was having them, the inmates and at least one of the staff technicians, that queer Lansford, and maybe even a few of the doctors. Everyone but him. That was the thing of it: everyone but him. It was almost like they were all getting together behind his back to fake up a gigantic mountain of bullshit to pile on top of him, this space-dream stuff.

"I know your turn will come," she said. "Oh, Ed, the dreams are so beautiful!"

"I wouldn't know," he said. "Let's go this way. Into the woods."

She giggled nervously. Almost a whinny.

Ferguson didn't think he'd slept with her. So far as his ring-recorder indicated, Alleluia was the only one since he'd been here. Women April's size had never been his thing, though he could certainly see the potential prettiness deep down inside all that flesh, the buried cheekbones, the nice nose and lips. About thirty-five, came from L.A. like him, very screwed up like everybody here. What bothered him more than the fat was the way her head worked, so ready to believe all sorts of fantastic things. That we all had lived lots of lives and could get in touch with our previous selves, and that some people really were able to read minds, and that gods and spirits and maybe even witches and elves were real and existed all around us, and so on. It made no sense to him, all her goofy beliefs. The real world hadn't treated her very well so she lived in a bunch of imaginary ones. She had showed him pictures of herself dressed up in costumes, medieval clothes, even one in a suit of armor, a fat lady knight ready to go off to the Crusades. Jesus. No wonder she loved the space dreams.

But he had to know if this crap was really happening.

It was quiet here in the forest. Wind in the treetops, nothing else. Good clean redwood smell. He was starting to like it here a little.

"Why don't you believe we really have the dreams?" she asked.

Ferguson looked at her. "Two things," he said. "One is that all my life I been dealing with people who experience things I don't experience. The ones who go to church, the ones who hang tinsel on their Christmas trees, the ones who think that prayers are answered. Those people have *assurances*.

You know what I mean? I never had an assurance of any damn thing, except that I had to make my own luck because there was no one out there going to make it for me. You follow me? Sometimes I'd like to pray too, just like everybody else, only I know there's no use in it. So I feel myself sitting outside what a lot of people know for certain. And when these sort of weird dreams come along, and everyone says how beautiful, how wonderful, and I don't get them—you know how I feel? Go on, tell me I'm paranoid. Maybe I am, or I wouldn't be in a place like this, but I never could believe in anything I couldn't touch with my own hands, and I'm not touching these dreams."

"You said there were two things, Ed."

"The other one is, you know I was supposed to go to jail?" He wondered why he was telling her so much about himself. There might be some way she could use this stuff to hurt him. No, he thought, not her. Sweet April. "Convicted of fraud is what I was. Selling trips to the planet Betelgeuse Five is what I was doing. We'd promise to send you I forget how many light-years, fifteen, fifty, not in the actual flesh but just your mind, by a process of metem—metem—"

"Metempsychosis?" April said.

"That's it, yeah. People signed up in droves. I'm surprised you weren't on our list. Christ, maybe you were. Everybody wanting to go, but of course it was just bullshit, we were going to have trouble with the process and refund all the deposits later on, but meanwhile we were making interest on the cash, you see? Plenty of it, millions. And then they got us. Me. I took the fall, some of the others got off. But what eats me, April, is now the scam is coming true, in reverse, goddamn Betelgeuse Five is metempsychosing to *Earth*. That's what's so unbelievable to me, that suddenly people's minds are in tune with other stars, the very thing I was peddling. I knew I was phony. But this—"

"No, it's real, Ed."

"How do I know? How do I *know*? Sometimes I think the
bastards are just fooling me. Making it all up just to mess
up my head." They were deep in the forest now. Just the
two of them. Is that really what I believe, he asked himself.
That it's like a conspiracy? Even Lacy, back in San Francisco,
seeing the big golden thing with horns: Alleluia had seen the
same thing. Could Lacy possibly be in on the deal too? No,
how could Lacy have managed to tell her dream to Alleluia?
She didn't even know that Alleluia existed. Even he had to
admit that it was crazy to doubt the dreams. But all the
same he did doubt. "Tell me about what you saw this
morning," he said. "The jellyfish people."

"I'm not supposed to discuss—"

"Jesus," he said. They were all alone, nobody around
but the chipmunks. He smiled and came close to her. For an
instant she gave him a worried, frightened look. "You could
be very attractive, you know?" Ferguson told her, and drew
her up against him. She was wearing a blue cashmere
pullover, fuzzy, soft. He slipped his hand up under it and
felt her breast, bare within, so big that he couldn't cover the
whole of it with his outspread fingers. She closed her eyes
and began to sigh. He found her nipple and rubbed his
thumb against it slowly, and in an instant it was hard as a
pebble. She pushed the lower half of her body against him
again and again and made little sighing sounds.

Then he took his hand away.

"Don't stop," she said.

"I want to know. I need to know. Tell me what you
saw."

"Ed—"

He smiled. He put his mouth over hers and slid his tongue
between her lips, and touched her breast again, outside the
sweater. "Tell me."

With a sigh she said, "All right. Don't stop and I'll tell
you. The sky on this world I dreamed is all lit up, it's a

million billion stars surrounding the planet, so there's day-time all the time, brilliant daytime. And these beings float through the atmosphere. They're gigantic, and they look something like enormous jellyfish, transparent, with dangling stuff, very intricate. Oh, Ed, I shouldn't be telling you this!''

He massaged her stiff nipple. "You're doing terrific. Keep going.''

"Each entity is a colony of beings, like. There's the dark brain in the middle, and then there are the coiling dangling things that hunt for food, and the ones with little oar-legs that propel the colony, and the ones that—that do the reproductive things, and—and, oh, I don't know, there must be fifty other kinds, all bound together, writhing clusters and tangles of them, each one with a sort of mind of its own, but all connected to the main mind. And on the outside of the whole thing are the perceptors that function in all this dazzling light like eyes, but they aren't really eyes because they're all over every bit of the outside—''

He said, "Did it look the same the other time you saw it?''

"I don't know, Ed. They picked me, remember? I lost it then. But I think it must have been the same, because it's a real projection of a real world, so how can it be different each time?''

He didn't know about real projection of a real world. But her description was the same, for sure. She was using some of the exact phrases she had the other day, two, three, four days ago, when she had first told him about the jellyfish people and the sky full of light. He couldn't remember what she had said that day any more than she could, but he had it all down on his recorder. And that was what she had said and he had transcribed, writhing clusters and tangles and a dark brain inside the transparent body.

"You mustn't say I told you, Ed.''

"No. Of course not."

"Hold me again, won't you please?"

He nodded. Her face came up toward his, eyes bright and misty, lips parted, tongue-tip visible. Poor fat broad. Proabably wishes she could leave her body behind and jump to that other world tomorrow and live like a jellyfish-being with dangling clusters of stuff. Happily ever after.

"Oh, Ed—Ed—"

Goddamn, he thought. There's no hiding from it: they all do have these dreams, everybody but me, sharing the same dreams, Christ only knows how. The bastards, the bastards. Everybody but me. He asked himself what use he could make out of all this. There had to be a use. All his life he had turned to his own use the fact that he missed out on a lot of things that other people experienced. All right, this too. Maybe they'll have some special need for somebody who's immune to the dreams and I can trade that for an end to the goddamn daily mindpicking, or something. Maybe.

April pressed herself close, pistoning her hips against him.

"Yeah," he said softly. A deal was a deal. She had told him what he wanted to know; now he had to come through for her. He slipped his hand under her sweater again.

5

ELSZABET said, "Output Dreamlist," and the data wall in her office lit up like a stock-exchange ticker display.

1) Green World   Six reports
Single green sun, heavy green
atmosphere, crystalline human-
oid inhabitants.

2) Nine Suns   Three reports
Nine suns, various colors, in
sky simultaneously; large extraterrestrial figure frequently
visible.

3) Double Star One   Seven reports
Large red sun, variable blue;
extraterrestrial being, horned,
associated with white stone
slab.

4) Double Star Two   Two reports
One yellow star, one white
one, both much larger than our
sun. Matter streaming from
both stars forming veil around
whole system emitting intense
red aura in sky of planet.

5) Sphere of Light   Six reports
Planet positioned within
globular star cluster so populous
that constant brilliant light
encloses it on all sides.
Inhabited by complex
medusoid/colonial atmosphere-
dwelling creatures.

6) Blue Giant   Two reports
Enormous blue star giving off
fierce output of energy.
Planetary landscape molten,
bubbling. Ethereal inhabitants
not clearly visualized.

* * *

"Data entry," Elszabet said.

She began to post the morning's haul of dream reports.

April Cranshaw, Blue Giant.

Tomás Menendez, Green World.

Father Christie, Double Star Two.

Poor Father Christie. He took the dreams worse than any of the others, always interpreting each one as God's personal message to him. He still hated to give them up. Every morning she had to go through the same struggle with him, usually needing to double-pick him to get him clean. Maybe if we weren't picking him, she thought, the dreams would lose some of their transcendental power for him, and he'd be easier about the whole thing. On the other hand, if he weren't getting picked he'd have to contend with the notion that God had come to him in half a dozen different bizarre alien guises over the past few weeks. And most likely he'd be in deep schiz by now, far beyond retrieval, if he had access to more than one dream at a time. Better that he should think each one was his first.

Elszabet continued with the day's entries.

Philippa Bruce, Sphere of Light.

Alleluia CX1133, Nine Suns.

She felt something that seemed like a headache beginning to invade her, just the ghost of it, a tickling little throb around her temples. Strange. She never got headaches. Hardly ever. Time of the month, maybe? No, she thought. After-effects of getting punched by Nick Double Rainbow? But that was over a week ago. General tension and stress, then? All this puzzling over weird dreams? Whatever, the sensation was getting a little worse. Pressure behind her eyes, unfamiliar, nasty. She touched the neutralizer node on her watch and gave herself a buzz of alpha sound. First time she'd done that in ages. The pressure eased off a little.

Going onward. *Teddy Lansford, Nine Suns*.

A knock at the door. Elszabet frowned and glanced at the viewscreen. She saw Dan Robinson outside, lounging amiably against the frame of the door.

"You spare a minute?" he asked. "Got something new for you."

She let him in. He had to stoop crossing the threshold. Robinson was an elongated man, basketball-player physique, all arms and legs. He practically filled the little room. Elszabet's office was nothing more than a small bare functional cubicle, floor of rough gray planks, tiny window, orange glow-light floating overhead. Not even a desk or a computer terminal, just a couple of chairs facing the floor-to-ceiling data wall. She liked it that way.

Robinson peered at the data wall. The Teddy Lansford entry was still showing. He nodded toward it.

"That's his fourth one, isn't it?"

"Third," Elszabet said.

"Third. Even so, why does he get the dreams and not the rest of us? It doesn't figure, that only one staff member should get the dreams."

"Teddy's the only one willing to admit it, maybe," she said. She didn't amplify his statement. Naresh Patel's lone Green World dream was still a confidential matter between him and Elszabet, and would stay that way as long as Patel wanted it that way.

"You suspect that other staff people are hiding them?" Robinson asked. His eyes were suddenly very wide, very white in his chocolate-toned face. "You think I am, maybe?"

"Are you?"

"You serious?"

"Well, are you?" she asked, a little too sharply. She wondered why she was being so sharp with him. He was wondering too, obviously.

"Hey. Come off it, Elszabet."

The headache was back. She felt the pressure again, stronger than before, a heavy throbbing at the temples. She shook her head, trying to clear it.

"Sorry," she said. "I didn't mean to imply—"

"You know I'm dying to experience one of those dreams. But so far it seems Lansford's the only lucky one."

"So far, yes."

Except for Naresh Patel, she thought. And that had been just one time.

"Why do you think that is?" Robinson asked.

"Not a clue." Elszabet hesitated and said—a stab in the dark—"Could it be that the dreaming or lack of it is a function of emotional resilience? The patients are extremely wobbly around the psyche, otherwise they wouldn't be here, after all. That must lay them open to any manner of disturbances that staff people wouldn't be vulnerable to. Such as these dreams."

"And is Teddy Lansford wobbly around the psyche?"

"Well, he's homosexual."

"So what?"

She rubbed her forehead lightly. Something hammering away in there. It embarrassed her to press for an alpha buzz in front of Dan Robinson.

"So nothing, I guess," she said. "A silly hypothesis." And Naresh Patel isn't particularly wobbly around the psyche either, Elszabet told herself. Or gay, for that matter. "Lansford's actually pretty sturdy emotionally, don't you think?"

"I'd say so."

She said, "I can't tell you, then. Maybe when we have more data we'll be able to figure it better. Right now I don't know." Brusquely she added, "You said there was something new you wanted to talk to me about?"

He looked at her. "Are you okay, Elszabet?"

"Sure. No, not really. Beginnings of a headache." Something beyond just beginnings, now. It was really banging away. "Why, does it show that much?"

"You seem a little touchy, is all. Impatient. Sharp. Short. Not much like your usual self."

Elszabet shrugged. "One of those days, I guess. One of those weeks. Look, I told you I was sorry for snapping at you like that before, didn't I?" Then she said more softly, "Let's start this all over, okay? You wanted to see me. What's up, Dan?"

"There's a new dream. Number Seven. Double Star Three."

"How's that? I thought we had all the reports for today."

"Well, now there's one more. This one courtesy of April Cranshaw, half an hour ago."

With a shake of her head Elszabet said, "We've already got April's entry. She reported the Blue Giant dream for last night."

"This isn't last night," Robinson said. "It's this morning, after pick."

That was startling. "What? A daytime dream?"

"So it seems. April was shy about admitting it. I think she was afraid we'd send her back for a second picking this morning. But it was on her conscience and she finally came in with it. This may not be the first daytime dream she's had."

"She's now had more dreams than anyone," Elszabet said.

"Right at the top of the sensitivity curve, yes. I think she knows that too. And is a little troubled about it."

"What kind of dream was this?"

"This is what I jotted down," Robinson said.

He handed her a slip of paper. Elszabet looked it over and said to the data wall, "Input Dreamlist." The screen gave her input format and she read the new dream in:

7) Double Star Three   One report
                         One sun much like ours in
                         size and color, but second
                         sun emitting orange/red light
                         also present, of larger size
                         than yellow one but more
                         faint. Intricate system of
                         moons. No life-forms re-
                         ported.

"That's handy, having that list," Robinson said.

"It is, yes," Elszabet said. She said to the data wall, "Output Dreamlist, Distribution Route One."

"What are you doing, printing it out for general reference use at the Center?"

"That's a good idea. I'll do that next."

"What's Distribution Route One, then?"

"I just sent it around to the other Northern California mindpick centers," Elszabet said.

Dan Robinson's eyes went wide again. "You did?"

"San Francisco, Monterey, Eureka. I called around this morning to tell them what's going on here, and Paolucci in San Francisco said yes, they were having something along the same lines, and he had heard the same thing from Monterey. So we're setting up a data link. Dream descriptions, tallies of incidence. We need to know what in God's name is happening. An epidemic of identical dreams? That's brand-new in the whole literature of mental disturbance. If mental disturbance is actually what we're dealing with."

"I wonder," Robinson said. "There's going to be some bitching, you going out to the other centers with this before bringing it up at a staff meeting here."

"You think so?" The pounding in her skull was getting to the impossible level now. Something in there trying to get out? That was how it seemed. "Excuse me," Elszabet said, and gave herself a buzz of alphas. She felt her cheeks reddening, doing that sort of modification in front of him. The pain eased just a little. Trying not to sound as irritated as she really was, she said to Robinson, "I didn't think it was classified stuff. I simply wanted to know if the other centers were experiencing this phenomenon, so I started calling, and they said yes, we are, send us your data and we'll send back ours, and——" Elszabet shut her eyes a moment and clenched her teeth hard and drew a deep breath. "Listen, can we talk about these things some other time? I need to get some fresh air. I'm going to run down to the beach, I think. This lousy headache."

"Good idea," Robinson said gently. "I could use some exercise too. You mind if I run with you?"

Yes, I do mind, she thought. Very much. The beach was her special place, her second office, really. She tried to escape to it a couple of times a week, whenever she had some serious thinking to do or just wanted to get away from the pressures of being in charge of the Center. It astonished her that the usually sensitive Robinson couldn't understand that she didn't want company right now, not even his. But she couldn't bring herself to tell him that. Such a sweet man, such a good man. Elszabet didn't want to seem to be snippy with him again. This is dumb, she told herself. All you have to say is that you need to be alone: he won't take offense. But she couldn't do it. She managed a smile. "Sure, why not?" she said, hating herself for caving in like this. She motioned to him. "Come on. Let's go."

The beach wasn't much: a little rocky cove walled in by flat-topped cliffs covered with iceplant. It was just under four kilometers from the main part of the Center, a nice easy twenty-minute lope down a narrow unpaved road bordered on both sides by sprawling red-barked madrone trees, and a low scrub of manzanita. They ran side by side, moving

smoothly and well. The throbbing in her head began to
diminish as the rhythm of the jog took over. She wasn't
having any trouble keeping up with him, though his legs
were even longer than hers. She knew how to run. In
college at Berkeley, she had been an athlete, a runner, track
team, all-state champion in almost every medium-distance
event, the 800 meters, 1500 meters, 1600-meter relay, and
more. Those long legs, the endurance, the determination.
"You ought to consider a career as a runner," someone had
told her. She had been nineteen, then. Fifteen years ago.
But what did that mean, a career as a runner? It was a waste
of a life, she thought, giving yourself up to something as
hermetically sealed, as private, as being a runner. It was a
little like saying, You ought to consider a career as a
waterfall, You ought to consider a career as a fire hydrant. It
was a useless thing to do with yourself, okay for a bit of
private discipline or for a collegiate extracurric, but you
didn't make a career out of it. For a career, she thought, you
had to make some real use of your life, which meant
entering into the human race, not the 1500-meter one. You
had to justify your presence on the planet by giving something to the others who were here in space and time sharing
it with you, and being the fastest girl in the class wasn't
close to being enough. Working at a center for the repair of
the poor bewildered burned-out Gelbard's syndrome people,
eventually coming to be in charge of it: that was more like
it, Elszabet thought. She ran on and on, saying nothing,
scarcely even aware of the silent graceful dark-skinned man
running beside her.

There was a steep tricky trail from the top of the cliff
down to the beach. The beach itself had just about enough
sand to spread three blankets on, side by side. In winter at
high tide there was hardly any beach at all, and if you went
there you had to huddle in an ocean-carved cave with the
chilly waves practically lapping at your toes. But this was a

warm summer afternoon, no fog, the tide low. She tossed
the beach blanket that she was carrying over the edge or the
cliff and went scrambling down after it. Robinson came
right behind her, taking the trail in big confident bounds.

When they reached the beach she said, "I'm going to
take my clothes off. I usually do here." She looked him in
the eye, a look that said, Don't get me wrong, I'm not
trying to be provocative. It also said, You're here but I don't
really want you to be, and I'm going to behave as if I were
here by myself.

He seemed to understand. "Sure," he said. "That's fine
with me." He tossed his shirt aside, kept his jeans on,
squatted down by the tide-pools at the upper end of the
beach. "Couple of starfish here," he said.

Elszabet nodded vaguely. She undid her halter and dropped
her shorts and walked naked to the edge of the water, not
looking toward him. Cold wavelets swirled up around her toes.

"Are you going in?" Robinson asked.

She laughed. "You think I'm nuts?"

She never went swimming here. No one ever did, winter or
summer. The water was cold as death all year round, as it was
along the whole Pacific Coast north of Santa Cruz, and a dark
reef just off shore made the surf turbulent and impassable. That
was all right with Elszabet. If she felt like swimming, there was
a pool at the Center. The beach meant other things to her.

After a while she glanced back at Robinson and saw him
looking at her. He smiled and did not look hurriedly away,
as if to look hurriedly away would be an admission of guilt.
Instead he kept his gaze on her another moment or two, and
then he returned his attention in a deliberate way to his
starfish. Maybe this is not such a good idea, Elszabet
thought. Nudity was no big deal at the Center, but there
were just the two of them here. And she knew Robinson
was interested in her, though he had never been overt about
it. She was an attractive woman, after all, and he was a

healthy outgoing man, and there were professional and intellectual ties. They were a plausible couple; everyone at the Center thought that. She sometimes thought that herself. But she wanted no romantic entanglements, not with Dan Robinson, not with anyone. This was not the time for that sort of thing for her. She wondered if she had actually meant to be provocative. Or teasingly cruel. She hoped not.

She decided not to worry about it. Cautiously she waded out until the water was ankle-deep on her. The cold drew a hiss from her, but it seemed to purge the throbbing in her temples.

Robinson said, still poking in the tide-pools, "I've been thinking about the dreams. One possible explanation. Which may sound weird to you but it seems less weird to me than trying to argue that a lot of people are having identical bizarre dreams through sheer coincidence."

Elszabet didn't feel much like talking about the problem of the dreams just now, or about anything else. But all the same she said politely enough, "What's your theory?"

"That we're getting some kind of broadcasts from an approaching alien space vessel."

"*What?*"

"Does that sound crazy to you?"

"A little farfetched, let's say."

"I'd say so too. But I've got a rationale to fit behind it. Do you know what Project Starprobe was?"

She was beginning to feel awkward, standing there naked, half turned toward him with her feet in the cold water. She walked a little way up the beach, not as far as her blanket, and sat down in the sand with her back against an upjutting rock and her knees drawn up to her chest. The warm sun felt good against her skin. She didn't put her clothes back on but she felt a bit less exposed, sitting down. It seemed to her that the headache might be returning. Just the merest tickle of it, across her brow. "Project Starprobe?"

she said. "Wait a second. That was some kind of unmanned space expedition, wasn't it?"

"To Proxima Centauri, yes. The star system closest to Earth. It was sent off a little way before the Dust War—oh, around 2050, 2060. I could look it up. The idea being to get to the vicinity of Proxima Centauri in twenty, thirty, forty years, go into surveillance orbit, search for planets, send back pictures—"

The headache again, yes. Definitely.

"I don't see what that has to do with—"

"Try this," Robinson said. "I haven't checked it out, but I figure Starprobe must have reached Proxima ten or fifteen years ago. About four light-years away, and I think the ship was supposed to reach a pretty hefty acceleration after a while, peak velocity close to a quarter the speed of light or so, and—anyway . . . let's say the probe got there. And Proxima Centauri has intelligent life-forms living on one of its planets. They come out in their little spaceships and they inspect the probe, they determine that it comes from Earth and is full of spy equipment, and they get kind of nervous. So they dismantle the probe, which maybe is why we've never received any messages back from it, and then they send out an expedition of their own to see what this place Earth is like, whether it's dangerous to them and so forth."

"And this spy mission announces its arrival by bombarding the Earth with random hallucinations of other worlds?" Elszabet asked. Dan was a sweet man, but she wished he would leave her alone for a little while. "It doesn't sound very plausible to me." She closed her eyes and tipped her face toward the sun and prayed that he'd let the discussion drop.

But he didn't seem to pick up the hint. He said, "Well, maybe they're not coming to spy, or to invade. Just as ambassadors, let's say."

Please, she thought. Make him stop. Make him stop.

"And somehow they give off telepathic emanations—they're alien, remember, we can't possibly figure how their thought processes would work—telepathic emanations that stir up pictures of distant solar systems in the minds of those most susceptible to receiving them." There was no stopping him, was there? She opened her eyes and stared at him, still too gracious to tell him to go away. The drumming in her head was building up. Before it had felt like something trying to get out. Now it felt like something trying to get *in.* "Or maybe sending the images is their way of softening us up for conquest by spreading confusion, fear, panic," he went on. "Yes? No. You still don't like it, do you? Well, that's okay. I'm just speculating a little, is all. To me it sounds goofy too, but not beyond all possibility. Go ahead, tell me what you think."

Robinson grinned at her like an abashed sixteen-year-old. Plainly he wanted some sort of reassurance from her, wanted to be told that his notion wasn't totally wild. But she could not give him that reassurance. Suddenly she did not care at all about his idea, about him, about anything except the spike of incredible pain that had erupted between her eyes.

"Elszabet?"

She lurched to her feet, rocked, nearly toppled forward. Everything looked green and fuzzy. She felt as though a thick blindfold of green wool had been tied around her forehead. And the wool was trying to poke its way into her mind—woolly green tendrils like a dense fog, invading her consciousness—

"Dan? I don't know what's happening, Dan!"

But she did. It's the Green World, she said to herself. Trying to break through into my mind. A waking dream, a crazy hallucination. Could that be it? The Green World?

I'm going crazy, she thought.

Gasping, sobbing, she stumbled down the little narrow beach and out into the water. It rose about her like ice, like flame, to her thighs, to her breasts. She tried to push at the thing that was creeping into her mind. She scrabbled at her scalp with her fingertips as if she could scrape it away. Then she blundered into a submerged rock, slipped, fell to her knees. A wave hit her in the face. She was freezing. She was drowning. She was going crazy.

And then it was over, as quickly as it had begun.

She was standing in shin-deep water, shivering. Dan Robinson was beside her. He had his arm around her shoulders and he was leading her to shore, guiding her up the strip of sand, wrapping her blanket around her. She was goosebumps all over, and the fierce cold had made her nipples rise and grow so hard that her cheeks flamed when she saw them. She turned away from him. "Hand me my clothes," she said, groping for her halter.

"What was it? What happened?"

"I don't know," she murmured. "Something hit me all of a sudden. Some kind of freakout. I don't know. Something weird, just for a second or two, and I guess I blanked out." She didn't want to tell him about the woolly green fog. Already the concept that it had been an image out of the Green World trying to break through into her consciousness seemed absurd to her, a silly horror-fantasy. And even if it had happened, she didn't dare confess it to Dan Robinson. He would be sympathetic, sure. He'd even be envious. She thought of how he had said sorrowfully only half an hour ago that he had never been lucky enough to experience one of the space dreams. But her own outlook on all this was altogether different. For the first time, the dreams frightened her. Let Father Christie have them; let April Cranshaw have them; let Nick Double Rainbow have them. They were emotionally disturbed people: hallucinations were routine stuff to them. Let Dan have them too, if he wants. But not me. Please, God, not me.

She was dressed, now. But she was still chilled bone-deep by that plunge into the Pacific. Robinson stood five or six meters away, staring at her, working hard at seeming not to be too worried about her. She forced a smile. "Maybe I just need a vacation," she said. "I'm sorry I upset you."

"Are you okay now?"

"I'm fine. It was just a quick thing. I don't know. Wow, that water is cold!"

"Shall we go back to the Center?"

"Yes. Yes, please."

He offered her a hand to help her climb up the cliff. Elszabet shook him off angrily and went up the trail like a mountain goat. At the top she paused only a moment to adjust the beach blanket around her waist, then took off without waiting for him, running at sprint speed down the unpaved road to the Center. "Hey, I'm coming!" he called, but she refused to let up and pushed herself without mercy down the road, going all out. She would not let him catch her. When she arrived at the Center she was dizzy and fighting for breath but she got there a hundred meters ahead of him. People stared at her in amazement as she thundered past.

She didn't pause until she had reached her office. When she was inside she slammed the door behind her, dropped to her knees, crouched there trembling until she was sure that she was not going to throw up. Gradually her heart stopped pounding and her breathing returned to normal. Terrible things were happening in her thigh muscles. She glanced up at her data wall. There was a message waiting for her, it said. She called it up. *Thanks for info. Our list of dreams exactly the same, detailed analysis to follow. Rumor of similar dream occurrence as far south as San Diego: am checking. More later. What in God's name is going on, anyhow?* It was signed *Paolucci, San Francisco.*

Three

With a thought I took for maudlin,
   And a cruse of cockle pottage,
With a thing thus tall, sky bless you all!
   I befell into this dotage.
I slept not since the Conquest,
   Till then I never waked,
Till the roguish boy of love where I lay
   Me found and stripped me naked.

And now I do sing, "Any food, any feeding
   Feeding, drink, or clothing?
     Come, dame or maid,
     Be not afraid,
Poor Tom will injure nothing."

                  —Tom O'Bedlam's Song

THE red-and-yellow ground-effect van was floating westward, floating westward, floating westward, on and on and on. The scratchers hadn't wanted to stay in the San Joaquin Valley after the killings in the farmhouse by the river fork. So westward they went, on a chariot of air, drifting a little way above the dusty August roadbed. Tom felt like a king, riding like that: like Solomon going forth in majesty.

They let him sit up front next to the driver. Charley drove some of the time, and Buffalo, and sometimes the one named Nicholas, who had a smooth boyish face and hair that was entirely white, and who almost never said a thing. Occasionally Mujer drove, or Stidge. Tamale never did, nor Tom himself. Mostly the one who drove, though, was Rupe, beefy and broad-shouldered and red-faced. He just sat there, hour after hour after hour, holding the stick. When Rupe drove, the van never seemed to drift more than a whisker's width from the straight path. But Rupe didn't like Tom to

sing when he drove. Charley did; Charley was always
calling for songs during his shifts. "Get out the old finger-
piano, man," Charley would say, and Tom would rummage
in his pack. He had picked up the finger-piano down San
Diego way three years ago from one of the African refugees
they had down there. It was just a little hollow wooden
board with metal tabs fastened to it, but Tom had learned to
make it sound as good as a guitar, picking out the melodies
with his thumbs against the tabs. He knew the words of a lot
of songs. He didn't know tunes for all of them, but by now
he had had enough practice so that he could make tunes up
that fitted the words. His voice was a high clear tenor.
People liked to hear it, everyone but Rupe. But that was
only fair, not bothering Rupe while he was driving.

> *O mistress mine, where are you roaming?*
> *O, stay and hear! your true love's coming,*
>   *That can sing both high and low.*
> *Trip no further, pretty sweeting,*
> *Journeys end in lovers meeting,*
>   *Every wise man's son doth know.*

"Where do you get those songs?" Mujer asked. "I never
heard no songs like that."

"I found a book once," Tom said. "I learned a lot of
poems out of it. Then I made up the music myself."

"No wonder I never heard none of those songs," said
Mujer. "No wonder."

"Sing the one about the beach," Charley said. He was
sitting just to the right of Tom. Mujer was driving, and Tom
between them in the front seat. "I liked that one. The sad
one, the beach at moonlight." They were getting close to
San Francisco now, maybe just another four or five hours,
Charley had said. There were a lot of little towns out here,
and most of them still were inhabited, though about every

third one had been abandoned long ago. The land was still
dry and hot, the heavy hand of summer pressing down. The
last time they had gotten out of the van to scratch for food,
that morning around eleven, Tom had hoped to feel the first
cool breeze blowing from the west, and to see wisps of fog
drifting their way: San Francisco air, clean and cool. No,
Charley had said, you don't feel San Francisco air until
you're right there, and then it changes all of a sudden, you
can be roasting and you come through the tunnel in the hills
and it's cool, it's like a different kind of air altogether.

Tom was ready for that. He was getting tired of the heat
of the Valley. His visions came sharper and better when the
air was cool, somehow.

He played a riff on the finger-piano and sang:

> *The sea is calm tonight.*
> *The tide is full, the moon lies fair*
> *Upon the straits; on the French coast the light*
> *Gleams and is gone; the cliffs of England stand,*
> *Glimmering and vast, out in the tranquil bay.*
> *Come to the window, sweet is the night-air!*

"Beautiful," Charley said.

"I don't like this goddamn song neither," said Mujer.

"Then don't listen," Charley said. "Just shut up."

> *Only, from the long line of spray*
> *Where the sea meets the moon-blanched land,*
> *Listen! you hear the grating roar*
> *Of pebbles which the waves draw back—*

"It don't make no sense," said Mujer. "It ain't about
anything."

"What about the end part?" Charley said. "That's where
it's really beautiful. If you got any soul in you. Skip to the

end, Tom. Hey, what's that town? Modesto, you think?
Modesto, coming up. Skip to the end of the song, will you,
Tom?''

Skipping to the end was all right with Tom. He could sing
the songs in any order at all.

He sang:

> Ah, love, let us be true
> To one another! for the world, which seems
> To lie before us like a land of dreams,
> So various, so beautiful, so new,
> Hath really neither joy, nor love, nor light,
> Nor certitude, nor peace, nor help for pain—

"Beautiful," Charley said. "You just listen to that.
That's real poetry. It says it all. Take the bypass, Mujer. We
don't want to get ourselves into Modesto, I don't think."

> —And we are here as on a darkling plain
> Swept with confused alarms of struggle and flight,
> Where ignorant armies clash by night.

"Do the rest of it," Charley said, as Tom became silent.
"That's it," said Tom. "That's where it ends. *Where
ignorant armies clash by night.*" He closed his eyes. He
saw Eternity come rising up, that ring of blazing light
stretching from one end of the universe to the other, and he
wondered if a vision was coming on, but no, no, it died
away as fast as it had risen. Too bad, he thought. But he
knew it would return before long; he could still feel it
hovering at the edge of his consciousness, getting ready to
break through. Someday, he told himself, a vision of brightness will come and completely take me and carry me off to
the heavens, like Elijah who was swept up by the whirlwind, like Enoch, who walked with God and God took him.

"Look there," said Charley. "The road to San Francisco turns off there."

The van swung toward the north. Floating, floating, floating toward the sea on a cushion of air. My chariot, Tom thought. I am led in splendor into the white city beside the bay. A chariot of air, not like that which came for Elijah, which was a chariot of fire, and horses of fire. And Elijah went up by a whirlwind into heaven. "There is a kind of chariot on the Fifth Zygerone World," Tom said, "that is made of water, I mean the water of that world, which isn't like the water we have here. The Fifth Zygerone people travel in those chariots like gods."

"Listen to him," Stidge said from the back of the van. "The fucking looney. What do you keep him for, Charley?"

"Shut it, Stidge," said Charley.

Tom stared at the sky and it became the white sky of the Fifth Zygerone World, a gleaming shield of brilliant radiance, almost like the sky of the Eye People's world except not so total, not so solid a brightness. The two huge suns stood high in the vault of the heavens, the yellow one and the white, with a rippling mantle streaming red between them and around them. And the Fifth Zygerone people were floating back and forth between their palaces and their temples, because it was the holiday known as the Day of the Unknowing when all the past year's pain was thrown into the sea.

"Can you see them?" Tom whispered. "Like teardrops, those chariots are, big enough to hold a whole family, the blood-parents and the water-parents both. And all the Fifth Zygerone people float through the sky like princes and masters."

His mind teemed with worlds. He saw everything, down to the words on the pages in their books; and he could understand those words even when the books were not books, the words were not words. It had always been like this for him; but the visions became sharper and sharper every year, the detail richer, more profound.

Charley said, "You just keep driving, Mujer. Don't stop nohow for anything. And don't say nothing."

"The Fifth Zygerone are the great ones, the masters. You can see them now, can't you, getting out of their chariots? They have heads like suns and arms sprouting all around their waists, a dozen and a half of them, like whips—those are the ones. They came to this star eleven hundred million years ago in the time of the Veltish Overlordry, when their old sun started to puff up and turn red and huge. Their old sun ate its worlds, one by one, but the Zygerone were gone by then to their new planets. The Fifth World is the great one, but there are nineteen altogether. The Zygerone are the masters of the Poro, you know, which is astonishing when you think about it, because the Poro are so great that if one of their least servants came to Earth, one of their merest bondsmen, he would be a king over us all. But to the Zygerone the Poro are nothing. And yet there is a race that is master over the Zygerone too. I've told you that, haven't I? The Kusereen, they are, and they rule over whole galaxies, dozens of them, hundreds, the true Imperium." Tom laughed. His head was thrown back, his eyes were closed. "Do you think, Charley, that the Kusereen yield to a master too? And so on up and up and up? Sometimes I think there is a far galaxy where the Theluvara kings still reign, and every half billion years the Kusereen Overlord goes before them and bows his knee at their throne. Except the Kusereen don't have knees, really. They're like rivers, each one, a shining river that holds itself together like a ribbon of ice. But then who are the kings the Theluvara kings give allegiance to? And there is also God in majesty at the summit of creation, triumphant over all things living and dead and yet to come. Don't forget Him."

"You ever hear crazy?" Stidge said. "That's crazy for you. That's the real thing."

"I like it better than his songs," said Mujer. "The songs give me a pain. This stuff, it's like watching a laser show, except it's in words. But he tells it real good, don't he?"

"He sees it like it's real to him, yeah," said Buffalo.

Charley said, "He sees it that way because it *is* real."

"I hear you right, man?" Mujer said.

"You hear me right, yeah. He sees worlds. He looks out across stars. He reads the Book of Suns and the Book of Moons."

"Oh, hey," Stidge said. "Hey, listen to Charley, now!"

"Shut your hole," said Charley. "I know what I'm saying, Stidge. You shut it or you'll walk the rest of the way to Frisco, man."

"Frisco," Buffalo said. "It ain't far now. Man, am I going to have some fun in Frisco!"

Charley said, speaking softly to Tom alone, "You don't pay any mind, Tom. You just go on telling us."

But it was over. All Tom saw now was the road to San Francisco, hardly any traffic, heat shimmering on the pavement and big tumbleweed balls rolling across the highway, fetching up against the old barbed-wire fencing. The Fifth Zygerone World was gone. That was all right. It would be back, or one of the others. He had no fear of that. That was the one thing he did not fear, that the visions might suddenly desert him. What he did fear was that when it came time for the people of the Earth to embrace the worlds of the Imperium he would be left behind, he would not be able to make the Crossing. There was a prophecy to that effect. It was an old story, wasn't it? Moses dying at the entrance to the Promised Land? I have caused thee to see it with thine eyes, but thou shalt not go over thither, said the Lord. Tears began to stream down Tom's cheeks. He sat there quietly weeping, watching the road unroll. The van moved silently toward San Francisco, floating, floating, on and on and on.

"San Francisco, forty-five minutes," said Buffalo. "My oh my oh my!"

2

THE tumbondé man said, "You wait here, we call you when Senhor Papamacer he ready to talk to you. You don't go out of this room, you understand that?"

Jaspin nodded.

"You understand that?" the tumbondé man said again.

"Yes," said Jaspin hoarsely. "I understand. I'll wait here until Senhor Papamacer is ready for me."

He couldn't believe this place. It was like a shack, four, five rooms falling apart, falling down; it was like the sort of stuff you would expect to find in Tijuana, except Tijuana hadn't been this run-down in fifty years. This, the headquarters of a cult that had the allegiance of thousands, that was winning new converts by the hundreds every day? This shack?

The house was in the southeast corner of National City somewhere right down next to Chula Vista, on a low flat sandy hilltop behind the old freeway. It looked about two hundred years old and probably it was: early twentieth century at the latest, patched and mended a thousand times, not the slightest thing modern about it. No protection screen, no glow-windows, no utilities disk on the roof, not even the usual ionization rods that everybody had, the totem poles that were thought to keep away whatever gusts of hard radiation might blow from the east. For all Jaspin could tell, the place had no electricity either, no telephone, maybe not even any indoor plumbing. He hadn't expected anything remotely as primitive as this. "Man, you be ready today, you come hear the word Senhor Papamacer has for you," they had told him. "We come get you, man, we take you to the house of the god." This? House of the god? Not even any sign of that, really, none of the tumbondé imagery visible from the front. It was only when you walked up the cracked and weedy wooden steps and around to the side entrance that you got a peek into the carport, where the papier-mâché statues of the divinities were stored, leaning casually against the beaver-board wall like discarded props from some laser-show horror program, old tossed-aside monsters. At a quick glance Jaspin had spotted the familiar forms of Narbail, O Minotauro, Rei Ceupassear. Maybe they kept the big Chungirá-He-Will-Come and Maguali-ga ones in some safer place. But in this neighborhood, where Senhor Papamacer was like a king, who would dare to mess around with the statues of the gods?

Jaspin waited. He fidgeted. At least in a doctor's office they gave you an old magazine to read, a cube to play with, something. Here, nothing. He was very frightened and trying hard not to admit that to himself.

This is a field trip, he thought. This is like you're going for your doctorate and you have to have an interview with the high priest, the mumbo man. That's all it is. You are doing anthropological research today.

Which was true, sort of. He knew why he wanted to see Senhor Papamacer. But why, for God's sake, did Senhor Papamacer want to see *him?*

One of the tumbondé men came back into the room. Jaspin couldn't tell which one: they all looked alike to him, very bad technique for someone who purported to be an anthropologist. In his narrow black-and-red leggings, his silver jacket, his high-heeled boots, the tumbondé man could have been a bullfighter. His face was the face of an Aztec god, cold, inscrutable, cheekbones like knives. Jaspin wondered if he was one of the top eleven apostles, the Inner Host. "Senhor Papamacer, he almost ready for you," he told Jaspin. "You stand up, come over here."

The tumbondé man patted him down for weapons, missing no part of him. Jaspin smelled the fragrance of some sweet oil in the tumbondé man's thick dark high-piled hair, oil of wintergreen, essence of citrus, something like that. He tried not to tremble as the tumbondé man explored his clothing.

They had stopped him after the rites when he and Jill were leaving two weeks ago. Five of them, surrounding him smoothly, while his head was still full of visions of Magualiga. This is it, he thought then, half dazed: they are on to human sacrifice, now, and they have noticed the scholarly-looking Jewboy with the skinny *shiksa* girlfriend, the wrong kind of ethnics in this very ethnic crowd, and in five minutes we are going to be up in the blood-hut next to the white bull and the three of us, Jill and the bull and me, will have our throats cut. Blood running together in a single chalice. But that wasn't it. "The Senhor, he has words for you," they said. "When the time is here, man, he wishes speak to you." For two weeks Jaspin had worried himself crazy with what this thing was all about. Now the time was here.

"You go in now," the tumbondé man said. "You very lucky, face on face with the Senhor."

Two more toreros in full costume came into the room. One stationed himself in front of Jaspin, one behind, and they led him down a dark hallway that smelled of dry rot or mildew. It didn't seem likely that they meant to kill him, but he couldn't shake off his fear. He had told Jill to call the police if he wasn't back by four that afternoon. Fat lot of good that would do him, most likely; but he could at least threaten the tumbondé men with it if things turned scary.

"This is the room. Very holy it is here. You go in."

"Thank you," Jaspin said.

The room was absolutely square, lit only by candles, heavy brocaded draperies covering the windows. When Jaspin's eyes adjusted he saw a rug on the floor, jagged patterns of red and green, and a man sitting crosslegged, utterly motionless, on the rug. To the right of him was a small figure of the horned god Chungirá-He-Will-Come carved from some exotic wood. Maguali-ga, squat and nightmarish with one great bulging eye, stood on the man's left. There was no furniture at all. The man looked up very slowly and speared Jaspin with a look. His skin was very dark but his features were not exactly Negroid, and his unblinking gaze was the most ferocious thing Jaspin had ever seen. It was the ebony face of Senhor Papamacer, no doubt of it. But Senhor Papamacer was a giant, at least when he was looming on the top of the tumbondé hill at the place of communion, and this man, so far as Jaspin could tell, considering that he was sitting down, seemed very compact. Well, they can do illusions extremely well, he thought. They probably put stilt-shoes on him and dress him big. Jaspin began to feel a little calmer.

"Chungirá-He-Will-Come, he will come," said Senhor Papamacer in the familiar subterranean voice, three registers below basso. When he spoke, nothing moved except his lips, and those not very much.

"Maguali-ga, Maguali-ga," Jaspin responded.

A glacial smile. "You are Jaspeen? You sit. *Por favor.*"

Jaspin felt a cold wind sweeping through the room. Sure, he thought, a cold wind in a closed room without windows, in San Diego, in August. The wind wasn't real, he knew;

the chill that he felt was. He maneuvered himself down to the red-and-green rug, creakily managing a lotus position to match Senhor Papamacer's. It seemed to him that something might be about to pop loose in one of his hips, but he forced himself to hold the position. He was frightened again in a very calm way.

Senhor Papamacer said, "Why you come to us in tumbondé?"

Jaspin hesitated. "Because this has been a dark and troubled time in my soul," he said. "And it seemed to me that through Maguali-ga I might be able to find the right path."

That sounds pretty good, he told himself.

Senhor Papamacer regarded him in silence. His obsidian eyes, dark and glossy, searched him remorselessly.

"Is shit, what you say," he told Jaspin after a bit, laying the words out quietly, without malice or rancor, almost gently. "What you say, it is what you think I want to hear. No. Now you tell me why white professor comes to tumbondé."

"Forgive me," Jaspin said.

"Is not to forgive anything," said Senhor Papamacer. "You pray to Rei Ceupassear, he give forgive. Me you just give truth. Why do you come to us?"

"Because I'm not a professor any more."

"Ah. Good. Truth!"

"I was. UCLA. That's in Los Angeles."

"I know UCLA, yes." It was like speaking to a stone idol. The man was utterly unyielding, the most formidable presence Jaspin had ever encountered. Out of some stinking brawling hillside *favela* near Rio de Janeiro, they said, came to California when the Argentinians dusted Brazil, now worshipped by multitudes. Sitting on the opposite side of this little green-and-red rug, almost within reach. "You leave UCLA when?"

"Early last year."

"They fire you?"

"Yes."

"We know. We know about you. Why they do that, hey?"

"I wasn't coming to my classes. I was doing a lot of funny things. I don't know. A dark and troubled time in my soul. Truly."

"Truly, yes. And tumbondé, why?"

"Curiosity," Jaspin blurted, and when the word came out of him it was like the breaking of a rope around his chest. "I'm an anthropologist. Was. You know what that is, anthropology?"

The chilly stare told him he had made a bad mistake.

Jaspin said, "Sometimes I don't know whether you understand my words. I'm sorry. An anthropologist. Years of training. Even if I wasn't a professor, I still thought of myself like one." Color was flooding to his cheeks. Go on, just tell him the real stuff, he thought. He's got your number anyway. "So I wanted to study you. Your movement. To understand what this tumbondé thing really was."

"Ah. The truth. It feels good, the truth?"

Jaspin smiled, nodded. The relief was enormous.

Senhor Papamacer said, "You write books?"

"I was planning to do one."

"You no write one yet?"

"Shorter pieces. Essays, reviews. For anthropological journals. I haven't written my book yet."

"You write a book on tumbondé?"

"No," he said. "Not now. I thought perhaps I might, but I wouldn't do it now."

"Why not?"

"Because I've seen Chungirá-He-Will-Come," Jaspin said.

"Ah. Ah. That is truth too." A long silence again, but not a cold one. Jaspin felt totally at this strange little man's mercy. He was wholly terrifying, this Senhor Papamacer. At length he said, as though from a great distance, "Chungirá-He-Will-Come, he will come."

Jaspin made the ritual response. "Maguali-ga, Maguali-ga."

Anger flashed in the obsidian eyes. "No, now I mean something other! *He will come,* I am saying. Soon. We will march north. It will be almost any day, we leave. Ten, fifty thousand of us, I don't know, a hundred thousand. I will give the word. It is the time of the Seventh Place, Jaspeen. We will go north, California, Oregon, Washington, Canada. To the North Pole. Are you ready?"

"Yes. Truth."

"Truth, yes." Senhor Papamacer leaned forward. His eyes were ablaze. "I tell you what you do. You march with me, with Senhora Aglaibahi, with the Inner Host. You write the book of the march. You have the words; you have the learning. Someone must tell the story for those who come after, how it was Papamacer who opened the way for Maguali-ga, who opened the way for Chungirá-He-Will-Come. That is what I want, that you should march beside me and tell what we have achieved. You, Jaspeen. You! We saw you on the hill. We saw the god coming into you. And you have the words, you have the head. You are a professor and also you are of tumbondé. It is the truth. You are our man."

Jaspin stared.

"Say what you will do," said Senhor Papamacer. "You refuse?"

"No. No. No. No. I'll do it. I've been committed to the march since July. Truly. You know I'll be there. You know I'll write what you want."

Quietly Senhor Papamacer said, in a voice rich with dark mysteries beyond Jaspin's comprehension, "I have walked with the true gods, Jaspeen. I know the seven galaxies. These gods are true gods. I close my eyes and they come to me, and now not even when they are closed. You will tell that, the truth."

"Yes."

"You have seen the gods yourself?"

"I have seen Chungirá-He-Will-Come. The horns, the block of white stone."

"In the sky, is what?"

"A red sun from here to here. And over here, a blue sun."

"It is the truth. You have seen. Not the others?"

"Not the others, no."

"You will. You will see them all, Jaspeen. As we march, you will see everything, the seven galaxies. And you will write the story." Senhor Papamacer smiled. "You will tell only the truth. It will be very bad for you if you do not, you understand that? The truth, only the truth. Or else when the gate is open, Jaspeen, I will give you to the gods who serve Chungirá-He-Will-Come, and I will tell them what you have done. You know, not all the gods are kind. You write not truth, I will give you to gods who are not kind. You know that, Jaspeen? You know that? I say it to you: Not all the gods are kind."

3

MORNING rounds, one of the regular chores. Routine was important, a key structural thing, for them and sometimes even for her. Right now especially for her. Go through the dorms, room by room, check all the patients out, see how well they were doing as their minds returned from their morning pick. Cheer them up if she could. Get them to smile a little. It would help their recovery if they'd smile more. Smiling was a known cure for a lot of things: it triggered the outflow of soothing hormones, that little twitch of the facial muscles did, sending all sorts of beneficial stuff shooting into the weary bloodstream.

You ought to smile more often yourself, Elszabet thought.

Room Seven: Ferguson, Menendez, Double Rainbow. She knocked. "May I come in? It's Dr. Lewis."

She hovered, waiting. Quiet inside. This time of morning they often didn't have a lot to say. Well, no one had said she couldn't come in, right? She put her hand to the plate. Every doorplate in the building was set to accept her print, Bill Waldstein's, Dan Robinson's. The door slid back.

Menendez was sitting on the edge of his bed with his eyes closed. There were bonephones glued to his cheeks, and he was moving his head sharply from side to side as if he were listening to some strongly rhythmic music. Across the room, Nick Double Rainbow lay stretched out belly-down on his vivid red Indian blanket, staring at nothing, chin propped up on fists and elbows. Elszabet went over to him, pausing by his bed to activate the privacy screen around it. A crackle of blurry pink light leaped up and turned Double Rainbow's corner of the room into a private cubicle.

In that moment, just as the screen went shooting up around them, Elszabet felt her mind invaded by a green tendril of fog. Almost as if the energy of the screen had allowed the greenness to get in. Surprise, fear, shock, anger. Something rising out of the floor to skewer her. She caught her breath. Her spine tightened.

No, she thought fiercely. Get the hell out of there. Get. *Get*.

The vagrant greenness went away. Once it was gone

Elszabet found it hard to believe that it had been in her just a moment ago, even for an instant. She let her breath out, commanded her back and shoulders to ease up. The Indian didn't seem to have noticed a thing. Still belly-down, still staring.

"Nick?" she said.

He went on ignoring her.

"Nick, it's Dr. Lewis." She touched his shoulder lightly. He jerked as if a hornet had stung him. "Elszabet Lewis. You know me."

"Yeah," he said, not looking at her.

"Rough morning?"

Tonelessly he said, "It's all gone. The whole thing."

"What is, Nick?"

"The people. The thing that we had. Goddamn, you know we had a thing and it was taken away. Why should that have happened? What the hell reason was there for that?"

So he was on his Vanishing Redman kick again. He was lost in contemplation of the supreme unfairness of it all. You could pick and pick and pick, and somehow you could never pick down far enough to get that stuff out of him. Which was what had dumped him into the Center in the first place: he had come here suffering from deep and abiding despair, the thing that Kierkegaard had termed the sickness unto death, which Kierkegaard said was worse than death itself, and which nowadays was called Gelbard's syndrome. Gelbard's syndrome sounded more scientific. Double Rainbow had lost faith in the universe. He thought the whole damn thing was useless and pointless if not actually malevolent. And he wasn't getting better. There were holes in his memory all over the place now, sure, but the sickness unto death remained, and Elszabet suspected it didn't have a thing to do with his alleged American Indian heritage but only with the fact that he had been unlucky enough to have been born in the second half of the twenty-first century, when the whole world, exhausted by a hundred fifty years of dumb self-destructive ugliness, was beginning to be overwhelmed by this epidemic of all-purpose despair. Bill Waldstein might actually be right that Double Rainbow wasn't an Indian at all. It didn't matter. When you had the sickness unto death, any pretext was enough to drag you down into the pit.

"Nick, do you know who I am?"

"Dr. Lewis."

"My first name?"

"Elsa—Ezla—"

"Elszabet."

"That's it. Yeah."

"And who am I?"

A shrug.

"You don't remember?"

He looked at her, an off-center look, dark eyes focusing on her cheek. He was a big heavy-set man, thick through the shoulders, with a blunt broad nose and a grayish tinge to his skin, not exactly the coppery hue his alleged race was supposed to have, but close enough. Since he had taken that swing at her a couple of weeks back he had never quite been able to look her in the eye. So far as anyone could tell, he had no recollection of having gone on a rampage, of having hit her and hurt her. But some vestige of it must remain, she suspected. When he was around her he looked rueful and embarrassed and also sullen, as though he felt guilty about something but wasn't sure what and was a little angry with the person who made him feel that way.

"Professor," he said. "Doctor. Something like that."

She said, "Close enough. I'm here to help you feel better."

"Yeah?" Flicker of interest, swiftly subsiding.

"You know what I want you to do, Nick? Get yourself up

and off that bed and over to the gym. Dante Corelli's got the rhythm-and-movement workshop going down there right now. You know who she is, Dante?''

"Dante. Yeah." A little doubtfully.

"You know the gymnasium building?"

"Red roof, yeah."

"Okay. You get down there and start dancing, and dance your ass off, you hear me, Nick? You dance until you hear your father's voice telling you to stop. Or until lunch bell, whichever one comes first."

He brightened a little at that. His father's voice. Sense of tribal structure: did him good, thinking about his father's voice.

"Yeah," he said. In his heavy way he started to push himself up from the bed.

"Did you have any dreams last night?" she asked offhandedly.

"Dreams? What dreams, how? I got no way of knowing."

He had dreamed Blue Giant, the harsh and piercing light: that was this morning's pick-room report. He seemed sincere in not remembering that, though.

"All right," Elszabet said. "You go dance now." She grinned at him. "Make it a rain dance, maybe. This time of year, we could use a little rain."

"Too soon," he said. "Waste of time, dancing for rain now. Rains don't come till October. Anyway, what makes you think dancing'll bring rain? What brings rain, it's the low-pressure systems out of the Gulf of Alaska, October."

Elszabet laughed. So he's not completely out of things yet, she thought. Good. Good. "You go dance anyway," she told him. "It'll make you feel better, guaranteed." She kicked the switch to knock the privacy screen down and went over to Tomás Menendez' side of the room. He was sitting just as he had been before, listening to his bonephones. When she activated his privacy screen she braced herself for another touch of the green fog, but this time it didn't come. Just about every other day now she had a whiff of it, an eerie sensation, that hallucination circling her like a vulture waiting to land. It was getting so that she was afraid to go to sleep, wondering whether this would be the night when the Green World finally broke through to her consciousness. That continued to terrify her, the fear of crossing the line from healer to hallucinator.

"Tomás?" she said softly.

Menendez was one of the most interesting cases: forty years old, second-generation Mexican-American, strong hulking man with arms like a gorilla's, but gentle, gentle, the gentlest man she had ever known, soft-spoken, sweet, warm. In his fashion he was a scholar and a poet, as profoundly involved in his own ethnic heritage as Nick Double Rainbow claimed to be with his, but Menendez seemed really to mean it. He had turned the area around his bed into a little museum of Mexican culture, holoprints of paintings by Orozco and Rivera and Guerrero Vasquez, a couple of grinning Day of the Dead skeletons, a bunch of lively brightly painted clay animals, dogs and lizards and birds.

The year before last, Menendez had strangled his wife in their pretty little living room down in San José. No one knew why, least of all Menendez, who had no memory of doing it, didn't even know his wife was dead, kept expecting her to visit him next weekend or the one after that. That was one of the strangest manifestations of Gelbard's syndrome, the motiveless murder of close relatives by people who didn't seem likely to be capable of swatting flies. Tell Menendez that he had killed his wife and he would look at you as though you were speaking in Turkish or Babylonian: the words simply had no meaning for him.

"Tomás, it's me, Elszabet. You can hear me through

those phones, can't you? I just want to know how you're getting along.''

"I am quite well, *gracias*." Eyes still closed, shoulders jerking rhythmically.

"That's good news. What are you playing?"

"It is the prayer to Maguali-ga."

"I don't know that. What is it, an ancient Aztec chant?"

He shook his head. He seemed to disappear for a moment, knees bobbing, fists banging lightly together. "Maguali-ga, Maguali-ga," he sang. "Chungirá-He-Will-Come!" Elszabet leaned close, trying to hear what he was hearing, but the bonephones transmitted sounds only to their wearer. The jacket of the cube he was playing with lay beside him on the bed. She picked it up. It bore a crudely printed label that looked homemade, half a dozen lines of type in a language that she thought at first was Spanish; but she could read a little Spanish and she couldn't read this. Portuguese? The label had a San Diego address on it. Tomás was always getting shipments of things from his friends in the Chicano community: music, poetry, prints. He was a much loved man. Sometimes she wondered if they ought to be screening all these cubes and cassettes that he received. They might deal with things that could impede his recovery, she thought. But of course whatever he played was picked from him the next day, anyway; and it obviously made him happy to be keeping up with his people's cultural developments. "Maguali-ga is the opener of the gate," he said in a firm lucid voice, as though the phrase would explain everything to her. Then he opened his eyes, just for a moment, and frowned. He seemed surprised to have company.

"You are Elszabet?" he asked.

"That's right."

"You have a message from my wife? She is coming this weekend, Carmencita?"

"No, not this weekend, Tomás." There was no use in explaining. "What was that, what you were playing?"

"It is from Paco Real, San Diego." He looked a little evasive. "Paco sends me many interesting things."

"Music?"

"Singing, chanting," Menendez said. "Very beautiful, very strong. Tell me, did I dream last night of the other worlds?"

"No, not last night."

"The night before, though?"

"Are you asking me or telling me?"

He smiled sadly. "The dreams are so beautiful. That is what I write down: the dreams are so beautiful. Even though I must lose them, the beauty is what stays. When will I be allowed to keep my dreams, Elszabet?"

"When you're better. You're improving all the time, but you aren't there yet, Tomás."

"No. I suppose not. So I must not know, when I dream of the worlds. Is it all right that I write down that the dreams are so beautiful? I know we are not supposed to write things to ourselves, either. But that is a small thing, to tell myself *about* my dream, though I do not tell myself the dream itself." He looked at her eagerly. "Or could I write down the dreams too?"

"No, not the dreams. Not yet," she said. "Do you mind if I hear the new cube?"

"No, no, of course, here. Here." He put the bonephones to her cheeks, pressing them on lightly, with a tender, almost loving touch. He tapped the knob and she heard a deep male voice, so deep it sounded like the booming of a great bullfrog, or perhaps a crocodile, chanting something steady and repetitive and vaguely African-sounding, a little barbaric, very powerful and disturbing. She heard the words that Menendez had been murmuring: Maguali-ga, Chungirá. Then there was a lot of what might have been Portuguese, and the sound of drums and some high-pitched instrument, and the noises of a crowd repeating the chant.

"But what is it?" she asked.

"It is like a meeting, a holy prayer. There are gods. It is very beautiful." He took the bonephones from her as tenderly as he had put them on. "My wife, she will not visit this weekend, eh?"

"No, Tomás."

"Ah. Ah, it is too bad."

"Yes." Elszabet switched off the screen. "You might want to go down to the gymnasium. There's a dance group there now. You'd enjoy it."

"Perhaps a little while."

"All right. Do you happen to know where Ed Ferguson is?"

"Ferguson, no. I think he goes off walking in the woods."

"Alone?"

"Sometimes the big woman. Sometimes the artificial one. I forget the names."

"April. Alleluia."

"One of them, yes." Menendez took Elszabet's hand carefully between his own. "You are a very kind woman," he said. "You will visit me tomorrow?"

"Of course," she said.

The strange discordant chanting still rang in her ears as she walked up the hallway to finish her rounds. Philippa, Alleluia, April. Alleluia wasn't there. All right, off in the woods with Ferguson: that was an old story. They deserved each other, she told herself, the cold-blooded swindler and the cold-blooded artificial being. Then she chided herself for lack of charity. Some hell of a healer you are, thinking of your patients that way. But as quickly as she had assailed herself Elszabet let herself off the hook. You're entitled to be human, she thought. You aren't required to love every-

body in the Center. Or even to like them. Just to see that
they get the treatment they need.

She broke into a slow trot and then into a jog, heading
back up the hill toward her office. The morning was lovely,
clear and warm. It was that time of the year when one
golden day followed another without variance or interruption; the summertime fog season was over, and as Nick
Double Rainbow had so thoughtfully reminded her, the
rainy season was still more than a month away.

I'll go to the beach this afternoon, Elszabet thought. Lie
in the sun, try to make some sense out of things.

It bothered her enormously that these strangenesses were
creeping into the Center: the shared dreams, puzzling not
only because they were shared but also because of their
bewildering content, all these other suns and worlds and
alien monsters. And the spread of the dreams to the staff:
Teddy Lansford and Naresh Patel and just yesterday Dante
Corelli, too, bewilderedly confessing a Nine Suns dream.
Elszabet suspected that other staff members might be concealing
space dreams of their own, too, just as she had not yet been
able to admit to anyone that she was now and then being
invaded—while actually awake, no less—by strands of imagery that seemed to come out of the Green World dream.
Everything was turning strange. Why? Why?

For Elszabet the Center was the one place in the world
where she felt at peace, where the crazy turmoil outside was
held at bay. That was why she had come here, to do her
work and be of service and at the same time to escape the
harshness and sorrows of that burned-out world beyond the
Center's gates. There were times here when she almost
managed to forget about what was going on out there,
although the steady influx of Gelbard's syndrome victims,
twitchy and hollow-eyed, constantly reminded her of that.
Still, the Center was a peaceful place. And yet, and yet, she
knew that was foolishness, hoping she could ever escape the

real world here. The real world was everywhere. And now the real world was getting unreal and the unreality was sliding through the gates like a fog.

As she approached her office Bill Waldstein came down the path from the GHQ building and said, "Where is everybody?"

"Who? Staff? Patients?"

"Anyone. Place seems awfully quiet."

Elszabet shrugged. "Dante's got a big dance group going. I guess just about everyone must be over at the gym. Who are you looking for? Tomás and the Indian are in their room, Phillipa and April are in theirs, Ferguson's fooling around in the forest with Alleluia—"

Waldstein looked drawn and weary. "Is it true that Dante had a space dream night before last?"

"You'd better ask her that," Elszabet said.

"She did, then. She did." He scuffed at the ground with his sandal. "Can we go into your office, Elszabet?"

"Of course. What's happening, Bill?"

He didn't speak until they were in the little room. Then, scrunching down against the data wall, he gave her a haggard look and said, "Confidential?"

"Absolutely."

"You remember when I was saying the space dreams had to be frauds, that the patients were making them up just to bedevil us? I haven't really believed that for a while, I guess. But I certainly don't now."

"Oh?" she said.

"Now that I've had one too."

"You?"

"I had Double Star Three last night. The whole thing, all the bells and whistles, the orange sun high and the yellow one down by the horizon, the double shadows. Then the yellow one set and everything turned to flame."

Elszabet watched him closely. She thought he was going to burst into tears.

"Wait," he said. "There's more. I improved on it. When April had it last week there were no life-forms, right? I got life-forms. Blue sphere-shaped creatures with little squid tentacles at the top end. Isn't that cute? Strolling around in a sort of amphitheater like Aristotle and his disciples. Cute. Very cute."

"How do you feel?" Elszabet asked.

Waldstein shuddered. "Dirty inside the head. Like I have gritty sand all over the lining of my skull."

"Bill—"

Compassion flooded her. This was the moment to tell him that he wasn't alone, that she had been feeling the Green World dream tickling at the edge of her mind, that she feared the same things he feared. She couldn't do it. It was a lousy thing, holding back on him when he was plainly in so much pain. But she couldn't do it. Letting him, anyone, know that her mind too was vulnerable to this stuff: no. No, she wouldn't. Couldn't. She felt like a hypocrite. So be it. So be it. She remained outwardly cool, calm, the sensitive administrator hearing the confession of the troubled staff member.

Give him something, Elszabet thought.

"I can tell you that you aren't alone in this," she said after a moment.

"I know. Teddy Lansford. Dante. Also I think Naresh Patel, from something he let slip a few weeks ago. And probably more of us."

"Probably," she said.

"So it isn't just a psychotic phenomenon limited to the patients."

"It never was limited to the patients. Almost from the beginning it's been reaching staff members."

"Who are psychotic also, then? Early stages of Gelbard's, do you think?"

She shook her head. "A, stop throwing around loaded words like psychotic, okay? B, sharing a manifestation like this with victims of Gelbard's doesn't necessarily mean that you're coming down with Gelbard's yourself, only that something very peculiar is going on that tends to affect the patients more readily than the staff, but affects staff too. C—"

"I'm scared, Elszabet."

"So am I. C, what we have here is a phenomenon not confined to Nepenthe Center, as I intend to make clear at the staff meeting tomorrow."

Waldstein looked startled. "What do you mean?"

"Move back and watch the data wall," she said.

He ambled to his feet and turned around. She activated the wall. A map of the Pacific states appeared.

"These dreams," she said, "have also been reported at the mindpick centers in San Francisco, Monterey, and Eureka." She touched a key and the screen lit up at those three places. "I've been in touch with the directors there. Same seven visualizations, not necessarily all seven in each center. Primarily experienced by patients, lesser frequency among staff."

"But what—"

"Hold on," she said. More lights appeared on the screen. "Dave Paolucci in San Francisco has been gathering reports of incidence of the space dreams outside Northern California, and it looks like his new data are coming on line right this minute." Patterns of color blossomed at the lower end of the state. "Look at that," Elszabet said. "I've got to call him. I've got to get the details. Look there: a heavy concentration of dream reports in the San Diego area, you see? And some from Los Angeles. And up there too: what's that, Seattle, Vancouver? Oh, Christ, Bill, look at that! It's everywhere. It's a plague.''

"Denver, too,'' Waldstein said, pointing.

"Yeah. Denver. Which is about as far east as we have reliable communication, but who knows what's going on beyond the Rockies? So it isn't just you, Bill. It's damn near everybody that's dreaming these dreams.''

"Somehow that doesn't make me feel much better,'' Waldstein said.

4

FERGUSON said, "What I'd like to do, I'd like to get myself the hell out of this place as fast as I can and start making some money out of all this nonsense.''

"How would you do that?'' Alleluia asked.

"Hell, wouldn't be much of a trick. The main side of the Center there's a gate, but on this side it's just the forest. You could slip off in the afternoon and find your way right through, just keep the sun at your back afternoons and in front of you mornings, maybe two or three days tops if you had your wits about you. Out to the old freeway and across to Ukiah, say—''

"No. I mean how would you make money out of it.''

Ferguson smiled. They were lying in a quiet mossy glade a twenty-minute stroll east of the Center, redwoods and sword ferns and a little brook. The ground was folded and tilted there in a way that would make it hard for anyone to blunder onto them. It was his favorite place. He had made sure to enter its location on his ring-recorder so he'd have no trouble finding it again, even though they might happen to pick the data from his mind every time after he had gone there. Some things you forgot, some you didn't: you never could be sure.

He said, "It's a cinch. The space dreams, they aren't just happening to the patients here. I know that for a fact."

"You do?"

"I listen very carefully. You know the technician, Lansford? He's had them two or three times. I heard them talking, Waldstein, Robinson, Elszabet Lewis. I think maybe that little Hindu doctor has had them. And even Waldstein, is what I think. But the dreams are also happening outside the Center."

"You know that?" Alleluia asked.

"I've got good reason to think so," Ferguson said. He ran his hand lightly up her thigh, stopping just short of the crotch. Her skin was smooth as silk. Smoother, maybe. It was half an hour since they had done it and he still felt sweaty, but not Alleluia. That was the thing about these artificial women—they were perfect, they never even worked up much of a sweat. "I have a friend in San Francisco, she told me about a dream weeks ago, same one you had once. You remember having that dream? With the horns, the block of white stone, the two suns?"

"I thought that you had that dream."

"Me? No. It was you. I never had any of the dreams, not one. The time I told you, it was that my friend had it, the one in San Francisco. If they're having them there, having them here, you can bet they're everywhere."

"So?"

He slipped his hand up to her breast. She stirred and wriggled against him. He liked that. He felt almost ready to go again. Just like a kid, he thought: always ready for an encore, even these days.

"You know what I was sent here for?" he asked.

"You told me, but they picked it."

"I had a scam going, offering to send people to other planets where they could make a new start, escape this mess on Earth, you know? Just give me a few thousand bucks and as soon as the process is perfected you'll be able to—"

Alleluia said, "You can still remember doing that?"

"It doesn't seem to go when they pick me."

"And you'll start your scam up again, is that it?"

"How can it miss? Everybody's presold. The dreams, they're like advertisements for the planets that I can supply, you see? There's the red-and-blue-sun world, there's the green-sky planet, there's the nine-suns planet—you see, I know them all, I have my ways, Allie. Seven of them, there are, seven dream-planets. You make your choice, you give me the money, I take care of things, I see to it that you're shipped to the right place. The dreams, I say, that's just the other planets sending out like travel posters to tell people how terrific they are. It can't miss, kid. I tell you: it can't miss."

"They'll catch you again," she said. "They caught you once, they'll catch you again. And this time they won't just toss you in Nepenthe Center."

"It won't happen, they catch me."

"No?"

"Never. First thing is, I get out of the jurisdiction. I go up north, Oregon, Washington. Then I use a dummy corporation—you know what that is?—and another dummy behind the dummy, a series of shells, everything through nominees. With a mail drop in Portland, say, or maybe Spokane, and—"

"Ed?"

"Yeah?"

"I don't give a crap, Ed. You know that?"

"Well, why should you? You don't give a crap about anything, do you?"

"One thing."

"Yeah," he said. "One thing. Thank God for that. But I don't understand. What good's a sex-drive in a synthetic? Sex was put in us originally so we'd reproduce, right? And you don't reproduce, not by sex. Right? Right?"

"It's there for a reason," she said.

"It is?"

"It's to make us think we're human," Alleluia said. "So we don't get maladjusted and unhappy and try to take over the world. We could, you know. We're highly superior beings. Anything you can do, we can do fifty times better. If we didn't have sexual feelings, we might think of ourselves as even more different than we are, some sort of master race, you know? But they give us sex, it keeps us pacified, it keeps us in our place."

"Yeah," he said. "I can understand that." Ferguson leaned across, kissed the tip of each nipple, lightly kissed her lips. "It makes a lot of sense," he said. He had never spent this much time around a synthetic before, and he was learning a lot from doing it. Like most people, he had tended to keep his distance, regarding the synthetics as creepy, weird. There weren't that many of them anyway, maybe half a million, something like that. Less. He remembered when they were being made, thirty years ago or thereabouts, just before the Dust War. Intended for military use, was what he remembered, perfect beings to fight a perfect war. A discontinued experiment of the good old days. But they weren't quite perfect, it seemed. They had a lot of genuine human quirks. Human enough to make them wind up in a therapy center the way this one had, apparently. Well, they were human enough to love to fuck, too. You take the pluses with the minuses, hope for the best. He cupped her breasts. Softly he said, "When I leave here, you leave here with me, okay? I'll show you all my little tricks."

"I'll show you some of mine," she said.

5

THE roadway looped like a great gray snake across the water, rising high above the water here, leveling off there, passing through a tunnel at one point, jumping up and becoming two huge suspension bridges later on. At the far end of it, white and glistening in the afternoon light, was San Francisco, tightly huddled on its little piece of the planet. Cool, cool air came flowing through the van's open windows.

"This bridge," Charley said, "it goes way back. They built it in the middle *ages*, and look at it still holding together. Through all the earthquakes and who knows what sort of other stuff, and it's still holding together."

"The Golden Gate Bridge," Buffalo said. "Incredible!"

"Nah, not the Golden Gate," Charley said. "That's the Golden Gate, over there on the side, going up north. This one's the Bay Bridge. That right, Tom?"

"I don't know," Tom said. "I've never been in San Francisco before."

Stidge laughed. "You been in the Eleventh Zorch Galaxy, but you never been in Frisco. That's pretty good."

"I never been here neither," Buffalo said. "What of it?"

"Well, we're here now," said Charley. "Pretty city. Prettiest damn city there is. I was a kid, I lived here six years. I bet it hasn't changed a whole lot. Somehow this place, it never changes."

"Even when there's earthquakes?" Buffalo asked.

"The earthquakes, they don't matter none," Charley told him. "They mess things up, the town gets put right back the way it used to be. I was ten years old they got clobbered. Six months you couldn't tell the difference."

"You were here for the Big One?" Mujer asked.

"Nah," Charley said. "Big One, that was a hundred years ago. They had that one, 2006. Big One Two, they called it. Big One One, they had that in 1906, the fire and everything, burned down the whole goddamn place. Then a hundred years after that they were getting ready for the anniversary celebration, you know, parades and speeches? Son of a bitch, Big One Two, two days before the anniversary, knocked everything down again. That's the kind of city this is."

"You weren't here for that," Mujer said.

"That was ninety-seven years ago," said Charley. "I guess I missed that one. Then they had the Little Big One, thirty years later, forty, I don't know. That was before my time, too. The earthquake I was here for, that one didn't get a name. Wasn't that big, but big enough. Knocked everything off the shelves, broke windows, scared the shit out of me. I was ten years old. House across the street came right off its foundations, sitting there with one wall down looking like a doll's house, all the rooms showing. That was more than an ordinary earthquake, they said, but not as big as a Big One. The Big One, it don't come more than once every hundred years or so."

"They about due, then," Tamale said from the back of the van.

"Yeah," said Choke. "Tomorrow afternoon, I hear. Half past three in the afternoon."

"Hot shit," Buffalo said. "That's just what I want, my first day in San Francisco. Start off with a real bang."

"What we do," said Mujer, "we get in the van just before it starts. We turn the engine on. Then we sit there floating on the air cushion until the ground stops moving, huh? We'll be okay. And then when it all stops, we get out and go looking around in the broken houses and fill up the van with whatever we like and we drive away north somewhere."

"Sure," Charley said. "You know what they do with looters, they get an earthquake? They string 'em up by their balls. That's the rule here, always was, always will be."

"And if they don't got no balls?" Choke asked. "Not everybody got balls, Charley."

"They put some on you in the sex-change ward of the hospital," said Charley. "*Then* they string you up by them. This town, they don't fool around with looters none. Hey, Tom, you ever seen a prettier city than that?"

Tom shrugged. He was far away.

"Hey, Tom? Where are you now, Tom?"

"Eleventh Zorch Galaxy," said Stidge.

"Hush it," Charley snapped. To Tom he said, "Tell us what you see, man."

Things were stirring and surging in Tom's mind. He was seeing the city called Meliluiilii on the world called Luiiliimeli, under the giant torrid blue star known as Ellullimiilu. That was one of the Thikkumuuru worlds of the Twelfth Polyarchy, Luuiiliimeli. High kings had reigned there for seven hundred thousand grand cycles of the Potentastium. "They have earthquakes there all day long," Tom said. "It doesn't trouble them at all. The ground is like molten, it boils and heaves like a cauldron, but the city just drifts above it."

"Where's that?" Charley asked. "Which planet?"

"Meliluiilii, on Luiiliimeli," Tom said. "It's one of the Pivot Worlds, the great ones that shape the Design. The sunlight on Luiiliimeli's so strong it hits you like a hammer. Blue sunlight, a hammer that burns. We'd melt in a flash. But the Luiiliimeli people, they're not even slightly like us. So they don't mind it any. It's not a planet for humans, it's a planet for *them*. This is the only planet for humans, the one we're on right now. The people on Luiiliimeli are like shining ghosts and the city, it's only a floating bubble. That's all, only a bubble."

"Listen to him," Charley said. "You think San Francisco is pretty? Loollymoolly, it's like a gigantic gorgeous bubble. I can almost see it floating there and shining when I listen to him talk about it. Fan*tas*tic."

Tom said, "All the cities are beautiful everywhere in the galaxy. There is no such thing as an ugly city, not anywhere. That one, now, that's Shaxtharx, the Irikiqui capital. That's on the big world in the Sapiil system, the empire of the Nine Suns. Everything is built out of a spiderweb material there, ten times strong as steel. It shimmers and bounces, and when there's an earthquake—they have earthquakes there often, very often, the gravity of the Nine Suns is always pulling the planet in all sorts of different directions—when there's an earthquake, you know, the city becomes even more beautiful, the way it moves. Almost like a tapestry, showing all the different colors of the suns. At earthquake time the Sapiil people come from all around to watch Shaxtharx shaking."

"You been there, huh?" Buffalo asked.

"No, not me. But I see it, you understand me? The visions come. I see all the worlds, and someday maybe I'll make the Crossing." Tom's eyes were shining. "You can't go across in the flesh. You'd die like a gnat in a furnace, any of those worlds. The only world for humans, it's this world, you follow what I'm saying? But when the Time of the Crossing comes we will be able to drop our bodies and go over into their bodies.''

"That was something, those cities he was telling us about,'' Buffalo said. "But he can't keep from running off at the mouth, can he? We drop our bodies, we go over into their bodies. Just like that. You know what he's talking about, Charley? You, Mujer? Drop our bodies, go over into their bodies.''

"Just as is said in the Bible,'' Tom went on. "In Corinthians, it's said. That we shall be changed in a moment, in the twinkling of an eye. For this corruptible must put on incorruption, and this mortal must put on immortality. That's the Crossing they're talking about, when we go over to the other worlds. Not to heaven: that's not what they mean. They mean we will go over to Luiiliimeli, some of us, and take on their very forms, and some of us will go to the Sapiil worlds and some to the Zygerone, or to the Poro, or will become Kusereen, even—we'll be scattered through the universe, which is the divine plan, the dispersion of the Spirit—''

"All right, Tom,'' Charley said gently. "That's enough for now, okay, Tom? We're coming off the bridge. We're in San Francisco. Right in the middle of town.''

"Hey, look at it!'' Buffalo cried. "You ever see beautiful? All those white buildings. All those green trees. Just breathe the air. That air, it's like wine, huh? Like *wine*.''

Tamale said, "Were you serious, Choke? About an earthquake tomorrow afternoon, half past three?''

"Well, they can predict them, can't they?'' Choke said. "They can measure the earthquake gas coming out of the ground days and days before.''

"So you know for sure? There's one tomorrow? What we doing here, then?''

"I don't know shit about tomorrow,'' Choke said. "I was only running my mouth, man. If there was an earthquake tomorrow, don't you think everybody would be packed and out of town by now? Jesus Christ, Tamale, how can you be so dumb? I was only running my mouth.''

"Yeah," Tamale said, with a little laugh. "Yeah. I knew that. I knew it, man.''

Tom sat quietly among them. The wonder of the visions still lay on his soul. Those marvelous unhuman cities, those noble beings moving about from place to place upon the faces of their amazing worlds. He thought of what he had said, that there was no such thing as an ugly city, not anywhere. He had never considered that point before, but it was true, and not just in the far galaxies. There was beauty everywhere in all places, in all things. Everything radiated the miracle of creation. San Francisco was beautiful, sure, but so were the desolate towns of the abandoned Valley behind them, the rusted crumbling wasteland towns, and so was everything else in the world, because everything had God's hand in its design. Mujer was beautiful. Stidge was beautiful. Once you begin looking at things with eyes that have been opened, Tom told himself, you see only beauty wherever you turn.

"Pull up here," Charley said. "We can park across the street, look around, ask some questions, find ourselves a place to stay. Rupe, you watch the van, you and Nicholas. We'll be back ten, fifteen minutes, maybe. Tom, you stay close to me. Are you with us, Tom? You back on Earth, man?''

"I'm here," Tom said.

"Good. You make sure you stay here a while, okay?'' Charley grinned. "What do you think of San Francisco? Pretty city?''

"Very pretty," Tom said. "The air. The trees.''

They headed up the street, scattering out, Buffalo going first with Choke right behind him, then Stidge and Tamale close together, Mujer near them, and Charley and Tom a little way back. It was important, Charley said, not to look like an invading gang. Sometimes the bandidos came in from the back country in gangs of ten or twenty to clean out the city, and they got into wars with the city vigilante commissions. Charley didn't want that. "We're just going to spend the summer here, keeping low, easy and cool, not attract any attention, okay? This is a good place to be, in the summer. And maybe when the rains begin we'll go somewhere else, up north, maybe, or maybe down to San Diego. It's nice and warm there, San Diego, in the winter."

Tom stared. It was a long time since he had been in a city, a real city. Things looked old here, even ancient, all the small wooden buildings that seemed to come out of a vanished era when life had had certainty and stability. There was something very peaceful about San Francisco, very comforting. Perhaps it was the scale, everything so small and close together. Or perhaps it was the way everything looked old. The cities he had seen before were not anything like this, the ones in Washington, in Idaho, in the other places up north where he had been. Even the cities that had come to him in his visions were not like this.

One thing that particularly struck him were the hills. The hills here were astounding. Tom looked up and saw the tiny white buildings climbing the hills, and it was hard to believe that they would build on hills like that. Of course he had seen worlds where they built their houses on glass-sided mountains that went straight up to the sky, houses jutting out from the side like eagles' nests, but that was on other worlds where everything was different, the air, the gravity. Some had no air at all. Maybe some had no gravity at all. There were all sorts of worlds. But this was the Earth and for a long time Tom had been living in places that were flat, and now he was in a city that seemed to be all peaks and valleys.

They moved warily to the end of the street and across.

There wasn't much traffic, a few old combustion cars and some ground-effect ones. The sky was a bright hard blue and the air was amazingly clear, sunlight bouncing almost visibly off the dazzling white facades. A cool dry wind, very sharp, was blowing from the west, where the ocean lay hidden from view by the hills.

Charley said, walking close by Tom's side, "That was beautiful, you know, what you were telling us on the bridge. About those cities. Sometimes you can get a little crazy, but all the same you got a wonderful mind, Tom. The things you see. The things you tell us."

"I know how lucky I am," Tom said. "The bounty of God has been conferred on me."

"I wish I saw a tenth the things you see. I do see them, you know. Some of them, anyway." Charley's voice was low, as it was sometimes when he didn't want the other scratchers to overhear him. But they were all up ahead, halfway up the block. "I been dreaming, almost every night, fantastic dreams. Fan*tas*tic. You know I saw that blazing bright world, the one you told me about, where the Eye People live? I didn't care to say while we were traveling. But I saw it just like you told it, that flood of light filling everything. And I saw another where there were two suns in the sky, a white one and a yellow, the damnedest shadows over everything and the sky all red."

"The Fifth Zygerone World," Tom said, nodding. "I thought you would. It comes through very strong."

"You know their names and everything."

"I've been seeing them practically all my life. Since I was small, when at first I thought everybody saw such things. It scared me, later, when I knew nobody else did. But I'm used to it now. And now others are seeing, too. And what I see, it gets clearer and clearer all the time."

"You think I'm starting to see them because I'm traveling close to you? Can that be it?"

"That could be," Tom said. "I don't know. Am I the source? Or are we all having the visions all at once? Maybe the other worlds are breaking through to the whole human race now, and no longer just me. I don't know."

Charley said, "I think some of the others are having the dreams too but they don't want to own it up. Choke, I think, and maybe Nicholas. Maybe everybody is. But they're all afraid to talk about it. They look a little strange some mornings, but nobody says anything. They think they'll be called crazy if they say they're seeing the things you see. They think they'll be made fun of. That's the thing they hate most, these guys, being made fun of. Worse than being called crazy."

"I don't mind it. I'm used to it. Either one, being made fun of, being called crazy. Poor Tom. Poor crazy Tom. Sometimes it can be pretty safe, being crazy. Nobody wants to hurt a crazy man. But the things that poor crazy Tom sees are real. I know that, Charley. And one day the whole world will know too. When we're called to the Crossing, I mean. When the skies open and we go forth unto the worlds of the Sacred Imperium."

Charley smiled and shook his head. "Now that's when I begin to feel funny about you, man, when you start talking like that. When you start to go on and on about—" He stopped in midstride. "You hear anything back there, Tom?"

"Hear what?"

"No, you wouldn't, would you." Charley turned, looking halfway back toward the place where they had left the van. Mujer, who had been up the street ahead of them, came galloping back and halted, panting, at Charley's side.

"That was Nicholas," Mujer said. "Calling for help."

"Yeah. God damn."

Charley swung around, and Mujer, and then the others, too, running past Tom, heading back in the direction of the van. Stidge went sprinting by, his eyes wild, his spike in his hand. Tom felt his skin prickling. Trouble coming, no doubt of it. He trotted behind them back toward the parking place. Nicholas was shouting now, again and again. Tom looked ahead and saw two strange men in worn jeans and loose white shirts on the far side of the van, running away, firing bolts of red heat as they ran. Rupe's blocky body lay sprawled in the street, face down. Nicholas was crouched behind the van, firing. By the time Tom reached the van it was all over, the strange men out of sight, the weapons put away. Charley was scowling and pounding his fists together in fury.

"You get a good look at them?" he said to Nicholas.

"No doubt of it. The two farm kids, the ones who got away from us when Stidge killed the father and the mother."

"Shit," Charley said. "Our quiet visit to San Francisco. Shit. Shit. Rupe's dead?"

"Dead, yeah," Mujer said. "Burn clear through the belly."

"Shit," Charley said. "All right. We got to go after them. Stidge, you got us into this, you track them down, wherever. We don't find them, they'll haunt us, pick us off easy. Move your ass, man. You got to go get them." Charley shook his head. "Go. Go." He looked toward Tom. "You see what I mean about killing? Once you begin you got to finish." He touched the laser bracelet on his right wrist. "You stay here with the van," he said. "*Inside* the van, don't open it for nobody. Try to keep your wits about you, you hear me, Tom? We'll be right back. God damn," Charley said. "And everything moving along so nice, too."

Four

When short I have shorn my sow's face
   And swigged my horny barrel
In an oaken inn I pawn my skin
   As a suit of gilt apparel.
The moon's my constant mistress
   And the lowly owl my marrow;
The flaming drake and the night-crow make
   Me music to my sorrow.

While I do sing, "Any food, any feeding,
   Feeding, drink, or clothing?
     Come, dame or maid,
     Be not afraid,
Poor Tom will injure nothing."

               —Tom O'Bedlam's Song

FOR Elszabet it was a quiet evening. She had a simple dinner about 1900 hours in the staff mess hall at the east end of the GHQ building: salad, grilled fish of some kind, small carafe of tangy white wine from one of the little wineries nearby. She shared her table with Lew Arcidiacono, who did most of the mechanical and electronic maintenance work at the Center, and his girlfriend Rhona, who was Dante Corelli's assistant in the physical therapy department, and Mug Watson, the head groundskeeper. None of them seemed to have much in the way of dinner conversation that night, which was fine with Elszabet. Afterward she went over to the staff recreation center and listened to Bach harpsichord concertos with holovisual accompaniment for an hour or so, and by 2130 she was making her way down the path to her cabin far over on the other side of the Center. A quiet evening, yes.

In the evenings things were always quiet for Elszabet. Generally her last sessions with patients took place about

1700—end-of-day counselling, periodic progress reviews, crisis intervention if any crises had popped up, stuff like that. Then she liked to meet briefly with individual staff members to check out special problems, theirs or their patients'. By 1830, usually, the work day was over, and the social part of the day, such as it was, was beginning. For Elszabet that part was never anything much. First an early dinner—she had no regular dinner companions, just sat at any table that happened to have a free space—followed by an hour or two in the staff rec center for a movie or a cube or a nighttime splash in the pool, and then back to her cabin. Alone, of course. Always alone, by choice. She might read for a while, or listen to music, but her lights invariably were out well before midnight.

Sometimes she wondered what they all thought of her, an attractive woman keeping to herself like that so much. Did they think she was peculiar and aloof? Well, they were right. Did they think she was antisocial or snobbish or asexual? An uppity bitch? Well, they were wrong. She kept to herself because keeping to herself was what she wanted to do these days. Was what she needed to do. The ones who knew her best understood that. Dan Robinson, say. She wasn't trying to snub anyone. Only to pull inward, to rest, to give her weary and eroded spirit time to heal. In a way she was as much of a patient here as Father Christie was, or Nick Double Rainbow, or April Cranshaw. Whether or not anyone else was aware of that, Elszabet was. She was living on the edge, had been for years, had taken the post at Nepenthe Center as much for the sake of healing herself as anything else. The difference was that instead of giving herself over to the mindpick every day so that the jarring dissonances could be scraped from her soul and a healthy new personality could form in the blank new places, she was trying to do it on her own, living cautiously, marshalling her weakened inner resources, letting her strength come gradually flowing back. This place was a sanctuary for her. Life outside the Center had worn her down the way it wore everyone down: the uncertainties, the tensions, the fears, the knowledge that the world that had been handed everyone was a badly broken one in danger of coming apart entirely. That, she had decided, was what Gelbard's syndrome was all about, really, the awareness that life nowadays was lived at the brink of the abyss. The Dust War had done that to people. For a hundred years everyone worries about the horrors of atomic war, the flash of terrible light and the shattered cities and the melted flesh, and then the atomic war comes, not with bombs but very quietly, with its lethal radioactive dust, far less spectacular but a lot more insidious, great chunks of land made permanently unlivable overnight while life goes on in an ostensibly normal way outside the dusted placed. Nations fall apart when bands of hot dust are spread through their midsections. There are migrations. There are upheavals of the body politic. There are ruptures of communication and of transportation and of ordinary civility. Societies fall apart. People fall apart. These were apocalyptic times. Something bad had happened, and everyone believed that something worse probably would happen, but no one knew what. These weird dreams, were they the harbingers? Who knew? Were they cause or effect? Was everybody going to go crazy? Was everybody *already* crazy? Elszabet thought she was in better shape than most, which was why she was here as one of the healers instead of as one of the patients. But she didn't kid herself. She was at risk in this maimed and broken world. She could fall into the pit just as Father Christie had, or April, or Nick. There but for the grace of God went she, and she didn't know how much longer God's grace would hold out. So nowadays she moved through her life with care, like someone crossing a field mined with explosive eggshells. The last thing she needed now was emotional turbulence of any kind, or emotional adventure. Let other people have the stormy love affairs, she thought. Let them have the winning and the losing. Not that she didn't miss it. Sometimes she missed it terribly. She missed that wonderful warm embrace, hands on her breasts, belly against her belly, eyes looking into her eyes, the sudden hard thrust, the warm flood of fulfillment, his, hers, theirs. She hadn't forgotten what any of that felt like. Or just the presence of the other, leaving sex out of it, just the comforting knowledge that there was someone else there, that you weren't minding the store all by yourself. She had had that once, or thought she had; maybe she would have it again someday. But not now, not here, not while the edge lay so close. The thing she feared more than anything else was having it again and losing it again. Better not to try for it. Not until she felt stronger inside. Sometimes she wondered: If not now, when? And had no answer.

She slipped out of her clothes and stood for a little while on her porch in the darkness.

The night was warm. Owls were talking in the treetops. The long golden Northern California summer still had a few weeks to run, maybe even many weeks. This was only September. Sometimes the rains didn't begin until the middle of November. What a change that was, when the unending months-long procession of sunny days suddenly yielded to the implacable downpours of the Mendocino County winter! It could rain for weeks at a time, December, January, February. And then it would be spring again, the trees greening up, the drenched land beginning to dry out.

She heard distant laughter. Staff people, fooling around up front. For some of them this place was just a big summer camp for grown-ups all year round. Do your work by day, fool around by night, hanky-panky in this cabin or that one, maybe on the weekend drive over to Mendocino, take in a club or a restaurant or something like that. Mendocino was the closest thing to a city that there was around here. Fifty years back it had actually had a little flurry of a boom, trying to set itself up as a rival to San Francisco for preeminence in Northern California at a time when San Francisco was suffering from a lot of self-inflicted wounds; but in the end what became clear was what everyone had really known all along, which was that San Francisco had been designed by geography to be a major city and Mendocino hadn't been. Even so, it still looked more or less citylike, and you could have a good time over there on the weekend, or so Elszabet had heard. Even in the present condition of the world you could have a good time, if you had the knack of shutting your eyes to what was really going on.

Again, laughter. Higher-pitched, this time. A squeal or two. Elszabet smiled and went inside and got into bed. A little music, she thought, while falling asleep. Bach? No, she'd had enough Bach for tonight. Schubert, the string quintet. Sure. Warm web of sound, deep, melodious, thoughtful. She flicked the stud to *automatic* so the system would shut down when the music was over, and turned on the cube. And lay there, half-listening, thinking more about tomorrow's staff meeting than she was about the music. Space dreams from Vancouver, space dreams from San Diego, space dreams from Denver. Everywhere. Paolucci was coming up from San Francisco to deliver a report. There was even a possibility that Leo Kresh had been able to make it all the way from San Diego. Something very odd was going on in San Diego, that was the word. But what was going on everywhere was odd. She had laughed at Dan Robinson's idea that afternoon when they were down on the beach, that the dreams were messages from an alien spaceship approaching Earth. Wild weird far-out notion, she had thought then. Now she wasn't so sure that it was all that wild. She wondered if Robinson had done any further work on that, to check out whether such a thing was possible. Tomorrow at the meeting I'll ask him if . . .

Still thinking about the meeting, she wandered off into sleep.

And somewhere during the night she had a space dream herself.

The greenness came first. Little wisps of thick furry fog, sidling into her mind. She was close enough to consciousness to know what was starting to happen. She was sleepy enough not to care. She had fought this thing off as long as she could. The invasion of the sanctuary, alien strangenesses creeping in from God knows where. Now she wasn't able to hold it back any longer. It was almost a relief, giving in to it at last. Go on, she told the dream. Go ahead and happen. It's about time, isn't it? My turn? Okay, my turn, then.

Green.

Green sky, green air, green clouds. The landscape was shades of green. Hillside, river far down below, meadows unrolling to the horizon. Everything looked soft and friendly, a gentle tropical landscape. Elegant trees without leaves, slender green trunks, green scaly branches coiling outward, bending back toward the ground. The sun faintly visible behind the veil of fog. The sun was green too, maybe, though it was hard to tell for sure, the way the light came blurrily through all that thick swirling fleecy fog.

Something was beckoning her.

Crystalline creatures, supple, almost delicate. Their long-limbed bodies glistened. Their dark eyes were bright and glittering, a row of three on each of the four sides of their heads. They were moving toward a shimmering pavilion on the hill just beyond her, and they were inviting her to come with them, calling her by name, Elszabet, Elszabet. But the way they were saying it was unearthly and awesome, a hushed reverberating whisper that resonated against itself again and again, an echo-chamber whisper that had in it an eerie whistling quality and an undertone like the roaring of distant winds. Elszabet, Elszabet.

I'm coming, she told them. And put her hand in their cool crystalline hands and let them carry her along. She floated just above the ground. Occasionally a strand of thick fleshy grass brushed her toes: when it did, she felt a sharp but not unpleasant tingling and heard the sound of bells.

She was entering the pavilion now. It seemed to be made of glass, but glass of a peculiarly yielding sort, warm and rubbery to the touch, like congealed teardrops. All about her moved the delicate crystalline people, bowing, smiling, stroking her. Telling her their names. The prince of this, the countess of that. A crystalline cat sauntered among them. It rubbed its crystalline ears against her leg; and when she looked down she saw that her leg was crystal too, that in fact she had a body just like theirs, shining and wondrous. Someone put a drink in her hand. It tasted like flowers; it erupted in a thousand brilliant colors as it made its journey through her body. Do you like it, they asked? Will you have another? Elszabet, Elszabet. There is the duke of something. Beside him are the duchess and the duke-other of something and the marquis of something else. Look, look, there is the city, coming into view now below! Will you have it? We will give the city your name if you like. There, it is done: Elszabet. Elszabet. They all congratulated her. They clustered close and she heard the faint tinkling of their arms and legs as they moved, a little silvery whispering sound, like Christmas-tree ornaments swayed by a breeze. Do you like it here, Elszabet? Do you like us? We have a poem for you. Where is the poem? Where is the poet? Ah: here. Here. Make way for the poem. Make way for the poet.

A crystalline she had not seen before, taller than any of the others, came up to her smiling shyly. Come, he said. I have a poem for you. They stepped outside the pavilion and greenness descended on them like emerald rain. He put something in her hands, an intricate little object that looked like a puzzle-box of glass, layer within layer, transparent to the core with a meshwork of dazzling glassy gears going round and round at the center. This is your poem, he said. I call it Elszabet. She touched it and a green flare of light sprang up from it and leaped across the sky, and from the pavilion came the tinkling sound of applause. Elszabet, they all said. Elszabet, Elszabet.

The green light deepened and thickened around her. She was swathed in it, now. The air seemed almost tangible. So warm, so woolly. So green, green, green.

Suddenly restless, she stirred, turned, sighed. Through the greenness she was able to glimpse a distant beacon of hard yellow light, and that bright beam aroused dismay in her and a kind of vague fear. A voice within her urged her to pull back, and after a moment she recognized the voice as her own. You must be careful, she told herself. Do you know where you are going? Do you know what will happen to you there? How tempting this is. How seductive. But be careful, Elszabet. If you get too far in, there may be no coming out again.

Or has that already happened? Perhaps you are already in too deep. Perhaps there will be no coming forth. She touched the poem again, and again green light leaped from it, and the poet smiled, and the crystallines applauded and whispered her name. How green everything is, Elszabet thought. How beautiful. How green, how green, how green.

2

So now they were going to kill again.

Tom stayed calm about that. You travel with killers, you

have to expect them to do some killing. Still and all, he didn't particularly like it. Thou shalt not kill, the Bible said, right out front. Thou shalt do no murder, said Jesus. You couldn't argue with commandments like that. Of course in wartime those commandments were suspended. You could make out a pretty fair case, Tom told himself, that these days it's a kind of wartime, every man's hand lifted against all others. Maybe.

He sat hunched up in the front of the van, looking at Rupe's body on the back seat. Rupe seemed to be asleep. His eyes were closed, his big meaty face was peaceful. His head lolled forward a little. You could practically hear him snoring. Mujer and Charley had propped him up in a sitting position back there, and Stidge had draped an old blanket across his lap to hide the laser burn that went through his shirt and his gut and out through his back. You looked at him, you thought he was asleep. Well, Rupe had never had much to say even when he was alive.

And now they were going off to kill again. A life for a life: two for one, in fact. No, it wasn't that, Tom thought. Not just revenge. They were going to kill because that was the only way they could feel safe: with those two gone. In wartime you have to eliminate your enemies.

Maybe they won't be able to find them, the two farm kids, Tom thought. The city has a million alleyways, a million basements. Those two kids could be hiding anywhere. They had a five-minute head start, didn't they? Well, two or three minutes, anyway. So maybe they'll get away. It was a shame to have more killing now, when the Last Days were so near, when the Crossing was almost about to begin. You die now, you miss out on the Crossing. What a pity that would be, to have to rot here in the soil of Earth with all the other dead ones from before, when everyone else was setting out on his way across the heavens. To miss out, right at the last minute. Those poor kids.

"Rupe?" Tom said. "Hey, you, Rupe?"

Very quiet back there. Tom took out his finger-piano, played a few random notes up and down the scale, hunting around for a tune.

"You mind if I sing, Rupe?"

Rupe didn't seem to mind.

"Okay," Tom said. And he sang:

> *Up the airy mountain,*
> *Down the rushy glen,*
> *We daren't go a-hunting,*
> *For fear of little men.*

"You ever hear that one, Rupe? I guess you never did. I guess you never will."

> *Wee folk, good folk,*
> *Trooping all together;*
> *Green jacket, white cap,*
> *And white owl's feather.*

He heard what sounded like someone rapping on the far side of the van. He didn't bother to look. Back so soon, Charley? Tom shrugged and went on singing:

> *High on the hilltop*
> *The old King sits.*
> *He is now so old and gray*
> *He's nigh lost his wits.*

The rapping again, louder. A voice, angry. "Open the goddamned window, will you? You hear me, open up!"

Frowning, Tom leaned over and peered out. He saw a stranger out there, a short man with curling golden hair and a short frizzy golden beard and cold blue eyes. The stranger looked bothered about something. Tom wondered what to do. *You stay here with the van,* Charley had said. *Don't open it for nobody.*

Tom smiled and nodded and moved away from the window. He started to feel a vision coming on. The usual roaring sound deep down in his mind, the whistling of the wind. The light of strange suns was kindled in his mind, blue, white, orange.

He still could hear the angry voice, though. "You move this van or I'll blow it away," the golden-haired man was saying. He pounded on the metal door, hard. "Who the hell said you could park here? Where's your goddamn permit? Hey, you ain't even got a license, this van. Will you open the fuck up?"

"Here is the Magister of the Imperium now," Tom said sweetly. "That shining, that glow hovering there. You can't see him, can you? *Them,* really. He's a corporate entity, three souls in one. Can you feel the power? A Magister like that, he has the power to loose and bind. They tell the tale among the Sorgaz warriors that at the time of the Theluvara withdrawal, the Great Abdication, a Magister of the Imperium was all that stood between the Sorgaz and the Fount of Force, and they would have been engulfed except for—oh, look at the colors, will you? Look there!"

"I can't hear what you're saying, you fucking idiot. Open the goddamn window, you want to talk to me."

Tom smiled. Tom said nothing. Tom was moving farther and farther away every moment. The angry voice went on and on.

"—under powers vested in me, City and County of San Francisco, Vigilante Street Authority, I declare this van in violation of Civic Code article 117 and I herewith—"

Then another voice, a familiar one.

"All right, fellow. We was just about to move along. My

friend in here, he's not permitted to drive, medical reasons. Neither of them.''

Charley.

Tom struggled back to awareness of the world about him. The pulsing blue sun faded, the white, the orange.

"It's okay," Charley said. "You can let us in, Tom.''

Tom saw Mujer and Stidge standing next to Charley. Across the street were Nicholas, Choke, Tamale, Buffalo. They had two other men with them, young-looking ones, pale frightened-looking ones. The kids from the farm. Too bad, Tom thought. Too bad.

Uncertainly Tom said, "This man, he was banging on the van. I wasn't sure—''

"It's okay," Charley said. "Just open up.''

Tom wondered why Charley didn't open the door himself. He had the key, didn't he? But Charley was starting to look impatient. Tom reached across and threw the latch, and when the door slid back Charley jumped out of the way and Mujer and Stidge grabbed the golden-haired man quickly under his arms and pushed him inside, throwing him face down on the floor. "What the hell," the golden-haired man said, his voice muffled. "I'm an officer of the San Francisco Vig—''

Stidge hit him on the back of the head with something and he was quiet.

Then the others were piling into the van too, Charley and Nicholas and Choke, Tamale and Buffalo, and the two boys from the farm. "Okay, come on, move it, Mujer!" Charley snapped. "We can't stay here." Mujer jumped behind the wheel and the van went floating off quickly down the middle of the street.

"What did he want?" Charley asked Tom. "What was he trying to tell you?''

"I'm not sure," Tom said. "Something about parking here. And not having a license. He was banging on the door, but you said not to let anyone in, and then you came back and—"

Charley muttered, "He really is a cop, then. A damned vigilante." He reached into the policeman's pocket, found a small shining computery-looking machine there, put it to his ear and listened a moment and nodded. The he stepped on it and ground it to pieces. "Now he's out of contact," Charley said. "But now we got to get rid of him. Getting rid of a cop: sheesh!"

"You leave the looney in charge of the van, that's what you get," Stidge said.

"All right," said Charley.

"Wasn't such a good idea parking the van there neither," Stidge said.

"All right. All *right*."

"Where you want me to drive?" Mujer asked.

Charley said, "Turn left here. Then keep going straight. When you see signs to the Golden Gate Bridge, you get on it, head north, get out of the city. And take it easy driving. Last thing we need now, stopped by highway patrol." He shook his head. "God damn, what a mess."

"We leaving San Francisco so fast?" Tamale said.

Charley swung around. "You feel like staying? We got a dead man on board, we got a kidnapped cop, we got two guys we got to get rid of, you want to stay? Check into a hotel and give a tea party for the mayor? Jesus, Tamale. Jesus Christ."

"That's the bridge sign there, right?" Mujer said.

"What you think that says?" Charley asked. "Golden Gate Bridge, big as life."

"I wasn't sure that was what it said," Mujer replied.

"Mujer, he got a little trouble reading," said Stidge. "He didn't learn how so good, huh? Huh?"

"Chinga tu madre," Mujer said. *"Pija! Hijo de puta!"*

"What's he saying?" Stidge asked.

"Telling you how much he likes your nice red hair," said Choke.

Buffalo said, "We not staying in San Francisco, then where we going to go, Charley?"

"I'll tell you later, okay?" Charley said. "Mujer, when you get off the bridge, you take the first exit and follow on down until you hit a country road. Then go out toward the beach." He shook his head again and slapped his hand against the side of it. "Dumb, dumb, dumb, this whole thing. We could've stayed in San Francisco all summer, and now look. Dumb. I don't remember ever screwing anything up this bad."

"This the right road?" Mujer asked.

"Yeah. Yeah. Stop here."

Tom said, "The Last Days are almost upon us. It will be the Time of the Crossing soon. Spare them, Charley. Don't deprive them of the Crossing."

Looking at him sadly, Charley said, "I wish I could, Tom. But we don't have no choice." He gestured to the others. "All right, get them out of the van. By the side of the road."

The San Francisco policeman was still lying face down, moaning a little. Stidge dragged him out. Nicholas and Buffalo hustled the two farm boys after him. They huddled together, trembling. One of them had wet his pants. They were eighteen, nineteen years old, Tom guessed.

Tom said, "And He had in His right hand seven stars, and out of His mouth went a sharp two-edged sword, and His countenance was as the sun shineth in His strength. And when I saw Him, I fell at His feet as dead. And He laid His right hand upon me, saying unto me, Fear not; I am the first and the last. I am He that liveth, and was dead; and beyond, I am alive for evermore, and have the keys of hell and death."

"That's enough for now, Tom," Charley said. "Line

them up by the edge of the ravine. That's right. Okay, step back.'' He cocked his laser bracelet and fired three quick bursts, the policeman first, the older farm boy, the other one. None of them made a sound as they died. "Son of a bitch,'' Charley murmured. "What a lousy unnecessary mess. All right, throw them down the ravine. Far down.''

Choke and Buffalo threw the vigilante cop. Nicholas and Mujer and Tamale and Stidge took care of the other two.

"Now Rupe,'' Charley said. "Take him a little way down the road, throw him over too.''

Choke looked up in surprise. "God's sake, Charley—!''

"What do you want to do, carry him along with us for a keepsake? Or give him a Christian burial? Come on. Throw him over. And then let's get the hell out of here.''

"You tell us where we're going?'' Buffalo said.

"Yeah. I can tell you, now that we don't have to worry about them overhearing. We going north, up to Mendocino County. Lots of woods around there, lots of good places to hide. Because that's what we need to do, now. We need to hide real good.'' He paused, watching as Nicholas and Tamale and Stidge dragged Rupe's heavy body from the van and hauled it to the edge of the ravine and sent it tumbling down into the dense underbrush far below. "Okay,'' Charley said. "Let's get moving.''

"We taking the looney?'' Stidge asked. "Ain't that a risk now that he's seen what he just seen?''

"He goes with us,'' Charley said. "Wherever we go. Right, Tom? You stay with us.''

"I am Alpha and Omega, the beginning and the ending, saith the Lord,'' Tom said, shivering a little, though it was much warmer on this side of the bridge than it had been in San Francisco. "Which is, and which was, and which is to come, the Almighty.''

"That's right, Tom,'' Charley said softly. "That's right. Come on, now. Into the van. Everybody into the van.''

3

"JESUS, the heat!" Jaspin said, amazed, as the tumbondé carávan started to flow down out of the mountains into the broad flat expanse of the San Joaquin Valley. He found himself smothered in a great stagnant apocalyptic mass of sizzling air that was almost too hot to breathe. Jaspin's battered old car was third in the long straggling procession, just behind the pair of creaky buses that housed the Senhor and the Senhora and the Inner Host. "I don't believe it. It's incredible, that heat. Where the hell are we going, into the Sahara?"

"Toward Bakersfield," Jill said. "We're just a little way south of Bakersfield."

"I know. But it's like the Sahara here. Like two Saharas piled one on top of the other. Christ, if we're really heading for the North Pole I wish we were a little closer to it now."

He thought the sky was about to break into flames. It was as though all the heat in the whole Valley had come rolling south like a white-hot bowling-ball and had banged up against the wall of the Tehachapi Mountains and now was lying here waiting to engulf them.

"I think we're stopping for the night," Jill said. "You see? The flags are going up."

"It's only three o'clock," Jaspin pointed out.

"Nevertheless. Look at the Senhor's bus. The flags are up."

She was right. He peered out the window and saw that a couple of tumbondé men were clambering around on the roof of the lead bus, putting up the gaudy banners that were the signal to halt and make camp for the night. The bus turned left off the edge of the freeway and into an open field. So did the second one. Jaspin, with a shrug, did the same. And behind him the whole strange caravan of buses and cars and wagons and trucks that had been coming down the pass like some weird motley giant caterpillar turned left too, one by one, following the bus of Senhor Papamacer out into the field.

Jaspin pulled his car up next to the second bus, the little orange-and-black one in which the eleven members of the Inner Host and most of the statues of the gods were traveling, and got out. He turned and shaded his eyes against the fierce mid-afternoon sun and looked back up the little ribbon of steeply rising roadway into the mountains out of which they had just descended. The line of vehicles stretched on and on as far as he could see back toward the summit. It probably went all the way back without a break to Gorman at the very least, and most likely a lot farther than that, on beyond Tejon Pass maybe, as far as Castaic, even. Incredible. Incredible. This whole thing is absolutely incredible, he thought. And for him one of the most incredible aspects was his own presence in it, right here in the front of the procession, just one notch behind the Inner Host. He was here as an observer, sure, as an anthropologist. But that was only half of it, maybe less than half. He knew that he was here as a follower of the Senhor also. He had made the surrender; he had accepted tumbondé; he was going north to await the opening of the way and the coming of Chungirá-He-Will-Come. Last night, lying in uneasy sleep on an air mattress next to the car on some desolate abandoned street in what once had been Glendale or Eagle Rock, he had had a vision of one of the new gods moving in serenity through a world where the sky and everything else were green; and the god, that shining fantastic creature, had greeted him by name and promised him great happiness after the transformation of the world. How strange all this is, Jaspin thought.

"Look at that, will you?" he said. "It's the Mongol horde on the march!"

"I wish you wouldn't talk that way, Barry."

"I say something wrong?"

"The Mongol horde. This isn't anything like that. They were invaders, evil marauders. This is a holy procession."

Jaspin looked at her strangely. She was drenched with sweat, shining with it. Her T-shirt was soaked, almost transparent: her nipples were showing through. Her eyes were glowing in a frightening way. The glow of the True Believer, he thought. He wondered if his eyes ever took on a glow like that. He doubted it.

"Isn't it?" she said. "Holy?"

"Yes. Of course it is."

"You sound so irreverent sometimes."

"Do I?" Jaspin said. "I can't help it, I suppose. My anthropological training. I can't ever stop being a detached observer."

"Even though you believe?"

"Even though."

"I feel sorry for you," she said.

"Come on. Ease off."

"I don't like it when you make jokes about what's happening. The Mongol horde, and all that."

"All right," he said. "I'm flippant. So shoot me. It's in my genes, being flippant. I can't help it. I've got five thousand years of flippancy in my blood." He reached out for her, lightly touching her bare arm, gliding his fingertip through the perspiration of her skin and leaving a streak. She pulled away from him. She was doing that a lot lately. "Come on," he said. "I'm sorry I was flippant."

"If this is the Mongol horde," Jill said, "you're one of the Mongols too. Don't forget that."

Jaspin nodded. "You're right. I won't."

She turned away, rummaging in the car, groping in the water-cooler. After a moment she came up with a bottle of water, took a deep pull, put it back without offering him any. Then she wandered away and stood staring toward Senhor Papamacer's bus.

The new Jill, he thought.

There had been a subtle change, he noticed, in her attitude toward him since they had set out from San Diego with the tumbondé caravan. Or perhaps it wasn't so subtle. She had cooled; she had become very distant. She was much less the timid waif now, much less tentative and subservient, much more self-assured. No more gratitude that the wonderful erudite Dr. Barry Jaspin of UCLA kindly permitted her to stick around. No more of that wide-eyed awe from her now; no more gaping at him as though he were the custodian of all human wisdom. And the sexual thing between them, which had been so free and easy the first couple of weeks, was fading fast, was hardly there any more. Well, some of that had been inevitable, Jaspin knew. He had been through it before with other women. He was human, after all, feet of clay right up to his eyebrows like everybody else, and she was bound to find that out sooner or later. She was starting to see that he was less wonderful than her fantasies had led her to think, and she was starting to look at him more realistically. Okay. He had warned her. I am not the noble romantic intellectual figure you think I am, he had told her, right up front. He might also have said he wasn't the awesome lover she imagined him to be, but no need, she had had time by now to discover that herself. Okay. Okay. Being worshipped wasn't all that great anyway, especially when it wasn't based on anything real. But something else was going on, something a little scary. She was still basically a worshipper at heart, a dependent personality: what she had done was shift her dependence from him to the gods of tumbondé. The awe she had had for him was reserved now, it seemed, for Senhor Papamacer as Vicar-on-Earth of Chungirá-He-Will-Come. She would, he suspected, do anything the tumbondé men asked her to do. Anything.

He stared toward the south again, looking up the high

mountain wall. The vehicles were still streaming down into the Valley, an unending flow of them. This was the fifth day of the journey, and day by day the size of the procession had grown. They had taken the inland route to avoid problems with traffic and with the authorities in the big coastal towns; they had gone up through places like Escondido and Vista and Corona, and then around the eastern edge of Los Angeles. It was a slow trip, with frequent stops for rituals and prayers and enormous communal meals. And it took forever to get things started up again when the order went out to head for the road. Probably the bulk of those who were here were people who had been part of the caravan since San Diego, Jaspin figured—tumbondé wasn't widely known outside the southern half of San Diego County, where the big refugee populations were—but as the vast procession had rolled along, a good many other people had joined in, perhaps a great many others. There might be fifty thousand people by now. A hundred thousand, even. Truly the Mongol horde on the march.

"Jaspeen?"

Turning, he saw one of the high tumbondé men, the one named Bacalhau. It was getting easier to tell them apart, now. Despite the intense heat, Bacalhau was wearing full tumbondé rig, boots and leggings and jacket, even the sombrero, or whatever it was, that flat black wide-brimmed hat.

"The Senhor, he want you," Bacalhau said. He glanced at Jill. "You, too."

"Me?" she asked, surprised.

Jaspin was surprised too. Not that Senhor Papamacer would summon him to an audience—he had done that yesterday evening, and also two days before that, each time treating Jaspin to a long rambling repetitious monologue describing how the first visions of Maguali-ga and Chungirá-He-Will-Come had happened to enter his soul two or three years ago, and how he had immediately understood that he was the chosen prophet of the new gods. But why Jill? Up till now the Senhor had shown no indication that he even knew Jill existed.

"You come," said Bacalhau. "You both."

He led them to the Senhor's bus. It was painted in the colors of Maguali-ga and bore the huge papier-mâché images of Prete Noir the Negus and Rei Ceupassear mounted on the hood on either side of the front window. Half a dozen other members of the Inner Host were lounging around its entrance when Jaspin and Jill approached it—Barbosa, Cotovela, Lagosta, Johnny Espingarda, Pereira, and one who was either Carvalho or Rodrigues, Jaspin was not sure which. Like Bacalhau they were all in formal tumbondé costumes, though some had loosened their collars.

"Maguali-ga, Maguali-ga," Lagosta said, sounding bored.

"Chungirá-He-Will-Come," Jill replied before Jaspin could make the ritual response.

Lagosta stared at her with a flicker of interest in his chilly eyes, but only for a moment. He gave Jaspin a frosty look too, as if saying, Who are you, pitiful *branco*, sad honky noodle, to rate so much of Senhor Papamacer's attention? Jaspin glowered back at him. Your name means lobster, he thought. And you, Bacalhau, that's codfish. Some names. Lobster, codfish. The holy apostles of the prophet.

"Pardon me," Jaspin said.

The Inner Host men sprawling on the steps of the bus moved aside making room for them to go in. Inside the bus the air was thick and stale, and there was the sour smell of some strange incense on it. They had pulled out all the seats and had divided the bus with brocaded curtains into three small rooms, an antechamber, a chapel in the middle, and living quarters for Senhor Papamacer and Senhora Aglaibahi down at the back.

"You wait," Bacalhau said.

He pushed aside the heavy curtain and went through into the chapel. The curtain closed behind him. Jaspin heard faint conversation in Portuguese.

"Can you understand what they're saying?" Jill asked.

"No."

"What do you think's going on?"

Jaspin shook his head. "Don't have the slightest," he whispered.

After a moment Bacalhau reappeared with a couple of other members of the Inner Host who had been inside. There was never a time when seven or eight weren't hovering close by the Senhor. Jaspin couldn't tell whether the role the Host was meant to play was that of apostles or bodyguards, or some of each. The Inner Host was made up entirely of youngish dark-skinned Brazilians, eleven lean cool unsmiling men who could pass just as easily for bandidos as holy apostles. There were a few Africans in the high councils of tumbondé also, Jaspin knew, but they didn't seem to rate the same access to the Senhor. Jaspin doubted that it was a racial thing, since the Brazilians were pretty much as black as the Africans; more likely Senhor Papamacer simply felt more comfortable with people from his own homeland.

"You come," Bacalhau said, beckoning.

They followed him into the dark musty interior of the bus. Jaspin struggled for breath. Last night when he had been in here it had seemed disagreeably hot and stuffy, but now, down amidst the blazing afternoon heat of the Valley, it was downright stifling. Every window was shut, the smoke of a dozen sputtering candles was rising in the chapel, there seemed to be no ventilation at all. Jaspin came close to gagging. He looked helplessly at Jill, but she didn't seem to be bothered at all by the foulness of the atmosphere. Her eyes had that glow again. It frightened him to see that look in her eyes.

Senhor Papamacer sat crosslegged at the far end of the bus, silent, waiting. To his left, along the side wall, was Senhora Aglaibahi, the divine mother and living goddess. The long narrow chamber was set up much like the room in which the Senhor had interviewed Jaspin back in Chula Vista: the darkness, the heavy draperies, the candles, the green-and-red rug, the little wooden images of Maguali-ga and Chungirá-He-Will-Come.

The Senhor made a tiny gesture of greeting with his left hand. His eyes came to rest on Jill. He studied her without speaking for what felt like forever.

"The woman," he said at last to Jaspin. "She is your wife?"

He reddened. "Ah—no. A friend."

"I thought a wife." The Senhor sounded displeased. "But you travel together?"

"As friends," Jaspin said uneasily, wondering where this was leading. He glanced toward Jill. She seemed off in some other world.

The Senhor said, "You know, I have the power of making you man and wife before all the gods. I will do this."

Jaspin was caught off guard. His cheeks grew even hotter. What the hell was this? Marry? *Jill?*

Cautiously he said, "Uh—I think it's best if she and I just remain friends, Senhor Papamacer."

"Ah. Ah." Jaspin felt a cold torrent of disapproval surging behind Senhor Papamacer's timeless expressionless features. From a million miles away the Senhor said, "As you wish. But it is good, being man and wife." Another barely perceptible gesture, this time toward the silent Senhora Aglaibahi. Jaspin's gaze followed the Senhor's hand. Senhora Aglaibahi sat without moving, scarcely seeming even to breathe. She seemed like some temple figurine, larger than life, something made of polished black stone: one of those Hindu goddesses, Jaspin thought, all breasts

and eyes. She wore a vaguely sari-like white muslin gar-
ment that was so loosely wrapped around her that it plainly
displayed the swaying globes of her bosom, the soft folds of
her belly. Her dark skin was shining in the candlelight as
though it had been oiled. Even after a week among these
people the Senhora remained a mystery to Jaspin, a lovely
voluptuous woman who might have been thirty or, just as
easily, fifty. Tumbondé mythology had it that she was a
virgin, but there was something else in the teachings about
the ability of gods and goddesses to replenish there virginities
as often as desired, and Jaspin doubted very much that the
Senhor and the Senhora were living together in chastity. As
he stared at her, the Senhora smiled. He imagined himself
suddenly being drawn toward those dark-nippled breasts and
given the milk of Senhora Aglaibahi to drink.

Jill said, unexpectedly, astonishingly, "I will be his wife
if that is your will, Senhor Papamacer."

"Hey, wait just a—"

"It is a good thing, yes, being man and wife. You do not
want this, Jaspeen?"

He faltered and did not reply. He felt as though he had
stepped in the path of a runaway steamroller. Marrying Jill
was the last thing in the world that might have been on his
mind when he walked into this bus five minutes ago.

"If you wish to attain the further knowledge, Jaspeen,
you must go onward into the mysteries. And for this you
must make the marriage."

Oh, so that's it, Jaspin said to himself.

Slowly he began to understand, then. Things had been
starting to turn a little unreal, but now they were making
sense again. This is mysticism country here, he thought.
The Senhor is talking the sacred marriage, the *hieros gamos,*
ye olde ancient primordial fertility thing. You want to learn
the inner secrets, you have to go through the initiation.
There are no two ways here. Jill must have grasped that

intuitively. Or maybe she's simply a better anthropologist that you are.

Plainly the Senhor was waiting for an answer, and only one answer was going to be acceptable. The steamroller had gone by, and he was flat as a tapeworm now.

He felt helpless. Okay, he thought. Okay. Go with it. Ham it up, Jaspin told himself. Rejoice, rejoice: you have no choice. In the most humble tone at his command he said, "I place myself in the Senhor's hands."

"You will take this woman in the marriage?"

Yes, yes, I will, certainly I will, he started to say. Whatever is pleasing to you, Senhor Papamacer. But he couldn't get the words out.

Jaspin turned toward Jill. Her eyes were glowing again. But not for me, he thought. Not for me.

He shook his head. For God's sake, he thought, am I really going to marry her, now? This scrawny goofed-up stringy-haired *shiksa,* this True Believer, this ragamuffin intellectual groupie? The idea was beyond belief. Everything in him balked at it. A voice within him cried out, What the fuck are you doing, man? *I place myself in the Senhor's hands.* What? Married? On five seconds' notice? To *her?* He imagined the scene, bringing her home to his parents. Mom, pop, this is my wife. Mrs. Barry Jaspin, yes, indeed. I was just waiting for the ideal mate to come along all this time, and now here she is. I know you'll love her. Yes. Yes. And then he thought, Stop being an asshole. This isn't anything legal. It won't mean a thing outside this bus. You can walk away from it any time. Marry her and be done with it, and think of it as part of your anthropological research. A tribal ceremony you're required to undertake so that the chief will go on allowing you to observe the other tribal rituals. And then he thought, Forget all that. Put from your mind all these thoughts of self and all this scheming for advantage. If you have any genuine hope of yielding

yourself to Chungirá-He-Will-Come at the time of the opening of the gateway, you must obey Senhor Papamacer in all
things. Jaspin felt his knees beginning to shake. He had
come to the truth about this thing at last. He might not be
doing this for love, but he also wasn't doing it out of any
cynical fingers-crossed-behind-the-back notion that he was
acting purely for opportunism's sake. No. That was just the
rationalization that he was using to hide from himself what
was really going on. But now he forced himself to admit the
real story. He was doing it because beyond anything else he
yearned to have his mind and soul flooded and possessed by
Chungirá-He-Will-Come; and unless be obeyed Senhor
Papamacer in all things that would not happen to him. So he
would do it. For God's sake.

"I will take her, yes," Jaspin said.

A flicker of a smile passed across Senhor Papamacer's
thin lips. "Kneel beside the Senhora," he said. "Both of
you."

4

THE conference room was swaying, sliding, trying to turn
green. Elszabet breathed deeply and struggled to keep everything in focus. She knew that she was nearing the edge
of hysteria. Maybe I should just tell them, she thought, that
I had a space dream last night and I am somehow unable to
shake myself free of it, and to hell with trying to be
professional up here.

No. No. Stay with it, she ordered herself. You can't just crap out right in front of everybody.

She brought herself back into the meeting. It was an effort, but she brought herself back in.

Briskly she said by way of getting things started, "We all agree, I think, that we're dealing with something that's very hard to comprehend. But I think the first thing that we need to acknowledge is that it's a phenomenon that can be measured and quantified and delineated in purely scientific terms."

That sounded good.

Naresh Patel looked up from the sheaf of printouts he was studying. "Can it? Tabulations like these, do you mean? Frequencies and geographical distribution of hallucinatory events, variable-similarity scales, imagery analysis, cognitive-filtering vectors, correlation of hallucination with Gelbard-Louit stability-index rating of hallucinator? But what if this is a phenomenon totally inexplicable by scientific means?"

What if it is, Elszabet thought. What if it isn't? Am I supposed to say something now?

Dan Robinson rescued her. She heard his voice, coming from what seemed like a very great distance.

"If it is," he said, "then we won't be able to explain it, will we? But why should we think it is, at this point? Pardon my hopeless western-materialistic bias, Naresh, but I happen to believe that everything in the universe has an underlying quantifiable rationale, which may not necessarily be accessible to human understanding because of limits in our current investigative techniques, but which is there nevertheless. Before the invention of the spectroscope, for example, it would have been the wildest sort of fantasy to claim that we could ever know which elements the stars were composed of. But for a modern astronomer there's no problem at all in looking at a star fifty light-years away, or, for that matter, five billion light-years away, and saying quite authoritatively that it's made up of hydrogen, helium, calcium, potassium—"

"Agreed," Patel said. "Yet I think it is conceivable that a seventeenth-century astronomer could have accepted the idea that it would someday be possible to discover such information. All that was missing was the spectroscope: a matter of technological progress, refinement of technique, not a quantum leap of conceptualization. And I agree with you also that all events do have some underlying rationale. To say otherwise would be to argue that the universe allows pure randomness, and I do not think that is the case."

The room was turning green again. Patel, Robinson, Bill Waldstein, and the rest were taking on a shining crystalline texture. Elszabet could hear what was being said, but she had no idea what it meant. She was not quite sure where she was, or why.

Patel went on, " . . . but I argue only that the event we consider here may not have a rationale that fits the dogmas of western scientific thought, and that therefore we will not approach any understanding of it by trying to measure and count."

"What are you really saying, Naresh?" Bill Waldstein asked.

Patel smiled. "For example, what if these shared multiple hallucinations are not hallucinations at all, but rather the first signs of the advent upon our world of the actual numinous force, the divine spirit, the Godhead, if you will?"

"Are you going Hindu on us now?" Waldstein said.

Crisply Patel replied, "There is nothing specifically Hindu, I believe, in what I have just suggested. Or eastern in any way, so far as I can see. I think that if we were to consult Father Christie on the subject of the Second Coming we might find that there are Christian elements to the concept, or Jewish messianic ones. I say simply that we are attempting to approach this matter in a scientific way when in fact it may be entirely outside the scope of scientific technique."

Dante Corelli said, "Come on, Naresh. Are you telling us just to shrug and give up and wait to see what happens? Now *that's* a Hindu notion if I ever heard one—"

"I do agree with Naresh on one point," Dan Robinson cut in. "Where he says these shared multiple hallucinations are not hallucinations at all."

Bill Waldstein leaned forward. "What do you think they are, then?"

Robinson looked toward the head of the conference table. "Elszabet, shall I respond to that?"

She blinked. "What, Dan?"

"Shall I respond? To Bill's query? Is this the time for me to explain my idea of what the space dreams really are?"

"What the space dreams really are," she said. She was lost. She realized that she must have been wandering in far-off realms. "Yes. Yes, of course, Dan," she said indistinctly.

The Green World lay just beyond the window. Rolling meadows, graceful looping leafless trees.

"Elszabet? Elszabet?"

"Go ahead, Dan. What's the matter? Go on."

She looked around. Dan, Bill, Dante, Naresh. Dave Paolucci from the San Francisco center down at the far end of the table. Leo Kresh, all the way up from San Diego. An important meeting. You have to pay attention. She stared at the grain in the redwood-burl tabletop. God help me, she thought. What's happening to me? What's *happening*?

Robinson was saying, ". . . Project Starprobe, which was sent toward Proxima Centauri in the year 2057, I think, and which may now be producing a response in the form of a broadcast signal from the inhabitants of that world, a signal that is increasing in intensity as it approaches the Earth. I want to suggest that a vastly superior civilization in the

Alpha Centauri system—Proxima Centauri is one of the three stars of that system, you know—has quite possibly sent a Starprobe of its own toward us, using a technology presently unknown to us but not in any serious way implausible, in order to make direct contact with human minds.''

"For Christ's sake," Waldstein muttered.

"Is it all right if I finish what I'm saying, Bill? This signal, let's say, was received at first only by those here who were most sensitive to such a thing, which for some reason happened to be patients suffering from Gelbard's syndrome in this sanitarium and elsewhere. But as the intensity of the signal has increased, incidence of receptivity has widened to take in a broad segment of the human population, including, as I understand it, a good many people right in this room. If I'm correct, then, what we're confronting is not in any way an epidemic of some new mental illness, nor is it—forgive me, Naresh—any kind of metaphysical revelation, but in fact is a significant historical development, the inauguration of communication with intelligent extraterrestrial life, and as such an event neither to be feared nor to be—"

"There's just one problem, Dr. Robinson." A new voice cutting in from the far end of the table, quiet, assured. "May I have the floor a moment? Dr. Robinson? Dr. Lewis?"

Hearing her name, Elszabet looked up, startled, realizing she had been drifting again. They were all looking at her.

"May I address this point, Dr. Lewis?" The voice from the far end again. It belonged to the man from San Diego, Elszabet realized, her counterpart, Leo Kresh, the head of the Nepenthe Center down there. A smallish man, about forty, balding, precise in movement and in speech. She stared at him but she had wandered too far from the discussion to know what to say.

Into her silence Dan Robinson said quickly, "Of course, Dr. Kresh, go ahead, please."

Kresh nodded. "That these images of other worlds might in some way be connected with Project Starprobe had also occurred to me, Dr. Robinson, and in fact I've done considerable investigaton of that possibility. Unfortunately it doesn't appear to work out. As you correctly state, the unmanned Starprobe vehicle was launched in 2057, just a few years before the outbreak of the Dust War. However, I've been able to determine that even at the quite extraordinary velocities that Starprobe was capable of attaining at its peak of acceleration, it would not have reached the vicinity of Proxima Centauri, which is 4.2 light-years from Earth, until the year 2099. So you can see that there has not yet been quite enough time even for Starprobe's own signal, which of course is a narrow-band radio wave traveling at the speed of light, to have returned from Proxima, let alone for any hypothetical inhabitants of that system to have sent us any kind of signal of their own. And of course if the Proximans— if there are any—had shipped a Proximan equivalent of Starprobe in our direction, as you suggest, there's no likelihood at all that it will be here for decades more. Therefore I think we have to rule out the hypothesis that the space dreams have an extraterrestrial origin, tempting though that notion may seem."

"Suppose," Robinson said, "that the Proximans have some way of sending a spaceship here at speeds *faster* than light?"

Gently Kresh said, "Pardon me, Dr. Robinson, but I'd have to call that an excessive multiplication of hypotheses. Not only are we required to postulate Proximans, but also you ask us to assume faster-than-light transit, which under the laws of physics as we currently understand them is simply not—"

"Hold on," Bill Waldstein said. "What are we talking

about here? Spaceships to and from other stars? Faster-than-light travel? Elszabet, for God's shake, rule all his stuff out of order. It's bad enough that the situation we're coping with is fantastic in itself—can you imagine hundreds of thousands of people having identical bizarre dreams all over the West Coast, and maybe everywhere else too?—without dragging in all his imaginary speculation besides.''

"In addition," said Naresh Patel, "it has been over two months since the first dreams were reported. Given what Dr. Kresh has told us about the time of Starprobe's arrival at this other star and the necessary time that must elapse before its radio signal can return to us, I believe it's clear that there is no connection between the dreams and whatever data the Starprobe satellite will eventually send back.''

"What's more," Dante Corelli offered, "we're getting views of at least seven different solar systems in these dreams, right? Starprobe went to just *one* system, as I understand it. So even allowing for these problems of transmission time that Dr. Kresh's been pointing out, how can it be sending back so many different sort of scenes? I think—''

"Point of order," Bill Waldstein shouted. "Elszabet, will you *please* let us move on to something more rational? We've got people here from San Francisco and San Diego who want to tell us what's going on at their centers, and . . . Elszabet? Elszabet? Is there something the matter with you?''

She struggled to understand what he was telling her. Her mind was full of green fog. Crystalline figures moved gracefully to and fro, introducing themselves to her, inviting her to incomprehensible social events, a cataclysm symphony, a four-valley splendor, a sensory retuning. Everyone will be there, dear Elszabet. Your poet will present his latest, you know. And there is hope of another green aurora, the second one this year, and then no more again for at least fifteen tonal cycles, so they say—

"Elszabet? Elszabet?"

"I think I'd like to go to the four-valley splendor," she said. "And maybe the cataclysm symphony. But not the sensory retuning, I think. Will that be all right, to skip the sensory retuning?"

"What's she talking about?"

She smiled. She looked from one to the other, Dan, Bill, Dante, Naresh, Dave Paolucci, Leo Kresh. Green light blazed upward from the center of the huge redwood table. It's all right, she wanted to say. I've gone out of my mind, that's all. But you don't need to worry about me. It's not unusual for people to go out of their minds these days.

"You aren't well, Elszabet?"

Dan Robinson. Standing beside her, resting his hand lightly on her shoulder.

"No," she said. "I'm really not very well at all. I don't think I have been all morning. Would you excuse me, everyone? I'm terribly sorry but I think I should lie down. Would you excuse me? Thank you. Thank you. I'm terribly sorry. Please don't interrupt the meeting. But I think I should lie down."

5

FERGUSON said, "What did I tell you? There's nothing to it. You just slip away through the forest and keep on going east, and you'll hit civilization sooner or later."

"You have any idea where we are?" Alleluia asked.

"On our way to Ukiah."

"Ukiah. Where's that?"

"East of Mendo, maybe thirty miles from the coast. You forget? They pick it out of you?

"I don't know much about this part of California," she said. "We're going to walk thirty miles, Ed?"

He looked at her. "You're a superwoman, right? What's the big deal about walking thirty miles? Little less than thirty, maybe. We do it in two days, tops. You can't handle that?"

"Not me. You. Are you in shape for that kind of hike?"

Ferguson laughed and rubbed his hand against the flawless skin of her upper arm. "Don't worry about me, baby. I'm in terrific shape for a man my age. I'm in terrific shape, period. Anyway, I get tired, we can always stop a couple hours. Nobody going to be coming after us here."

"You sure of that?"

"Sure I'm sure," he said. He grinned. "Imagine," he said. "No pick tomorrow morning. No more head-scrambling. We'll go through a whole goddamn day remembering everything that happened to us the day before."

"And what we dreamed the night before too."

"What we dreamed, yeah." The grin, which had slowly been fading, turned into a frown. "You dream last night? A space dream?"

"I think so."

"You get them just about every night."

"Do I?" she asked.

"That's what you've been telling me every morning before pick. I've got it all down, right here on my little ring. A different planet every night, the nine suns, the green world, the one where the whole sky's full of stars. Last night it was the big blue star in the sky and the shining bubbles floating in the air."

"I don't remember," Alleluia said.

"Well, sometimes you do and sometimes you don't."

"And you? You never get the dreams, do you?"

"Never once," he said, and felt the bitterness starting to rise. "Everybody gets them but me. I don't know. I'd like to see those places just once. I'd like to know what the hell is going on in everybody's mind. I've got it on my ring that first thing in the morning I have to ask myself, Did you dream a space dream? And I never have. Christ, I hate not feeling what other people feel."

"You ought to try being artificial for a while, then. See what it's like being really different."

"Yeah. Sure. Just what I need." Ferguson smiled. "Well, at least I won't get picked tomorrow. They won't stick their goddamn electronic scalpels into my head. Maybe two or three days away from those bastards and I'll start to dream, you think? What do you think, Allie?"

"The trouble with you," she said, "is that you want it too bad. You have to stop wanting it if you hope to get it. You see that, Ed?"

"You make it sound so simple."

"A lot of hard things are simple."

"Forget it," he said. "I can live without the goddamn dreams. I'm just glad to be away from that place."

"So am I," she said, and gave his forearm a squeeze that he supposed was meant to be joyful and affectionate. It sent such a jolt of pain through him that he wondered for an instant if she had broken his arm.

They were about three hours out of the Center now. It was late afternoon, still a couple of hours to go before dark. The air was still warm, though there was the first hint in it of the oncoming evening chill. They were in dense redwood forest, moist and soft underfoot even after the long months of summer drought. There were ground squirrels running around everywhere, and now and then some shy skittish little deer peered at them from behind one of the giant trees.

Getting away had been easy, just as Ferguson had expected. After lunch, during free-time, they had simply wandered off into the woods on the inland side of the Center. Nothing unusual about that. Kept right on wandering, that was the unusual part. Stopping in his favorite little screwing-glade to pick up the canvas bag he had stashed there the day before. He had filled the bag with bread, apples, some squeeze-cans of juice, and he had put a detailed memo about it on his recorder-ring, telling his post-pick self of the next day exactly where to find it. And now they were on their way. Christ, it felt good to be free! Out of the pokey at last. Well, the Center wasn't exactly like a prison—more like a strict boarding school, Ferguson thought—but he had never been much for boarding school either. Or anyplace else where people could tell him what he was supposed to do twelve, sixteen hours a day.

He had a sort of plan. Get to Ukiah, first: that was a fair-sized town, his recorder said, thirty, forty thousand people. A downright metropolis these days, post-Dust War days, when kids were few and far between and the population was way down, off as much as eighty-five percent from twentieth-century peaks. Sometimes Ferguson tried to imagine the world with all those people in it, five or six million in L.A. alone, more than that in New York. They said sixteen million in Mexico City. Could you believe it? Wasn't anyone in Mexico City now, zero, *nada,* everybody scattering when the Nicas dusted the place. And maybe a million in L.A., if you counted in every town from Santa Barbara down to Newport Beach as being L.A. Well, so we get to Ukiah, he thought, find ourselves a motel, tidy up, regroup, and reorganize. Then phone Lacy and have her wire some money to me from San Fran. She'd be liquid enough to advance him something, he hoped. Christ knows she made a pile when she was working for me: must have hung on to enough to spare me a little. He wasn't carrying any, of course. There was no need for it at the Center, and they didn't encourage you to keep it on hand; when you had a weekend's external leave they simply set up a credit line for you at the place where you'd be staying and at the place where you'd be eating. They didn't want their inmates getting beyond reach.

He'd get beyond reach, all right. Couple days in Ukiah making arrangements, then off to Idaho—no visa needed to get into Idaho, right?—and from there, after maybe six weeks' residence to make it official, apply for entry into Oregon. They had some sort of republic in Oregon now, Oregon and maybe half of what had been Washington State, and once he was across the line there'd be no way of getting him back to California. A matter of sovereign independence, and the way Oregon felt about the Californios, they'd never extradite *anybody*. So then with Oregon as his base he could start making some profitable use of the space dreams. He wasn't exactly sure how just yet, probably some variation on the former Betelgeuse Five scam, guaranteed transmission to the newly developing other worlds, the seven planets so widely being exhibited in your nightly dreams. It would help some if he could see the dreams *himself*, but that wasn't essential so long as he had Alleluia beside him. And Alleluia beside him at night, too, that tremendous panther body of hers every night—

"Hey, what's the hurry?" he called to her. Suddenly she was striding along like a house on fire, leaving him far behind.

She turned and gave him a mischievous smile. "You having trouble keeping up, Ed?"

"Screw you," Ferguson said amiably. "We all know you're a superior life-form. You don't have to prove the goddamn point. Now slow down a little and let's hike it together, okay?''

"Right now I feel like moving fast," she told him. "Getting my heart pumping some."

"You get out of sight, you'll get lost altogether. You may be perfect but you don't know where you're heading, do you? Go on. You just charge off through the woods. Maybe I'll see you again, maybe not."

Her laughter came floating back to him. Feeling anger rising, Ferguson began to walk faster, keeping his eyes fixed on her. Bitch, he thought. Challenging him like this. A real bitch. But you have to admit she's a magnificent bitch.

He had never known a woman anything like her, and he had known a lot of women. So tall and supple, practically his own height. And beautiful: all that jet-black hair, those breasts, those legs. And strong: the long flat muscles rippling beneath her satiny skin, that aura she had of tremendous power just barely held in reserve. And strange: you could never predict what she would do. The way her mind worked, she seemed like a Martian sometimes. A woman from Betelgeuse Five. Ferguson wondered what sort of problems had landed her in mindpick. The first thing they told you at Nepenthe Center was that you weren't to discuss your past with your fellow patients; the past was where your wounds were, they said, and you were supposed to let it all slough off under the pick. When you reintegrated in the final phase of the treatment, they told you, the useful part of your past would come back, the wounds would be forever gone; so it wasn't useful to cut the memory grooves any deeper by talking about where you were coming from. Ferguson had broken that rule, of course. He broke all the rules, just as a matter of habit. But Alleluia hadn't told him a thing about the disturbances that had brought her to the Center. She had gone into fits of crazy depression, maybe, the Gelbard stuff, and maybe even killed people with her bare hands to cheer herself up, for all he knew. Whatever it was, she kept it to herself. Maybe she didn't even know. Maybe she had already sloughed all her memories off under the pick, he thought. A strange woman. But gorgeous. Gorgeous.

He was damned if he'd let her get this far ahead of him. She was almost out of sight up there. He started into a half-trot, breathing hard, breaking into a light sweat, stumbling a little on the soft loose forest duff. Ferguson was surprised at how short a time it took for him to get out of breath. Then he began to feel the beginning of some pain behind his breastbone, nothing too agonizing, just a sharp little pressure. No big deal. But a little on the scary side all the same.

Hell, he thought, huffing and puffing, you ought to be able to outrun a *girl*, right?

Wrong, he told himself. Don't be an asshole. That was no girl, that was a superhuman artificial being, and she had a hundred-meter head start on him. Besides, he was fifty years old. Not exactly a boy any more. It was nutty to go chasing after her like this through the woods.

But he kept on all the same. His shirt was soaked now and his heart was pounding and there were sharp little pressures all up and down his chest, but he couldn't let himself be bested this way. "Goddamn you, Allie, wait up for me!" he yelled, running even harder. He couldn't even see her now: a close-set stand of enormous redwoods rose like a wall before him. Screw her. I'll just let her run away and get lost, he thought. I've got all the food, right? But still he didn't slow down. And then he caught his foot in some sort of gopher hole and went toppling heavily to the ground, and felt the ankle twist beneath him as he landed.

Pain blazed in his whole leg. He sat up, touching himself here and there. The ankle was throbbing. He tried carefully to stand and discovered that he couldn't: the leg wanted to buckle when he put the slightest weight on it. How was he going to get to Ukiah now? He cupped his hand to his mouth and called to her: "Allie? Allie? Come on back, I hurt myself!"

Five minutes, no sign of her. Ferguson massaged his ankle, hoping it would unsprain itself fast; but when he tried again to get to his feet it felt worse than before. His foot was beginning to swell up.

"Alleluia? God damn you, Alleluia, where are you?"

"Easy, easy. I'm right here."

He looked up and saw her loping toward him like a gazelle, running in high splendid bounds. When she halted beside him she was not in the least winded: her breathing was as calm as if she had been sauntering.

"What happened to you?" she asked.

"Tripped. Sprained it. I can't walk, Allie!"

"Sure you can. I'll make a crutch for you."

"Jesus, a crutch? I don't know how to use a crutch. And what am I going to do, hobble for thirty miles? Why the hell did you have to go running off like that? I wouldn't have tripped if I hadn't been chasing after you. And—"

"Take it easy," she said. He watched in astonishment as she bent a little tree to ground level, broke off the top third of its trunk, and began stripping away the branches. "You don't have to go that far. There's a road just up ahead. We'll flag somebody down and ask for a ride into Ukiah. They don't want to go to Ukiah, we'll persuade them."

"A road?"

"A little paved highway, just on the other side of those big trees, maybe five minutes up ahead. I was there when I heard you calling. A few cars going by, even. Don't worry, okay?" She scooped him to a standing position as if he were a sack of feathers and propped the improvised crutch under his armpit. It was a little too long. Supporting him with one arm, she brought the crutch up across her shin and snapped off the tip. "There," she said. "Ought to be the right length now." If he hadn't seen it done, he wouldn't have believed that she had been able to snap a green sapling as thick as her wrist with one quick little gesture. How hard would it be for her to break someone's arm or leg?

The crutch helped. It was a clumsy business, but he limped along, letting his injured foot dangle. She walked beside him, her arm around his shoulders, giving him an extra lift. The ground sloped upward until they reached the dense stand of redwoods, but then on the far side it angled down and leveled out and before long they emerged into a clear space and saw the highway. It was an old two-lane county road, potholed and worn, no vehicle-control devices visible at all in it, the sort of road they had had a hundred fifty years ago. He listened for cars but heard nothing: total silence. Behind them, the sun was getting low, starting to drop toward the Pacific.

"Something's coming," Alleluia said.

"I don't hear a thing."

"Neither do I. But I can see it, down the raod. And now I can hear the engine, more or less. Probably a ground-effect car, since it's so quiet."

He saw no sign of anything, not even a speck in the distance. Her senses were awesome. A couple of minutes went by, and then he began to make it out, a dark van coming toward them from the south. "Okay," he said. "I'm going to creep a little way back into the woods. You stand out here and flag them down."

"Will they stop?"

"People got to be out of their minds not stopping for a woman looks like you, out here by yourself with night coming on. They'll stop. When they do, you tell them your husband's back there with an injured leg, will they mind driving us to Ukiah. I'll be coming out. Not much they can do about it then, when I come out. Meanwhile you get close to the driver. He show any sign of pulling out, you reach in

the window, you put your hand on his throat, right? Not to
hurt him, you understand, just to keep him cooperative."

"Okay," she said. "You better get out of sight."

"Yeah," Ferguson said, and went hobbling off into the
underbrush. He settled in behind a tree to watch. A moment
later the van appeared. It was a ground-effect job, all right,
a real antique, maybe even a prewar model, with big garish
bolts of lightning painted in red and yellow along its sides.
Alleluia was standing in the middle of the road, wigwagging
her arms; and, sure enough, the van slowed to a stop a short
distance in front of her. He saw a couple of men in the front
seat. They probably figured they were in for a night's hot
fun, terrific brunette, lonely country road. They tried anything with Allie, though, they'd find out different in a hurry.

He heard them talking with her. Ferguson started to
emerge from his hiding place. We won't even bother hitching
a ride, he thought. I'll just have Allie toss them out into the
shrubbery and we'll drive to Ukiah ourselves and take it on
north tomorrow morning to Oregon.

Then he got a closer look at things and realized that
beside the ones in the front seat there was a whole mob of
men in the back of the van—three, four, maybe five of
them. Scratchers, most likely. Or maybe even bandidos.

Damn, he thought. Even she can't take on seven guys. I
can't even take on one, with my leg like this. Abruptly he
saw how their escape from the Center was going to end:
with him lying in the weeds with his throat slit, and
Alleluia, kicking and scraming all the way, being dragged
off somewhere for a night of gangbanging.

They were getting out of the van. Four, five, six, seven,
yes. No, eight. Coming up to Alleluia, clustering around
her, looking her over appreciatively. One of them, an
evil-looking cat with a greasy face and a lot of untidy red
hair, was staring at her breasts as if he hadn't touched a
woman in three years. Another, with washed-out blue eyes

and a face full of acne scars, was actually licking his lips. Ferguson wanted to turn and get away, but it was too late, too late, they had seen him. At his hobbling pace they'd catch him in half a second.

"That your husband over there?" one of the scratchers asked, a stocky, tough-looking one with a short thick black beard. He pointed toward Ferguson. What a dumb way to die this is going to be, Ferguson said to himself. He prayed for Alleluia to go into action, grab three or four of them and snap their necks the way she had snapped that sapling, fast, before they knew what was happening. But she didn't seem about to do that. She looked calm and cheerful and relaxed. Goddamn weird woman. He halted, leaning on his crutch by the side of the road, wondering what was going to happen next.

What happened next was that still another of the scratchers, a tall skinny one with long arms like a monkey's and wild gleaming eyes, came over and peered at him in a peculiar intense way, staring into his face as if trying to read a map, and said earnestly, "Are you hurting a lot? I don't mean your leg, I mean your soul. I think your soul's hurting some. Just remember, this is none other but the house of God, and this is the gate of heaven."

"What the hell," Ferguson said, his voice thick with fear and bewilderment.

"Don't pay him no mind," said the red-haired scratcher. "He ain't nothing but a looney, that one. That crazy bastard Tom."

"Crazy, huh?" Ferguson said. He looked slowly around, beginning to think maybe they would come out of this in one piece after all. The thing was to stay cool, to start talking and talk a whole lot, to make himself seem useful to these men. "If he's a real mental case," he said, "you guys are in the right place, then. Take him over to the Center on the other side of that redwood forest there and he'll feel completely at home. With all the other nuts they got there. Feed him, give him a bath, treat him nice and kindly, that's what they'll do for him over there, your crazy friend Tom.''

The dark-bearded man moved closer to Ferguson. ''Center? What sort of center you mean?''

Five

The palsy plagues my pulse
   When I prig your pigs or pullen,
Your culvers take, or mateless make
   Your Chanticleer, or sullen—
When I want provant with Humphrey
   I sup, and when benighted,
I repose in Paul's with waking souls
   Yet never am afrighted.

But I do sing, "Any food, any feeding,
   Feeding, drink, or clothing?
     Come, dame or maid,
     Be not afraid,
Poor Tom will injure nothing."

                      —Tom O'Bedlam's Song

SENHOR Papamacer said, "The beginning, that is what is important, Jaspeen. I tell you this already? Well, you listen again: it is the most important. How the gods first visited themselves into me, the new gods."

Jaspin waited patiently. The Senhor had told him this already, yes, more than once. More than twice, in fact. But there was never any percentage, Jaspin knew, in trying to direct these conversations. The Senhor said only what the Senhor wanted to say. That was his privilege: he was the Senhor. Jaspin was merely the scribe.

Besides, Jaspin had learned that if he was content to sit still while the Senhor was running through familiar stuff, sooner or later the Senhor would dredge up some new revelation. This afternoon, for instance, Jaspin noticed a large cardboard portfolio on the floor next to the Senhor. The Senhor was sitting with the stubby fingers of his left hand spread out wide over the portfolio, a sure sign that it was important. Jaspin wanted to know what was inside it, and he had a notion that if he simply sat still and waited, he would find out. He sat still. He waited.

"It was in the beginning with a dream," Senhor Papamacer said. "I lay in the dark one night and Maguali-ga he show himself to me and say, I am the opener of the gate, I am the bringer of what is to come. And I know at once that this is the god speaking from across the ocean of stars, and that I am the chosen voice of the god. You know?"

Yes, Jaspin thought. He knew. He knew what came next, too. *And I arose in the night and I went to the window, and the nine stars of Maguali-ga were shining in the heavens, and I reach my arms out and I feel the great light of the seven galaxies upon me.* He knew it all word by word, by now. Senhor Papamacer was dictating a scripture to him and wanted to make sure he got it down right. *There was no doubt. I felt the truth at once.*

He studied the lean sculptured face, the obsidian eyes. This little man who meant to change the world and maybe would: this prophet, this holy monster, latest and perhaps last in a long line of prophets. Moses, Jesus, Mohammed, Senhor Papamacer. The Senhor liked to bracket himself with them: Moses, Jesus, Mohammed, Senhor Papamacer. Maybe he was right.

"And I arose in the night," said the Senhor, "and I went to the window, and the nine stars of Maguali-ga were shining in the heavens—"

Ah, yes. And the great light of the seven galaxies.

"The thing that I know instantly," the Senhor said, "is that these gods are real and they will come to Earth to rule us." That was the interesting thing, Jaspin told himself, that great bounding leap of faith. Knowing *instantly*. Faith in the substance of things hoped for, the evidence of things not seen. Six months ago that would have been incomprehensible to Jaspin; but *he* had seen also: Chungirá-He-Will-Come on the scorching hillside back of San Diego, and then

Maguali-ga so many times in his dreams, and Rei Ceupassear, Narbail of the thunders, O Minotauro. He too had seen; he too had believed instantly. To his own amazement. "How do I know this, you ask?" Senhor Papamacer went on. "I know it that I know it, is all. That is sufficient only. *Verdademente a verdad,* truly the truth. You know that you know."

"Just as when Moses asked God to tell him His name," Jaspin ventured eagerly, "and all that God would answer was, 'I AM THAT I AM.' And that was good enough for Moses."

Senhor Papamacer gave him a frosty look. Jaspin was here to listen, not to supply commentary. Jaspin wanted to sink out of sight.

But after a moment the Senhor continued as though Jaspin had not spoken. "One must believe, you know, Jaspeen? In the face of the absolute truth one believes absolutely. So it was with me. I yielded myself to the truth and one by one the gods made themselves known to me, Rei Ceupassear and Prete Noir the Negus and O Minotauro and Narbail and the others, each gave me the vision in turn. I saw their worlds and their stars and I knew that they love us and watch over us and are making ready for their coming among us. I was the first to know this, but because I held the truth others came to me and I shared my knowledge with them. Now there are many thousands of us, and one day all the world will be joined with us: joined in blood, in the rite of tumbondé, to make ourselves worthy of the final god who will bring the blessings of the stars."

Hesitantly, feeling he had to say something, Jaspin intoned, "Chungirá-He-Will Come, he will come."

For once it was the right thing. The Senhor nodded benevolently. "Maguali-ga, Maguali-ga," he replied. Together they made the sacred signs.

Then the Senhor said suddenly, surprisingly, "You know

what I was, before the gods came to me? You will not know.
This you must put in your book, Jaspeen. I drive the taxi, in
Chula Vista. Twenty years I drive there, and before that I
drive in Tijuana, and when I am young I drive in Rio,
before the big war. Take me here, take me there, can you
drive any faster, keep the change." He laughed. Jaspin had
never heard the Senhor laugh before: a dry harsh shivering
laugh, reeds rubbing together in a windswept arroyo. "All in
one night I am made new by the gods, I never drive again.
You put that in the book, Jaspeen. I give you photographs:
my taxi, my chauffeur license. Mohammed, he drive cam-
els, Moses he was a shepherd, Jesus a carpenter. And
Papamacer a taxi-man."

There they were again, the big four, Moses, Jesus,
Mohammed, Papamacer. Jaspin tried to imagine this formidable deep-voiced coiled spring of a man, this charismatic
prophet of the high gods of the stars, buzzing around San
Diego in some old jalopy of a cab scrounging up fares and
tips. The Senhor reached for the cardboard portfolio. The
taxicab photos, Jaspin figured. But instead Senhor Papamacer
said, "When you close your eyes, Jaspeen, you see the
gods, yes?"

"Some nights, yes. I dream the visions two, three times a
week."

"You see all seven loving galaxies?"

"By now, yes," said Jaspin. "All seven."

"And you believe, these are the homes of the gods,
verdademente a verdad?"

"I believe it, yes," Jaspin said. He wondered what the
Senhor was getting at.

"You ever wonder, maybe it is only dream, maybe it is a
foolishness of the night that you have, that I have, that all of
us have?"

"I believe the gods are true gods," Jaspin said.

"Because you have the faith. Because you know that you know."

Jaspin shrugged. "Yes."

"I have here the proof absolute," said the Senhor. He opened the portfolio. Jaspin saw a thick stack of holgraphic repros inside. Senhor Papamacer passed the top one across to Jaspin. "You know this place?" he asked.

Jaspin stared. Even in the dim light of Senhor Papamacer's bus the holo gleamed with an inner radiance. It showed a string of dazzling suns—he counted six, seven, eight, nine—strewn out across a dark purple sky, and an alien landscape, eerie and bewildering, all harsh angles and impossible perspectives. And in the foreground stood a massive six-limbed figure with a single great glowing compound eye in the center of its broad forehead. Jaspin began to tremble inside.

"What is this, a photograph?" he asked.

"No, not a photograph. A painting only. But a very real painting, no? What is this place? Who is that standing there?"

"That's Maguali-ga," Jaspin murmured. "The nine suns. The Rock of the Covenant."

"Ah, you know these things. You recognize."

"It looks exactly the way I've seen them myself."

"Yes. Yes. How interesting. You look at this one, now." He passed Jaspin a second holo. It was a different view of the world of Maguali-ga now: the angle much steeper, and instead of Maguali-ga by himself there were five such beings. This repro too could have passed for a photograph; but now that Jaspin had been given the clue he was able to see that in fact it was only a painting, probably computer-generated and very realistic but nonetheless a work of the imagination. "And this," said the Senhor, laying a third view of Maguali-ga's planet down in front of Jaspin: somewhat different technique, considerably different subject matter—

this time a strange stone building was in view, high-vaulted and rugged, and Maguali-ga standing at its threshold—but there was no question that it depicted the same world as the other two.

"Now these," the Senhor said, and dealt three more pictures from his pack. Red sun, blue sun, fiery arch in the sky, golden figure in the foreground with curving ram's-horns. Each of the three was clearly the work of a different artist; but all three showed the same thing, identical in all details. Jaspin shivered. "Chungirá-He-Will-Come."

"Yes. Yes. And these?"

Three more. Green world, thick wisps of fog, shimmering crystalline figures moving about. Three of a world of blazing light, the entire sky one vast sun. Three of a fiery world whose sun was blue, and there was Rei Ceupassear, soring high overhead in a shining radiant bubble. Three of a world whose suns were yellow and orange—

"What are these things?" Jaspin asked finally.

The Senhor beamed like an ebony Buddha. He had never looked so joyous. "It is truly the truth, and I know that I know it. But others are not so sure, and there are some who will oppose us. So I have had the truth made into pictures for them. You know, there are devices, they turn the pictures in a man's mind into a picture on a screen, and then it can be made like this. I sent for three different people and I said, Make pictures of the worlds of the gods. Put them into this machine, so everyone can see the visions that you see. Well, Jaspeen, you can see. If you make the photograph, three people, you point the camera at the same street in Los Angeles, you still get the same picture. And here too we have the same picture, although it just comes out of people's minds. So everyone is seeing the same thing. Look, this is Maguali-ga, this is Narbail, this is where O Minotauro dwells—who can doubt it now? These things are true and real. When they come into our minds, they are coming from true places. Because we all see the same. There can be no doubt now. You agree? There can be no doubt!''

"I never doubted," said Jaspin, dazed. But he knew that he was lying. Some part of him had maintained its skepticism all along. Some part had insisted that what he was experiencing was only some sort of crazy hallucination. But if everyone was having the same hallucinations—exactly—down to the little details—these weird little plantlike things here that he had seen so often but which he had never mentioned to anyone else, here they were, in this holo and in that one and here too—

He was altogether stunned. He had not asked for these proofs; he had been willing to act on faith alone; but the holograms before him were overwhelming.

"Truly the truth," Senhor Papamacer said.

"Truly the truth," Jaspin murmured.

"You go now. Write down what you feel, how you think this minute. Now. You go, Jaspeen."

He nodded and rose and went stumbling through the dim musty bus, groping in the darkness of the chapel, then out the front way. A few men of the Inner Host were sprawled on the steps of the bus: Carvalho, Lagosta, Barbosa. They smirked up at him. White eyes flashed mockingly in dark faces. He moved sideways through them, carefully, not giving a damn about their smartass smirks: the presence of the gods was still on him. Go write down what you feel, how you think. Yes. But first he had to tell Jill.

Dusk was coming on. The air was cool. They were somewhere up near Monterey now, inland a little way, camped in what had been somebody's artichoke field before a hundred thousand pilgrims had driven their buses and vans and trailers into it. Jaspin heard the sound of chanting in the distance. Three enormous campfires were blazing, sending black columns of smoke into the darkening sky. He looked into his car for Jill. Not there.

From behind him he heard laughter. More Inner Host: Cotovela, Johnny Espingarda, leaning against their little orange-and-yellow bus. He glanced toward them.

"Something funny?"

"Funny? Funny?"

"Either of you see my wife?"

They laughed again, forcing it a little. They were deliberately trying to make him feel uncomfortable. He despised them, these chilly-faced inscrutable Brazilian bastards, these apostles of the Senhor. So smug in their assumption of superior holiness.

"Your wife," Johnny Espingarda said. He made it sound dirty.

"My wife, yes. Do you know where she is?"

Johnny Espingarda balled his hand into a fist, put it to his mouth, coughed into it. Cotovela seemed to be choking back laughter. Jaspin felt the awe and astonishment that the Senhor's holograms had aroused in him vanishing under the weight of his anger and irritation. He swung around, turned away from them, peered around for Jill in the gathering darkness. He walked to the far side of car, thinking she might have spread a blanket over there. No Jill there either. When he came around to the front again, though, he saw her, walking toward the car from the general direction of the Inner Host bus. She looked flushed, sweaty, rumpled; she seemed to be fumbling with the belt of her jeans. Behind her, Bacalhau had emerged from the bus and was saying something to Cotovela and Johnny Espingarda: Jaspin heard their rough laughter. Oh, Christ, he thought. Christ, no, not Bacalhau.

"Jill?" he said.

Her eyes were a little out of focus. "You been visiting the Senhor?"

"Yes. And you?"

She seemed to be making an effort to see straight; and

then suddenly she was, her eyes locking on his, her expression a chilly, defiant one. "I've been interviewing the Inner Host," she said. "A little field anthropology." She giggled.

"Jill," he said. "Oh, Christ, Jill."

2

STANDING between these two strange new people, the beautiful dark-haired woman who was not real and the scowling-looking man with the injured leg, Tom was sure he felt a vision coming on. Right here, in front of everyone on this lonely back-country road as the sun was going down.

But somehow it didn't arrive. There was the roaring in his brain, there was the first beginning of luminous flickering, but that was all. The vision stayed on hold. Something else was happening, maybe, some sort of omen unfolding within him.

He looked at Charley. He looked at the dark-haired woman and at the scowling-looking man who had hurt his leg. Charley was asking questions about the place that the scowling man had called a center. Where is it, who runs it, what do they do there? Tom listened with interest. He found himself thinking that he might like to go to that center, go there this evening, sit down and rest for a while in its gardens. He had been on the road too long, wandering this way and that, and he was tired.

"You mean this place, it's a kind of a funny farm?" Charley asked.

"Not exactly," the scowling man said. "They got a lot of troubled people there. I think not quite as troubled as your friend here, most of them. But troubled, you know? Deeply upset inside. And they take care of them there. They got ways of soothing them and caring for them."

Tom said, "Tom could use some soothing. Poor Tom."

No one appeared to notice that he had spoken. He glanced toward the sky, still afternoon-blue but growing dark around the edges. The sun was hidden now by the tops of the tremendous redwood trees. The forest began just a little way off the road and went on and on and on. Overhead he saw stars appearing and drifting around the sky, colored pinpoints of light, red and green and orange and turquoise.

Tiny floating sparks. But each one at the heart of an empire spanning thousands of worlds, and each of those empires bound in a confederation encompassing whole galaxies. And on those worlds a billion billion wondrous cities. Compared to the smallest of those cities, Babylon was a village, Egypt was a puddle. And the light of all those stars was focused now on this unimportant little world, this sad Earth.

Charley said, "Who are you two, anyway?"

"I'm Ed. That's Allie, here."

"Ed. Allie. Okay. Out for a stroll in the woods."

"Uh-huh. A little hike. I put my foot in a gopher hole and twisted my ankle."

"Yeah. You got to be careful." Charley was measuring them. "And what's the name of this place, this center?"

"The Nepenthe Center," the man named Ed said. "Some foundation runs it. They take people in from all over California. It's almost like a country hotel, hiking and recreation and everything, except they also give you treatment there for your troubles. He'd like it there. It's just around on the far side of that forest, between the woods and the coast. There's a big gate out front, and signs. You can't miss it. If you wouldn't mind driving Allie and me over to Ukiah first, and then there's a road that goes straight out from Ukiah to Mendocino, and you can pick up a road off that takes you to the Center.''

"How come you know so much about it?" Charley asked.

"My wife's been treated there," Ed said.

"Allie? What was wrong with her?"

"No, not Allie." Ed looked uncomfortable. "Allie's a friend. My wife—" he shrugged. "Well, it's a long story."

"Yeah. I bet."

Tom realized that Charley was going to kill these people when he was finished talking to them. He had to. They could identify him now. If the local police came around and said, "We're looking for some scratchers who killed a vigilante officer in San Francisco, did you see anybody unusual driving around up here," these two could say, "Well, we saw eight men in a van drive through this way, and this is what they looked like." Charley couldn't risk that. Charley said he didn't like to kill, and very likely he meant it. But he didn't mind killing, either, when he felt that he had to.

The woman said, "Tell me something. Do you people have space dreams?"

The man turned to her, his face getting red, and said, "Allie, for Christ's sake—"

Yes. He'd kill them sure as anything, Tom knew. The idea that he had to do it was starting to show in Charley's face: that the man was dangerous to him, the man might somehow tip off the police. The only reason Charley had stopped in the first place was that he thought the woman was by herself on the road. The scratchers had wanted to use her. But then when the man appeared, limping out of the underbrush—that changed everything. The man had to die because he was too dangerous to Charley. And that meant the dark-haired woman had to die too. Once there's killing, there's got to be more killing. That was what Charley had said a long time ago.

The woman was saying, sounding stubborn, "No, I want to know. It's important. These are the first people we've seen since—since. I just wonder. Whether they have space dreams too."

"Space dreams?" Tom said, as if hearing for the first time what she was saying.

She nodded. "Like visions. Other worlds. Different suns in the sky. Strange beings moving around. I've been having dreams like that, and I'm not the only one. A lot of people I know. Not Ed, though. But a lot of others."

"Harbingers," Tom said to her. "The Time of the Crossing is coming near." He saw Stidge turn to Tamale and tap his forehead and make a circle in the air with his fingers. Well, that was Stidge. Tom said, "I get the visions all the time. Do you ever see the green world? And the world of the nine suns?"

"And there's one with a red sun and a blue one too," she said, sounding excited. "It's all coming back to me now. I thought I had lost them, but no, I can find them in my mind now. Why is that? That stuff was gone. But I remember a big blue sun sizzling in the sky—shining cities that looked like floating bubbles—"

"Yeah," Charley said. "I know that one. I heard about it from Tom. That's the Loollymoolly planet, right, Tom?"

"Luiiliimeli," Tom said. He felt excited too, now. Maybe Charley wouldn't kill them after all, now that he had found out that the woman had the dreams too. Charley could get interested in people, and that made a difference sometimes. Tom said to the woman, "What other places have you seen? Was there one where the whole sky was filled with light just radiating down from all over?"

"Yes," she said. "There's one of those too. And—"

"It's getting late," Charley said. Charley's eyes looked dark and hooded suddenly, and his voice was flat. Tom knew that look and that voice. Chilly look, scary voice. "We been having a nice talk here, haven't we? But it's getting late."

He's going to kill them anyway, Tom thought. No matter what.

It was no good, this killing. All this killing had to stop. He had already explained that to Charley. The Time of the Crossing was too close at hand now. It wasn't fair to deprive anybody of their chance to go to the stars, now that the Time of the Crossing was almost here.

Charley turned and said, "Stidge—Mujer—"

"Wait," Tom said. He had to do something, he knew, right now, right this minute. "Here. Here. It's starting to come on. I feel the rush beginning."

He had never faked a vision before. He hoped he'd be able to bring it off.

Charley said, "Save it, Tom. We got things to do."

"But this one's special, what I'm seeing," he said, begging for time. That was all he could do now, beg for time and hope for something to happen. "The whole sky is moving! You see the stars? They're drifting around like goldfish up there." He threw his head back and waved his arms around and tried to look ecstatic, hoping he might somehow bring a real vision on. But nothing was coming. Desperately he said, forcing it, "Can you see the Kusereen princes? They move freely through the Imperium. They don't need spaceships or anything. It would take too long, getting from world to world by spaceships, but they understand how to make the Crossing, you know? All of them do. They can leave their bodies behind and enter into whatever kind of body the host world has."

"Tom—"

"This woman here, this Allie. She's really Zygerone,

Charlie. She's a Blade of the Imperium. And the man, he's a Kusereen Surveyor. They're visiting us, preparing us for the Crossing. I can feel their inner presences." Tom felt himself beginning to tremble. He was at the edge of believing his own story. The man and the woman were staring at him, astounded, bewildered. He wanted to wink at them and tell them to go along with everything, but he didn't dare. Words poured from his lips. "I've felt the consciousnesses of these two many times, Charley. She's a true Fifth Zygerone herself, even though consciously right now she doesn't really have access to her own identity. They lock it away, so they don't get into trouble. And him, I can't even begin to tell you what he is, he's so powerful in the Kusereen hierarchy. I tell you, we're in the presence of great beings here. And it could even be that the whole destiny of the human race is going to be settled right out here on this road tonight and—"

"Shit, just listen to him," Mujer said.

Charley said, "Take him back into the van. Nicholas, Buffalo. Don't hurt him any, just take him in there, keep him occupied. Go on. Go on, now."

"Wait," Tom said. "Please. Wait."

Suddenly there was a droning noise in the sky.

"Christ," Mujer said, "what's that? Helicopter?"

Tom blinked and stared. A dark gleaming shape hovered above them, descending gently.

"Son of a bitch," Charley muttered.

"Cops?" Buffalo asked.

Charley glared at him. "You going to stay around to ask them? We got to scatter. *Scatter.* Into the woods, every which way. Go on, run! Run, you idiots!"

The scratchers disappeared into the dusk as the helicopter floated down to land by the side of the road. Tom stood still, watching it in fascination. He heard Charley yelling to him from somewhere in the woods but he paid no attention. The helicopter was small and sleek. It bore the words *Nepenthe Center Mendocino County* along its glossy pearl-colored sides in bright blue lettering.

A hatch opened and two men jumped out, then a woman, then a third man. "All right, Ed," one of them said. "Alleluia. It's time to go home now."

"For the love of suffering Jesus," the man named Ed said. "You been flying all over the county after us?"

The woman said, "It's not all that hard tracing you. You've both got homing-vector chip implants, you know. I guess you forgot that, right?"

"Jesus," Ed muttered. "They pick you, how can you win?" He swung about and started toward the woods in a hopeless hobbling clumsy way. When he had gone eight or nine steps he tripped over his crutch and went sprawling and lay there cursing and pounding his fist against the ground. The woman and one of the men went to him, helped him up, began leading him toward the helicopter.

The woman named Allie did not move at all at first. Tom had expected her to try to escape into the forest too, but she stood as though she had been turned into a statue. And when she did move it was not away from the people who had come to get her but straight toward them, with amazing speed. She was on them in an instant. She knocked one of the men almost to the far side of the road with one swipe of her arm and seized the other one around the neck.

"Okay," she said. "You leave us the hell alone," she said, "or I'll pull his head off, you hear? Now take your hands off Ferguson. You hear me, Lansford? Let go of him."

"Sure, Alleluia," said the man who was holding the man with the injured foot. He stepped away from Ed, and so did the woman on the other side of him. "No problem," the man said. "You see? Nobody's holding Mr. Ferguson."

"All right," Allie said. "Now I want you to get into that helicopter of yours and take yourselves right back to—"

"Alleluia?" said the woman.

"Don't talk to me, Dante. Just do what I say."

"Absolutely," the woman named Dante said. She brought her hand up and something bright flashed in it, and the woman named Allie made a soft little sound and fell to the ground.

Tom said, "Did you kill her?"

"Anesthetic pellet. She'll be asleep about an hour, time enough to get her back and cooled off. Who are you?"

"Tom's my name. Poor Tom. Hungry Tom. You're from the center? Where people go to rest and be soothed?"

"That's right," the woman said.

"I want to go there. That's where I need to go. You'll take Tom with you, won't you? Poor Tom? Hungry Tom? Tom won't hurt anyone. Tom's been with the scratchers long enough." They were staring at him. He smiled. "That's their van, the scratchers. Charley and his boys. They all ran off into the forest, but they aren't far away. They thought you were the police. When you go they'll come back for me if you leave me. I've been with them long enough. They hurt people sometimes, and I don't like that. Tom's hungry. Tom's going to be cold, out here by himself. Please? Please?"

3

FOR a little while that morning, while she was trying to get ready for the meeting with Kresh and Paolucci, Elszabet had seriously considered asking to undergo mindpick herself. That was how scary it had been, coming up out of the Green World dream and discovering that vestiges of the strangeness were still clinging to her, a dream that would not go away.

Of course, pick really wasn't an available option, and she knew that. Nobody on the staff had ever been picked: it was strictly for patients only. You didn't just reach for pick the way you might for a martini or a traquilizer whenever you felt the need to mellow yourself out. Setting someone up for pick was a big deal involving weeks of testing, fitting the electroneural curves just right so no damage would be done. Pick was supposed to be a therapeutic process, not a destructive one. When chopping away at somebody's memory-banks, you had to be sure you chopped only at the pathological stuff, and that required elaborate prepick measuring and scanning.

All the same, the moment of awakening had been so terrifying for her that she had simply wanted to unhappen the dream as fast as she could, by any means available. Get it out of her mind, obliterate it, forget it forever.

What was frightening about the dream was how beautiful it had been.

Seductive, that cool green fog-wrapped world. Irresistible, those elegant shimmering many-eyed people. Delicious, the intricate baroque dance of their daily existence. Those magnificently civilized beings, moving gracefully through lives untouched by conflict, ugliness, decay, despair: a civilization millions of years beyond all the nasty grubby sweaty little flaws of human existence, all those disagreeable things like aging and disease and jealousy and covetousness and war. Having once plunged into that world, Elszabet did not want to leave. Awakening had been like the explusion from Eden.

Of course there were no such places, she knew, except in that land of dreams. It was pure fantasy, a phantom of the night. Nevertheless she wanted to go back there. It seemed unfair, a brutal imposition, to have to wake up: as cruel as a snowstorm on a summer afternoon.

The powerful pull of the Green World had drained her vitality all morning. Going through her rounds, calling on Father Christie and Philippa and April and Nick Double Rainbow and all the rest, she had been barely able to pay attention to their problems and needs and complaints; her mind kept drifting back to the other place and its dukes and countesses, its parties, its symphonies of form and color and psychological interplay. She had already forgotten the names of those among whom she had moved in her dream, and the details themselves were blurring: they had more than two sexes, she knew, and there was something about a new summer palace, and a poet and his poem. Knowing that she was starting to forget filled her with despair. She grasped at the fading memories. She yearned to go back to that blessed world.

No one had told her that the space dreams were this wondrous. Was it that she had dreamed more intensely than anyone else? Or that they forgot within an hour or two of awakening? Or that they kept the richness and complexity of what they had seen to themselves, a sweet hoarded interior treasure?

Elszabet had feared the dreams before she had ever had one. Now she feared them even more, now that she knew what risk to her sanity they presented. How could she let dreams be the answer? A dream so lovely as that one could beckon her straight into madness, she realized. The edge was always near, perilously near. Dreams were unreal. Dreams were the negation of reality. That land of dreams, the poet had said, so various, so beautiful so new: it really offered nether joy nor love nor light, nor help for pain.

By mid-morning, though, she was beginning to think that she had shaken the dream-world off. She had the distraction of the two visitors, Paolucci from San Francisco and Leo Kresh from San Diego, to draw her back to reality.

Dave Paolucci had arrived with a bunch of charts and graphs showing his latest information on the geographical range of the space dreams, and a packet of cubes containing spoken accounts of them that patients at his center in San Francisco had recorded. Elszabet felt comfortable and assured in Paolucci's presence. He was a comfortable sort of man, round-faced and sturdy, with dark olive skin and deep-set amiable eyes. She had trained with him in mindpick technique at the San Francisco headquarters before coming up here to Mendocino; in a way Paolucci had been her mentor. Later in the day she intended to tell him about her own dream experience of last night and ask him to counsel her.

Kresh, the San Diego man, was not at all a man to feel comfortable with. Tidy, fastidious, a little on the pedantic side, he seemed in full command of himself and of his emotions and probably did not have a great deal of sympathy for those who were not. It was a considerable concession for him to have traveled this far, seven or eight hundred kilometers, for this meeting. Perhaps he had simply wanted to get out of Southern California, teeming with its multitudes of second-generation Dust War refugees, to spend a few days in the cool clean air of the redwood country. When Elszabet met with him shortly before the general staff meeting was due to begin he showed relatively little interest in what had been going on at Nepenthe; he wanted to tell her instead about some religious phenomenon that was centered in the refugee-inhabited towns surrounding San Diego proper. "You know about tumbondé?" Kresh asked.

"I'm not sure that I do," she said.

"I'm not surprised. It's been a purely local San Diego thing. But it isn't going to be much longer."

"Tumbondé," Elszabeth said.

"It's a hybrid Brazilian-African spiritist cult, with some Caribbean and Mexican overtones. A former San Diego taxi driver who calls himself Senhor Papamacer runs it, and there are thousands of followers. They hold ritual ceremonies, apparently pretty wild stuff, in the hills east of San Diego. The essential thing of it is apocalyptic: our present civilization is near its end and we are about to be led to the next phase of our development by deities who will break through to our world from remote galaxies."

Elszabet managed a smile. She felt a tendril of the Green World brush across her consciousness, and shivered. "These are very strange times..."

"Indeed. There are two notable aspects of tumbondé that are relevant to us, Dr. Lewis. One is that there seems to be a remarkable correlation between the space gods that Senhor Papamacer and his followers invoke and worship and the unusual dreams and visions that have been reported lately by a great many people, both at mindpick centers and in the general population. I mean the imagery appears to be the same: evidently the tumbondé people have been receiving the space dreams too, and have used them as the basis for their—ah, theology. In particular their god Maguali-ga, who is said to be the opener of the gate who will make possible the breakthrough of the space deities on the Earth, seems identical with the massive extraterrestrial being who is invariably seen in the so-called Nine Suns dream. And their supreme redemptive figure, the high god known as Chungirá-He-Will-Come, appears to be the horned being experienced by those who have the dream termed Double Star One, with the red sun and the blue one."

Elszabet frowned. Those names were familiar somehow: Maguali-ga, Chungirá-He-Will-Come. But where had she heard them? She was so weary this morning—so preoccupied with the vision that had come to her in the night—

Kresh went on, "As I'll explain more fully at the meeting, it's possible that these tumbondé manifestations, which have been widely publicized in San Diego County and elsewhere in Southern California, may actually be encouraging a wider locus for the space dreams through mass suggestion: that is, people may *think* they are having the dreams when in fact all that is happening is an influence from media coverage. Of course, that couldn't be a factor here, where tumbondé has not yet been publicized. But that brings me to my second point, which is a rather urgent one. A significant aspect of tumbondé theology is the revelation that the point of entry for Chungirá-He-Will-Come is the North Pole, identified in tumbondé terminology as the Seventh Place. Senhor Papamacer has vowed to lead his people toward the Seventh Place in time for the advent of Chungirá-He-Will-Come. And, though evidently you haven't heard the news yet, the migration has now begun. Anywhere between fifty and a hundred thousand tumbondé followers are traveling slowly northward in a caravan of cars and buses, gathering new supporters as they go. I understand that they're somewhere in the vicinity of Monterey or Santa Cruz by now—Dr. Paolucci probably has more accurate word on that—"

Maguali-ga, Elszabet thought. Chungirá-He-Will-Come. She remembered now: Tomás Menendez, the cube he had been playing on his bonephone, the strange barbaric African-sounding chanting she had heard. Those names had been repeated again and again: Maguali-ga, Chungirá-He-Will-Come. Menendez had friends in the Latino community in San Diego who sent things to him here. So tumbondé evidently had at least one adherent already in Northern California, she thought. One right here at the Center, in fact.

"But it's quite possible," Kresh continued, "that the tumbondé marchers will pass right this way, along the coast at Mendocino, and there are so many of them that they

could very well spill over onto the property of your Center. I
think it might be a good idea to give some thought to setting
up special security precautions.''

Elszabet nodded. ''We certainly should, if a hundred
thousand people are heading our way,'' she said. ''I'll bring
it up at the staff meeting today. I'd like to talk about all
these things at the meeting. Which is just about due to
begin, by the way.''

As it turned out, Elszabet wasn't able to talk about much
of anything at the meeting. The thing that she most dreaded
plagued her all during it: the Green World, seeking once
more to rise up through her conscious mind and carry her
away. She fought it as long as she could. But when eventually it overcame her she had had to leave the room. After
that she wasn't sure what had happened for a time; they had
given her a sedative and had her lie down, and when she
returned to consciousness there was a new mess to deal
with. Dan Robinson brought her the news: Ed Ferguson and
the synthetic woman Alleluia had run away. Homing-vector
tracers were in use, though, and the fugitives had been
located east of the Center in the redwood forest. An hour or
so from now, when they emerged into some open place, Dan
would send out the helicopter to pick them up.

''Who's going to go?'' Elszabet wanted to know.

''Teddy Lansford, Dante Corelli, and one of the security
men. And I suppose I will also.''

''Count me in too.''

Robinson shook his head. ''The copter only holds six,
Elszabet. We need to leave room for Ferguson and Alleluia.''

''Let Dante stay behind, then. I ought to supervise the
pickup operation.

''Dante's a strong and resourceful woman. They could be
dangerous, especially Alleluia. I'd like Dante to go.''

''Then Lansford—''

''No, Elszabet.''

"You don't want me to go."

Robinson nodded. As though speaking to a child, he said, "Right. At last you see it. I don't want you to go. You practically became delirious at the staff meeting, you've been under sedation for the past two hours, you're wobbly as hell. It makes no sense for you to go chasing off in a helicopter after a couple of unruly runaways who happen to be the two least predictable and most amoral individuals we have here. Okay? Do you agree that you're going to skip the pickup mission?"

She couldn't argue with that. But the rest of the afternoon was a fidgety time for her. Runaways were serious business: she was responsible not only for the mental condition of the patients but for their physical well-being as well. It was very much against the rules for any of them to leave the Center grounds without permission, and permission was granted only with stringent precautions. There were legal aspects: Ferguson was here in lieu of a jail term, after all. And the synthetic woman, though she was not actually regarded as a criminal, was uncontrollably violent at times, extremely dangerous to others because of her superhuman strength. In her pre-Center days she'd done more than a little damage to people during wild moments of blackout. Elszabet didn't want either one of them wandering around loose. They would need extensive double-picking when they got back, and maybe some preventive reconditioning as well—and what if they somehow gave the pickup squad the slip, or harmed a staff member while they were being apprehended—?

So there was that to worry about. And the aftermath of her dream still to wrestle with. And she supposed she also had to give some thought to that horde of tumbondé people heading this way, although that was far from being an urgent problem right now if they were still somewhere south of San Francisco. Sufficient unto the moment were the headaches thereof.

It was a long couple of hours.

The helicopter returned toward sunset. Elszabet, feeling tired but much more calm than she had been during the day, went out to greet it. Alleluia was out cold: they had had to hit her with an anesthetic dart, Dante said. Ferguson, looking rumpled and sullen and abashed, came limping out: he had hurt his ankle pretty badly romping around in the forest, though otherwise he was okay. "Put him under pax and let him sleep it off," Elszabet said. "We'll double-pick him in the morning after we find out where he thought he was going. Ask Bill Waldstein to look at that ankle, too. Set up an immediate pick for Alleluia when she wakes up, and make sure she's secured against any kind of violent outbreak. We'll pick her again tomorrow, too." Elszabet paused. Someone unexpected was coming from the copter: a tall, thin, shabby-looking man with intense, burning eyes. She glanced toward Don Robinson. "Who's that?"

"His name's Tom," Robinson said. "If he's got any other name we don't know it. He was with a band of scratchers when we found Ferguson and Alleluia. The scratchers ran for it, but Tom stuck around and asked us to take him in. Pretty far gone, you ask me: paranoid schizophrenic's the quick two-dollar diagnosis. But very gentle, harmless, hungry."

"I suppose we can give him a bath and a few meals," Elszabet said. "The poor scruffy bastard. Look at those eyes, will you! They've seen the glory, all right!" She started to walk toward the newcomer, who was prowling around in a vague perplexed way. Then she paused and looked back at Robinson. "Hey, I thought you told me the copter only held six!"

He grinned at her. "So sue me. I lied."

"Tom's hungry," the scratcher said. "Tom's cold. Will you take care of me here?"

"We'll take care of you, yes," Elszabeth said. She went

over to him. How strange he is, she thought. The strangeness seemed to radiate from him like an aura. Schizophrenic, maybe: it was, as Dan Robinson said, a pretty good two-buck diagnosis. Certainly he was a little off center. Those eyes, those fiery biblical eyes—the eyes of a madman, sure, or the eyes of a prophet, or both. "You're Tom?" she asked. "Tom what?"

"Tom o' Bedlam," he said. "Poor Tom. Crazy Tom."

He smiled. Even his smile had a fierce strange intensity. She put out her hand to him. "Come on, then, Tom o' Bedlam. Let's go inside and get you cleaned up, okay?"

"Tom's dirty. Tom's cold."

"Not for long," she said. She took him by the wrist. As she touched him she felt a curious sensation, as though something were twisting and churning in the depths of her mind; and for an instant she thought the Green World hallucination was going to repossess her right then and there. But that faded as quickly as it had come. Again Tom smiled. His eyes met hers, and something—she had no idea what—passed between them in that moment, some silent transfer of force, or power. I think we may have something special here, Elszabet told herself. But what? What?

4

In the morning Tom woke a little before sunrise, as he usually did. But for a moment he was bewildered at not being able to see the dawn sky, black shading into blue overhead and the last stars still glowing faintly. Above him all he could make out now was darkness, and beneath him he felt the unaccustomed softness of a bed, and he wondered where he was and what had happened to him.

Then he remembered. This place called the Center. The woman named Elszabet, taking him to the little wooden cabin at the edge of the woods last night and saying, "This will be where you stay, Tom." Showing him how to work the sink and the shower and the other attachments. He remembered her telling him, "You get yourself cleaned up and I'll be back in half an hour or so to take you down to the mess hall, okay?" Giving him fresh clothing, even. Pair of jeans, soft flannel shirt, pretty good fit. And coming back for him and taking him over to the big building where they were serving food. Dinner served on dishes, not something cooked on a stake over a fire by the side of the road. He remembered all that now.

So he hadn't dreamed it. He was really here. This beautiful quiet place. He got up and walked out of the cabin porch and stared at the thick mists coiling like lazy snakes through the trees.

It had felt great sleeping in a bed again, an actual honest bed with pillows and clean sheets and a sleep-wire to hold in your hand if you didn't feel sleepy, and all the rest. Tom couldn't remember the last time he'd been in a bed, not really. When he was with the scratchers he had slept on one of the blow-up mattresses that they kept in the back of the van. Before that, coming down from Idaho, he had slept outdoors, mostly. Here and there, under trees or in little caves or right out in open fields, and sometimes, but not often, in some old burned-out house in one of the dead towns. And before that? He wasn't sure. But it didn't matter. He was here now.

It was a good place, this Center. He felt different here, more peaceful, more in command of himself, closer to the center of his being. That was interesting, the way he felt so different here.

In the dimness he could see the indistinct forms of buildings, some cabins like his own close by and then a big open lawn and some more small cabins and then bigger buildings farther away on the hill over there.

He looked up through the mists into the sky.

The stars seemed very close to the Earth here. He couldn't see them, not with sunrise just a short time away. But he could feel them, the shining presences of them, like a series of invisible glittering spheres lined up one after another up there. This must be a very holy place, he thought, to have the stars so close. All the worlds he had visited so often in his visions seemed practically within his grasp: just reach out, just touch!

Tom tingled with awe. Those wondrous galaxies, those millions upon millions of worlds bustling with life! "Hello," he called. "Hello, you Poro and you Zygerone. You Thikkumuuru people. And you fabulous Kusereen, hello, hello!" The heavens declare the glory of God: and the firmament showeth His handiwork. What a privilege it had been to behold all this, the multitude of worlds, the fullness of the universe. For how many billions of years had those great races been masters of the stars, building their civilizations and their empires, linking world to world, soaring across those black incredible spaces, becoming almost as gods themselves? And he had seen it all, image upon image pouring into his astounded brain. At first it had seemed like mere craziness, sure. But then he began to recognize the patterns; yet even so there was too much to comprehend or even to begin to comprehend. It was as if he had picked up an envelope and taken out a letter and the letter contained every word in every book that had ever been published; and all those words had come roaring into his mind at once. That could have driven anyone crazy. But he had lived with

these things so long that he had come to make a little sense
out of them. He knew which races ruled the star-kingdoms
now, and which had ruled in the eons gone by. He knew
which were obedient subjects waiting their own time of
greatness yet to come. It was all there, in the Book of Suns
and the Book of Moons, which he had been allowed to read.
He alone was the chosen one through whom the peoples of
the universe were permitting themselves to be made known
to Earth. Now the news was spreading, though; and soon
everyone would know it; and then the moment for which
Tom lived would come, when the peoples of the Earth went
forth into those shining worlds themselves, soaring across
the gulfs of space to become citizens of the vast galactic
realm.

The first light of dawn came into the sky and the mists
started to burn away. Tom felt the phalanx of the galaxies
recede and disappear. For a moment, standing there on the
porch, he felt a terrible pang of separation and loss. Then
the feeling eased and he grew calm again. He went back
inside, washed, put on his new jeans, his new shirt. Knelt
for a long time beside his bed in prayer, giving thanks for
the blessings received. And decided to go out, finally, and
see if he could get himself some breakfast.

He wasn't sure which building it was. Everything looked
different by daylight. While he was wandering around he
ran into the man with the bad leg, the one called Ed, who
had tried to escape. Ed appeared to be wandering around
too, walking without any real purpose. He didn't look very
good this morning. His face was puffy and his eyes were red
and bleary and his mouth was clamped in a tight scowl, and
he was moving in a wobbly blithery way, as though he
might be drunk. At this hour of the morning.

They stood facing each other on the path.

"Hey," Tom said, "you wake up on the wrong side of
the bed?"

Ed stared at him in silence for a long moment. He didn't seem drunk close up. Sick, maybe, but not drunk. "Who the hell are you?" he asked finally.

"I'm Tom. I was in the helicopter with you yesterday when they brought us in from oustide. Don't you remember that?"

"I don't know," Ed said. "I don't know any goddamn thing right now. I'm just coming up from pick. You know what that is don't you, fella?"

"Pick?"

"You new here?"

"I came in last night with you on the helicopter."

"You got a lot to learn, then." Ed shifted his weight, favoring his sore leg. He was leaning on a white plastic crutch. "Pick is when they put electrodes on our head," he said, "and flash a flickering light in your eyes and send some kind of juice down into your brain. Wipes out your short-term memory. You forget most of what happened to you yesterday. You even forget what you dreamed last night. That's what they do here."

Tom blinked. "Why would they do that? It ought to be against the law, doing that to somebody's brain."

"They do it to heal you. To cure you when they think your mind is mixed up. That's how they cure you, by mixing it up even more. You wait. They'll pick you too, fella. Tom, whatever your name is. Soon as they measure your brain-waves they'll go to work on you."

"Me? No," Tom said, a little nervously. This man was making him very uncomfortable. This man, this Ed, there was something wrong with him inside. Tom had seen that right away, when Ed had first come straggling out of the woods back there on that little highway. His soul was injured; his spirit was all closed in on itself, full of pain and hatred. Like Stidge, that was how he was, a mean and bitter man who thought that everybody was out to get him. Tom smiled and said, "Not me. They won't do that to me."

"You wait."

"Not me," Tom said again. He laughed. "Poor Tom, nobody wants to hurt Tom. Tom doesn't do any harm."

"You really are a nut, aren't you?"

"Poor Tom. Tom's a nut, yes. Poor Tom, silly Tom."

"Christ, where'd they find you?" Ed's scowl deepened. "You say you came in here with me last night, on the helicopter? From where? What was I doing outside the Center in the first place?"

"You tried to run away," Tom said. "You and the woman named Allie. They caught you."

"Ah," Ed said, nodding. "So that's what."

"Brought you back in the helicopter. Just last night. You don't remember?"

"Not a goddamn thing," Ed said. "That's what they do to you here. They take your memory away."

"No," Tom said. "I don't believe that. This place is a *good* place. They wouldn't hurt anybody's mind here."

"You wait, fella. You'll find out."

Tom shrugged. There was no sense arguing with him. He was sick in the head, everything all twisted up in him. You just had to look at him to know it. Tom felt sorry for people like that. Once we make the Crossing, he thought, everyone will be truly healed of pain. In the embrace of the star-folk all sufferers will be given ease at last.

"You know where I can find some breakfast?" Tom asked.

"Up there. Gray building on the hill, you go around to the right side."

"Much obliged. You going that way?"

Ed made a sour face. "They filled me full of dope last night. The idea of food makes me sick to my stomach."

"I'll see you, then," Tom said. He headed up the hill at a

good clip. The morning air was fresh and bracing, though he suspected the day was going to get hot later on. As he neared the complex of buildings midway up the hill the woman, Elszabet, stepped out of one of them and waved to him.

"Tom?"

"Morning, ma'am."

She walked toward him. A nice-looking woman, he thought. Not sensationally beautiful, the way that Allie woman was, but of course Allie was artificial, they could make them as beautiful as they wanted. And Elszabet was pretty. Tall and slender with very long legs and wonderful warm rich gray eyes. And a very good person, too, kind and gentle. That was obvious right away, how tender and loving she was, and full of life. He hadn't known many people like that, with the kindness and goodness right out front where you could feel it. Although there was something tight inside her, like a clenched fist. Tom wanted to reach into her and pry that fist open. She'd look even prettier then.

"Going up for breakfast?" she asked.

Tom nodded. "It's in there, right?"

"That's right. I'll walk over with you. Sleep well?"

"Best I've had in months. Years. Real sound sleep."

"I bet it was so sound you didn't even dream."

"Oh, I dreamed, all right," Tom told her. "I always dream."

She gave him that pleasant smile of hers. "I'll bet you have interesting dreams, don't you?"

Tom walked along beside her, not saying anything. She had said something about dreams last night too, he remembered. When she had taken him to his cabin after dinner, just some offhand remark, something about how she was going to go to sleep herself right away because she was tired, she had had a strange dream the night before and it had upset her. He thought then that she was hoping he would ask her about that dream of hers, but he hadn't felt like it. Now she was talking about dreams again. And both times she had seemed sort of tense when the subject came up, her nostrils quivering a little, color coming into her cheeks. Why were they so interested in dreams here? He recalled that man Ed saying, telling him about the pick thing. *You even forget what you dreamed last night.* Tom began to feel a little uneasy.

She said after a moment, "When you get a chance, Tom, would you like to come over to my office for a talk? It's in that building just down here—you ask anyone inside, they'll tell you where to find me. I'd like to know a bit more about what was happening yesterday with Ed and Alleluia out beyond the forest, okay? And a few other things I'd like to talk about with you."

"Sure," he said. "Sure, I'll stop by." Why not? These people were feeding him and sheltering him. She was entitled to ask him a few things.

They paused outside the big gray building. She stood close beside him, looking straight into his eyes. She was almost as tall as he was, and she was very close to him. He found himself hoping she would take him in her arms and hold him tight; but all she did was rest her hand on his forearm for an instant, giving him a little squeeze. And he saw her nostrils quiver again, and the two little red dots appear in her cheeks. As though she was a little afraid of him. As though she knew somehow that he could reach in and open that tight fist within her soul. And she was afraid of that, afraid of him.

Well, that makes two of us, he thought. Because I'm a little afraid of you, Miz Elszabet.

She let go of him and walked away, turning to wave. He waved back and entered the mess hall. There were just a few people in it, most of them sitting far apart from one another. Tom took a seat by himself, off to one side. A machine on the table lit up and asked him what he wanted. Coffee and rolls, he decided. It told him which buttons to push. He had learned how to do that last night at dinner. He had expected that a machine would come down the aisle bringing him his dinner, too, but that wasn't how it worked: a boy came by with a cart. This morning it was a girl. The rolls were so good that he ordered a second breakfast, more of the same and a grapefruit, too. It seemed you could have whatever you wanted here, and as much as you wanted, and not pay. Poor Charley, he thought—getting scared and running away like that. If he hadn't run away, he might be eating free grapefruit and coffee and rolls this morning too. Tom wondered what had become of them, Charley and Buffalo and Stidge and the rest. Probably in Ukiah by now, or maybe on their way to Oregon, wandering on and on and on in their aimless way. He hoped they stayed out of trouble, wherever they went. Just took it easy, Tom hoped, and not get themselves killed this close to the Time of the Crossing, because all their worries would be over when they went out to the stars. If they lived long enough to get to go.

When he was finished eating Tom sat by himself for a while, just savoring the pleasure of sitting still and not having to jump back in the van and ride off somewhere with the scratchers. He wondered how long they would let him stay here. A week, maybe? That would be nice, staying here a week. And then maybe he'd be able to catch a ride down to San Francisco. He had liked that city. So clean, so pretty. Too bad they'd only stayed there a couple of hours. But he would go back. It was getting to be October, now. Winter coming on in those parts of the country that had real winter. If he had to spend another winter on the Earth, he thought, at least let it be a California winter. He didn't know when the Crossing would begin—maybe next week, maybe by Christmas, maybe not until spring. You could freeze to death wandering around east of the mountains, but out here on the coast you were pretty safe from the weather.

"Hey, you, Tom!"

He looked up. The man named Ed was standing by the door of the mess hall. He had another man with him, a short pudgy curly-haired one wearing a Catholic priest's outfit. They seemed to be looking for company. Tom beckoned them over.

"I thought the idea of food made you sick right now," Tom said.

"Well, I got to feeling a little better after a time. The fresh air. Tom, this is Father Christie. Father, Tom."

"You the chaplain here?" Tom asked.

The priest smiled. He seemed like a sad little man. "Chaplain? Oh, no, no, I'm just a patient, same as you."

Tom shook his head. "I'm not a patient."

"You aren't? But you can't be staff, surely."

"Just a visitor," Tom said. "Just passing through. But very pleased to make your acquaintance, Father. I've done some preaching myself, up Idaho way, Washington State. Different sort of thing from yours, of course. But I was pretty good. The congregation, they didn't much mind how crazy I got. They thought the crazier the better, the crazier the holier."

"We aren't supposed to use the word crazy here," said Father Christie.

"Perfectly good word," Tom said. "What's wrong with saying crazy? What's wrong with *being* crazy?"

"You telling us you're crazy?" Ed asked.

"You know it. I see visions. Isn't that crazy? Other worlds swimming before my eyes. Always have, since I was a kid, visions pouring in like—like crazy."

Ed and Father Christie exchanged glances. Ed said, "Other worlds? Like space dreams?"

"Space dreams, yes. But not just when I'm asleep."

"Father Christie here has space dreams too. Everyone in this whole fucking place has them. Excuse me, Father. Everyone has them but me, that is. I don't get them. But I know all the dreams. The green world, the nine suns, the red star and the blue one—"

"Wait a second," said Father Christie mildly. "You say there are several kinds of space dreams?"

"Seven of them," Ed said. "You don't know that, because you get picked every morning, you don't remember anything about your dreams. But there are seven. I have ways of keeping little records. You had one this morning, Father, the green world again. But they picked it. The bastards. Excuse me again, Father."

Tom listened in wonder.

The priest shook his head and said, "I don't know. I just don't know. Say, what about breakfast?"

"Got a better idea," Ed said. He reached into his breast pocket and drew forth some little squeeze-flasks. "Too early in the day, maybe? A quick drink? I got Canadian here, bourbon, Scotch. Here, here's one special for you, Father: a flask of Irish. Tom? You a drinking man?"

Father Christie said morosely, "I can't use this, Ed. You know that."

"You can't?"

"I guess you forgot, on account of being picked. But I'm an alcoholic. I've got a conscience chip in my gullet. Any booze hits my throat, the chip's going to make me throw up. You don't remember that, huh? Here, maybe your friend Tom wants it."

"Conscience chip," Ed muttered. "Right, I forgot. All these scientific things they stitch into us. Conscience chips to keep you from drinking. Homing-vector implants in case we run away. The bastards, they stick a sliver of this and a sliver of that in us and they operate us like machines. You be a smart guy, Tom, you get yourself out of here fast, you hear?''

"They've been nice to me so far."

"You be a smart guy anyway. You want one of these?"

"Thanks," Tom said. "No."

"Well, I do. Down the hatch!" Ed pressed the squeeze-tab and put the flask to his mouth. "Ah, that's what I needed!" He looked a little more cheerful. "So you get visions of other worlds too, huh? God, I'd like to see one of those! Just one. Just to find out what all the fuss is about."

"You never have?"

"Not once," Ed said. His red-rimmed eyes seemed to blaze suddenly with rage and anguish. "Not even once. You know how much I envy all of you, with your green worlds and your blue ones and your nine suns and all the rest of it? Why don't I see too? Some goddamn tremendous thing is going on all around me, some weird colossal thing that nobody can understand but that's plainly of gigantic tremendous importance, and *I'm* shut clean out of it. And that stinks. You know? It *stinks*."

So that's it, Tom thought.

Now he understood where the pain lay inside this man, and what he might be able to do about it, maybe. He wanted to do something about it.

Tom said, "Give me one of those drinks."

"Which one you want?"

"That doesn't matter."

"Bourbon," Ed said. "Here, have the bourbon."

Tom took the squeeze-flask from him, studied it a moment, pressed the tab. The top popped open and he put it to his lips and let the dark liquor roll down his throat. It hit all at once, hard and hot and good. It was a long time since Tom had had a drink, and he sat there relishing it, feeling it go to work in the crevices of his soul. Good, he thought. I can handle this. This is going to work out just fine.

He turned to Ed. "You got to stop worrying about those space dreams, okay?"

"Stop worrying, the man says. I'm not worrying. I'm just a little pissed off. Am I a freak or something? Why don't I see what the others all see?"

"Easy up," Tom said. He took a deep breath and put his hand over Ed's hand and leaned close and said, "You *will* see. I promise you that. You'll have the dreams too, Ed, just like everybody else. I know you will. I'm going to show you how, all right? All right?"

5

"MONDAY, the eighth of October, 2103," Jaspin said. He was sitting in the back seat of his car, speaking into the golden gridwork of a hand-held mnemone capsule. "We are well up into Northern California now, camped in open country about fifty miles east of San Francisco Bay. The march is about to take on a new aspect, because Senhor Papamacer has decided to swing due west here and go through Oakland before we resume our northward journey. We have avoided passing through cities up till now, ever since setting out from San Diego. I think the Senhor would actually like to cross the bay and enter San Francisco, which he says is a profound focus of galactic forces. But even he sees that that's logistically unwise, maybe even impossible, because San Francisco is so small and is accessible only by bridge, except from the south. Trying to bring a mob this size into San Francisco would cause major disruptions both for the city and for us. There would be no place to camp, and the main routes out might become blocked, possibly causing a breakup of the entire march. So we will go no further than Oakland, which is readily accessible by land and has adequate camping space in the hills just east of the city. While we are there, of course, thousands of its citizens will certainly join the march, and perhaps an even larger number will come over from San Francisco to enroll. It's just as well that there are no more major population centers along the coast between here and Mendocino, because we're quickly reaching a point where our numbers are becoming unmanageably unwieldy. This is already the greatest mass migration since the end of the Dust War, certainly, and since Senhor Papamacer intends to get at least as far north as Portland before the onset of winter, and maybe even to Seattle, the possibility exists that serious disorders will—"

"Barry?"

Jaspin looked up, annoyed at the interruption. Jill stood by the window, thumping on the roof of the car to get his attention.

"What is it?" It was two or three days now since he had had a chance to bring his journal up to date, and there was plenty of important material he wanted to enter. Whatever she wanted, he thought, couldn't it have waited anther half an hour?

"Someone to see you."

"Tell him five minutes."

"Her," Jill said.

"What?"

"A woman. Red frizzy hair, looks sort of trampy in a high-class way. Says she's from San Francisco."

"I'm trying to dictate my notes," Jaspin said. "I don't know any redheads from San Francisco. What does she want with me?"

"Nothing. She wants an audience with the Senhor. Got as far as Bacalhau, Bacalhau says she should talk to you. I think you're now the high muckamuck in charge of excitable Anglo broads around here."

"Christ," Jaspin said. "Okay, five minutes, tell her. Just let me finish this. Where is she now?"

"At the Maguali-ga altar," Jill said.

"Five minutes," he said again.

But his concentration was broken. In his journal entry he had wanted to discuss the way the racial makeup of the tumbondé procession was changing as the march went along—the original San Diego County group of followers of Senhor Papamacer, heavily South American and African in ethnic origin, having been diluted now by hordes of Chicanos from the Salinas Valley farming communities out back of Monterey; and now up here in the north there had been an Anglo influx too, rural whites, causing some alterations in the general tone of the whole event. The newcomers had no real idea of the underlying Dionysiac flavor of tumbondé, the pagan frenzy and fervor; all they seemed to hear was the promise of wealth and immortal life when Chungirá-He-Will-Come finally came waltzing through that gateway at the North Pole, and they wanted to be in on that number, oh, yes, Lord. Already that was creating disorder in the march, and it was going to get worse, especially if Senhor Papamacer continued to reign in absentia, as he had been doing for days, from the seclusion of the lead bus. But getting his observations on all these matters down on the mnemone capsule would have to be postponed now. Jaspin realized he should have gone off by himself for an hour or two to do his dictation, but too late for that now. He turned off the capsule and got out of his car.

It was a hot muggy afternoon. Heat had plagued them all the way up the center of the state, and there was still no sign of the rainy season. They said that up here it sometimes began raining in October, but apparently not this October. The low rounded hills of this unspectacular countryside were tawny with the dry summer grass. Everything here was shriveled and parched and golden-brown while it waited for winter.

From hill to hill, all across the saddle of this valley, all you could see was tumbondé: pilgrims everywhere, a surging sea of them. In the center of the whole circus were the buses in which the Senhor, the Senhora, the Inner Host, and the holy images were traveling. Nearby was the big patch of consecrated ground with the altars and the bloodhut and the Well of Sacrifice and everything all set up, just as though this were the original communion hill back of San Diego. Wherever they went, they set up all that stuff. And then beyond the central holy zone there was a horde of patch-work tents, thousands upon thousands of pilgrims, innumerable smoky campfires, children yelling, cats and dogs running around, every imaginable sort of ramshackle vehicle parked in random chaotic clusters. Jaspin had never seen so many people together in one place. And the numbers grew from day to day. How big would the army of tumbondé be, he wondered, a month from now? Two months from now? He wondered also, sometimes, what was going to happen when they reached the Canadian border—the Republic of British Columbia's border, actually. And what was going to happen if they kept on going north and north and north for month after month, and winter closed in on them, and Chungirá-He-Will-Come did not make an appearance. There will be no more winter, Senhor Papamacer had promised, once Maguali-ga opens the gateway. But Senhor Papamacer had spent all his life in Rio, in Tijuana, in San Diego. What the hell did he know about winter, anyway?

Screw it, Jaspin thought. The gods would provide. And if not, not. Mine not to reason why. I lived by reason all those years and what good was it ever to me? Chungirá-He-Will-Come, he will come. Yes. Yes.

The woman was easy to find. She was standing by the Maguali-ga altar, just as Jill had said: staring at the nine globes of colored glass as if she expected the bulgy-eyed god to materialize before her eyes at any second. She was shorter than Jaspin was expecting—somehow he had thought she would be tall, he didn't know why—and not quite as flashy, either. But she was very attractive. Jill had said she was trampy in a high-class way. Jaspin knew tramps and he knew high class, and this one wasn't really either. She looked shrewd, she looked energetic, she looked like she'd been around some. An enterprising woman, he figured.

"You wanted to see me?" he asked. "I'm Barry Jaspin. The Senhor's liaison aide."

"Lacy Meyers," she said. "I've just come over from San Francisco. I need to see Senhor Papamacer."

"Need?"

"Want," she said. "Want very much."

"That's going to be very difficult," Jaspin told her. He realized that somehow he was standing closer to her than was really necessary, but he didn't move back. Quite an attractive woman, in fact. About thirty, maybe a little more, the red hair close to her head in a caplike coif of tight ringlets, her eyes a deep lustrous green. Delicate tapering nose, fine cheekbone, the mouth maybe a little coarse. "Is this for a media interview?" he asked.

"No, an audience. I want to be received into his presence." She was wound up tight: one poke and she'd explode. "He may be the most important human being who has ever lived, do you know? Certainly he is to me. I just want to kneel before him and tell him what he means to me."

"So do all these people you see here, Ms. Meyers. You understand that the Senhor's burdens are very great, and that although he would make himself available to all his peoole if that were possible, it isn't—''

The green eyes flashed. "Just for a minute! Half a minute!''

He wanted to help her. It was completely impossible, he knew. But even so, he found himself wondering whether he might be able to find a way. Because you find her attractive, is that it? If she were plain, or old, or a man, would you even consider it?''

He said, "Why is it so urgent?''

"Because he's opened my eyes. Because I've gone through my whole life not believing in any goddamned thing except how to make life softer for Lacy Meyers, and all of a sudden he's made me see that there's something really holy in this universe, that there are true gods who guide our destinies, that it isn't all just a dumb joke, that—that—I don't really need to tell you, do I, what a religious conversion is like? You must have been through it too, or you wouldn't be here.''

Jaspin nodded. "I think we actually have a lot in common.''

"I know we do. I saw it right away.''

"And you've been following the path of tumbondé even up here in the Bay Area? I didn't think it had—''

"I didn't know anything about tumbondé until a couple of weeks ago, when you people started getting up into this part of the state. But I've known about the gods all summer. I had a vision in July, a dream, a red sun and a blue one, and a block of white stone, and a creature with golden horns reaching out toward me—''

"Chungirá-He-Will-Come,'' Jaspin said.

"Yes. Only I didn't know it then. I didn't know what the hell it was. But the dream kept coming back and coming back, and coming back, and each time I saw it more clearly, the creature moved around and seemed to say things to me, and sometimes there were others like him in the dream, and then there were other dreams—I saw the nine suns of Maguali-ga, I saw the blue light of—what's the name, Rei Ceupassear?—I saw all sorts of things. I tell you, I thought I was going nuts. That the whole world was going nuts, because I know everybody else was having these visions too. But I didn't know what to make of it. Nobody did. Until I read about Senhor Papamacer. And I saw the pictures he had—the pictures of the gods—''

"The computer-generated ones, the holographic repros."

"Yes. And then it all fell into place for me. The truth of it, that the gods were coming to Earth, that they were going to bring the jubilee, that the millennium was coming. And I saw that Senhor Papamacer must truly be their prophet. And I knew that I was going to come over here and join the pilgrimage to the Seventh Place and be part of what was going to come. But I want to thank the Senhor personally. I want to go down on my knees to him. I've been looking for some sort of god all my life, you know? And absolutely sure I could never find one. And now—now—''

Jaspin saw Jill coming toward them. Worried, maybe, that he might be getting something on with this woman? Flattering that she even gave a damn, she who came in every night reeking of Bacalhau's sweet greasy hair-oils, with Bacalhau's sweat mingling with her own. Screwing her way right through the Inner Host and back again, and he could hardly remember the last time she'd been willing to make love with him, his wife Jill. Jealous, now? Jill? Not very likely.

What the hell, even if she was, Jill had no right to complain. He'd been damned miserable all month long on Jill's account. If he happened to find some woman attractive now, and she happened to feel the same way about him—

Lacy was saying, "The ironic thing, all this space stuff, is that a couple years ago I was actually involved in a fraud, a scam that involved promising to send people off to other stars. It was like we were selling them real estate that didn't exist, the old underwater development bit: give us your money, we'll put you on the express to Betelgeuse Five. A man named Ed Ferguson, a real shifty operator, he was running it, and I was working the marks for him. Well, they caught him, they were going to send him in for Rehab Two, but he had a good lawyer—''

Jill walked up next to Jaspin. "He being of any help to you?'' she said to Lacy.

"I was just telling Mr. Jaspin, the irony of it, that I used to work with a man who was running a crooked thing involving journeys to other stars. Before any of these visions from the stars began reaching Earth. He would have gone to jail, but he got himself sent to one of those mindpick places instead, up near Mendocino, where they're supposed to be turning him into a decent human being. Some chance.''

"My sister April's in the same place,'' Jill said. "Nepenthe, it's called. Near Mendocino.''

"Your sister?'' Jaspin said. "I didn't know you had a sister.''

Lacy laughed. "It's a really small world, isn't it? I bet your sister and Ed are having a terrific wild affair up there right this minute. Ed always had an eye for the women.''

"He won't have an eye for April,'' said Jill. "She's fat as a pig. Always has been. And very weird in the head, too. I'm sure your friend Ed can do a lot better than April.'' To Jaspin she said, "When you're finished here, Barry, go over to the Host bus, huh? They're setting up for the Seven Galaxies rite tonight and Lagosta wants you to help out plugging in the polyphase generator.''

"Okay,'' Jaspin said. "Five minutes.''

"Nice meeting you, Ms.—uh—'' Jill said, and drifted away.

"Not very friendly, is she?'' Lacy said.

"Downright rude and nasty," said Jaspin. "Getting religion has made her go sour somehow. She's my wife."

"Your wife?"

"So to speak. More or less. One day the Senhor decided we ought to be married. Spur of the moment, married us on the spot, month or so ago. It's for the rituals, the initiations, some of it: you have to be part of a couple. It isn't what you'd call a happy marriage."

"I wouldn't think so."

Jaspin shrugged. "It won't matter, once the gate is open, will it? But until then—until then—"

"It can be rough, yeah."

"Look," he said, "I've got to go help set up for tonight. But I want to tell you, I'll try to arrange an audience with the Senhor for you. Won't be easy, because he's been pretty scarce the last few weeks. But maybe I can get you in. That isn't just bull. If I can do it I will. Because I know what it feels like, being a standard shabby twenty-second-century human being just faking your way through life and suddenly being lifted up and shown that there's something worth living for besides your own crappy comfort. Like I say, we have a lot in common. I'll try to get you what you've asked me for."

"I appreciate that," she said.

She offered him her hand. He debated pulling her toward him, just on an impulse, and kissing her. He didn't do that. But there was no mistaking the warmth in her eyes and the gratitude. And the possibilities. Especially the possibilities.

Six

I know more than Appollo
*   For oft when he lies sleeping*
I behold the stars at mortal wars
*   And the wounded welkin weeping.*
The moon embraces her shepherd
*   And the queen of love her warrior,*
While the first doth horn the star of morn
*   And the next the heavenly farrier.*

While I do sing, "Any food, any feeding,
**   Feeding, drink, or clothing?**
**   come, dame, or maid,**
**   Be not afraid,**
Poor Tom will injure nothing."

                      Tom O'Bedlam's Song

ELSZABET felt a dream starting to come over her while she was still awake. In the beginning it had been terrifying when that happened, when the tendrils of unreality began to invade her conscious mind. But not any more. A lot of things that once had been terrifying to her terrifed her no longer. She wasn't sure whether she ought to be troubled by that.

She was lying in the hammock that hung from wall to wall along one corner of her cabin. Reading a little, dozing a little, not quite ready to get into bed. It was about an hour before midnight of a cool autumn evening, wind off the sea blowing through the treetops. And suddenly she was aware that the dream was there, hovering just outside the gates of her consciousness. She lay there, letting it happen, welcoming it.

Green World again. Good. Good.

By now she had had all the other dreams too, the complete set of seven, sometimes two or three of them the

235

same night. It was a week now since the wandering mystery-
man Tom had showed up at the Center, and all week the
dreams had been coming to her thick and fast. Was there a
connection? It seemed that there had to be, though it was
hard for her to understand how it was possible. In the week
Tom had been there Elszabet had seen Nine Suns, she had
see Double Star One and Two and Three, she had seen
Sphere of Light and Blue Giant.

But of all the dreams, Green World was the one she
cherished. In the other strange worlds of the dreams she was
only a disembodied observer, an invisible eye floating above
the bizarre alien landscape; but when she entered Green
World it was as a participant in the life of the planet,
plunged deep into its rich and sophisticated culture. She was
coming to know the place and its people; they were coming
to know her. And so every night, drifting off to sleep,
Elszabet found herself hoping she would be allowed to go
once more to that lovely place where she felt—God help
her—where she was starting to feel so thoroughly at home.

Here it comes now. Green World, hello, hello.

It was as though she had never been away—never gone
off on a sojourn to that scraggly troublesome place called
Earth where she spent the other part of her life. It was
Double Equinox day and the triads were gathering in the
viewing-chamber. Here were the Misilynes, arm in arm in
arm, and just behind them came the delicious elegant
Suminoors, and those, those there, weren't they the Thilineeru?
The Thilineeru had doubled with the Gaarinar, so the gossip
had it, and evidently the gossip was true, for there were the
Gaarinar and they glistened with an unmistakable overtone
of Thilineeru texture, a sheen like the ringing of bells.

And who was this? This heavy dusky figure with that
single huge glowing eye rising like a fiery yellow dome
from his broad head? He strolled serenely through the room
followed by a vast entourage, and from all sides people

came toward him to pay their respects. Elsazbet thought she had seen him before. Or someone of his kind, at any rate. But she wasn't sure where.

Ah. They were announcing him now: a shimmering tremolo of silvery sound dancing through the air, telling everyone at once that this was none other than the Sapiil envoy, His Excellency Horkanniman-zai, minister plenipotentiary of the empire of the Nine Suns and high representative of the Lord Maguali-ga to all outer-sphere natons. How imposing a set of titles; how imposing a personage! Elszabet waited her turn to greet him. Come, said Vuruun, who had been ambassador to the Nine Suns himself in the time of the Skorioptin Presidium of blessed memory, let me introduce you. And brought her forward until His Excellency Horkanniman-zai noticed her. The envoy of the Sapiil extended a thick black whiplike limb in greeting; and she touched it with one of her own crystalline fingers, as she had seen the others doing, and felt herself flooded with the light of nine dazzling suns.

It is a gift, said the envoy of the Sapiil gently.

And then he turned away, airily remarking to one of the Suminoors that this was the finest evening he had spent since that time last year, at the investiture of the Kusereen Grand-Delegate on Vannannimolinan, when the Poro skydancers had impulsively dedicated a whole season's performances to him and—

Elszabeth heard no more of that story. The Sapiil envoy had moved along. He stood with his broad back to her now, framed by throbbing green light in the faceted north window of the viewing-chamber. But no matter: there were other diversions. Visitors had come from all over the galaxy to see the Double Equinox. Some wore the bodies of their native worlds; others, not as compatible with local conditions, had donned crystalline. The room buzzed with the chatter of fifty empires. Three Blades of the Imperium and a

Magister, someone was saying. Can you imagine? All in the
same room. And someone else said, They were Ninth
Zygerone, I'm sure of it. Have you ever seen Ninth before?
And a soft whisper: She is of the Twelfth Polyarchy, under
the great star Ellullimiilu. Years since one of them has been
here. Well, of course it *is* the Double Equinox, but even
so—

From somewhere far away a knocking sound, insistent,
annoying. *Rat-tat-tat, rat-tat-tat*.

"Elszabet?"

She stirred. Looking about, turning to one of the Gaarinar
to ask something about the princess of the Polyarchy, the
being from Ellullimiilu.

Rat-tat-tat. Rat-tat-tat.

"It's me, Elszabet. Dan. I have to talk to you."

Dan? Dan? She sat up, blinking, muddled, still more than
half-entangled in the delicate sarabandes and minuets of the
Green World folk. Who was Dan? Why was he making that
sound? Didn't he know it was the night of the Double
Equinox and—

More knocking. "Are you all right? Look, if you don't
answer me I'm going to come in there and see if you're—"

"Dan?" she said, trying to shake free of her confusions.
"Dan, what's the matter? What time is it?"

"It's almost midnight. I didn't mean to intrude or anything, but—"

"Okay. Just a second." She thumbed her eyes. Almost
midnight. She was in the hammock, a book turned face
down across her lap. Must have dozed off, then. Dreaming.
The Green World—the Double Equinox, was it? An ambassador there from the Nine Suns, and someone else from
Blue Giant, and a Ninth Zygerone whatever that was—oh,
God. *God*.

The ragged end of the interrupted vision scraped and
screeched in her brain. She put her hands to the sides of her

head. The pain was almost unbearable. To have been wrenched away from all that so suddenly, so roughly—

"Elszabet?"

"I'm coming," she said. She swung her legs over the side of the hammock, paused for a moment with her feet just touching the floor, took three deep breaths, wondered whether she'd be able to keep her balance when she stood up. She was shaking. To get drawn in so deeply, to become so enmeshed, so dependent—like a drug, she thought. Like a narcotic. "Just a second, Dan. I'm—waking up slowly, I guess—"

"I'm sorry. Your light was on. I thought—"

"It's all right. Just a second." She steadied herself. The last strands of green radiance were fading from her mind. She went to the door.

He loomed in the doorway, a dark figure against the darkness, his eyes very white, very wide. When he stepped inside she saw that he was glistening with perspiration, that his face was actually flushed: a distinct undertone of light pink beneath the chocolate. She hadn't known that it was possible. She had never seen him this agitated before. Relaxed, mellow Dan. She closed the door behind him and looked about for something to offer him, a drink, a popper, anything to calm him. He shook his head. "Mind if I?" she said, as the box of poppers wandered into her hand. Another shake. She pulled one out. The tranquilizing vapor traveled from her nostrils to her cerebral cortex in half a microsecond. Ah. Ah. That's better.

"What happened, Dan?"

He was sitting on the edge of her bed, looking like a man who had just run ten kilometers and was having some trouble catching his breath. "I feel a little foolish now, getting so worked up," he said. "It just seemed to me that I had to run in here right away and tell you, that's all."

He was being exasperating, though he probably didn't

intend to be. She said, a little irritably, "Dan, what *happened?* Are you going to let me in on it or not?"

Sheepishly he said, "I finally had one just now. A space dream. My first."

"Now I see why you're so keyed up."

"After all these months trying to analyze other people's imagery data without really having the foggiest idea what the hell they were actually experiencing—"

"Oh, Dan. Dan, I'm so glad that it happened at last—"

"It was Double Star One. I closed my eyes, and bang! There I was, red sun, blue sun, alabaster block. And the big thing with horns standing on top of it. Two or three more just like it a little distance away, doing something like drilling a well. But the clarity of it, Elszabet! The absolute conviction that this was reality. Hell, I don't need to tell you. But I couldn't help being overwhelmed—all this time, wondering whether I was ever going to experience it, wondering what was wrong, why I was blocking—" He grinned. "So I had to tell someone. You. Came running over, and your light was on, and—you're annoyed, aren't you? That I woke you up for something so trivial?"

Gently she said, "It's only that I was right in the middle of a dream myself. You know how it is when someone pulls you out of a dream. Any dream?"

"And it was a space dream?"

"Green World. Richer and more complex than ever before."

"I'm sorry."

She shrugged. "I'm glad for you. I'm glad you came to tell me. And don't call it trivial. Whatever else these dreams are, they aren't trivial."

"Why do you think I finally had one tonight, Elszabet?"

"I guess it was finally your turn."

"A random process, you mean? No, no, I don't think so."

"What do you mean?"

He was silent a moment. "I'm always a fast man with a theory. But a lot of times my theories don't stand up so well, do they?"

"I'm not the Board of Examiners. What are you thinking, Dan?"

"Tom."

"Tom?"

"His being here. A proximity effect. Look, have you gone over the stats for the week? The frequency of space dreams has tripled since he's been here. You've experienced that yourself, haven't you?"

"Yes. That's right."

"And you said just now that the dream you were having, the one I busted into, was the richest, the most complex you've had. Right? So what do we have? The frequency of dreams has increased among dream-susceptible subjects. The intensity of dreams has heightened too, apparently. And now someone who has demonstrated one hundred percent dream-nonsusceptibility since the whole thing began finally gets one too. Something's going on. And what's the variable factor that's changed here this week? Tom. A very strange, probaby schizophrenic individual wanders in, someone who we all agree gives off a distinct aura, a definite vibration of psychic force—am I right, weren't you the first to remark on it, hasn't every conversation you've had with him left you feeling that he has some kind of peculiar power?"

"Absolutely," Elszabet said. "But what are you getting at? That *Tom's* the source of the space dreams?"

"It makes more sense than my last idea, that they're some kind of broadcast from an incoming extragalactic spaceship, doesn't it?"

"You want my honest opinion?"

"Go on."

"The same thing occurred to me, I have to admit. That

there's some link between Tom's presence at the Center and
the way the dreams have been coming more often. But all
the same, I think I'd rather believe the spaceship theory.''

"Leo Kresh punctured that one. There hasn't been time
for our Starprobe to reach its destination and generate a
response from the inhabitants of—''

"Why does Starprobe have to have anything to do with it,
Dan? Suppose it's unrelated. A spaceship, all right, coming
in from God knows where, beaming us movies of other
solar systems. Not in any way connected with the fact that
we sent out an interstellar probe a generation or so ago.''

"Now you're the one who's multiplying hypotheses,''
Robinson said. "Sure, that's what it could be, but we've got
no reason in the world to think that that's actually what's
going on. Whereas we do have Tom right here at a time
when the pattern of dreams is definitely changing.''

"Coincidence,'' Elszabet suggested. "Why should proximity to Tom have the slightest relevance?''

"Are you just playing devil's advocate, or do you have
some reason for not wanting to accept the Tom hypothesis?''

"I don't know. Part of me says yes, yes, it has to be Tom,
isn't that obvious? And the other part says that it makes no
sense. Even assuming it's at all possible for somebody to
transmit images into someone else's mind . . . and where's
the substantiation for that? . . . don't forget that the dreams
have been going on all across the West, Dan. He can't be
everywhere at once. San Diego, Denver, San Francisco—''

"Maybe there are several sources. Several Toms roaming
around out here.''

"Dan, for God's sake—''

"Or maybe not. I don't know. What I think is that this
man is in the grip of a psychosis so powerful that he's
somehow able to broadcast it to others. A kind of psychic
Typhoid Mary capable of scattering hallucinations across
thousands of kilometers. And the closer you get to him,

Elszabet, the more intense and the more frequent the hallucinations are, although I'll concede that proximity may be
just one determining factor, more significant in the case of
low-susceptibility types like me. But what about someone
like April Cranshaw, who seems to have unusually high
susceptibility? She's been snarled up in dream after dream
all week, awake or asleep.''

"How about Ed Ferguson?" Elszabet asked. "So far as I
know, he's the only one on the premises outside of you
who's never shown any susceptibility at all. I'll be more
willing to buy your idea if it turns out that Ferguson's
finally getting dreams too.''

"What do you want to do, wake him up right now and
ask him?''

"Tomorrow morning's early enough, Dan.''

"Sure. Sure, that makes sense. And we ought to interview April, too. Get her into the same room with Tom and
watch what happens. Whether there are any hypersensitivity
effects under direct proximity. That should be easy enough
to arrange." He leaned forward, peering intently at the bare
wooden floor. After a time he said, "You know, Elszabet, I
thought the dream I had was the most beautiful thing I've
ever seen in my life. That weird landscape—those colors—
the sky, lit up in four or five colors, like the greatest sunset
that's ever been—''

"Wait until you see the rest of them," Elszabet said.
"The Sphere of Light. The Nine Suns. The Green World.
Especially the Green World.''

"More beautiful even than Double Star One?''

"Frighteningly beautiful," she said in a very quiet
voice.

"Frighteningly?''

"Yes," she said. "The dream I was having when you
came knocking on the door—I was annoyed with you, yes,
for interrupting it. The way Coleridge must have been

annoyed, when he was dreaming "Kubla Khan" and the
person from Porlock came and bothered him. Do you know
that story? But in a way I'm glad you broke in on it. Those
dreams are like drugs. Half the time now I'm not sure
whether I'm living here and dreaming about *there,* or the
other way around. Do you understand me, Dan? It scares
me that I'm so drawn in. Any kind of fantasy that draws you
so deeply, that becomes so real for you—I hardly need to
say it, do I, Dan? There are times I think, coming up from
one of those dreams, that I'm gradually losing my own
sanity, what little sanity I may have." She shivered and
folded her arms across her chest. "Chilly in here. Summer's
just about over, I guess. Do you know what else, Dan? Now
the dreams are beginning to overlap for me. Tonight I saw
figures out of Nine Suns and Blue Giant mixing in a party
on Green World. As though it's all flowing together in one
big lunatic movie-show. That's new. That's really bewildering."

"It's all very bewildering, Elszabet."

She nodded. "I wish I had even the faintest idea what the
hell's going on. An epidemic of identical dreams involving
hundreds of thousands of people? How? How? Broadcasts
from an alien spaceship? An itinerant psychotic scattering
wild visions around at random? Maybe we're all going
psycho. The last gaudy convulsion of western industrial
society: we all go nuts and disappear into our own
dreams."

"Elszabet—"

"I don't know. I don't know anything."

"It's late. We should try to get some sleep. In the
morning we'll start doing some further checking up on all
this, okay?"

Robinson got up and walked toward the door. Elszabet
felt a sudden rush of fear—of what, she wasn't sure. In a
hoarse voice that was little more than a whisper she said,

suddenly, unexpectedly, "Don't go, Dan. Please. Will you stay here with me?"

2

THE woman, this Elszabet, hadn't slept well last night. Tom could see that right away. She was all jangled up, the fist inside her heart closed even tighter than usual. And dark rings under her eyes, and her cheeks all drawn and hollow. Too bad, he thought. He didn't like to see anyone unhappy, especially not Elszabet. She was so kind, good, wise: why should she have to be this troubled?

"You know," he said to her, "you remind me a little of my mother. I just now realized that."

"Did you like your mother, Tom?"

"You always ask stuff like that, don't you?"

"Well, if you say I remind you of her, I want to know how you felt about her. So I know how you feel about me. That's all."

Tom said, "Is that it? Oh. How I feel about you is very good. That you listen to me, that you pay attention, that you like me. I don't really remember very much about my mother. Her hair was fair, I think, like yours, maybe. What I mean is that you're the sort of person I would have liked my mother to be, if I knew what my mother was like. You know what I mean?"

She seemed to know what he meant. She smiled; and the

smile softened some of the tightness that was within her. She ought to smile more often, Tom thought.

"Where did you grow up?" she asked him.

"A whole lot of places. Nevada, I think. And Utah."

"Deseret, you mean?"

"Deseret, yeah, that's what they call it now. And Wyoming, though of course you can't live in a lot of Wyoming, on account of the dust that blew in from Nebraska, right? And some other places. Why?"

"Just wondering. I didn't think you were from California."

"No. No. I been to California before, though. Three years ago, I think. In San Diego. Stayed there five, six months. Nice and warm, San Diego. All kinds of strange people there, though. They don't even speak English, a lot of them. Foreigners. The Africans. The South Americans. I knew a few of them there."

"What brought you to San Diego?" she asked.

"Traveling. I got caught in the hot wind one day. You know what I mean, the hot wind? Radiation. This was when I was back living in Neveda. I can feel it, you know, when there's radiation blowing on the wind, hard dust, makes my head tingle inside, right over here, the left side. And I felt it coming, but where can you go? That mean east wind, picking the stuff up Kansas way, maybe, blowing it and blowing it and blowing it, clear out to Nevada. No place to hide, that happens. You don't get that stuff here, do you? This far west. But I got a dose, and I was sick for a while, my hair fell out, you know? So I thought I'd rest me in San Diego until I was better. Then I moved on. Got tired of the foreigners. I never stay the same place long. You never know, someone's going to hurt you."

"No one's going to hurt you here, Tom."

"Oh, *you* won't hurt me. But that don't mean no one will. Not even here. Poor Tom's always wandering. And the wandering won't stop, will it, till we get to the Last Days and make the Crossing. But the Last Days are almost here, you know.''

She leaned forward, body tensed. That always happened when he came around to that subject. This was the third or fourth time he had talked with her this week, here in this little office of hers with the big green screen on the wall, and each time, the moment he had mentioned the Crossing or the other worlds or anything like that, he had seen the change in her right away.

She said, ''Do you want to tell me some more about the Crossing this morning?''

''What do you want to know?''

''All about it. Whatever you want to tell me.''

''There's so much. I don't know where to begin.''

She said, ''We're all going to go to the stars, is that it? To jump across space somehow and take up new lives on other worlds?''

''That's it, yes.'' She had a little machine in front of her, something to record his words. He saw a red light glowing. Well, that was all right. He trusted her. He had never trusted many people, but he trusted her. She wouldn't do anything to hurt him. ''I mean, we're not going to go in our actual bodies. We're going to drop our bodies behind us here, and just our essences are going to go over to the new worlds.''

''And they'll give us bodies there? If we go to the Green World, say, will we get the crystalline bodies, with the gleaming skins and the rows of eyes?''

Tom stared at her. ''You know about the Green World?''

''I know about them all, Tom.''

''And you know that they're real?''

Softly she said, ''No, I don't know that. I just know that I've seen them in my mind, and so have a lot of other people. I've walked around on the Green World with the crystalline people, Tom. In my mind. And I've seen the people of the other worlds, too, the Nine Suns people with the one big eye, and the Sphere of Light people with all the dangling appendages—''

"Sphere of Light, yes, that's a good name for it. That's the Great Starcloud, that light. Those are the Eye People that live there. All these places are real, you know."

"How long have you known about them?"

"Ever since I can remember."

"And you're how old, did you say?"

He shrugged. "Thirty-five, I think. Maybe thirty-three. Somewhere around there."

"Born just before the Dust War?"

"No, just after it started," he said.

"Your mother was in the radiation zone when it broke out?"

"On the edge," Tom said. "Eastern Nevada, I'm pretty sure that's where we lived. Or maybe across the line in Deseret. Utah. I know she got a little radiation, just a touch, while she was carrying me. She was sick a lot afterward, died when I was a kid. It was a lousy time."

"I'm sorry."

"Yeah." She really was. He could feel it. How nice she is, he thought. I hope she has a good Crossing, this Elszabet, this good kind woman.

"And the visions? They go right back to your childhood?"

"Like I said, as far back as I can remember. At first, like, I thought everybody must see these things, and then I found out nobody else did and I thought I was crazy." He grinned. "I guess I *am* crazy, huh? You live with stuff like this in your mind all these years, it makes you kind of crazy for sure. But now everybody's seeing the stuff I see. Last couple of years, people around me have been talking, saying they have dreams, they see the Green World and the rest. A few. There was this black man in San Diego, a foreigner, South American, drove a taxicab: I stayed in his house a while, town called Chula Vista, he rented a room to me. He started seeing them, the visions. Dreaming them, I mean. Told all his friends. *He* seemed real crazy to me. I got out of there. And then other people, the scratchers I was traveling with, some of them saw them—and here you say you see them too—everybody's starting to see them, right? And me, I see them better, clearer, sharper. I get a lot more detail now. The power's been deepening in me almost day by day: I can feel it changing. That's how I know the Time of Crossing is coming near. They picked me, the space people, who knows why but they picked me as a kind of forerunner, the first one to know about them, you follow me? But now everybody will know. And then one by one we'll start to go to their worlds. It's all part of the Kusereen plan. The Design."

"Kusereen?"

"They rule the Sacred Imperium. They're the current great race, been in charge millions of years, everybody reveres them, even the Zygerone, who are extremely great themselves, especially the Fifth Zygerone. I think the Fifth Zygerone will be the next great race. It does change, every I don't know how many millions of years. It was the Theluvara before the Kusereen, three billion years ago. It says in the Book of Suns that the Theluvara may still exist, somewhere way out at the end of the universe, but nobody's heard anything from them for a long time, and—"

"Wait a second," Elszabet said. "I'm getting lost. The Kusereen, the Zygerone, the Theluvara—"

"It takes time to learn it all. I was jumbled up about it maybe ten years until it came clear. There are a zillion races, you know—practically every sun has planets, and the planets are inhabited, even ones that you wouldn't think couldn't possibly have life on them because their sun is too hot or too cold, but there is life all the same. Everywhere. Like on Luiiliimeli where the Thikkumuuru people live, it's a planet of this big hot blue star Ellullimiilu that's like a furnace, the ground itself melts there. But the Thikkuumuru don't care about that, because they don't have flesh, they're like spirits, you know?''

"Blue Giant," said Elszabet, almost to herself. "Yes."

"And the Kusereen, we were talking about their plan: they want new races all the time, they want life moving around from world to world so nothing gets old, nothing gets stale, there's always change and rebirth. That's why they keep making contact with the young races. Like us, we're only a million years old, that's no time at all to them. But now they want us to come to them and live among them and exchange ideas with them, and they know it has to be soon, because we've been in big trouble here, always on the edge of blowing ourselves up or dusting ourselves to death or something, and this is the last chance, right now. So we're going to make the Crossing. And—"

"Are there wars among these races?" Elszabet asked. "Do they fight with each other for supremacy?"

"Oh, no," Tom said. "They don't have wars. They're way beyond that. Any race that thought it wanted to make war, it destroyed itself long ago, millions, billions of years ago. That always happens to the warlike races. The ones that survive understand how stupid war is. Anyway, it's impossible to have wars in the stars because the only way you can get from star to star is by making the Crossing, and you can't Cross unless the host world is willing to receive you and opens the way for you, so how could there ever be an invasion? There was a time once during the Veltish Overlordry in the Seventh Potentastium when—"

"Wait," she said. "You're going too fast again. You know what I'd like to do? I'd like to make a list. All the different worlds, their names, the physical form of the people who live on each planet. We'll put it into the computer, put it right up on the wall here where the big screen is. Just so I can get everything sorted out. And then after that I want you to tell me about the histories of these different worlds, whatever you know, the dynasties of ruling races and all that, just talk it all out and we'll organize it later. Will you do that with me?''

"Yeah. Yeah, you bet I will. It's important that everybody knows these things, so that when we make the Crossing we aren't all bewildered. That we know about the Design, that we know which the Pivot Worlds are, and all.'' Tom felt the fever of joy rising in him so strong that he thought it might even call up a vision right here. This woman, this wonderful woman—he had never known anyone like her. "Where I think it begins,'' Tom said, "is with the Theluvara, when they ruled the Imperium—''

She held up her hand. "No, not right now, Tom. I'm awfully sorry. There isn't time this morning. I've got to get out and see the people I look after here, the sick people. Suppose I give you a day to think about things, okay? And then we'll meet again here tomorrow, and the same time every morning until you've told me all you want to tell me. Is that all right?''

"Sure. Whatever you like, Elszabet.''

There was a knock at the door. On the little screen just next to the door Tom saw the image of the person standing outside, a big soft round-bodied sweet-faced woman in a pale pink sweater. Tom had seen her around before. "Come in, April,'' Elszabet called, and pushed something that automatically opened the door. "Tom this is April Cranshaw. She's one of the people I look after here. I thought you and she would like to get to know each other a little better, maybe. Take a walk with her now, just stroll around the grounds—I think you two will like each other very much.''

Tom turned to the fat woman. She looked very young, almost like some sort of huge little girl, although he could tell that actually she must be at least as old as he was and it was simply the flesh of her, like baby fat, that smoothed out all the lines in her face. And she was wide open, as wide open as anyone he had ever known. As tightly as that man Ed Ferguson was shut, that was how wide this April was open. Tom had the feeling that all he needed to do was touch his fingertip to her plump wrist and every vision he had ever seen would go pouring into her, she was that wide open. She seemed to know it, too: she was staring at him in a timid, fearful way. Look, he wanted to say, I'm not going to hurt you. I'm not Stidge, I'm not Mujer. I won't do anything bad to you.

"Is that all right with you, April?" Elszabet asked. "Will you take Tom for a walk?"

In a soft fluttery voice April said, "If you want me to."

Elszabet frowned. "Is something wrong, April?"

The fat girl was bright red. "Should I say? In front of—"

"It's all right. Just tell me."

"I guess I'm a little upset this morning," she said, soft-voiced, breathy-sounding, little girl within big huge body. "I know you want me to go for a walk with him, but I just feel kind of upset."

"About what?"

"I don't know." A wary look in Tom's direction. "The space dreams. The visions. They're coming so close together, Dr. Lewis. Sometimes I almost don't know where I am, they're so strong. Whether I'm here or on one of those worlds, I mean. And since I walked into your office just now—I mean—that is—"

"Go on, April." Elszabet was leaning forward again, giving the fat girl her fullest attention, no longer looking at Tom at all.

"I mean it's—getting—very—hard—for—me—to—think—straight—"

"April? April?"

"She's going to fall down," Tom said. He rushed toward her as she tottered and managed to get his arms around her just in time, under her breasts, and hold her up. She was heavy. She was incredibly heavy. Must weight two, three times as much as me, he thought, struggling with her. Elszabet went around to the other side and helped him. Together they eased her down to the floor. She lay there on her back, gasping. Elszabet turned to him with a nervous smile and said, "Will you go out and down the hall, Tom, and ask Dr. Robinson to come in here? You know who he is, the tall dark-skinned man? Go send him here, Tom. Will you, please?"

"Did I do that to her?" Tom asked.

"It's hard to know that, isn't it? But she'll be all right in a minute or two."

"I guess I'll have to take that walk with her some other time," he said. "Okay. Dr. Robinson. I'll go send you Dr. Robinson. Thanks for talking to me, Miss Elszabet. It means a lot to me, having someone to talk to."

He went out, down the hall.

"Dr. Robinson? Dr. Robinson?"

That poor fat girl, Tom thought. Passing out like that. It'll be a blessing, dropping the body, that one. The poor fat girl. I wish her an early Crossing, he thought. But that's what I wish us all, every one of us, an early Crossing. I hope we can go next week, even. Tomorrow, even. Tomorrow.

3

WHEN Ferguson came back to the dorm after morning therapy he found two letters lying in the middle of his bed.

He scooped them up, dropped them on the floor next to the
bed, and sprawled out, bone-weary. He could play the
letters later. Wasn't ever anything in the mail worth knowing, anyway. Dr. Lewis went through everybody's letters
first, cut out anything that might be considered disturbing.

Tired. Suffering Jesus. First an hour-long interview with
Dr. Patel, the precise little British-accented Indian, who
always came at you with questions from six different unexpected angles. He was still working on space dreams, how
Ferguson felt about them, the fact that other people were
having them and he was not. Or was he? "You are not now
by any chance beginning to experience the perceptions of
that sort, are you, Mr. Ferguson?" Screw you, Dr. Patel. I
wouldn't tell you even if I was. And then an hour jumping
up and down like a lunatic in the rec center, physical
therapy session led by that ferocious dykey broad Dante
Corelli—holy Jesus, they make you dance until you drop
and don't even apologize—

If only I had managed to get the hell out of this place
when I tried it, Ferguson thought. But no, no, they had their
goddamn little chip in me, they just sent out their copter and
reeled me in like a fish—that was how it was, wasn't it, I
actually did escape, me and Allie, we were gone three
goddamn hours, was it? Five, maybe. And then they reeled
me in.

He looked around the room. Same old dismal roommates.
Nick Double Rainbow zonked out on his bed, brooding
about Sitting Bull, Red Cloud, Kit Carson, Buffalo Bill.
Poor bastard, he must wipe out General Custer ten times a
day in his head. Lot of good it does him. And over there,
the other sad case, the Chicano, Menendez. Chanting and
muttering to himself all the time, praying to the Aztec gods.
Nice peaceful guy, probably dreaming of putting us all on
the altar and cutting out our hearts with a stone knife. Jesus.
Jesus, what a looney bin!

Ferguson picked up one of his letters and stuck the little cube into the playback slot. On the three-by-five screen the image of a good-looking blonde woman appeared. She'd have been terrific if she didn't look so solemn.

"Ed," she said. "This is Mariela. Your wife, in case they've picked that out of you."

Well, they had. How were you supposed to deal with all this? Ferguson halted the letter and touched his ring. "Request wife," he said.

Back at him came the data he had stored:"Wife: Mariela Johnston. Birthday August seventh. She'll be thirty-three this summer. You married her in Honolulu on July fourth, 2098—"

He let it play on to the finish, wondering how the people in charge here expected him to make sense out of anything, since they didn't know he had this little ring-recorder to fill him in on his own history. He activated the letter-cube again and Mariela returned to the screen. "I just want you to know, Ed, that I'm going back to Hawaii. I'm booked on a boat next Tuesday, which is a day after you'll get this. It isn't that I don't love you any more, because that isn't so, but I felt after that visit I had with you at the mindpick center in July that there simply wasn't anything happening between us any more, that maybe you didn't even remember who I was, that you certainly didn't care for me any more, and so I want to go away from California before they release you. For both our sakes. I'll be filing the papers in Honolulu, and—"

All right, Mariela. Who cares anyway?

He killed the cube and put the other one in. This letter was from a gorgeous hot-looking redhead who called herself Lacy. "Request Lacy," he told his ring, and found out that she was a San Francisco woman, evidently a girlfriend of his, partner in the Betelgeuse Five deal. Okay. He got her back on the screen, thinking maybe she was going to tell him she had arranged to come up here for a visit, and wondering if that would cause him any problems with Alleluia.

But that wasn't what she was planning at all.

"Ed, I have to tell you something marvelous, which is that I've found happiness and meaning in my life for the very first time," she said. "Do you remember that time in the summer when I said I had had a weird dream, the strange planet, the creature from outer space with the horns? That was the beginning of it for me. It was a religious revelation, though I didn't understand that then. But since then I have discovered the tumbondé movement, which maybe you don't know much about—it started in San Diego, a great man named Senhor Papamacer, who is leading us toward a union with the gods, and I have gone into it heart and soul. I have joined the march north, hundreds of thousands of us following the leadership of the Senhor, and I feel completely transformed and even redeemed. It's as though I've been purified of all the shady bad things I used to do—forgiven, handed a clean slate. And all because of the vision I had, that weird figure under those two strange suns—"

Jesus, Ferguson thought bleakly. Listen to her. Like a convent girl, she sounds. And these crazy dreams, changing everybody's lives. The whole world's gone nuts. Everybody but me.

"—And we are marching toward the Seventh Place where the final redemption will be offered. What I mean to say is that we will probably be passing close to Mendocino in a little while, and I think if you could somehow get yourself out of the Nepenthe and join us, if you could give yourself over to tumbondé and accept the guidance of Senhor Papamacer, you too would find yourself transformed, you would feel all the bitterness and unhappiness that has marked your life fall away from you in a moment, as it has from me, and—''

Sure. Just waltz out of here and sign on with the Senhor, whoever he might be. Was that all that it took? Dr. Lewis has already played this letter, Lacy baby. If there was a chance in a million that I could get away from this place to join you, do you think I'd be hearing you now? Do you?

''—Am confident that the blessing of Maguali-ga will be conferred upon you also, that the shining light of Chungirá-He-Will-Come will enter your soul—if only you would join us, dear Ed, come forth to us as we undertake our pilgrimage toward the Seventh Place—''

He scowled and shut off the cube. What crazy shit. Going off to have a union with the gods? The other one, going back to her family in Hawaii, at least that made a little sense. But this—this crazy stuff—

So he was rid of them both, that was how it looked. All right. All right. There was still Alleluia, who was as good as both of them put together. Somehow there was always another woman better than the last one when he needed her. Ferguson shook his head, trying to clear it. He wondered what Alleluia was doing now. He'd see if he could find her. Maybe a little walk in the woods—their customary midday frolic—

''Ed?'' called a voice from outside. ''Ed, you there?''

Ferguson frowned. ''Who is it?''

''Me, Tom. You got some free time?''

One more lunatic. Well, why not? ''Sure,'' he said. ''Hold on, I'll let you in.''

He opened the door. Tangle of wild hair, strange wild staring eyes. There was something wrong with this guy, no question about it. Definitely not playing with a full deck. Ferguson stood there uncertainly, wondering what, if anything, was on Tom's mind.

''Today's the big day for you,'' Tom said.

"Yeah? It is?"

"You remember last week, the first time we talked? When I said I'd show you how to have the space dreams?"

"You said that?"

"In the mess hall, yes. We were sitting with the little priest, and you gave me some bourbon and then—"

"I don't remember shit about last week," Ferguson said wearily. "Don't you know that? I remember that we met somewhere, I know your name's Tom, all the rest is gone. Picked. That's what they do in this place, they ream out your mind. You know that, don't you?"

Tom made a funny little gesture, as though he were dismissing what Ferguson had just said as so much noise. "Well, if you don't remember, I do. I can feel your misery, friend. And I mean to help you up from all that. Come on, let's go for a little walk. Into the woods a ways, where it's quiet, where it's peaceful. You still haven't had a space dream, right?"

"No," Ferguson said. "As far as I can remember, no, I haven't. Except—" He paused.

"Except what?"

Ferguson frowned. "I'm not sure. But there was something. Hold on, let me check." He went into the john so that Tom would not see what he was doing, and touched his ring and requested his file of unusual events, week of October eighth. His own voice, small and quiet, came up out of the recorder, running through all sorts of stuff, anything that had happened to him in the past few days that he had thought might be worth saving from pick. Most of it was just junk. But then came an entry for two nights earlier: "Something a little like a space dream last night, maybe. Just the outside flicker of it, anyway—a feeling that the world was wrapped up in green fog. I think that's something like one of the dreams they have, the Green World dream. That was all I got, the fog. I don't think that's the real thing. But it was a beginning, maybe.''

Tom was looking at him strangely when he came out.

"You talking to yourself in there?"

"Yeah," Ferguson said. "A little conference with myself. Listen, one of the space dreams, it has to do with green fog, doesn't it?''

"That's the Green World. A very beautiful place.''

"I wouldn't know. All I saw was fog. In my sleep, night before last. Green fog.''

"That's all? Just fog?''

"Just fog.''

"Okay," Tom said. "The dreams are trying to break through, then. You've made a start. Maybe because I'm right here the influence is stronger. But you see? You can do it just like anybody else, Ed. You come along with me now. Out into the woods.''

"What for?''

"I told you. I'm going to give you a space dream. But we ought to go where nobody can bother us, because you got to concentrate. Okay, Ed? Come on. Come on, now.''

"It isn't going to work. You tell me: How can I have a dream when I'm wide awake?''

"Just come with me," Tom said.

Ferguson shrugged. Nothing to lose, was there? Might as well try it. He nodded to Tom and they went out into the warm autumn morning, around the side of the gymnasium and onto the path into the woods. They passed a couple of people as they walked: Dante Corelli, April Cranshaw, Mug Watson the gardener. Dante smiled and waved to them, the gardener paid no attention, fat April gave them a quick frightened look and immediately turned the other way, as if she had seen a couple of werewolves out for a stroll. Poor nutty fat broad, Ferguson thought. Thing that would make her feel better would be getting laid once or twice. But who would want to, with her? Not me, you betcha. Holy Jesus, not me.

"What about here?" he said to Tom.

"Fine. This is just fine. Sit down here on this rock. Next to me, that's right. Now the thing you have to know," Tom said, "is that the universe is full of benevolent beings. Okay? There are more suns than anybody can count, and all of those suns have planets, and those planets have people on them, not people like us, but *people* all the same. They're all alive and out there right this minute, going about their lives. Okay? And they know that we're here. They're beckoning to us. They love us, every one of us, and they want to gather us to their bosom. You with me, Ed? You got to believe this. Through the vehicle of dreams they have contacted me, and I am the emissary, I am the forerunner who will lead everyone into the stars." He was leaning close to Ferguson now, his dark strange eyes drilling in hard. "Does this sound like a lot of crazy stuff to you, Ed? You must try to believe. Just for the time being, put aside all your anger, put aside all your hatred, all the deadly stuff that sits inside you like a lump of ice. Tell yourself this guy Tom is crazy, sure, but you'll pretend, just for a minute, that he knows what he's talking about. Okay? Okay? You'll pretend. Nobody's going to know that Ed Ferguson allowed himself to believe something weird for sixty seconds. Tom won't tell anybody. Believe me, Tom won't tell. Tom loves you. Tom wants to help you, Ed, to guide you. Give me your hands, now. Put your hands in mine."

"What the fuck," Ferguson said. "Holding hands, now?"

"Believe in me. Believe in *them*. You want to go on feeling the way you've felt all your life? Just for once, let everything go. Let it all open up. Let grace come flooding in. Give me your hands. What do you think, that I'm some sort of queer? Uh-uh. Just trying to help you. The hands, Ed."

Tentatively, uneasily, Ferguson put out his hands.

"Now relax. Let yourself go. You know how to smile? I don't think I ever see you smile. Do it now. Fake it, if that's what you have to do. Just a silly grin, corners of the mouth turn up, don't worry how silly it is. There. There. That's it. I want you to keep on smiling. I want you to tell yourself that within you is an immortal spirit created by God, who has loved you every instant of your life. Smile, Ed! Smile! Think of love. Think of the worlds out there waiting for you. Think of the new life that will be yours when you drop the body and make the Crossing. You can be anyone you want up there, you know. You don't have to be you. You can be tender and loving and kind and *nobody will laugh at you for being that way.* It's a new life. Keep smiling, Ed. Smiling. Smiling. That's it. You don't look silly at all, you know? You look wonderful. You look transformed. Now give me your hands. Give—me—your—hands—"

Ferguson felt helpless. He wanted to resist, he wanted to put up a wall against whatever it was that was trying to batter its way into his mind, and for a moment he had the wall actually built; but then it collapsed and he was unable to resist in any way. His hands drifted upward like a couple of balloons, and Tom reached for them, grasped them firmly in his, and in the moment of contact something like an electrical force went jolting through Ferguson's brain. He wanted to pull away but he couldn't. He had no strength at all. He sat there feeling the power of the galaxies come flooding through him and there was no way he could resist it.

And he saw.

He saw the Green World, with long slender shining people moving delicately around in a glittering glass pavilion. He saw the blue sun, pouring out pulsing streams of fire. He saw the planet of the nine suns.

He saw—he saw—he saw—

A torrent of images. Dizzying him, dazzling him. His mind whirled with the multitude of them. The whole thing, all the dreams at once, world upon world upon world. Landscapes, cities, strange beings, the empires of the stars. He trembled and shook. Nothing would hold still. A strange joy overwhelmed him, a hurricane of bliss. He cried out and toppled, slipping forward, falling practically at Tom's feet, and lay there sprawled on his belly with his forehead pressed against the damp soil, while the first tears that he could remember shedding came welling up and spilling out in hot streams down his cheeks.

4

THE moon was a bright gleaming sickle out there over the Pacific and Venus was gleaming right alongside, a cold clean point of white light. It was a clear, mild night, the air free of fog but nevertheless a little soft around the edges, maybe a hint of the oncoming rainy season that was still hanging back, lurking somewhere north of Vancouver. Jaspin said, "What was the name of that little town we passed yesterday?"

"Santa Rosa," Lacy said. "It used to be a pretty good-sized city."

"Used to be," Jaspin murmured. "This is the Land of Used-to-Be."

They were sitting on the side of a low snubby hill, rounded and curved almost like a breast, that rose out of a broad sloping pasture, a sea of grass. This unspoiled Northern California landscape up here above San Franciso was very different from what he was accustomed to growing up in Los Angeles, where the scars inflicted in the prewar days of vast population and intensive development were everywhere, ineradicable.

Though the moon was only a crescent it cast stark shadows: the gnarled solitary oak trees, upjutting rocks, the rough surface of withered brown grass—everything stood out sharply. The ocean was a couple of kilometers in front of them. Behind them lay the enormous chaos of the tumbondé caravan, practically an ocean itself, an innumerable multitude of vehicles stretching a bewildering distance back toward the inland freeway and beyond. In San Franciso and Oakland the Senhor had gained so many new adherents that the size of the procession was just about doubled now. The Pied Piper of Space, Jaspin thought, scooping up eager followers with both hands as he marched merrily along toward the Seventh Place.

Jaspin let his hand rest lightly on Lacy's shoulders. This was the first time he had managed to find her in three days, since they had broken camp outside Oakland. He had begun to wonder whether she had turned around and gone back to San Francisco for some reason, even after telling him how much tumbondé meant to her. But she hadn't, of course. She was simply off somewhere, swept up in the maelstrom of worshippers. The procession was so big now that it was easy to get lost in it. Jaspin had finally spotted her tonight, trying to get through the frantic mob in front of the platform where Senhor Papamacer was supposed to appear. "Forget it," he had told her. "The Senhor's changed his mind. He's having a private communion with Maguali-ga tonight. Let's go for a walk." That was two hours ago. Now they were on the coastal side of the hills and the sounds of the caravan were faint in the distance.

"I never realized California was this huge," Jaspin said. "I mean, what the hell, I've seen it on maps. But you don't understand the size of it until you set out to march up the length of it from the bottom to the top."

"It's bigger than a lot of countries," Lacy said. "Bigger than Germany, England, maybe Spain. Bigger than a lot of important places. That's what Ed Ferguson told me once. My former partner. Have you ever been to another country, Barry?"

"Me? Mexico, a few times. Doing field research."

"Mexico's right next door to where you lived. I mean really another *country*. Europe, for instance."

"How would I have gotten to Europe?" he asked. "Magic carpet?"

"People go to Europe from America, don't they?"

"From the East Coast, maybe. I think they run some ships back and forth. But not from here. How would you do it from here, with the whole dusted zone in between that you'd have to get across?" Jaspin shook his head. "There was a time when people went all over the world in an afternoon, you know. Australia, Europe, South America, wherever, you just got on a plane and you went."

"They still have planes. I've seen them."

"Sure, planes. Maybe some of them still fly across oceans, I don't know. But the politics is all wrong now. With the old countries broken up into all sorts of pieces, Republic of This and Free State of That, fifty visas needed to get from here to there—no, it's a mess, Lacy. Maybe a mess that's completely beyond fixing by now."

"When the gate is open and Chungirá-He-Will-Come has arrived, everything will be put to right," Lacy said.

"You really believe that?"

She turned her head sharply toward him. "Don't you?"

"Yeah," he said. "Yeah, I do."

"You don't entirely, do you, Barry? There's still something holding back somewhere in you."

"Maybe."

"I know there is. But it's all right. I've known people like you before. I was one myself. Cynical, doubting, uncertain—why not? What else would anybody with half a grain of sense be, growing up in a world where you travel half an hour outside the cities and you're in bandido territory, and everything for a thousand kilometers on the other side of the Rockies is a radioactive mess. But it can all drop away from you, all those doubts, all those wiseacre attitudes, if you just let it happen. You know that."

"Yes, I do."

"And we're at the end of a long bad time, Barry. We've come down to the bottom, where there's hardly any hope left, and suddenly there's hope. The Senhor has brought it. He tells us the word. The gate will open; the great ones will come among us and make things better for us. That's what's going to happen, and it's going to happen very soon, and then everything will be okay, maybe for the first time ever. Right? Right?"

"You're a very beautiful woman, Lacy."

"What does that have to do with it?"

"I don't know. I just thought I'd tell you."

"You think I am, huh?"

"You have any doubt?"

She laughed. "I've heard it before. But I'm never sure. There isn't a woman alive who thinks she's really beautiful, no matter what men tell her. I think my hair is very good, my eyes, my nose. But I don't like my mouth. It spoils everything."

"You're wrong."

"On the other hand I think my body is quite satisfactory."

"Is it?" he said.

Her eyes were very bright. Jaspin saw the sickle moon

reflected in them, and he thought he could even make out the brilliant white point that was Venus. With the arm that was around her shoulders he pulled her toward him; he brought the other arm up and let his hand wander lightly across her breasts. She was wearing a soft green sweater, very thin material, nothing underneath. Yes, he thought, quite satisfactory. He wanted to put his head between her breasts and rest there. Vaguely he wondered where Jill was, what she was doing now. His wife. A farce, that was. He hadn't even seen her in two days. Apparently she had lost interest in the Inner Host, or more likely they had lost interest in her. He'd been right about her the first time: a drifter, a waif, scruffy, useless. Lacy was a different story: shrewd, wise, a woman who had seen a lot and who understood what she had seen. If in her earlier life she'd been a con artist, a swindler, so what? So what? You were a con artist yourself, Jaspin told himself, remembering his UCLA days when he'd made a career that hadn't amounted to much more than hastily patching together his lectures out of other people's ideas. A scholar, you think? No, a phony. You might just as well have been peddling real estate on Betelgeuse Five. But none of that mattered any more. We will soon all be changed, he thought. In a moment, in the twinkling of an eye.

He began to pull her sweater upward. Smiling, Lacy moved his hands away and drew it up herself, and tossed it aside. Her jeans followed a moment later. She seemed almost to glow in the moonlight, skin very pale, curling red hair standing out luminously against it.

"Come on," she whispered hoarsely.

They moved close together. This felt strange to him, dreamlike, very beautiful and very peculiar both at once. He had never been much of a romantic, especially when it came to this; but somehow it seemed different this time, unique, brand new. Was it the imminence of the coming of the

gods? That had to be it. Here on this hillside north of San
Francisco under the moon and the stars, Venus shining
bright: he knew that the bad time was ending, and he could
feel all the raw and pimpled places on his soul beginning to
heal. Yes. Yes. Chungirá-He-Will-Come, he will come. And
when I stand forth to face him, I will not be alone.

Indeed we have all been changed, Jaspin thought. In a
moment. In the twinkling of an eye.

"You know what?" he said. "I love you."

"Which means you're finally learning to love yourself,"
Lacy said. "That's the first step in loving someone else."
She smiled. "You know what? Me too. I love you, Barry."

That was the last thing that either of them said for quite a
while. Then after a time Lacy said, "Wait a minute, okay?
Let me get on top. Is that all right with you? Ah. That's it,
Barry. Right. Oh, yes, *right*."

5

"PROXIMITY, that definitely appears to be the key thing,"
Elszabet said. "Or at least one of the key things." She was
in her office, early afternoon, looking up at Dan Robinson,
who was leaning in a loosejointed way against the wall by
the window. He seemed to be all arms and legs, standing
like that. The sky, as much of it as was visible through the
tiny north-facing window, was graying up, heavy clouds
beginning to move in. She said, "You were right. If what

happened to April is any indicator, proximity has to be a significant factor. I'm prepared to concede that now."

"You are. Well, that's something."

"How's she doing?"

"She'll be okay," Robinson said. He had just come from the infirmary. "We've got her paxed out, hundred milligrams. Lordy, that girl is big! She had a little surge, is all. Rush of blood to the head, essentially."

"More like a hot flash, I'd say. You should have seen her. Red as a beet. As a tomato."

Robinson chuckled. "Some tomato. Exactly what happened, anyway?"

"Well, as you and I discussed, I cooked things up so there'd be an occasion for her to come into my office while Tom was here. The moment she saw him, she started to hyperventilate."

"Hippopotamus in heat?"

"*Dan.*"

"Just a flash image. Sorry."

"It wasn't a sexual thing with her, I'm pretty certain. Even though she was blushing like a girl who'd been goosed on her first date. Tom doesn't seem to arouse sexual feelings in people, did you notice that?"

"Not in me, at any rate," Robinson said.

"No, I wouldn't think so. Not in anyone, apparently. He seems—well, asexual, somehow. He's very masculine but nevertheless it's hard to imagine him with a woman, wouldn't you say? There are men like that. But he stirred some sort of excitement in April, and it was *fast*, change of breathing, mottled blotches on her cheeks, then this bright red flush."

"Like an allergic reaction. Adrenaline surge."

"Absolutely. She weaved around a little and told me she was feeling upset. About what, I said, and she said it was on account of her dreams, her visions, that lately they were coming much more closely together and they were more vivid.''

"Proximity effect. Tom.''

"Said she was having trouble thinking straight. Sometimes hard for her to tell which was the real world and which was the dream.''

"You made a similar remark last night.''

"Yes,'' Elszabet said. "I remember. Hearing it from April was—well, disturbing. Her speech became slurred and she swayed back and forth. Then she started to pass out. Tom and I caught her just in time and managed to lower her to the floor. The rest you know.''

"Okay,'' Robinson said. "Seems pretty conclusive that Tom's presence here is hyping up the hallucination level.''

"Yet the dreams have been experienced across enormous distances. Proximity seems to intensify, but it's not essential.''

"I suppose.''

"We've got the distribution charts. Space dreams reported simultaneously from all over the place. If he's the source then he must be a tremendously powerful transmitter.''

"Transmitter of dreams,'' Robinson said softly, shaking his head. "Doesn't all this sound completely buggy to you, Elszabet?''

"Let's just work with it,'' she said. 'A hypothesis. He boils with images, fantasies, hallucinations. He boils over. Broadcasts them from the Rockies to the Pacific, San Diego to Vancouver, as far as we know. Susceptibility varies from practically none at all to extreme. Perhaps some correlation with emotional disturbance level . . . victims of Gelbard's syndrome appear to pick up the stuff much more readily than others. But that's not a complete correlation, because people like Naresh Patel and Dante Corelli are definitely not emotionally disturbed, and they've been getting the space dreams almost as long as some of the patients, whereas someone like Ed Ferguson, who *is* a patient, has proved completely resistant to—"

"Do you really think Ferguson has Gelbard's, Elszabet?"

"He's got something, I'd say."

"He's got a bad case of scruple deficiency, that's all. The more I observe him, the more convinced I become that the guy's simply a con artist who wangled treatment here because it sounded better to him than being tossed in jail for Rehab Two. Now, if you want to tell me that anybody as casual about matters of morality as Ferguson must *ipso facto* be emotionally disturbed, you might have a case, but even so, I think—" Robinson paused. "Which reminds me, have you run a check on whether Ferguson's showing any proximity effects? He had breakfast with Tom last week, and he's been seen talking with him a couple of times since."

Elszabet said, "I had Naresh run through Ferguson's pick reports for space-dream symptomata. Evidently there have been no dreams per se, but the night before last Ferguson did turn up with a trace of something. Just the merest shadowy outline of a bit of Green World imagery. I tried to call him in for a conference this afternoon but he wasn't around. Went off for a walk in the woods, they told me."

"Another escape attempt, you think?"

"No, although I'm having him monitored closely anyway. But he's out there with Tom. Been out there quite a while."

Robinson's eyes narrowed. "A very odd couple, those two. The saint and the sinner."

"You think Tom's a saint?"

"Just a quick glib phrase."

"Because I do. It's an idea that's been tickling at me the last few days. He's so strange, so innocent—like a holy fool, like the chosen of God, you know? Like an Old Testament prophet. Saint's not a bad label for him either. He wanders in the wilderness—what's the line, 'despised and rejected of men—'"

"'A man of sorrows, and acquainted with grief.'"

"That's it," she said. "And all the time he's carrying inside him this tremendous gift, this power, this blessing—he's like an ambassador from all the worlds of the universe—"

"Hey," Robinson said. "Hold on a little, there. A saint, you say. A messiah, actually, is what you seem to mean. But now you're talking as though the stuff he's giving out, if indeed he's the one who's giving it out, is an authentic vision of actual and literal other worlds."

"Maybe it is, Dan. I don't know."

"Are you serious?"

She tapped the little mnemone capsule on her desk. "I've been interviewing him. He's been filling me in on the background of the places in the dreams—the names of the worlds, the races that inhabit them, the empires, the dynasties, fragments of the history, a whole vast intricate interwoven structure of galactic civilization, tremendously dense in detail, internally consistent so far as I've been able to follow what he's saying, which I confess is not really very far. But what emerges nevertheless is very damned convincing, Dan. He's definitely not improvising. He's lived with that stuff a long time."

"So he has a rich fantasy life. He's spent twenty-five years dreaming up those details. Why shouldn't it be intricate? Why shouldn't it be convincing? But does that mean those empires and dynasties actually exist?"

"The things he says coincide in every detail with things that I've experienced myself while undergoing space dreams."

"No. Not relevant, Elszabet. If he's transmitting images and concepts and you and a lot of other people are receiving them, that still doesn't mean that what he's transmitting is anything but hallucinatory in origin."

"Granted," Elszabet said. "Okay, we have a phenomenon here. But of what kind? If Tom is indeed the source, then it would appear that he possesses some sort of extra-sensory power that allows him to transmit images to other people by mind-to-mind contact.''

''Sounds a little farfetched. But not inconceivable.''

''I can make out a valid case for the ESP angle. He told me this morning that he was born right after the outbreak of the Dust War, and that his mother was in Eastern Nevada when she was carrying him. Right on the edge of the radiation zone.''

''Telepathic mutation, is that what you're saying?''

''It's a reasonable hypothesis, isn't it?''

''Bill Waldstein should only hear all this stuff. He thinks *I'm* prone to cooking up wild theories,'' Dan said.

''This one doesn't seem so wild to me. If there's an explanation for Tom's abilities, a light touch of radiation at the time of conception isn't the most fantastic possible idea.''

''All right. A telepathic mutant, then.''

''A phenomenon, anyway. Okay. Now, as to the content of the material that he's producing, perhaps he's in the grip of some powerful fantasy of his own invention that by virtue of his extrasensory abilities he's able to scatter around to any susceptible mind within reach. Or, on the other hand, perhaps he's uniquely sensitive to messages being beamed our way telepathically by actual civilizations in the stars.''

''You want to believe that very much, don't you, Elszabet?''

''Believe what?''

''That what Tom is transmitting is real.''

''Maybe I do. Does that worry you, Dan?''

He studied her for a long moment. '' A little,'' he said at last.

''You think I'm going around the bend?''

''I didn't say that. I do think you've got a powerful need

to find out that the Green World and the Nine Suns planet and the rest are actual places."

"And therefore that I'm being drawn into Tom's psychosis?"

"And therefore that you're a little more deeply committed to escapist fantasies than might be altogether healthy," he said.

"Well, I feel the same way, okay?" Elszabet told him. "If you're worried about me, that makes two of us. But it's such a damned attractive notion, isn't it, Dan? These beautiful other worlds beckoning to us?"

"Dangerous. Seductive."

"Seductive, yes. But sometimes it's necessary to let yourself get seduced. We've got such a shitty deal, Dan, this poor broken-down civilization of ours, living like this in the ruins and remnants of the prewar world. All these shabby little countries that used to be pieces of the United States, and the anarchy that's going on outside California and even inside a lot of it, and the sense that everybody has that things are just going to go on getting worse and worse, uglier and uglier, shabbier and shabbier, that progress has absolutely come to an end and that we're simply going to keep slipping farther back into barbarism—is it any wonder that if I start dreaming that I'm living on a beautiful green world where everything is graceful and civilized and elegant I'm going to want to find out that it really exists? And that we're soon going to be able to go to that green world and live there? It's such an irresistible fantasy, Dan. Surely we need some fantasies like that to sustain us."

"*Go* there?" he said, looking startled. "What do you mean?"

"I didn't tell you. Tom's whole notion. When I play you his capsule, you'll hear it. It's an apocalyptic concept: the Last Days are at hand, and we're going to drop our bodies— that's his phrase, drop our bodies—and be translated to the worlds of the space dreams and live there forever and ever, amen."

Robinson whistled. "Is that what he's peddling?"

"The Time of Crossing, he calls it. Yes."

"The opposite of what this other bunch, these Brazilian voodoo people, are saying. The way they have it, the space gods are coming to *us*, isn't that what Leo Kresh told us? Whereas Tom—"

Elszabet's telephone made a little bleeping sound. "Excuse me," she said, and glanced behind her at the data wall to see who was calling. *Dr. Kresh, the wall screen said, calling from San Diego.*

They exchanged looks of surprise. "Speak of the devil," Elszabet murmured, and thumbed the phone. Kresh's face blossomed on the screen. He had gone back to Southern California late the previous week, and right now he seemed as though he had been through some changes since his visit to Nepenthe: he was uncharacteristically rumpled-looking, flushed, plainly excited.

"Dr. Lewis," he blurted, "I'm glad I was able to reach you. Quite an astonishing development—"

"Dr. Robinson is with me here," Elszabet said.

"Yes, that's fine. He'll want to hear this too, I know."

"What's happened, Dr. Kresh?"

"It's the most amazing thing. Especially in view of some of the ideas I heard Dr. Robinson propose while I was up there. In relation to Project Starprobe, I mean. Are you aware, Dr. Robinson, Dr. Lewis, that there's a ground station in Pasadena that has been tuned all these years to receive signals from the Starprobe vehicle? It's operated by Cal Tech, and somehow they've kept it maintained, just in case—"

"And there's been a signal?" Robinson said.

"It began coming in late last night. As you know, Dr. Robinson, the Starprobe hypothesis had occurred to me independently, and in the course of my investigation I learned about the Cal Tech facility and established contact with it. So when the signal began arriving—it's a tight-beam radio transmission at 1390 megacycles per second, coming to us from Proxima Centauri via a series of relay stations previously established at intervals of—''

"For Christ's sake," Robinson broke in, "are you going to tell us what it was that came in or aren't you?"

Kresh looked flustered. "Sorry. You understand, this has been a very confusing experience for me, for everyone—" He caught his breath. "I'll put the images on the screen. You're aware, I think, that the probe was programmed to enter the Proxima Centauri system, scan for planets that might be habitable, take up orbit around any that it found and drop down into the atmosphere of any planet that showed clear indication of life-forms. The nine hours of transmission that have come in so far actually cover a real-time period of about two months. This is Proxima Centauri, viewed at a distance of point-five astronomical units."

Kresh disappeared from the screen. In his place appeared the image of a small, pallid-looking red star. Two other stars, much brighter, were visible in a corner of the screen.

"The red dwarf is Proxima," Kresh said. "Those are its companion stars, Alpha Centauri A and B, which are similar in spectral type to our sun. The Cal Tech people tell me that all three stars appear to have planetary systems. However, the Starprobe vehicle found the planets of Proxima to be of the greatest interest, and so—"

On the screen now appeared a featureless green ball.

"My God," Robinson muttered.

Kresh said, "This is the second planet of the Proxima Centauri system, located point-eighty-seven astronomical units from the star. Proxima Centauri is a flare star, I'm told, subject to fluctuations of brightness that would be dangerous to life-forms at any closer range. But the Starprobe vehicle detected signs of life on Proxima Two, and reconformed itself for a planetary approach—"

On the screen, thick swirling mists, heavy, impenetrable-looking. Green.

Green.

"Oh, my God," Robinson said again. Elszabet sat tensely, hands balled into fists, teeth digging against her lower lip.

Another shot. Below the cloud cover.

"You will see," said Kresh, "that even though Proxima Centauri is a red star, the cloud cover is so dense that from the surface of the second planet it appears green. The cloud cover also, the Cal Tech people tell me, sets up a sort of greenhouse effect to keep the temperature of the planet within a range suitable for the metabolism of living creatures, despite the low energy output of the primary star Proxima Centauri—"

Another shot. Low orbit now, virtually skimming the clouds. High-resolution cameras coming into play. A focus shift; then new images, fantastically detailed. A gentle landscape, lush green hills, shining green lakes. Buildings down below, mysterious structures of disturbingly alien design, unexpected angles, baffling architectural convolutions. Another increment of camera capacity. Figures moving about on a lawn: long, tapering, frail-looking, with crystalline bodies bright as mirrors, rows of faceted eyes set on each of the four sides of their diamond-shaped heads. "My God," Dan Robinson said over and over again. Elszabet did not move, scarcely even breathed, would not let herself so much as blink. That is the Misilyne Triad, she thought. Those must be the Suminoors, and those, the Gaarinar. Oh. Oh. Oh. She was numb with awe and wonder. She wanted to cry; she wanted to drop to her knees and pray; she wanted to run outside and cry hallelujah. But she was unable to move. She remained perfectly still, frozen with astonishment, as image succeeded green image on the screen. Everything unbearably strange. Everything bizarrely alien.

Everything also completely and utterly and entirely *familiar,* as though she were looking at photographs of the town where she had lived when she was a child.

Seven

The Gypsy snap, and Pedro
  Are none of Tom's comradoes;
The punk I scorn and the cutpurse sworn
  And the roaring-boys' bravadoes;
The meek, the white, the gentle,
  Me handle, touch, and spare not,
But those that cross Tom Rhinoceros
  Do what the panther dare not.

Although I do sing, "Any food, any feeding,
  Feeding, drink or clothing?
    Come, dame or maid,
    Be not afraid,
Poor Tom will injure nothing."

—Tom O'Bedlam's Song

I T was starting to get dark, earlier than usual. Some clouds starting to drift over from the north, maybe even a little rain tonight, Tom thought. The first of the season. Last night clear and sharp and cool, the moonlight strong and bright; tonight, maybe, rain. A change in the weather, perhaps heralding other, bigger changes just ahead. Go back to the room, take a nice shower, fix yourself up for dinner. Afterward have a talk with some of the people here, this Ferguson, the fat girl April, some of the others. The Time of the Crossing was getting close. Like the coming of the rain: the season was changing.

"Let's go," he said to Ferguson. "We been out here for hours. Time to head back."

"Yeah," Ferguson said. "Sure." He sounded half-awake, or less than half: vague, dreamy, furry. He had been that way since Tom had given him the vision. Sitting quietly under the giant trees, smiling, shaking his head from time to time, saying almost nothing at all. It was as though the

Green World dream had stunned him. Or was it something else, Tom wondered? Was it that somebody had turned to him at last and said, Look, man, I care for you, me, an absolute stranger with not a damn thing to gain, I just want you to stop hurting and this is what I can do for you. Maybe no one had ever said anything like that to him before, Tom thought.

"Come on, then. Up."

"Yeah. Yeah. I'm coming."

"Give you a hand. Here."

Tom pulled Ferguson to his feet. He was a big powerful man, plenty of beef on him. Getting him up was work. Ferguson wobbled a little, rocking back and forth. Easy, Tom thought. Get your balance. He hoped Ferguson wasn't going to fall. He remembered what it had been like catching hold of April when *she* went over. Easy. Easy.

Ferguson managed to steady himself. They started toward the trail back to the Center.

"You think I'm going to get the space dreams all the time now?" Ferguson asked. "Without you having to do that to me, I mean?"

"Sure," Tom said. "Why not? You're wide open. You always were, except you wouldn't let it. Now you know how to let it."

"What a beautiful thing. That green world. I understand now, the fuss. I want to see the other ones too, you know? All seven of them."

Tom said, "There are more than seven."

"There are?"

"The seven are just the main ones, the strongest visions. There are others. Thousands. Millions. An infinity. Some have come to me only once, for a fraction of a second. Some only a couple of times, years apart. But the main seven, they come all the time. Those are the ones that I can give to others, the strong ones, the main ones."

"Jesus," Ferguson said. "Millions of worlds."

"Look up there," said Tom. "You know how many stars you can see when the sky is clear? And those are just the bright ones near by. This galaxy, it's a hundred thousand light-years from end to end. You know how many stars there are in a hundred thousand light-years? And that's just this galaxy. They've got nebulas out there that are whole galaxies in themselves. Andromeda. Cygnus A. The Magellanic Clouds. Full of stars, and all the stars have planets. Makes you dizzy, just to think. This funny little planet . . . what gall, saying we're the only stuff there is in the universe. You know?"

"Yeah," Ferguson said. "Yeah. Jesus, what was I doing all my life? What was I thinking of?"

Lost in the vision, still. Floating along with his head in the stars. He seemed to be altogether different now, that cold knot in his breast gone, his face smoother, younger-looking, more at ease. Well, Tom thought, that won't last. You don't get completely transformed in one single flash, no matter what. The old sad mean bitter cold Ed Ferguson might come back, probably would, an hour from now, a day, a week, sooner or later. Unless something big was done to change him, very soon now, while he was still open and vulnerable. Tom gave that some thought.

"Tom?" a sudden voice whispered out of the underbrush. "Hey, you, Tom!"

He looked around. A face in the shadows, blue eyes, thin lips, little scars all over the cheeks. A hand beckoning to him, pointing, signaling him to get rid of Ferguson and come over there.

Buffalo, it was. Hiding there like a ghost.

Tom shook his head. Pointed toward the Center, pointed at Ferguson.

Buffalo gestured again, more urgently. Whispered again.

"Come here, will you? Charley's here. Wants to see you."

"All right," Tom said, frowning. "Wait."

He trotted forward, catching up with Ferguson, who by now was twenty, thirty paces ahead. "You go on back," he said. "I'm going to stay out here another five minutes, okay?"

Ferguson didn't seem curious about that. Right now the Green World was more vivid to him, he figured, than anything that might be going on here in the woods. "Yeah," Ferguson said. "Sure."

"I just need to be alone a little bit."

"Yeah. Sure."

He went trudging on. Tom hesitated, watching him go; then he turned back into the deeper forest. Buffalo stepped out from behind an enormous tree.

"That was the guy from the highway, wasn't it? The one who hurt his leg, the one with the dark-haired girl?"

"That's right," Tom said. "Why are you here? What does Charley want with me, Buffalo?"

"To see you, man. To talk to you. He misses you, you know that? We all do." Buffalo winked. "Hey, you look good, Tom! Got yourself cleaned up a little, huh? New pair of jeans, new shirt, everything fresh. This a pretty good place here, this Center?"

"It's all right," said Tom. "A lot of fine people here. I like it."

"I bet. Well, come on. Come on. This way, right back here. Charley wants to see you."

Buffalo led the way between the great trees, across a meadow thick with clumps of leathery ferns. A few more of the scratchers were hunkered down in a secluded little glade near a stream that had just about run dry. Charley was there, looking tired and gloomy. Mujer. Stidge. White-haired Nicholas. They all seemed even scruffier than usual, a worn-out, beat-up group of men. Tom wasn't happy to see them. He hadn't expected ever to see them again.

"There he is!" Charley called out. "Son of a bitch, look at the new outfit! They gave you a bath, too, put some food in your belly, huh? Hey, there, Tom! Tom, how you been?"

"Charley."

"Sight for sore eyes," Charley said. "You been doing okay. Hasn't been going so good for us, you know."

"No?"

"We ran into a little trouble, up Ukiah way. Tamale and Choke, they were ambushed and killed."

"I thought they were back out there with the van."

"Van's in here," said Charley. "We floated it right between the trees, got it a little ways back in the meadow. Tamale and Choke, uh-uh. Rest of us, we were lucky to get away."

"Not so lucky, them," Tom said. "The Time of the Crossing's almost here. What a time to get killed, missing out on all the splendor, on the redemption."

"Give you a bath, it don't change you any, I see," Charley said, smiling faintly. "The green world and the Loollymooly planet and all the rest. That's okay. We dream the visions too. Loollymooly and everything. Mujer, Buffalo, me. Stidge says he doesn't. That right, Stidge? You never get a vision, huh, you sour-faced bastard?"

Stidge said, "Why don't you get off my back, Charley? But for me you'd be dead back there with Tamale and Choke."

"That's right," Charley said. "Stidge saved us, do you know that, Tom? Very quick with his spike, Stidge is. There were these three vigilantes at the roadblock, big energy-wall up, and somehow Stidge slipped around behind them—" He shrugged. "It's been a rough couple weeks, Tom. We missed you."

"I bet you did."

"No. Seriously. You were our luck, Tom. So long as you were with us, everything seemed to go okay. All your nutty stuff, your visions, your worlds, they were like a charm for us. We got into trouble, we got right out again. Since they took you away in that copter it's been lousy. Choke, Tamale, they shot them into pieces. Didn't even ask questions. That's why we came back here, Tom."

"Why?"

"For you. We're going to make a run for the south, warm weather, Mexico, maybe. Rainy season's coming on any minute. We'll head down the Valley, maybe over into the desert, cut around San Diego and down into Baja. You come with us, okay? We got plenty of room in the van, now."

"The Crossing's almost here, Charley. Doesn't make any sense, going to Mexico or anywhere else now. A couple of weeks, we'll be up there in the sky."

He heard Stidge snickering, Mujer muttering.

Charley said, "That so? Hell, you can do the Crossing just as easy from Baja, can't you? And be a lot warmer until it happens, right?"

"I'm going to stay here, Charley."

"At the goddamn Center?"

"Yeah. There are people here I want to help. When the Time of the Crossing comes, I want to guide them. I tell you what, though. You stay here, I'll help you too. You were good to me. I want you to be among the first to Cross. You stay out here in the woods, in the van, and I'll come to you when it begins. Okay? That's a promise. Let me help Ferguson over, and April, and Dr. Elszabet and some of the others and then I'll be back here to help you. Another week, maybe. Maybe even less, Charley."

"You want him," Mujer said, "let's just put him in the van and go, you hear, Charley?"

Charley shook his head. "No. I don't want that." To Tom he said, "You come with us, Tom."

"I told you, I got things to do here."

"You know what's going to happen to you, you stay here? You'll get run over by the lunatic crazy army that's marching this way. They'll be here, another day or two, the whole goddamn swarm of them, and when they come they'll tear the place apart."

"I don't know anything about that, Charley," Tom said, frowning.

"Nobody told you? That's all we heard out there, last couple of days. About a million and a half crazies, some gang of nuts, marching toward the North Pole, they say. Going there to meet God. Some kind of god, anyway. Started in San Diego, been collecting people all up the coast. Heading straight this way, like a plague of locusts, chewing up everything in sight. That's why we're going to get out of this end of the state. Double back around them to the east, head south while all the fun and games is going on up here. It won't be safe for you, Tom. Come on with us. We'll clear out in the morning."

"It won't matter what's going on here, when the Crossing begins."

"It's supposed to be like a traveling riot," Charley said. "It's real wild. Guy like you, you don't want to be mixed up in stuff like that."

"It won't matter," Tom said. "Look, I got to get back. I want to wash up, have dinner, talk to a few people. You come on to the Center with me, all right? They'll take you in. They're really good there. Dr. Elszabet, she'll welcome you the same way she did me. And then we'll all be together when the Crossing starts. What do you say, Charley?"

"Nothing doing. We're clearing out. This won't be no place to be when those marchers get here. You come give us good luck again, Tom."

"The place for good luck is right here."

"Tom—"

"I got to go now."

"You think about it," Charley said. "We'll camp out here tonight. In the morning, you come back, we'll still be here. You can go south with us."

"You want him, we ought to just grab him," Mujer said again.

"Shut up," Charley said. "See you tomorrow, Tom?"

"You come into the Center tomorrow," Tom said. "Tonight, even. They got good eating there."

He turned and walked away into the shadows. It was much darker now. Definite hint of rain, maybe tonight, maybe not until morning. Were they going to run up behind him and grab him? No, he thought, Charley wasn't like that. Charley had a sort of honor about him. Tom felt sorry about the scratchers. Come with us, be our luck: yeah. But he couldn't. His place was here. Maybe in the morning he'd hike back out again and try to talk them into staying. He hoped they wouldn't try to grab him then. Not with the Crossing so close—to take him away from his new friends here, before he could help them—no, that would be bad. He'd have to think about it some.

He was back in the main part of the Center in twenty minutes. Into his little cabin, edge of the woods. A good long shower, and he sat crosslegged on the floor beside his bed for a time, doing his thinking. Then over to the big building, the dinner place. The others were there already, Ed Ferguson and Father Christie, and the beautiful artificial woman Alleluia, and fat April, all sitting together at one of the long tables. Ferguson was still glowing. You could see the glow on him from halfway across the room. It was a good feeling, Tom thought, knowing that by the laying on of hands he had brought a joyous vision to that unhappy man. He went over to them.

Alleluia said, "He told us you gave him a space dream."

"I showed him how to open himself to a vision, yes," Tom said. "Can I sit with you?"

"Here," said Father Christie. "Right here, next to me. You're a remarkable person, you know that, Tom?"

"I wanted to help him."

"How'd you do it?" Alleluia asked.

"I spoke with him for a while. I showed him the powers that lay within him. That was all."

"It's amazing," said Alleluia. "He's like someone else now."

"He's like himself now," Tom said. "The real self that was inside him all along. We are all becoming ourselves. We will all be fulfilled soon."

This is the moment, he thought. Tell them. About the Crossing. Tell them now.

But then April said to him in a small little voice, "You know what? You scare me." She was on the far side of the table, shrinking back from him as though she was afraid she'd catch a disease from him. She was trembling and her face was red. Tom hoped she wouldn't go into another fit and fall over.

"I do?" he said.

"You have the visions inside you, don't you? Like a power all coiled up in there. And when I'm this close to you I can feel it," April said. Her cheeks were burning. She wasn't able to look him in the eye. "The other worlds, pressing in. It's frightening. The other worlds are very beautiful, you know. But it's all frightening. I wish none of this was happening."

"No, child," Father Christie said. "What's happening is the imminence of the advent of the Lord upon the Earth. There's nothing to fear. This is the moment we've been awaiting for more than two thousand years."

Tom looked at Ferguson. He was far away, smiling in the deepest bliss.

He said to April, "Don't be afraid. Father Christie's right. This is a wonderful thing that's about to happen."

"I don't understand," April told him.

"Yeah," Alleluia said. "What are you talking about, anyway?"

Tom looked from one to the other—Alleluia, Father Christie, poor terrified April, the blissed-out Ferguson. All right, he thought. This is the moment. At long last, the Time is here. Let it begin.

"It's a long story," he said.

And he began to tell them all about the wonderful thing that was soon to come.

He began to tell them all about the Crossing.

2

ELSZABET said, "The latest estimate from the county highway authorities is that there are three hundred thousand of them. The woman I spoke to said that the figure might be off by as much as fifty thousand either way, but there was no real hope of getting an accurate count because they were spread out so wide and because it was hard to tell how many were traveling in each vehicle. I think you all understand that even if the estimate is too high by a hundred thousand, we've got a real problem on our hands."

"What makes you think they'll be coming anywhere near us?" Dante Corelli asked.

Elszabet took a deep breath. She was feeling ragged.

Dreams and visions were surfacing with bewildering frequency now, for her, for everyone. Just an hour ago the full Nine Suns had erupted in her brain, this time richly detailed and sequential, not only the huge cyclopean alien form against the rocky landscape but a whole elaborate rite involving beings of several planetary types, almost a ballet. And looking at the faces of her staff around the big conference table, she knew the same thing must be happening to them. Dante, Patel, Waldstein, even Dan Robinson, who had had so much trouble experiencing the dreams once upon a time: everyone was fully receptive now, everyone was being bombarded by the vivid throbbing pulsating images of strange worlds.

"They have to pass reasonably close," she said. "Where they are now, there aren't that many options for going north. You can't drive thousands of cars and buses and trucks through a forest. And they'll start butting up against the mountains of the coastal range, which will force them closer and closer to the ocean. It's already too late for them to turn inland and go up by Ukiah way, because there aren't any decent roads that a mob that big can use to cross the mountains from where they're located now. So they can't help but be funneled toward Mendocino, and as they come swarming through there it's pretty likely that some of them will start spilling over onto our land. Perhaps a lot of them, or the whole horde, maybe. What I want to do is put up an energy wall across the whole western side of our property so that when they come up the coast they'll have to keep toward the ocean."

"Do we have the equipment for that?" Bill Waldstein asked.

"I talked to Lew Arcidiacono about that just now. He says we probably do, or at least enough to protect us on the side facing Mendocino. What we might have to do is keep moving the equipment around from place to place on an ad hoc basis all along our western perimeter until these tumbondé people have gone past.''

. Dan Robinson said, ''Sounds like we'll need the entire staff for that.''

''More than just the staff,'' said Elszabet. ''Lew tells me that we'll need dozens of people out there on the line, some to patrol, some to haul equipment, some to operate the generators. That's going to take everybody we have, and then some.''

''Patients, too?'' said Dante Corelli.

Elszabet nodded. ''We may have to use some of them.''

''I don't like that,'' Dan Robinson said.

''The most stable ones. Tomás Menendez, say, Father Christie, Philippa, Martin Clare, maybe even Alleluia—''

''Alleluia is stable?'' Waldstein asked.

''On her good days she is. And think of how strong she is. She could probably carry a generator in each hand. We might want to give each patient a twenty-milligram nick of pax before we send them out, but I think there's no question we're going to have to use some of them on the lines.''

''Furthermore,'' Naresh Patel said, ''if we do have to have the entire staff on the front line, it would be a good idea to keep the patients out there with us so we can keep watch on them for the duration of the emergency.''

''Good point,'' Robinson said. ''We can't just leave them back here to amuse themselves while we're setting up the energy wall.''

Waldstein said, ''Are you sure this is going to happen, Elszabet? This ferocious onslaught of berserk cultists?''

''They aren't necessarily ferocious or berserk. But there's an awful lot of them and they're in the county and coming in this direction, Bill. Would you like to gamble that they'll politely go around us without trampling so much as a blade of grass at the Center? I wouldn't. I'd rather risk wasting a little effort in protecting ourselves than fold my arms and find out that we're smack in their path.''

"Agreed," Dante Corelli said.

"We have no choice, I think," Dan said.

"I think you're the only one here who has serious doubts, Bill," Elszabet said.

"Not serious doubts. I just wonder if it's all really necessary. But you're right that there's a real risk of trouble and we're better off taking whatever precautions we can. I'd like to know something else, though. While we're busy fending off this potential invasion, what are we going to do with this Tom thing of yours?''

"Tom?"

"You know. Your fiery-eyed psychotic friend who's been filling all our heads with his craziness. Do you think it's safe to let him run around loose?''

"What are you suggesting, Bill?" Dan Robinson asked.

"I'm suggesting that we can't function effectively if we're having hallucinations like this every ninety minutes or so. That's been my experience the last two or three days, and I think everyone else can report the same thing. Drifting in and out of Nine Suns, Green World, the Double Star planets—we have a powerful and dangerous telepath in our midst. He's messing up our heads. We're entirely at his mercy. And now if there's a real crisis marching up the road toward us—''

Robinson said, "Tom isn't psychotic. Those aren't hallucinations.''

"I know. What they are is newsreel shots of actual other planets, right? Come off it, Dan.''

"How can you doubt that now?''

Waldstein stared at him. "Are you serious?''

"Bill, you saw the stuff Leo Kresh sent us, the relay photos from the Starprobe satellite. We have unquestionable proof now that Green World, at least, exists. Surely you

won't try to dispute the fact, after seeing that material, that
what we've been calling the Green World dream is a
detailed and exact view of one of the planets of the star
Proxima Centauri. And that Tom, far from being psychotic,
actually has some kind of telepathic means of picking up
images from distant solar systems and relaying them to other
minds over a wide geographical range."

"That's bullshit," Waldstein said.

Elszabet said, "Bill, how can you—"

Waldstein swung around fiercely toward her, hunching
forward, face flushed. "How do we know those pictures
came from Proxima Centauri? How do we know that Tom
doesn't have some way of hocus-pocusing the receivers at
Cal Tech that picked those relays up, the same way he
hocus-pocuses our minds? I'll grant you that he's a telepath
with astounding abilities. But not that he's scanning planets
dozens of light-years away. The whole thing's his own
cockeyed fantasy, top to bottom, and he's spewing it out
into millions of other people. I feel invaded by this crap
myself. I feel soiled. I think he's a menace, Elszabet."

Quietly she said, "I don't. I believe his visions are
genuine ones and that the Starprobe relay confirms it. He's
in tune with the whole cosmos. He's opening the universe to
us in the most amazing way—"

"Elszabet!"

"No, don't look at me that way, Bill. I'm not crazy. I've
spent hours talking with him. Have you? He's a gentle holy
man with the most fantastic power any human being has
ever had. And if what he's told me is true, his powers are
ripening to the point where it will actually be possible for
human beings to travel instantaneously to the worlds we've
been seeing in our—visions. He says that we're going—"

"For God's sake, Elszabet!"

"Let me finish. He says a time is coming soon—the Time
of the Crossing, he calls it—when our minds will begin

jumping across space to those worlds. We'll all abandon Earth. Earth is done for; Earth has had it. The universe is calling us. Does that sound crazy, Bill? Sure it does. But what if it's true? We already have the evidence of the Starprobe photos. I don't think Tom's a madman, Bill. He's a disturbed individual in some ways, yes, he's been whipped around by the enormous thing within him, he's pretty far off center, sure, but he's not crazy. He might just be able to open the whole universe to us. I believe that, Bill."

Waldstein looked stunned, shaking his head. "Jesus Christ, Elszabet. Jesus Christ!"

"So the answer to your question is no, I don't think we need to restrain Tom in any way while the tumbondé people are passing through. And afterward I think it would be a good idea for us to drop everything else and devote our skills to finding out what Tom is really all about. Okay? And unless there are serious objections, I'd like to get back to the topic of how we can prepare ourselves for the possibility that hundreds of thousands of trespassers may soon—"

"May I say just one more thing, Elszabet?"

Elszabet sighed. "Go ahead, Bill."

"Starprobe or no Starprobe, I'm still not convinced that this man is in any genuine contact with real-world extraterrestrial planets. But *if* he is, and *if* this Crossing you speak of is in any way possible, then I don't think we should just lock him up. I think we should kill him right away—"

"Bill!"

"I mean it. Don't you see the danger? Suppose he can really do it. Send the minds of everybody who's ever had a space dream off to other planets. Leaving what behind, empty husks? Wipe out the whole human race, depopulate the Earth? Doesn't that idea bother you in the *slightest?*" Waldstein shook his head. He pressed his hands against his face. "Jesus, I can't believe I'm sitting here seriously discussing this lunacy. One last try: Either Tom is crazy and dangerous to everybody's mental health because of his ability to transmit hallucinations, or he's sane and dangerous to everybody's life because he's getting ready to empty the world of people. Okay? Okay? Whichever way it is, he's a menace."

Naresh Patel said calmly, "I have a proposal. Let's devote our energies now to the task of defending the Center against the trespassers. I gather that they are moving steadily toward some destination far to the north of us and will be a potential threat to us only for the next day or two. After that, let's examine Tom closely and attempt to determine the nature and range of his abilities; and if protective action seems desirable to take then, we can consider it at that time."

"Seconded," said Dan Robinson.

"Bill?" Elszabet said.

Waldstein clapped his hands together in a gesture of resignation. "Whatever you want. I hope to hell he leaves for Mars in half an hour. And takes the entire bunch of you with him."

3

FERGUSON didn't sleep at all that night. He lay awake the whole night long, and the whole night long his head swarmed with wonders. The space dreams came to him by twos and threes. He wasn't sure they could really be called dreams because he wasn't asleep: but he saw the other worlds, turning under their suns of many colors. He saw strange intricate creatures moving about, speaking in languages no human ear had ever heard. He saw gleaming wondrous cities of strange design. He saw—

He saw—

He saw—

A couple of times he cried out in the dark, the things that he was seeing were so beautiful.

"You okay?" Tomás Menendez asked from the far side of the room.

"The visions don't stop," Ferguson said.

"Do you see Chungirá-He-Will-Come? Do you see Maguali-ga?"

Ferguson shrugged. "I see the whole shebang. It's the most amazing thing ever happened to me."

Out of the darkness Nick Double Rainbow muttered, "Son of a bitch, I'm trying to sleep!"

"I'm having visions," Ferguson said.

"Well, fuck your visions."

"It is the great time," said Tomás Menendez. "The opening of the gate will soon occur. Now you must fill your heart with love, Nick, and let the gods spill through into you. As Ed is doing. Do you see how happy Ed is now?"

Nine suns blazed on the screen of Ferguson's mind. A gigantic weird-looking thing with one brilliant eye on the top of its head turned toward him and held out many arms and called him by his name. Then the image went away, and he saw a different landscape, a white sun in the sky and a yellow one, and even weirder-looking beings that seemed to be riding around in automobiles made of water were traveling to and fro. And then—and then—

It isn't ever going to stop, Ferguson thought. On and on and on, one after another. You wanted space dreams, Ed baby? Okay, now you've got space dreams.

Joy overflowed in him and tears came to his eyes again.

He had never cried so much in his life, not since he was a baby. He couldn't stop. He was like a fountain. But that was all right. The tears were washing his soul. It felt good to cry. Tom had touched something inside him, Tom had opened him up somehow, and now the tears were rushing through him like the spring thaw, washing away all kinds of ancient grime and garbage. They should see me now, he thought. Blubbering like this. Everyone who knew me in Los Angeles, they wouldn't believe it. Poor Ed has flipped his lid. Crying all the time, and loving it. Poor Ed. Poor nutty Ed.

Look, that's the blue star, the one that's so hot it melts the ground. The shimmering floating city. The shining ghostlike people. Gorgeous! Gorgeous!

His pillow was soaked with tears.

God, it felt good. Cry all you want, Ferguson told himself. And then cry some more. Clean yourself out, fellow. Whatever thing is happening to you, it's all right. Just let it happen. The way Tom had said: *Just for once, let everything go, let it all open up. Let grace come flooding in.*

He couldn't just lie still. He got up, walked around the room, held on to the door, to the cabinet, to the sink, anything that would steady him. The world swayed around him. He was spinning, spinning—it would be so easy, he thought, just to let go, let himself go floating off into space—

Tomás Menendez stood beside him. "It is a wonderful time, no? The gods are breaking through. Chungirá-He-Will-Come arrives on Earth, or perhaps we will go to Chungirá, I do not know which. But everything will be changed."

"Shut the fuck *up*." From Nick Double Rainbow.

Ferguson smiled. "Now I see the red sun and the blue one, and a bridge of light streaming between them. Christ, that red sun, it takes up half the sky!"

"It is the vision of Chungirá" said Menendez. "Come let us go outside. Stand under the stars, let Chungirá enter your soul."

"A big white wall of stone," Ferguson murmured. "It's the thing Lacy saw. Alleluia. Now me. The golden thing with the curving horns."

Menendez had him by the elbow, guiding him into the hallway out to the steps of the dormitory building. Ferguson didn't care. He would go wherever Menendez wanted to take him. He saw only the giant red sun, throbbing and pulsing, and the blue one beside it, pounding his mind like a gong. And the wonderful being with the curving horns. Reaching toward him. Calling to him. An arch of blazing light stretching across the heavens.

He followed Menendez out of the building. Light sprinkles of moisture struck his cheeks. The air smelled different: clean, fresh, new. Somewhere during the night the rainy season had begun: soft rain, gentle rain, quietly pattering down. He had almost forgotten what rain was like, all these dry months. But here it was, finally. That was all right, Ferguson thought. I'll just stand here in the rain, get myself clean outside as well as in. It seemed to be almost morning. Ferguson didn't feel at all as though he had gone without sleep. His mind was alert, active, wide open. The horned figure was going through the same movement again and again, turning, reaching out, raising its arms, turning sideways. And turning again.

Ferguson stared. He saw the staff office building, the red building, the dark looming massive trees beyond. But all those things were misty and insubstantial, almost transparent. What had real density and substance was the shining white block and the huge figure that stood on top of it. And the red sun, and the blue one. He lifted his face toward them. Rain streamed down his forehead. He had no idea how long he stood there. A minute, an hour, how could he tell?

Then the vision faded. The real world returned, solid, visible. Ferguson looked around, feeling a little dazed.

He was standing on the front porch of the dormitory building with Tomás Menendez beside him. It was raining lightly. The sky was gray but getting brighter. A figure in a yellow rain-slicker came jogging by, heading toward the far side of the Center. Teddy Lansford, it was.

"What is it, time for pick already?" Ferguson called.

Lansford paused a moment, running in place in the rain. "No pick today," he said.

"You kidding?"

"Not today. Not for anybody. Dr. Lewis says."

"Why?" Ferguson asked, baffled. "What's so special, today?" But Lansford was gone already, sprinting off into the rainy morning. Ferguson swung around and saw other figures emerging from the dorm, crowding out onto the porch as if to see if it was really raining. April, Alleluia, Philippa, a couple of the others. "No pick today!" Ferguson said to them. "It's a pick holiday!"

"Why?" April asked.

"Dr. Lewis says," Ferguson told her with a shrug.

Which set them all into excited discussion. Ferguson stood to one side, scarcely listening. It didn't matter to him, one way or the other, about pick this morning. What had happened to him couldn't be taken away. If they picked the visions from his mind new visions would come. He was fundamentally different now, that much he knew. He was changed forever. Just as well there was no pick today, he figured, because he wanted time to think, to analyze what had happened to him yesterday, how Tom had changed him. Taking him by the hands, opening him to the visions— Ferguson didn't want to lose his memories of all that. But he realized it would be no big deal if he did. The important thing was not what had happened but who he was now, and who he was was someone else from the person who had been riding around in his head yesterday. He leaned against the porch wall. The wind picked up a little, blowing rain inward at him. He didn't move. It felt fine, the rain. This early in the season the rain wasn't too cold.

Dante Corelli appeared out of the mists. She looked as if she'd been up all night too. She trotted up on the porch and clapped her hands. "All right, everybody. Get yourselves up to the mess hall and have some breakfast, and then assemble in the gymnasium. Pick's canceled today."

Alleluia said, "What's going on, Dante?"

"A little trouble, nothing too major. There's a big parade, sort of, coming this way, thousands of people who have been marching all the way from San Diego. Some kind of religious thing, that's what I hear. They're supposed to be traveling through Mendocino today, but we think that some of them might just go astray and wind up in here and cause some difficulties. So we're going to put up energy walls around the Center and keep them out. That's all. Nothing for anybody to get worried about, no cause for alarm, but it's going to be a sort of unusual day."

Tomás Menendez, standing next to Ferguson, said as if to himself, "The Senhor is here! It is the Senhor!"

"What was that?" Ferguson asked.

"He has come here because this is the Seventh Place!" Menendez said.

"Who has?" Ferguson asked. But Menendez, his face flushed, his eyes glowing strangely, turned and walked past him, back into the dormitory, without replying. Well, okay, Ferguson thought. Like Dante says, it's going to be a sort of unusual day.

Dante trotted on toward the headquarters building. "Remember, everyone," she called, looking back at them. "Breakfast right away, and then over to the gym."

Ferguson went inside to get dressed. Father Christie came up beside him. "How are you this morning, son?"

"I didn't sleep. Fantastic stuff going on in my head all night."

"But are you well?"

"The best I've ever been, Father. These visions. The things I've seen. I don't know, I can't stop—crying—crying from happiness—look, I'm doing it again—"

"Let it happen," said the priest. He was crying too, suddenly. "These are the great days, the days of the prophecy, when He brings every work into judgment. I was up all night too, do you know? Reading the Bible, that's what I was doing." The priest laughed. "You won't believe how long it has been, the Bible and me. But I read right through the night. The Revelation of Saint John, over and over. The Lamb which is in the midst of the throne shall feed us, and shall lead us unto living fountains of waters: and God shall wipe away all tears from our eyes. But first we must weep, if He is to wipe away our tears. Isn't that right?"

"I never was able to cry, Father. But now I can't seem to stop."

"Go on. Cry all you like. This is the day when the seventh seal shall be opened, and the seven angels will sound the seven trumpets. Believe me, son. You aren't Catholic, are you?"

"Me? No."

"That makes no difference. I'll bless you all the same when the time comes. How could I deny the blessing to anyone on this day?"

"What's going to happen today?" Ferguson said. He felt very easy, relaxed. He was just floating along.

"The Omega and the Alpha," said a voice from the other end of the hall. "The end and the beginning."

Ferguson felt new visions stream through his mind. Shining worlds sprang up and blazed in him. He was floating still.

"Tom?"

"This is the day when it begins," Tom said, coming toward him. "The Time of the Crossing. I feel it within me, the strength, the power. Will you be the first to go, Ed?"

"Me? Go?"

"To make the Crossing."

Ferguson stared. "Where to?"

"I think, to the Double Kingdom. They are willing to receive you. I can feel it, their willingness. Their two suns burn like fire in my heart today, the red and the blue."

Ferguson became aware that April was standing beside him, that Alleluia had appeared from somewhere and was at his elbow too. Indistinctly he said, "We're supposed to go get breakfast right away, and then—the gym—"

Tom's eyes were fixed on his. "Accept the Crossing, Ed. Someone must be the first, and you are the chosen one. Open the way for the rest of us. Once the first Crossing is made, the next ones will be easier, and it will get easier and easier and easier. Will you? Now?"

"You want me—to go to some other *star*—"

"You will drop this body, yes. For a better one in a better place. This corruptible must put on incorruption. This mortal must put on incorruptibility. And death is swallowed up in victory."

Ferguson studied him uneasily. They were all crowding close about him now. "Wait a second," he said. He wasn't floating so much now. He felt heavier now. "I'm not sure. Ease off a little. I'm not sure. What all this means."

"No one will force you," Tom said.

"Just let me think. Let me think."

Tomás Menendez appeared. His face was radiant. "This is the day when Chungirá will come!"

"Yes," Tom said. "And Ed, here, he's going to be the first to make the Crossing into the stars. I know he will. He'll go to the Double Kingdom."

"He will go the Chungirá," Menendez said. "And that will be the signal; and then Chungirá will come to us. Yes. Yes, I know it." Menendez seemed to be speaking out of a trance. "The Senhor is very close. I can feel him. Come, we will send Ferguson to Chungirá; and then I will go to the Senhor, I will welcome his coming. I will be Maguali-ga; I will be the opener of the gate." He put his hand on Ferguson's wrist. "You are ready, Ed? You will accept?"

Ferguson shook his head slowly, trying to understand. He would drop the body. He would make the Crossing. He would go to some other planet. The first twitches and flickers of fear began to awaken in him. What were they trying to say? What did they want to do to him? He would die, right? That was what all this meant, this dropping the body. Yes? No? He didn't understand any of this. For a moment all the old suspicions flared in him. They were trying to put something over on him, weren't they? They wanted to use him. They wanted to hurt him.

He said, "Am I going to die?"

"Your life will only just be beginning," Tom said.

They surrounded him, moving in close, smiling, stroking him. April, Alleluia, Father Christie, Menendez, Tom. Telling him that they loved him, that they envied him, that they would follow him very soon. But he had to be the first. He was the one who was ready. Is that so? he wondered. Am I ready? How do they know?

"Someone must be the first," Tom said.

"Let me think. Let me think."

"Let him think," said Father Christie. "He mustn't be pushed."

Ferguson sucked his breath in deep and hard down to the bottom of his lungs. Visions were starting to rise in him again. The Green World, gentle glistening glades. The world of light. All the worlds of the heavens shining in his mind. Vast beings walking to and fro. They wanted to send him there. They wanted him to be the first. He felt that cold knot of suspicions loosening, melting, draining away.

He wasn't interested in dying. But would it be dying if he made the Crossing? Would it? *Would it?*

"Don't say anything," someone said. "Just let him work it out."

Hey, why not? Ferguson thought. Feeling lighter again. The floating sensation coming back.

Do it, he thought. For once in your crappy life, do it. You be the one to go. Show them the way. Do it for them. Maybe even do it for yourself, who knows, but at least do it for them. For once in your life, just once. What do you have to lose? What's so wonderful for you here on Earth that you want to stay? Do it, Ed. Do it. Do it.

He blinked, shook his head, smiled. "Yes," he said. "Go ahead. Send me. Wherever you want."

"Are you certain?" Tom said.

Ferguson nodded. It surprised him, how calm he was. How completely willing, eager, unafraid, now. Father Christie, by his side, was murmuring in Latin. Praying for him? Probably. All right, let him pray. A little praying couldn't hurt. Everything was going to be okay. He was smiling. He was totally at peace. He couldn't remember ever having felt this way before.

"Everyone join hands," Tom said. His voice seemed to be coming from a vast distance. "Join hands, stand close around us, focus your minds. Help me help him to Cross, all of you. I can't do it alone, but with your help we can

manage it. And you, Ed. Put your hands in mine. The way
you did yesterday in the forest. Put your hands in mine.''

4

ELSZABET left her office, went down the hall to the double
door at the end and stepped through, out into the storm. It
was about eight in the morning and everything seemed under
control so far. She paused on the porch to check the little
communications system she was wearing. "Lew?" she said.
"Lew, can you hear me?" Transmitter and receiver and
bone-induction speaker, the three units together smaller than a
fingernail, taped just back of her right ear. Tiny microphone
mounted along her cheek. Military equipment: if there was
going to be a war today, she would have to be the general.

Arcidiacono said, "I hear you clear, Elszabet." It sounded
as if he were standing right next to her.

The rain was starting to get serious now. It was riding a stiff
wind down from the north and pounding hard against the sides
of the buildings in gusty cascades. Elszabet figured that was a
bit of luck on their side. The marchers, the tumbondé people,
were less likely to go wandering where they didn't belong if it
was raining, wasn't that so? They'd stay inside their buses and
vans and just keep right on going toward the North Pole, or
wherever it was that their prophet was leading them.

So she hoped, anyway. All the same, it seemed like a
good idea to get the energy walls up and keep them up until
the marchers had gone through. Just in case a couple of

hundred thousand strangers saw the Center sitting there at the edge of the woods looking warm and snug and decided to come in out of the wet for a while.

She said to Arcidiacono, "What's going on out there?"

"All quiet. We're still setting up the generators. You get any news from the county police about the tumbondés?"

"Just talked to them. They say the marchers haven't broken camp yet this morning."

"Where are they staying, do you know?"

"Seems like they're all over. There's one main batch of them just outside Mendo but they spread far and wide, both sides of Highway One. Closest group maybe two-point-five kilometers south and west of us."

"Jesus," said Arcidiacono. "Pretty close."

"You ready to handle it, if they start coming through in an hour or so?"

"Whenever. We'll be ready here. I'm not worrying."

"Okay," Elszabet said. "If you're not worried I'm not. Everything's going to be okay, Lew. Sure you have enough people?"

"For now," the technician said. "Little later, once they get on the move, I'll want more. So we can start shifting the equipment from place to place."

"We'll all be out there by then. I'll check back every fifteen minutes."

"Do that, yes," said Arcidiacono.

Elszabet gave the receiver a light tap, switching it over to B frequency, Dante Corelli in the gym fifty meters away. "It's me, Elszabet," she said. "Just testing. Everything okay there?"

"Pretty much. Patients are straggling in from breakfast."

"They know what's going on?"

"More or less. I've told them the general outlines. Nobody's particularly alarmed. Bill Waldstein gives each one a little shot of pax as they show up—we minimize it, we say it's just to keep them relaxed, nothing to fret about.

A lot of visions happening. Everybody here's pretty spacy right now, Elszabet.''

"I'm not surprised."

"I wonder, on account of the rain, do we really want to bring them out to the perimeter? We could just keep them all here, pax them out, couple of supervisory personnel—''

"Let's wait and see," Elszabet said. "Maybe the whole thing's going to be a false alarm anyway."

"You think so?"

"That would be nice, wouldn't it?"

"Listen," Dante said, "I'm still missing a few of them. Maybe you ought to phone up to the mess hall and get them hustling across here, okay?''

"Who's not there yet?"

"Well, April, Ed Ferguson, Father Christie. No, here comes Father Christie now. So it's just April and Ed. Otherwise the whole crew's in the gym."

"Tom there too?"

"No. No, I don't know where he is."

"We ought to know. If he turns up, call me."

"I will," Dante said.

"And I'll check on the other missing ones. I'm talking to you from right outside the mess hall now anyway. If they're in there I'll have them over to you in five minutes of less."

Elszabet walked around to the mess hall side of the GHQ building and peered in. No one in sight except one of the kids from town who cleaned up the dirty trays and swept the floor. "I'm looking for a couple of patients," she said. "April Cranshaw? Big round plump woman, about thirty years old? And Mr. Ferguson? You know which one he is?"

The boy nodded. "Sure, I know them, Dr. Lewis. I don't think either one came in for breakfast today."

"No?"

"That April, she's hard to miss, you know."

Elszabet smiled. "I'd like to find them. If they wander in

while you're still here, will you call over to the gym, tell Dante Corelli? Then send them over there.''

"Sure thing, Dr. Lewis."

"And have you seen Tom? You know, the new one, the one with the peculiar eyes?"

"Tom, yeah. He hasn't been here this morning either."

"Strange. Tom's someone who hates to miss a meal. Well, same thing there. If you see him, call Dante."

"Right, Dr. Lewis."

Elszabet went outside again. She felt curiously peaceful, an eye-of-the-hurricane kind of feeling. First thing, she thought, head over to the dorm, see if maybe April was still in bed, or Ferguson. Morning like this, they might just have decided not to get up, especially since there had been no pick-call today.

The rain whipped at her face. Nastier and nastier, almost like a real midwinter storm. The ground was soaking everything up, it was so dry after five straight months of fair weather, but if the stuff continued to come down like this they'd be sloshing around in mud by tonight. In the summer months you tended to forget, she thought, how messy the rainy season could be.

First find April and Ferguson, yes. Then track down Tom. And then she'd have to get herself out toward the front gate to see how Lew Arcidiacono was coming along with the energy-wall installation. After that it would just be a matter of waiting out the day, doing what she could to make sure that the marchers from San Diego went around the Center instead of straight through it. The marchers were a problem she didn't really need at this time, a stupid extraneous distraction. She knew that Tom was the big event that she should be dealing with right now, Tom and his visions, his almost magical powers, Tom and his galactic worlds—the worlds that she understood now, thanks to the Starprobe cameras, to be the real thing, actual authentic inhabited planets that were sending beckoning images of themselves through the strange mind of this one man of Earth—

As if on cue something tickled at the corners of Elszabet's mind. Eerie light began to glow behind her eyes. No, she thought furiously. Not now. For God's sake, not *now*.

Everything she saw was casting twin shadows, one outlined in yellow, one in reddish orange. In the sky a pale pink nebula sprawled like some great octopus across the horizon. And creatures moving around, spherical, blue-skinned, clusters of tentacles wiggling on their heads. She recognized that landscape, those stars, those spherical beings. Double Star Three was drifting into her mind. Right this minute, out here in the driving rain, as she walked from the mess hall toward the dorms, she was sliding away into the other world.

No, she thought. No. No. *No*.

She staggered a couple of steps, went lurching into a big rhododendron in the middle of the lawn, grabbed a couple of its branches and held on tight, dizzy, swaying, fighting the vision back. This is a rhododendron bush, she told herself. This is a rainy morning in October, 2103. This is Mendocino County, California, planet Earth. I am Elszabet Lewis and I am a human being native to planet Earth and I need to have all my wits about me today.

A rasping voice behind her said, "You all right, lady? You need some help?"

She swung around, startled, disoriented. Double Star Three shattered into fragments and fell away from her, and she found herself facing three strangers. Rough-looking types, nasty-looking. One with a thick black beard and deep-set eyes almost buried in black rings, one with a lean face scarred all over with the deep craters of some skin disease, and one, short and ugly with a wild thatch of red hair, who seemed even meaner than the other two.

Elszabet faced them and, as coolly as she could, brushed her hand against her hair, switching the transmitter on. It should still be tuned to B frequency. Dante Corelli would be picking it up right over there in the gym.

"Who are you?" she said. "What are you doing here?"

"You don't need to be scared, ma'am," said the one with the scarred face. "We don't mean no harm. We thought you was sick or something, hanging there on that bush."

"I asked you who you were," she said, a little more crisply. It annoyed her that the scar-faced man thought she was frightened, even though it was true. "I asked you what you were doing here."

"Well, we—we—" the one with the scars began.

"Shut up, Buffalo," the one with the black beard said. Then to Elszabet: "We were just passing through. Trying to find a friend who seems to have strayed in here."

"A friend?"

"Man named Tom, maybe you know him. Tall, skinny, a little strange-looking—"

"I know who you mean, yes. Do you know that you're on private property, Mr.—Mr.—"

"I'm Charley."

"Charley. You're with the tumbondé march, is that it?"

"You mean the San Diego mob? All those crazies? Hey, no, not us. We're just traveling through. We thought maybe we could find our friend Tom, take him with us, move along before the crazies hit. You know how many they got out there, just down the road?"

Elszabet could see Dante now emerging from the gym, two or three others with her. They were keeping back, watching cautiously, listening in on Elszabet's conversation with the three strangers. Elszabet said, "Your friend Tom's not around right now. And in any case I don't think he plans to go anywhere. What I suggest you do is take yourselves off our grounds right away, for your own good, okay? As you say, there's quite a mob just down the road, and if they break in here I can't be responsible for your safety. Besides which, you happen to be trespassing."

"You just let us talk to Tom a minute, then we—"

"No."

Dante was gesturing as if to say, Give me a signal, I'll knock them out. Dante was terrific with the anesthetic-dart gun at almost any range up to a hundred meters. But Elszabet wasn't so sure. Certainly these three were armed: knives, spikes, maybe guns. That looked like a laser bracelet on the black-bearded man's wrist. If Dante opened fire, one of them might have time to fire back and it wouldn't be anesthetic pellets he'd be firing.

The red-haired one said, "Charley, look behind us."

"What's back there, Stidge?"

"Couple of people. Watching us."

Charley nodded. Very carefully he turned and looked.

"What you want to do?" Stidge asked. "Grab this one, make her help us find Tom?"

"No," said Charley. "Nothing like that, Stidge." To Elszabet he said, "We don't mean no trouble. We're going to move along. You see our friend Tom, you give him our regards, okay?" He was gesturing to the others, and they were starting to slip away toward the woods, the scar-faced one first, then Stidge. Charley remained where he was another moment, until the other two were out of sight in the trees. "Hope we didn't trouble you any, ma'am," he said. "We're just passing through, on our way. All right?" He was edging away as he spoke. "You tell Tom that Charley and the boys were looking for him, okay?"

Then he was gone too. Elszabet realized that she was shivering: soaked through and more than a little shaken up. A delayed reaction was sweeping over her. Her teeth chattered. Some flickering fragments of space visions were dancing at the outer reaches of her mind, like pale transparent flames dancing on the embers of a bonfire.

Dante came running toward her, Teddy Lansford just behind.

"Everything all right?" Dante asked.

Elszabet brushed at the rain streaming across her forehead

and fought back a shudder. "I'll be okay. I'm a little wobbly, I guess."

"Who were they?"

"I think they were the scratchers Tom used to travel with. Looking for him. They want to get out of the neighborhood before the tumbondé people pass through and they want to take Tom with them wherever they're going."

"Grubby bastards," Dante said. "As if we didn't have enough problems to deal with today, we have to have scratchers too."

"Should we call the police?" Lansford asked.

Dante laughed. "Police? What police? Any police this county has, they're down by Mendo trying to control the tumbondé mob this morning. No, we'll have to watch out for those three ourselves. In our spare time." She looked at Elszabet. "You're still pretty shaky, aren't you?"

"I was trying to sidetrack a space vision. And then I turned around and there were three scary-looking strangers standing right behind me. Yeah, I'm still shaky."

"Maybe this'll help," said Dante. She stepped closer and put her hands on Elszabet's back and shoulders, and began to move things around in there, rearranging bones and muscles and ligaments as though she were shuffling papers on a desk. Elszabet gasped in surprise and pain at first, but then she felt the tension and distress beginning to leave her, and she swayed back against Dante, letting it happen. Gradually a sense of some balance returned to her. "There," Dante said finally. "That a little better now?"

"Oh, my. Absolutely tremendous."

"Loosen up the back, it loosens up the mind. Hey, did you ever find out where April and Ferguson were?"

Elszabet put her hand to her lips. "God. I forgot all about them. I was on my way over to the dorm when the vision started to hit and then—"

Suddenly the voice of Lew Arcidiacono said out of the

speaker just back of her right ear, "Elszabet? I think it's starting now. We've got the word that there's a whole mess of tumbondé people not very far down the road and they're probably going to be heading smack in our direction very soon."

Elszabet switched to A frequency. "Terrific. How are you doing with the energy walls?"

"We've got a solid line of defense up all along the probable line of approach. But if the march gets sloppy they may begin to come at us from one of the unshielded sides. I can use all the extra personnel you can send down here now."

"Right. I'll have Dante head out your way with everyone she has. Stay in touch, Lew."

"What's happening?" Dante asked.

"They're getting near us," Elszabet said. "The tumbondé crowd, just a little way down the road."

"Here we go, huh?"

"We'll be able to handle it. But Lew's calling for help on the front line. Take everybody from the gym and go on down there pronto, okay? I'll look in at the dorm for April and Ferguson and meet you there in five minutes."

"I'm on my way," Dante said.

Elszabet summoned up a fragile grin. "Thanks for the backrub," she said.

The dormitory building lay twenty paces to her right. She trotted over, slipping and sliding on the muddied path and rain-slicked grass. The storm was getting worse all the time. Half-stumbling, Elszabet pulled herself up onto the dorm porch and went clomping into the building, leaving big muddy tracks. "Hello?" she called. "Anybody here?"

All quiet. She wandered down the hallway, peering into this room and that, the little dens where her unhappy patients passed their unhappy days. No sign of anyone around. At the far end of the hall she paused at number seven, Ed Ferguson's room. As she touched her hand to the doorplate she heard odd crooning sounds coming from inside, deep, heavy, slow.

April squatted crosslegged in the middle of the floor, rocking steadily back and forth, singing tonelessly to herself, sobbing a little. Behind her, half-obscured by the big woman's bulk, Ed Ferguson was sitting motionless on the floor, leaning against one of the beds, his head thrown back and his arms dangling alongside his hips. He looked drugged.

Elszabet went first to April and dug her fingers into the soft flesh of the big woman's shoulder, trying to slow her rocking.

"April? April, it's me, Elszabet. It's all right. Don't be afraid. What's the matter, April?"

"Nothing. There isn't anything the matter." Thick husky voice, heavy with emotion. "I'm fine, Elszabet." Tears running down her face. She would not look up. Rocking even harder now, she began to sing again. "It's raining, it's pouring, the old man is snoring—"

The song gave way to the sort of rhythmic humming a woman who was holding a baby might make, and then to unintelligible crooning. But April seemed calm, at least. She seemed lost in some private world. Elszabet rose and walked over to Ferguson. He didn't move at all. The look on his face was unfamiliar, a strangely benign expression that completely altered his normal tense and sour appearance; at a quick glance she might not have been able to recognize this man as the grim, bitter, gloomy Ed Ferguson. He was transfigured. His eyes were wide and shining with some ineffable bliss; his face was relaxed, almost slack; his mouth was drawn back in a broad smile of the deepest happiness.

So extraordinary was that beatific expression of Ferguson's that it was another moment before Elszabet realized that his eyes were remaining open without blinking, that he didn't seem to be drawing a breath.

She knelt beside him, alarmed. "Ed?" she said sharply, shaking him. "Ed? Can you hear me?" She put her hand to his chest and felt for a heartbeat. She listened for the sounds of breathing. She grasped his limp cool wrist and searched as best she knew how for a pulse. Nothing. Nothing. Nothing at all.

She looked across at April, who was rocking harder and harder. She was singing another children's song, one that seemed almost familiar, but her voice was so blurred and indistinct that Elszabet was unable to make out any of the words. "April, what happened to Ed Ferguson?"

"To Ed Ferguson," April repeated very carefully, as if examining those sounds to discover some possible meaning in them.

"To Ed, yes. I want to know what happened to Ed."

"To Ed. To Ed. Oh, *Ed*." April giggled. "He made the Crossing. Tom helped him do it. We all held hands, and Tom sent him to the Double Kingdom."

"He what?"

"It was very easy, very smooth. Ed just let go. He just dropped the body, that's all he did. And off he went to the Double Kingdom."

Good God, Elszabet thought.

"Who was here with you then?"

"Oh, everybody."

"*Who?*"

"Well, There was Tom, and Father Christie, and Tomás and . . ." April's voice trailed off. She disappeared once more into gibberish and began rocking again. In the middle of it she became still and turned to Elszabet and said in a completely lucid voice, "I'm scared, Elszabet. Tom said that we're all going to be going over there soon. To the stars. Is that right, Elszabet? It's the time, he said. He has the full power now, and he's going to send us all, one by one, just like he sent Ed. I suppose I'll go soon. Isn't that so? I don't know where I'll be going, though. I don't know what it'll be like for me there. It can't be any worse than it's been for me here, can it? But even so, I'm scared. I'm so scared, Elszabet." And she began to sob again, and then to sing once more.

Elszabet shook Ferguson again. His head lolled over.

Dead? Really? The idea stunned her. She felt her cheeks flush hot with guilt. Ferguson, dead? One of my patients, dead? That lolling head, those sightless eyes. Elszabet shivered. All this talk of Crossings, of shining alien worlds, seemed bizarre and absurd to her now against this ugly unanswerable reality. Over and over again she heard herself thinking, *One of my patients is dead.* No patient had ever died at the Center before. Suddenly—with all the chaos swirling outside, the riot and the skulking scratchers and Tom going around doing God only knew what kind of witchcraft—there was just one thought in Elszabet's head, which was that someone who had been entrusted to her care had died. All the work she had done this year with Ferguson, the elaborate tests, the closely watched charts, the counselling, the carefully monitored pick program—and there he was. Dead.

Maybe he wasn't, not really. Maybe he was just in some kind of deep trance. She was no doctor. She had never seen a dead person this close. There were states of consciousness, she knew, that seemed just like death but were merely suspended animation. Maybe he was in one of those. She said to April, "What exactly did Tom do to him, can you tell me? When he made the Crossing. What was it like?"

But April was far away. Elszabet crouched beside Ferguson, feeling numb. Rain drummed hard on the rooftop. Somewhere down near the main road a huge mob of cultists was wandering around just outside the Center, and on the other side in the woods three sinister-looking scratchers were lurking about, and Tom had gone God knew where, and here was Ferguson dead or maybe in a trance, and April—

She heard footsteps in the hall. Jesus, what now?

Someone out there calling her name. "Elszabet? *Elszabet?*"
Bill Waldstein, it sounded like.

"I'm in room seven."

Waldstein came running in at full tilt, nearly tripped over
April, and brought himself to an abrupt skidding halt.
"Dante was worried about you and sent me over to see how
you were doing," he said, then noticed Ferguson. "What
the hell—?"

"I think he's dead, Bill. But you'd know better. Please
take a look at him . . ."

Waldstein stared. "Dead?"

"I think so. But check it. You're a doctor, not me."

Waldstein bent over Ferguson, probing him here and
there. "Like an empty sack," he said. "There's nobody
here."

"Dead, you mean?"

"Sometimes it's hard to be completely sure just by
looking. But he seems plenty dead to me. Nobody home at
all. Christ, look at that empty grin on his face."

"April says that Tom showed him how to make the
Crossing."

"The Crossing?"

"He's gone off to some star, April says. They all held
hands and sent him somewhere."

Waldstein glanced at April: rocking, crooning, sobbing.
He turned his head slowly from side to side. "Ferguson
went to another star, you're telling me? To another *star?*
Jesus, Elszabet!"

"I don't know where he is. I've told you what April told
me. He's dead, isn't he? What from? If he *didn't* make the
Crossing, what did he die of, a man in apparent perfect
health? She said they all held hands, Tom, Father Christie,
Tomás—"

"And you believe this?"

"I believe they did what April says they did, yes. That

they joined hands and performed some sort of rite. And I even half-believe that Tom really did send him off to one of the star worlds . . . more than half-believe, maybe. Look at his face, Bill. Look at his face. Have you ever seen such a blissful expression? It's the way somebody would look who knows he's going straight to heaven. But Ferguson didn't believe in heaven.''

"And now he's on some star?''

"Maybe he is," Elszabet said. "How would I know?''

Waldstein stared at her. "We ought to find Tom and kill him right this minute.''

"What are you saying, Bill?''

"Listen, there are no two ways about this. Are you going to let him wander around this place murdering people?''

Elszabet gestured helplessly. She didn't know what answer to make. Murder? That wasn't the right word, she thought. Tom wouldn't murder anyone. But yet—but yet—if Tom had touched Ferguson as April had said, and Ferguson had died—

Waldstein said, "If Tom is for real, if he's genuinely able to lift people out of their bodies and ship them who knows where and leave nothing but an empty shell behind, then he's the most dangerous man in the world. He's a one-man horror show. He can just walk around from place to place, making Crossings or whatever for people until there's nobody left alive. Just snap his fingers and send people to the goddamn stars—you think that's a good thing? You think that's something we should allow him to do?'' She looked at him but still couldn't find anything to say. He went on, "That's if you *believe* any of this crazy garbage. And if you don't, well, we still have the problem of finding out how he managed to kill Ferguson and—''

There was a sudden crackling noise out of the speaker taped behind Elszabet's ear. She heard Arcidiacono's voice, ragged, muffled, almost hysterical.

"Say that again?" she told him.

Waldstein began to speak. She held up her hand to shush him. "Not you, Bill." Into her microphone she said, "I didn't hear what you were just saying, Lew. Slow down. Give it to me clearly."

"I said Tomás Menendez just switched off one of the energy walls and the tumbondés are pouring through our line."

"Oh, Lew, no. *No*."

"We had everything under control. Colossal mob of them out there, but they couldn't get in. Menendez was carrying generators around. Working as hard as anybody. Then he seemed to spot someone he knew out there in that mob, and he yelled that he was the opener of the gate, or something. And he opened it. He turned the wall right off. We've got thousands of them coming into the Center right this minute, Elszabet. Millions of them. I don't know. They're all over the place. Another two minutes, they'll be down your way."

"Oh, my God," she said. A strange tranquility began to come over her. She felt almost like laughing.

"What's he telling you?" Waldstein asked.

Elszabet closed her eyes and shook her head. "The wall is down, the tumbondé people are coming in. Oh, Jesus, Bill. That's the finish. Here we go. Jesus, here we go."

Eight

With a heart of furious fancies
  Whereof I am commander,
With a burning spear and a horse of air
  To the wilderness I wander.
By a knight of ghosts and shadows
  I summoned am to tourney
Ten leagues beyond the wide world's end
  Methinks it is no journey.

Yet will I sing, "Any food, any feeding,
  Feeding, drink or clothing?
    Come, dame or maid
    Be not afraid,
Poor Tom will injure nothing."

—Tom O'Bedlam's Song

JASPIN hunched forward, gripping the stick as tightly as he could, using body English to keep the car from flipping over or skidding into a tree. There was no road any more. They were driving across slick slippery sodden grass, some sort of lawn churned into a quagmire by the wheels of the vehicles ahead of him. The rain was coming down so hard it flowed across the windshield in thick streams.

Jill said, "I'm sure this is where my sister is. Find a place to park and I'm going to get out and look for her."

"Park? With umpteen thousand cars coming right behind me?"

"I don't care. You pull up by one of those buildings. I'm going to go in there and get her. She isn't right in the head. If I don't protect her, somebody's going to find her and rape her or maybe kill her. This isn't a procession any more, Barry. It's a crazy mob now."

"So I notice."

"Well, you stop and let me go find April."

"Sure," he said, nudging the brake panel. "You can get out right here and go find her."

The car squiggled over the oozing mud and slid to a stop practically up against some big leafy bush. He kept the engine running.

"Park by one of the buildings," Jill said. "Not here."

"I'm not parking anywhere," Jaspin told her. "I'm going to try to circle around and find some road out of here up that way. But you go on. You go look for your sister."

"You're not going to stop?"

"Look," he said, "this is a dead end, you see? Christ only knows why the Senhor turned in this way, but what we have is some buildings right in front of us and a goddamned redwood forest behind the buildings, and in back of us we've got the whole tumbondé pilgrimage rumbling forward like a herd of maddened dinosaurs. I stay in here, I'm going to get squeezed flat up against those buildings or those trees. So you go look for your sister. I'm going to make a left turn up that dirt road and keep on going as far as I can, and if the road gives out I'm going to get out of my car and go on foot. Because what's going to happen in here this morning is the Black Hole of Calcutta. People are going to get trampled by the thousands. Now you get out and you go look for your sister, if that's what you want. Come on. Out."

She gave him a venomous look. "How will I find you again?"

"That's your problem." Jaspin pointed off to the left. "You head that way, and maybe when things calm down a little I'll come back and look for you. Maybe. Go on, now."

"You bastard," she said. She glared at him again. Then she shook her head and got out of the car. He watched her for a moment, running off toward the old weatherbeaten gray wooden buildings just ahead. Instantly she was soaked through. She looked like a giant half-drowned chicken sprinting through the rain.

He wondered about Lacy.

She had her own car, somewhere back in the main body of the procession. Not too far back, he hoped. He had told her last night, when the forecast of rain came in, that she should try to move forward, drive as close to the front as she could. He knew the rain was going to scramble everything up, though he hadn't expected this, the sudden swerve off Highway One onto the county road, the blundering crashing intrusion on this peaceful rural neighborhood. It was impossible to figure what, if anything, the Senhor had had in mind, turning in this direction. He had just turned. There had been energy walls blocking their way, and then for some reason they went down and everybody went rolling right on. And now here they were. What a lousy mess, Jaspin thought.

Jill disappeared between two of the buildings. Two to one I'll never see her again, he told himself. Well, what the hell. He got the car moving again. He felt the wheels digging ruts in the lawn and heard sucking sounds as they pulled free of the muck. Easy, easy—there, he was on a gravel road now, heading up along the front of a shallow-crested hill—just keep your head down and go right on slithering until you're out of here, kid—

But there was no place for him to go. The gravel road ended at a kind of garbage dump, and there was just what looked like a vegetable garden on the far side and then the forest. Dead end no matter where you went. Jaspin looked back and saw hundreds of cars and vans piling up insanely in the triangular area between the two groups of buildings, with more and more and more coming on from the west. The ones to the rear didn't seem to realize that there was no road in front, and kept on going, grinding blithely on into

what was sure to be the biggest vehicular cataclysm in
human history.

It didn't make sense to drive back down the gravel road
and join the frolic. Jaspin abandoned his car at the edge of
the vegetable garden and made his way through the down-
pour as far as an enormous wide-branching tree. Standing
under it, he was able to keep more or less dry, and he had a
good view of the carnage.

They were just ramming helplessly into each other down
there, the big vans going right up over some of the small
cars. Like dinosaurs, yes, Jaspin thought, exactly like a
herd of dinosaurs running amok. He saw the Senhor's bus
and the bus of the Inner Host right in the middle of it all.
Banners were waving in the rain on top of the Senhor's bus,
and someone had mounted the statues of Narbail and Rei
Ceupassear on the hood. The giant papier-mâché images
were beginning to melt.

Jaspin wished he'd been driving with Lacy instead of Jill.
At least that way he would know where she was, now. Jill
probably wouldn't have cared. But the Senhor did. The
Senhor had found out that he was getting it on with
someone other than his divinely chosen wife Jill, and the
Senhor hadn't liked it. Bacalhau himself had conveyed that
information to Jaspin: You touch the red-haired woman, you
make the Senhor very angry. So Jaspin and Lacy had been
going easy the last couple of days. It was never wise to
make the Senhor angry. And now Lacy was down there lost
in all that madness and—

No. There she was. Clearly visible, red hair blazing in the
midst of a crowd of maybe a thousand people who had left
their cars and were lurching around chaotically on the lawn.

"Lacy! *Lacy!*"

Somehow she heard him. He saw her looking about. He
jumped up and down, wigwagging frantically until she saw
him.

"Barry?"

"Get out of there," he called. She started up the gravel road toward him, and he ran to meet her. She was drenched, her tight neat ringlets uncurling, her hair plastered to her skull. Jaspin held her for a moment, trying to steady her. She was quivering, whether from fright or chill he wasn't sure.

Her eyes looked wild. "What happened? Why did we come in here?"

"God only knows. But this better be the Seventh Place, because we aren't going to go any farther, for damned sure." Sadly he said, "Holy Jesus, what a catastrophe this is turning into."

"Do you know what this place is?"

"Some kind of boarding school, you think?"

"It's the Nepenthe Center," she said. "The mindpick place. I saw the sign when we went through the gate. This is the place where my old partner Ed Ferguson was undergoing treatment."

"Well, it's out of business as of right now," said Jaspin. "It's going to be a complete ruin in a little while. Look how they're just swarming right through it."

"I've got to find Ed," Lacy said.

"Are you kidding?"

"I mean it. He's probably wandering around dazed in that mob. I want to get him out and up here before he gets hurt. He lives in some kind of dormitory. We ought to be able to find it."

"Lacy, it's crazy to go down there."

"Ed may be in trouble."

"But is he worth risking your life for? I thought you said he was a louse."

"He was my partner, Barry. Louse or not, I need to try to get him out. It's not that I love him or even like him. But I can't just stand by and watch this place get torn apart with him in it and not try to help him.''

"Like Jill," Jaspin said. "Jill's in there already, looking for her sister."

"I'm going in there too. You going to wait here?"

"No," Jaspin said. "I'll come with you. What the hell."

2

Buffalo had been saying all morning, We got to get out of here, Charley, that mob is coming, that mob is going to stampede right through this place. But Charley had said no, let's hold on a little longer, Tom's got to be around here somewhere and I want to take him.

Stidge couldn't understand either of them. That Buffalo, he was just a shit-ass. He looked real tough, sure, but inside him there was just brown shit from head to knees. You hit a little trouble, first thing he wants to do is clear out. Charley, now, he wasn't really afraid of anything—say that for him— but sometimes it was real hard to figure him. Like this thing he had for the looney, Tom. Take him along, all the way from the far side of the Valley, clear to San Franciso, now up here to Mendo, for what? For goddamned what? Gives me the creeps, Stidge thought, just looking at that guy's eyes. And now Charley waiting around in the forest in the rain trying to find him, take him along again. Made no sense at all.

Charley said, "They had energy walls up. Then they took

them down. I wonder why they did a thing like that. They're wide open, now.''

"Maybe Tom did it," Buffalo said. "Found the generator and shut it down, let them all come running right through."

"Why'd he want to do that?" Charley asked. "I don't think he would. Must have been someone else, or maybe the power just conked out on its own. Tom likes this place. He wouldn't want a mob running over it."

Stidge said, "Man's crazy. Crazy man would do anything."

Charley grinned. "You think Tom's crazy, Stidge? Shows how little you know."

"Says he's crazy himself, out of his own mouth. And the visions he has—"

"Crazy like a fox," said Buffalo.

"Yeah," Charley said. "Listen, Stidge, those visions of his, they're not crazy, they're true visions. He sees right into the stars. That make any sense to you? Nah, I bet it don't. But I tell you, he's not crazy. Only way he can keep from scaring people with that power of his, he has to say he's crazy. But you can't understand stuff like that, can you? All you understand is hurting people. Times I wish I never met you, Stidge."

"All I understand," Stidge said, "is that one of these days that Tom's going to bug me too much, I'm going to put a spike in him. All summer long you been riding me, Stidge don't do this, Stidge don't do that, Stidge let Tom alone. I'm pretty sick of your Tom, you hear me, Charley?"

"And I'm pretty sick of you," Charley said. "I tell you one more time, anything happen to Tom, you're done, Stidge. You're done." He turned toward Buffalo. "You know what we ought to do? We ought to take one more look around those buildings, find Tom, pick up anything light enough to carry that might be worth something and get the hell away from here."

"Yeah," Buffalo said. "Before they come rampaging into the woods and tip over our van or something."

Stidge said, "Instead of Tom, the one we ought to find is that woman, the tall one we saw before. Or that hot-looking one who was out on the road with the limping guy. Find one of them, bring her along, that's what makes sense to me."

"Count on you, saying something like that," said Charley. "Just what we need, kidnap a woman now. Tom's what we want. Find Tom, get away from here. You clear on that, Stidge?"

"I don't know why the hell—"

"You clear on that, Stidge?"

"Yeah," Stidge said. "I hear you, man."

"I hope you do. Come on, now."

"You two go look for Tom," Stidge said. "I got another idea. You see that bus out there, the one with the cockeyed statues on top, all the flags? I think I'll take a sniff in there. I bet it's the treasure bus."

"What treasure you talking about?" Charley asked.

"The marchers' treasure. I bet it's their holy bus, all kinds of rubies and emeralds and diamonds in there. I'll just take a little look. That okay with you, Charley? While you're hunting around for Tom?"

Charley was silent a moment. Finally he nodded. "Sure," he said. "Grab yourself a sack of rubies."

3

JUST as Jill stepped up on the porch of the long wooden building that she thought might be the dormitory, a lanky dark-haired man came running out of it and slammed straight into her. They collided with a solid thunk and went bouncing back from each other, and they stood there for a moment looking at each other, both of them a little stunned.

He was wearing a white coat and had the look of someone who might be on the staff. "Sorry," Jill said. "Hey, can you tell me, is this where they keep the patients?"

"Get out of my way," he said. He had a sort of crazed look in his eye.

"I just want to know, is this where—"

"What do you want here? What are all you people doing here? Get *out*." He waved his arms at her. It was the craziest thing she had ever seen.

"I'm looking for my sister. April Cranshaw. She's a patient here and I want to—"

But he was gone, sprinting past her like a maniac, disappearing into the storm. All right, Jill thought. Be like that. See if I care. She wondered how crazy the patients here must be, if that was what the staff was like. Man looked like a doctor, maybe a psychiatrist. They were all crazy anyway. Of course, the fact that thousands of cars had just driven onto the grounds and the whole Mongol horde was charging around on the lawn out there might have upset him a little.

She went into the building. Yes, it did look like a dorm. Bulletin board up, notices posted, a lot of little rooms opening off the hallway.

"April?" she called. "April, honey, it's Jill. I came to get you, April. Come on out, if you're in here. April? April?"

She looked in one room after another. Empty. Empty. Empty. Then in a room down at the end of the corridor she saw a man sitting on the floor, but he was either drunk or dead, she couldn't tell which. She shook him, but he didn't wake up. "Hey, you. You! I'm trying to find my sister." But it was like talking to a chair. She started to go out, but then she heard sounds coming from the bathroom, someone singing or humming. "Hello?" Jill said. "Whoever's in there."

"You want to use the bathroom? I can't let you. I have to be in it. I'm supposed to stay in here until Dr. Waldstein comes back, or Dr. Lewis."

"April? That you, April?"

"Dr. Lewis?"

"This is Jill. For Christ's sake, your sister Jill. Open the door, April."

"I have to stay in here until Dr. Waldstein or Dr.—"

"So stay in there. But open the door. I need to pee, April. Do you want me to pee in my pants? Open it."

A moment of silence. Then the door opened.

"Jill?"

It was like the voice of a little girl. But the woman who was behind it was like a mountain. Jill had forgotten how huge her older sister was; either that or April had really been piling it on since she'd come up here. Some of both, Jill thought. April looked weird, too—weirder than Jill remembered, totally spaced-out, her eyes gleaming and strange, her face very white, the fat cheeks sagging.

"Are you here to help me make the Crossing?" April asked. "Mr. Ferguson made the Crossing a little while ago. And Tom says we all will. We'll go to the stars today. I don't know if I want to go to the stars, Jill. Is that what happens today?"

"What happens today is that I'm going to get you out of this place," Jill said. "It isn't safe here any more. Give me your hand. Here. Come on, April. Nice April. Pretty April."

"I'm supposed to stay in the bathroom. Dr. Waldstein is coming right back and he'll give me an injection so I'll feel better."

"I just saw Dr. Waldstein running like a lunatic in the

other direction," Jill said. "Come on. You can trust me. Let's go for a little walk, April."

"Where will they send me? To the Nine Suns? To the Green World?"

"You know about them?" Jill asked, surprised.

"I see them every night. I can almost see them now. The Sphere of Light. The Blue Star."

"That's right. Maguali-ga will open the gate. Chungirá-He-Will-Come, he will come. There's nothing to worry about. Give me your hand, April."

"Dr. Waldstein—"

"Dr. Waldstein asked me to get you and bring you outside," Jill said. "I just spoke with him. Tall man, dark hair, white coat? He said, Tell April I won't have time to come right back, so you get her."

"He said that?" April smiled. She put her hand in Jill's and took a step or two out of the bathroom. Come on, April. Come on. That's right. Jill led her sister across the room, past the dead or unconscious man sitting on the floor, toward the door. Out into the hall, down the corridor. They were almost to the exit when the outside door opened and two people came running in. Barry, for Christ's sake. And that red-headed woman of his.

"Jill?"

"I found my sister. This is April."

"Then this is the dormitory?" the redhead asked.

"Right. You looking for someone too?"

"My partner. I told you, he was a patient here."

"Nobody else around in here. No, wait, there's one guy. In the last room on the left, down the hall. I think he's drunk, though. Might even be dead. Sitting on the floor, big grin on his face. What's happening outside?"

"The Inner Host is trying to get everything calm," Jaspin said. "They've fanned out through the crowd, carrying the holy images. It's almost a riot but they may just be able to quiet things down."

"And the Senhor? The Senhora?"

"In their bus, far as I know."

Jill said, "The Senhor ought to come out. That's the only way to quiet things."

"I'm going down the hall," the redheaded woman said.

Jill told Jaspin, "You ought to go to the Senhor, ask him to speak to the crowd. Otherwise you know it's all going to turn berserk, and then what happens to the pilgrimage? Go talk to him, Barry. He'll listen to you."

"He won't listen to anyone. You know that."

From down the hall the woman called, "Can you come here, Barry? I found Ed, but I don't think he's alive."

"He made the Crossing," April said, like someone talking in her sleep.

"I better go," Jaspin said. "What are you going to do?"

"Take April, find a safe place, wait for everything to settle down."

"Isn't this a safe place right here?"

"Not when ten thousand people decide to come in out of the rain all at once. Old rickety building like this, they'll knock it right over."

The redheaded woman was returning, now. "He *is* dead," she said. "I wonder what happened. Poor Ed. He was a bastard, but still—dead?—"

"Come on, April," Jill said. "We got to get out of here."

She led her sister around Jaspin and out on the dormitory porch. The scene in front of her was wilder than ever. Cars were stacking up like flood debris. People everywhere, yelling, bewildered, churning around like bees in a hive. No room for anybody to move: they were all butted up one against the next. In the center of everything was the Senhor's bus. In front of it the eleven members of the Inner

Host could be seen, all decked out in their high tumbondé
drag and carrying the soggy images of the great gods. They
were moving slowly forward, cutting a path through the
throng. People were trying to give way before them but it
was hard: they had no place to go.

Then Jill saw a stocky little man with a big mop of red
hair climb up the side of the Senhor's bus, do something to
the protective screen on one of the windows that somehow
disconnected it, and go wriggling inside.

"Oh, Jesus," she said. "Barry? Barry? Come on out
here! It's important!"

Jaspin poked his head out the door. "What is it?"

"The Senhor," Jill said. "I just saw some kind of
scratcher break into his bus. The Host is out marching the
statues around, and nobody's guarding the Senhor, and
somebody just broke into the bus. Come on. We've got to
do something."

"Us?"

"Who else? April, you stay here until we get back, you
understand? Don't go anywhere. Not anywhere at all." Jill
beckoned fiercely to Jaspin. "Come on, will you? Come
on."

4

Tom felt the ecstasy rising and rising and rising. It was as
though all the worlds were coming to him at once, the light
of a thousand suns illuminating his spirit, Ellullilimiilu and

Nine Suns and the Double Kingdom and all the myriad
capitals of the Poro and the Zygerone and the Kusereen
flooding through him at the same time. It seemed to him that
even the awesome ancient godlike Theluvara themselves
were warming his soul from their eyrie at the farthest
reaches of space.

He had done it. He had initiated the Time of the Crossing
at last. He still quivered with the power of the sensation that
had engulfed him at the moment when he had felt the soul
of that man, that Ed, rising from his body and arching
upward, soaring toward its destination in the distant galaxies.

Now, ablaze with joy, Tom wandered like a Blade of the
Imperium through the Center, from one deserted building to
the next. Two of his followers were with them, two of those
who had loaned him their strength when he had lifted that
man, that Ed, to his Crossing. But there had been two
others when they had done that, the Mexican man and the
heavy-set woman, and they had disappeared when all the
shouting and excitement began.

I need to find them, Tom thought. I may not be strong
enough with just these two to undertake the rest of the
Crossings.

The strength that he had received from the other four,
when he had sent the man to the stars, had been essential.
That he knew. It had taken immense energy to achieve the
Crossing. In the instant of the separation of Ferguson's body
and his soul Tom had been able to feel every particle of his
own vitality at risk. It had been like the dimming of the
lights in a room when too much energy was required at one
time. And then the other four, the Mexican and the heavy-
set woman and the artificial woman and the priest, had
come to his rescue, had sent their own power roaring
through the chain of linked hands, and Tom had been able to
accomplish the Crossing for Ferguson. There were other
Crossings now to do. He had to find the missing two.

Prowling from building to building, he scarcely noticed the rain. He was vaguely aware of the great mob of strangers that had erupted into the Center grounds and was crashing about in the open space between the dormitory and the staff cabins, but that didn't seem important. Whoever they were, they meant nothing to Tom. In a little while everything would be calm again, and all these frantic strangers would be setting forth on their journeys to the stars.

A voice at Tom's elbow said, "It was the real thing, wasn't it? The actual Crossing?"

Tom looked down and saw the priest. "Yes."

"Where did he go, do you know? Ferguson."

"The Double Kingdom," Tom said. "I'm certain of it."

"And which is that, then?"

"One sun is blue, and one is red. It is a world of the Poro, who are subject to the Zygerone. Who are ruled by the Kusereen, who are the highest masters of all, the kings of the universe. They have gathered him in. He is among them at this moment."

"Already there, do you think?" Alleluia asked. "So far away?"

"The journey is an instant one," Tom said. "When we Cross, we move at the speed of thought."

"One sun is blue, one is red," Father Christie murmured. "I know that place! I've seen it!"

"You'll see them all," said Tom. He spread out his arms to them. Down below on the lawn, cars and trucks were smashing against each other with idiotic fury. "Come, follow me. We'll go out there and find other people who are ready to Cross, and we'll guide them to their new homes. But first we have to see where our other helpers have gone. The fat woman, the Mexican—"

"There's April," Father Christie said. "Outside the dormitory."

Tom nodded. She was standing on the porch in the rain, turning from side to side, smiling uncertainly. Tom ran over to her. "We need you. For making the rest of the Crossings."

"I'm supposed to wait here for my sister."

"No," Tom said. "Come with us."

"Jill said she'd be right back. She went down that way, where all the people are running around and shouting. Are you going to send me to some planet?"

"Afterward," Tom said. "First you'll help to send others. And then, when I can spare you, I'll send you after them." He reached for her hand. Her fingers were plump and limp and cold, like sausages. Her hand lay squidlike in his. He tugged at her. "Come. Come. There's work for us to do." In a slow shuffling way she followed him out into the rain.

5

THE lawn in front of the dorm was a sea of mud. Jaspin, sloshing along behind Jill, had a sudden vision of it all turning to quicksand, everybody sinking down beneath the surface of the earth and disappearing, and the whole place restored to peace again.

Jill was moving like a demon, clearing the way, shoving, pushing, elbowing. Jaspin followed along in her wake. A kind of general screaming was going on, nothing coherent, simply an all-purpose roar of confusion that sounded like the grinding of giant machinery. Little openings formed in the crowd, just for a moment, and closed again. A couple of times Jaspin stumbled and nearly went down, but he kept his balance by grabbing the nearest arm and hanging on. If you fall you die, he thought. Already he could see people crawling around at ground level, dazed, unable to get up, vanishing in a forest of legs. Once it seemed to him that he had trampled someone himself. But he didn't dare look down.

"This way," Jill yelled. She was practically to the Senhor's bus now.

Someone's flailing arm caught him in the mouth. Jaspin felt a jolt of pain and tasted salty blood. He struck back instantly, automatically, bringing the sides of his hands down like hatchets on the man's shoulders. Maybe not even the one who had bumped him, he realized. He heard a grunt. Jaspin couldn't remember the last time he had hit anyone. When he was nine, ten years old, maybe. Strange how satisfying it felt, striking out like that in response to the pain.

Just ahead Jill was struggling with a big hysterical farmboy-looking guy who had caught hold of her right in front of the door to the bus. "Maguali-ga, Maguali-ga," he was roaring, gripping her with his arms around her waist. He didn't seem to be defending the Senhor's bus or doing anything else that had any purpose; he was just out of control. Jaspin came up behind him and hooked his arm around the big man's throat. He squeezed hard until he heard a little hoarse yoiking gagging sound.

"Let go," Jaspin said. "Just take your hands off her."

The man nodded. He let go and Jaspin swung him around and heaved, sending him reeling off in the other direction. Jill dashed up the steps and into the bus, Jaspin right behind her.

The interior of the bus was an island of weird tranquility in the maelstrom of chaos. Dark and silent, smelling of sour incense. Flickering candles. The heavy draperies seemed to filter out the drumming of the rain and the booming cries of the mob. Cautiously Jaspin and Jill moved to the rear of the antechamber and pulled back the brocaded curtains that concealed the middle section of the bus, Senhor Papamacer's chapel.

"Look, there he is," Jill whispered. "Oh, thank god! Is he all right, do you think?"

The Senhor appeared to be in a trance. He sat immobile in his familiar lotus pose, face to the wall, staring rigidly at an image of Chungirá-He Will-Come. Around his neck was the enormous golden breastplate, studded with emeralds and rubies, that he wore only on the most solemn occasions. Plainly he was off on some other world. Jaspin started to go over to him; but he heard a sound like a panicky whimpering cry coming from the farthest room, the living quarters of the Senhor and the Senhora. A woman, crying out in some unknown language—an unmistakable plea for help—

Jill turned to him. "The Senhora's in there, Barry—"

"Yeah." He took a deep breath and lifted the curtain.

On the far side, the innermost kingdom of the Senhor, everything was in disarray. The draperies were dangling, the wooden images of Maguali-ga and Chungirá-He-Will-Come had been knocked over, and the Senhor's storage cabinets were overturned. The contents of the cabinets had been spilled out helter-skelter onto the floor—ceremonial robes, ornate helmets and sashes and boots, all the flamboyant regalia of the tumbondé rites.

In the rear corner of the bus Senhora Aglaibahi stood backed up against the wall. Just in front of her was the stocky red-headed scratcher, the one whom Jill had seen clambering into the side window of the bus. The Senhora's white sari was ripped down the front and her heavy breasts, gleaming with sweat, had tumbled into view. Her eyes were bright with terror. The scratcher was holding her by one wrist and was trying to get hold of the other. Probably he had come into the bus with burglary in mind, but there must not have been anything here that he considered worth taking, so he was turning his attention now to rape.

"Leave her alone, you son of a bitch," Jill said in a voice of such ferocity that Jaspin was momentarily astounded by it.

The scratcher whirled around. His eyes went from Jill to Jaspin and back to Jill. It was the look of a cornered beast. "Watch it," Jaspin said. "He's going to come right at us."

"Stay back," the little man said. He was still gripping Senhora Aglaibahi by the wrist. "Get over there, by the wall. I'm getting out of here and you aren't going to try to stop me."

Jaspin now saw a weapon in his other hand, one of those things they called spikes, deadly little things that delivered lethal electrical charges.

"Careful," he said quietly to Jill. "He's a killer."

"But the Senhora—"

"You stay back," the little man said again. He tugged at the Senhora's arm. "Come on, lady. Let's you and me get off the bus, okay? You and me. Let's go."

Jaspin watched, not daring to move.

The Senhora began to wail and howl. It was a high keening unearthly cry that might have been the song of Maguali-ga himself, an intense rising-and-falling screech, a terrifying sound that very likely could be heard all the way to San Francisco. The red-haired man shook her arm fiercely and said, "Cut that out!"

Then things began to happen very fast.

The curtain lifted and the Senhor appeared in the doorway looking dazed, as though he were still at least in part deep in his trance. For a long moment he stared in amazement at what was going on; then the awesome deep-freeze look came into his eyes, and he raised both his arms like Moses about to smash the tablets of the Ten Commandments, and he cried out unintelligible words in a colossal voice, as if trying to knock the intruder over by sheer decibel impact alone. In the same instant Jill sprang forward and attempted to pry the Senhora loose. The scratcher turned to her and in one quick unhesitating movement drew his spike across Jill's ribcage from side to side. There was a little flash of blue light and Jill went crashing back against the wall. Then the scratcher released Senhora Aglaibahi and lunged forward, trying to get past the Senhor. As he came up alongside him he paused, as if noticing for the first time the jeweled breastplate the Senhor was wearing. The scratcher yanked at it but the clasp held firm. The scratcher did not let go. He started up the middle of the bus toward the front exit, dragging the Senhor along by the breastplate.

Jaspin looked back at Jill. She lay crumpled and motionless, her arms and lets twisted into knots. The Senhora was in a heap on the other side of the bus, trembling, sobbing convulsively. The scratcher, pulling Senhor Papamacer with him, was halfway across the chapel now, heading toward the antechamber. Jaspin looked around for a weapon. The best thing he could find was the little statue of Maguali-ga. He snatched it up and ran toward the other end of the bus.

The Senhor and the scratcher had reached the driver's compartment of the bus. As Jaspin came toward them they stepped outside, onto the little platform that led down to ground level. There they halted, still struggling, the scratcher yanking and pulling on the breastplate, Senhor Papamacer booming out curses and pounding the scratcher with his fists, both of them in full view of the astonished crowd of the Senhor's followers.

Jaspin peered out into the surging rain-drenched mob. There was real hysteria out there now. He could hear them yelling, "Papamacer! Papamacer!" But no one went to the Senhor's aid. Jesus, Jaspin thought, where's the Host? They must see what's going on. Why don't they come help the

Senhor? Then he realized that it was impossible for anyone around the bus to move, they were all so tightly jammed. A human gridlock out there.

Then it's up to me, Jaspin told himself.

He lifted the statue of Maguali-ga like a club and maneuvered for an opening, trying to get into position to bring it down on the arm that held the spike. But the two of them were thrashing too wildly for him to be able to get a clear shot at the weapon.

Maybe now—now—

Jaspin swung the statue with all his force. It came down hard, but on the wrong arm, the one with which the scratcher was trying to pull Senhor Papamacer's breastplate loose. The scratcher grunted sharply and let go of the Senhor, who was slammed by his own momentum against the open door of the bus. Jaspin tried to push him back inside, but to his amazement Senhor Papamacer shook his head and rushed forward, seizing the scratcher by both his shoulders, pulling him around, shaking him furiously, showering him with what sounded like Brazilian obscenities. All the monstrous intensity of Senhor Papamacer's soul was pouring forth in a frenzied attack on this grubby stranger who dared to violate the holy sanctuary. The scratcher, blinking and gaping, did not seem to know what to do in the face of such an insane onslaught.

A couple of members of the Host were getting through the crowd, now. Jaspin saw them down below, ten, fifteen meters from the steps of the bus.

The scratcher saw them too. He brought his spike up in a sudden desperate swipe and jammed it against Senhor Papamacer's chest. There was another puff of blue light and the Senhor, arms and legs convulsing, sprang high into the air, fell back, dropped heavily to the ground. The scratcher, without pausing, jumped down beside him, made one last unsuccessful grab at the breastplate, then darted off to the

left, disappearing into the crowd just as Bacalhau and
Johnny Espingarda came running up.

Bacalhau knelt beside the Senhor. With trembling hands
he touched the Senhor's cheek, his forehead, his throat,
then looked up, and his face was the face of someone who
had seen the end of the world.

"He is dead," Bacalhau cried in a voice like thunder. "Is
dead, the Senhor."

And then everything went wild.

6

ELSZABET realized that somehow she had crossed from the
dormitory to the gymnasium, though she had no recollection
of having done it. Now she stood just at the edge of the little
rose garden outside the gym, numb, watching in disbelief as
the mob of tumbondé people tore the Center apart.

It was very much like a dream. Not a space dream, but
the ordinary sort of anxiety dream, she thought, the kind in
which it's the opening day of classes and you don't know
where the course you've registered for is supposed to meet,
or the kind in which you're trying to get from one side of a
crowded room to the other to speak to someone important,
and the air is thick as molasses, and you swim and swim
and swim and can't get anywhere.

These people, these cultists, were going to destroy everything. And there was nothing she could do about it. She
knew what she had to do: round up the patients, get them to

a safe place, if there was any such thing left. And find Tom before he carried out any more Crossings. But she was frozen where she stood. She felt paralyzed. She had tried to protect the Center and she had failed, and now it seemed too late to do anything. Except stand and watch.

It was getting very crazy out there now.

It had been bad enough at the beginning, when they were simply pouring in with their cars and vans and parking them all over the place, banging up against one another in a great screech of crumpling metal, and then getting out and running round and round until there was no room for anybody to move. But now it was much worse; now it had entered an entirely different and more frenzied phase.

The real trouble had started after that little black man in the strange costume had been killed on the steps of that multicolored bus right in the middle of everything. He must have been their leader, their prophet, Elszabet decided. She had seen the whole thing, just as she was coming out of the dorm to go in search of Tom. The little black man and the other one, the red-headed hoodlum who had accosted her earlier, coming out of the bus and fighting just outside it. The third man coming out of the bus waving that heavy wooden statuette around, trying to club the scratcher with it. And then the scratcher hitting the cult leader with his spike—that was when things had gone truly berserk.

In their grief and tumbondé people were ripping everything apart. They surged back and forth like the tides of a human ocean, crashing into cabins and knocking them off their foundations, pulling up bushes and shrubs, overturning their own vans. The craziness was feeding on itself: the rioters appeared to be trying to outdo each other in displays of rage and sorrow, and it looked as though even those who had no idea what had touched off the upsurge of violence were joining the rampage.

From her vantage point at the edge of the Center Elszabet had a view of almost everything that was happening. The

GHQ building seemed to be on fire, black smoke rising
from it in the rain. Down the other way the pick cabins were
being smashed to splinters—all that intricate and costly equipment, Elszabet thought sadly, everything so painstakingly matched
and calibrated, and all the files, all the records—and beyond
them she could just make out the staff cabins, her own cabin,
nestling in the woods, people swarming all over them, hurling
things out the windows, kicking in the walls, even tearing up
the ferns on the hillside just outside. Her books, her cubes, her
records, the little journal that she sometimes kept—everything
out in the mud by now, she supposed, trampled underfoot—

There was nothing she could do but watch. In ghostly
calmness she scanned the scene from north to south, from south
to north, strangely calm, paralyzed by shock and despair,
watching. Watching.

Then she caught sight of Tom. That was Tom over there,
surely. Yes. Appearing out of nowhere a little way uphill,
drifting past the far side of the dormitory building, going
around to the left. Down toward the middle of the madness.

Like everybody else he was flecked with mud and soaked to
the skin, clothing sticking to his spare fleshless body. And yet
he seemed uncaring of that, invulnerable to the weather, as if he
were surrounded by some invisible sphere of protection. He was
walking slowly, almost casually. He had a sort of entourage
with him: Father Christie, Alleluia, April, Tomás Menendez. They
were all holding hands, as though they were frolicking off to a
picnic in the forest, and they all seemed extraordinarily
serene.

I've got to go to them, Elszabet thought. April and the
others are in no shape to be left wandering around on their
own in this riot. And I've got to get him away from them
too. Before he helps any more of them make the Crossing.
Find them a safe place, she thought. And then take Tom and
put him somewhere safe too, where he can't harm anyone
and no one can do any harm to him.

But she made no move to leave the rose garden. Taking so much as a single step seemed impossible.

"Elszabet?" someone called.

She turned slowly. Bill Waldstein, flushed-looking, big smears of black mud all over his white clinical jacket.

"What are you doing out here?" he asked.

"Watching it. It's worse even than we imagined it could be."

"For Christ's sake, Elszabet. You look absolutely stupe-fied, do you know that? Where's April?"

Elszabet pointed vaguely toward the middle of the lawn.

"I left her with you," Waldstein said. "I was just going over to the infirmary to get a sedative for her. How could you leave her alone? Why did you come out here? What's the matter with you, Elszabet?"

She shrugged. "Look at what's going on."

"Come on, snap out of it. We need to round up the patients before they get hurt. And we need to find Tom and seal him away somewhere so he can't—"

"Tom?" she said. "Tom's right over there."

Waldstein peered into the dimness. "Jesus, yes. And April's with him, and Menendez, and Father Christie—" He stared at her. "You're just letting him waltz away with them like that? You know what he's likely to do to them?" Suddenly Waldstein looked as berserk as any of the tumbondé people. "I'm going to kill him, Elszabet. He's brought all this insanity down on us, with plenty more to come. He's got to be stopped. I'm going to kill him—"

"Bill, for God's sake—"

But Waldstein had already broken into a run. She watched him run across the swampy lawn, fall, scramble to his feet, fall again, scramble up. With agility he sidestepped a group of tumbondé people who were carrying what looked like pipes torn from some building's heating system, waving them around like baseball bats. He ran up toward Tom, shouting and gesturing. Elszabet saw Tom turn toward

Waldstein with a benign smile. She saw Waldstein leap at Tom and both men go sprawling. Then she saw Alleluia pluck Waldstein free of Tom the way one might pluck an insect from one's arm, and hurl him at least fifteen or twenty meters through the air, sending him crashing into the trunk of a towering pine.

Even at this distance, Elszabet plainly heard the sound of the impact as Waldstein struck the tree head first. He dropped without a quiver and lay without moving.

Dante Corelli came around the side of the gymnasium at a fast jog just at that moment and pulled up next to Elszabet. Elszabet turned to her and said almost in a conversational tone, "That was Bill, did you see? He jumped on Tom and Alleluia simply picked him up and—"

"Elszabet, we've got to get out of here. We're all going to get trampled to death."

"I think Bill must be dead, Dante. I heard the way his head hit the tree—"

"Dan's on his way down from GHQ. He'll be here in a minute and then the three of us are going to run for the woods, do you hear me, Elszabet? Look, there's a whole new mob charging up the hill right now. You see them coming? Holy Christ, do you see them?"

Elszabet nodded. Confusions gripped her spirit. She knew she was sinking deeper into that strange paralysis of the will. Simply paying attention to what was happening was an effort. A mob, Dante had said? Where? Yes. Oh, yes. There. They were streaming up out of the central chaos like some unstoppable torrent, overrunning everything in their way. They were heading toward the place where Tom and his little band of followers stood. "Oh, God," Elszabet murmured. "Tom. *Tom!*"

Father Christie went running forward to meet the tumbondé people, waving his arms, crying out to them. Offering a blessing, perhaps. The comfort of the Church in a time of chaos. They swept up and over him and he disappeared beneath their feet. Alleluia was next. She planted herself squarely in the path of the advancing mob and with astonishing energy that seemed almost diabolical began scooping them up and flinging them against the trees, one, five, a dozen of them, tossing them to their deaths, until she too was pulled down and was lost to view.

"Tom," Elszabet said quietly. She could no longer see him, or April, or Menendez.

She heard Dante saying to someone, "It's like she's gone out of her mind. She just stands here, watching."

"Hey. Elszabet." It was Dan Robinson. He touched her arm. "We have to get out while we still can, Elszabet. The Center's in ruins. The mob's completely out of control. We'll slip off into the forest and take the rhododendron trail, okay? We should be able to get deep enough in so they won't bother us there and—"

"I have to find Tom," Elszabet said.

"Tom's probably dead by now."

"Maybe he is, maybe he isn't. But if he's alive we have to find him. And find out what he is. There are things we have to know about him, about what he's doing, don't you see that? Please, Dan. Do you think I'm crazy? Yes, you do, both of you. I can see that. But I tell you, I've got to find Tom. Then we can leave. Not until then. Please try to understand. Please."

7

Tom held the fat woman with one hand and the Mexican man with the other and stood his ground calmly while the crazy people went rushing by. He knew they wouldn't hurt him. Not now, not while the Crossing was actually under way. He was safe because he was the chosen vehicle of the star people, and surely everyone knew that.

It was too bad, he thought, losing the priest and the artificial woman. Now they would never have a chance to make the Crossing. But even without them, it would still be possible for him to invoke the power. It was getting easier. With each new one he sent, his strength grew. A great tranquility was on his soul, a sense of the divine righteousness of his mission.

"Here," Tom said. "This is the next one that we'll send."

"Double Rainbow," the Mexican man said. "Yes, he is a good one. We will give him to Maguali-ga."

This one was an Indian. Tom realized that right away. He had seen a lot of Indians in his time. This one was a thick-bodied flat-nosed man with dark glossy hair, maybe a Navaho, maybe something else, but certainly an Indian. The Indian was standing with his back to a burning building, hurling clods of mud at the rioters as they ran by and calling out things to them in a language Tom didn't understand. The Mexican went up to the Indian and said something to him, and the Indian's eyebrows lifted and he laughed; and the Mexican said something else and the two men clapped each other on the back, and the Indian came striding over to Tom.

"Where you going to send me?" he asked.

"The Nine Suns. You will walk with the Sapiil."

"Will my fathers be there?"

"Your new fathers will welcome you into their number," said Tom

"The Sapiil," said the Indian. "What tribe is that?"

"Yours," said Tom. "From this moment on."

"You will go to Maguali-ga," said the Mexican. "You

will never know pain again, or sorrow, or the emptiness in the heart. Go with God, friend Nick. It is the happiest moment for you, now."

"Stand close around him," Tom said. "Everybody join hands."

"Maguali-ga, Maguali-ga," the Mexican said. The Indian nodded and smiled. There were tears in the corners of his eyes.

"Now," Tom said.

It was quick, a fast sudden surge and the big man slid easily to the ground and was gone.

Easier and easier all the time, Tom thought.

He led the fat woman and the Mexican past a place where a small building had been all broken up into slats, and started to go down toward the center of things, toward the bus that was sitting right in the middle. He thought he might sit on the steps of the bus and use that as a kind of platform for performing the Crossings. But he had gone only a few steps when a man and a woman came up to him. They looked pale and uneasy, and they were holding hands as if their lives depended on staying together. The woman was small and good-looking, with curling red hair and a pretty face. The man, who was slender and dark, had a bookish look about him.

The man pointed toward the Indian, who was lying in the mud with the smile of the Crossing on his face. "What did you do to him?"

"He has gone to Maguali-ga," Menendez said. "This man, he holds the power of the gods in his hands."

The man and the red-haired woman looked at each other.

The man said, "Is that what happened to the other man, the one in the dormitory?"

"He went to the Double Kingdom," Tom said. "I have sent some to Ellullimiilu today also, and some to live with the Eye People. The whole universe is open to us now."

"Send us to the Nine Suns!" the woman said.

"Lacy . . ." the man said.

"No, listen to me, Barry. This is real, I know it. They join hands and he sends you. You see the smiles on those faces? The spirit went out of him, you saw that. Where did it go? I bet it went to Maguali-ga."

"The man's dead, Lacy."

"The man has left his body behind. Listen, we stay here any longer, we'll get trampled to death anyway. You see how they're pulling the place apart since they saw the Senhor get killed? Let's do it, Barry. You said you had faith, that you had seen the truth. Well, here's the truth. Here's our moment, Barry. The Senhor had it upside down, that's all. The gods aren't coming to Earth, you see? We're supposed to go to *them*. And here's the man to send us."

"Come," Tom said. "Now."

"Barry?" the woman said.

The man looked stunned. He was afraid, untrusting. He blinked, he shook his head, he stared around. To help him, Tom sent him a vision, just the edge of one, the nine glorious suns in full blaze. The man drew in his breath sharply and pressed both his hands against his mouth and hunched his shoulders up, and then he seemed to relax. The woman said his name again and put her hand on his arm, and after a moment he nodded. "All right," he said quietly. "Yes. Why the hell not? This is what we were all looking for, wasn't it?" To Tom he said, "Where are we going to go?"

"The Sapiil kingdom," Tom said. "The empire of the Nine Suns."

"To Maguali-ga," said Menendez.

Tom reached for the hands of the fat woman and the Mexican. He rocked back and forth on his heels a moment.

"Now," he said.

Both at once, this time. He took the energy from the fat

woman and the Mexican and passed it through himself and
sent the man and the woman to the Sapiil. The ease of it
surprised him. He had never done that before, two at the
same time.

The man and the red-haired woman slid to the ground
and lay face up, smiling the wonderful Crossing-smile.
Tom knelt and lightly touched their cheeks. That was a
beautiful smile, that smile. He envied them, walking
now among the Sapiil under those nine glorious suns.
While he was still here slopping around in the mud. But
that was all right, Tom thought. He had his tasks to do
first.

He started down the hill again. All about him were people
screaming and shouting and waving their arms hysterically
in the air. "Peace to you all," Tom said. "It is the Time of
the Crossing, today, and everything is going well." But the
people came rushing past, confused and angry. For a moment Tom was swept up in the confusion, jostled and
buffeted, and when he was in the clear again he could no
longer see the fat woman and the Mexican. Well, he would
find them again sooner or later, he told himself. They knew
he was heading toward the bus, and they would go there to
wait for him, because they were his assistants in bringing
about the Crossing, they were part of the great event that
was unfolding here today in the rain and the mud and the
chaos.

Someone caught him by the arm, held him, stopped
him.

"Tom."

"Charley? You still here?"

"I told you. I was waiting for you. Now come on with
me. We got the van still sitting out there in the forest,
in the clearing. You got to get yourself away from here."

"Not now, Charley. Don't you understand that the Crossing is going on?"

"The Crossing?"

"Six, eight people have set out on the journey already. There will be many more. I feel the strength rising in me, Charley. This is the day I was born for."

"Tom—"

"You go to the van and wait for me there," Tom said. "I'll come to you in a little while and help you make your Crossing, as soon as I can find my people, my helpers. You'll be on the Green World an hour from now, I promise you that. Away from all this craziness, away from all this noise."

"Man, you don't understand. People are getting killed here. There are trampled bodies all over the place. Come on with me, man. It isn't safe for you here. You don't know how to look after yourself. I don't want to see anything happen to you, Tom, you know? You and me, we've traveled a long way together, and—I don't know, I just feel I ought to look after you." Charley took Tom's arm again and pulled gently. Tom felt the warmth of this man's soul, this scratcher, this wandering killer. He smiled. But he could not leave, not now. He peeled Charley's hand from his arm. Charley scowled and shook his head, and started to say something else.

Then the crazy mob came swirling back in their direction and Charley was borne away, carried off by the tide of humanity like a twig on the breast of a raging river.

Tom stepped out of their way and let them go thundering past. But he saw it was impossible to get to the bus now. Things were too wild down there in the middle of the lawn.

He thought he saw the fat woman off toward one side, and went off in her direction. But as he was clambering over the tumbled boards of some shattered little cabin he lost his footing on the slippery wood and slid downward into the shambles of planks and joists. For the moment he was stuck, his leg jammed deep down into it. There was a stirring in front of him and someone began to crawl out from the pile of wood.

Stidge, it was.

The red-haired man's eyes opened wide at the sight of Tom. "What the fuck. It's the looney. Hello, looney, you fucking troublemaker. How come Charley's not right there holding your hand?"

"He was here. He got swept away by the mob."

"That's too goddamn bad, isn't it?" Stidge said.

He laughed. He reached into his tattered jacket and drew out his spike. His eyes were gleaming like marbles by moonlight. He poked the tip of the spike against Tom's breastbone, hard, once, twice, three times, a sharp painful jab each time. "Hey," Stidge said "Got you where I want you, looney. Charley beat me up once on account of you, you remember? That first day, out in the Valley, when you came drifting in? He kicked the shit out of me because I laid a hand on you. I never forgot that. And then there were other times later, when I got in trouble on account of you, when Charley talked to me like I was nothing but a piece of crap. You know?"

"Put the spike away, Stidge. Help me get loose, will you?" He pushed at the timbers pinning his leg. "Poor Tom's foot is stuck. Poor Tom."

"Poor Tom, yeah. Poor fucking Tom."

"It's the day of the Crossing, Stidge. I've got work to do. I have to find my helpers and send people where they're meant to go."

"I'll send you where you were meant to go," Stidge said, and flicked the stud on the spike to turn on the power. "Just like I did to that crazy jig on the bus back there. For once I got you and no Charley around, and—"

"No," Tom said, as Stidge drew the spike back and jammed it toward Tom's chest.

He brought his hand up fast and seized Stidge's wrist, holding it steady for a moment, summoning all his strength to keep that deadly little strip of metal from touching him. He trembled against Stidge and for a long instant they struggled in stalemate. Then Stidge began forcing his arm forward, slowly, slowly, bringing the tip of the spike closer to Tom's chest. It took all that Tom had to hold that thing away from him. Stidge was pushing it closer and closer. Tom was shivering. Firey pain shot up and down his arm and into his chest. He looked into Stidge's hard glaring eyes, right up against his own.

And Tom picked up Stidge's soul and hurled it to Luiiliimeli.

He did it easily, smoothly, like skipping a stone across a pond. He did it all by himself, because he had to do it and his helpers were nowhere in sight. There was just no effort in it at all. He simply focused his energies and gathered the force and lifted Stidge's soul and threw it toward the heavens. Stidge stared at him in astonishment. Then the surprise went from his face and the Crossing-smile appeared, and the spike dropped from Stidge's dead hand, and he slumped down onto the pile of timbers.

Tom huddled over him, amazed, shaken, trembling, feeling sick to his stomach.

I did it all by myself, he thought.

It was just like killing him, he thought. I picked him up and threw him.

I never killed anybody before, he thought.

Then he thought, No, no, Stidge isn't dead, Stidge is on Luiiliimeli now, in the city of Meliluiilii under the great blue star Ellullimiilu. They have him and they'll heal him of all the sickness in his soul. It wasn't a killing any more than the other Crossings were. The only difference is that I did it all myself, that's all. And if I hadn't, he would have killed me sure as anything with that spike, and then there would be no more Crossings for anyone.

You understand that, Stidge? I didn't kill you, Stidge. I did you the biggest favor of your life.

Tom felt himself starting to calm down some. The queasiness left him. He probed at the scattered timbers, trying to get his foot free.

"Here. I'll help you."

It was the fat woman, climbing clumsily toward him. Her face was flushed, her eyes were strange. Her clothing was torn in two or three places. "Got my foot stuck somehow," Tom said. "Give me a hand—here—here—"

"That's the man who killed the other one outside the bus, isn't it?" she said. "Everybody was looking for him. He's dead, right?"

"He made the Crossing. I sent him to Luiiliimeli. I can do the Crossings without any help, now."

"I think this is the one that's holding you," she said. "Here." She wrenched a huge beam upward and tossed it aside. Tom pulled his leg free and rubbed his shin. She smiled at him. He felt the sadness coming from her, behind the smile.

He took her hand and said, "Where would you like me to send you?"

"What?"

"I can spare you now. I can give you your Crossing."

She jerked her hand free of his as if his touch were burning her. "No—please—"

"No?"

"I don't want to go anywhere."

"But this world is lost. There's nothing left here but pain and grief. I can send you to the Green World, or the Nine Suns, or the Sphere of Light—"

"It frightens me to think about that. It's like dying, isn't it? Or maybe worse." Her face grew panicky and she knelt and scrabbled around at her feet, grasping at the spike that had dropped from Stidge's hand. "I'm afraid. To start all over, to face a whole other world—no. No. I'd rather just die. You know?" The strangeness had gone from her eyes. She seemed to have come up out of some long tunnel into the open air. Her voice, which had always seemed to Tom like a little girl's voice, was a normal voice now. She was still talking. "I'm sick of being me. Carrying around this great awful body. Always afraid. Always crying." She was fumbling with the stud of the spike, trying to figure out how to use it. She didn't seem to know how. But then it began to glow and Tom realized she had turned it on after all. She was holding it between her breasts. Her hand was shaking.

"No," he said. He couldn't let her do that. He clamped his hand around her fleshy wrist and sent her to the Fifth Zygerone World.

As she dropped her body it fell with a terrible crash, landing beside Stidge. But she was smiling. She was smiling, that was the thing. Tom picked up the spike and switched it off and hurled it as far as he could, off into the shrubbery.

He crouched for a moment, catching his breath, getting his balance. He glanced at the two smiling bodies in front of him, thinking, It was like killing, but I didn't kill them, no, I just sent them away. Stidge would have killed me and she would have killed herself, and I couldn't let either of those things happen. So I did what I had to do. That's all. I did what I had to do. And this is the day of the Crossing, which is the most wonderful day in the history of the world.

He felt better now. He made his way carefully down from the fallen building. The riot was still going on. More buildings seemed to be burning. He looked straight ahead, through a clearing that had suddenly appeared, and saw the tall woman, the one who had been so kind to him, the doctor, the one who was called Elszabet, just across the way. She was staring at him.

Tom smiled at her. She seemed to be calling to him, beckoning him. He nodded and went to her.

8

"THERE he is," Elszabet said. "I've got to talk to him. Will you wait for me?"

She turned toward Dan Robinson, toward Dante. But at that moment a bunch of howling, screeching rioters swept through the place where they were standing, and when Elszabet looked again neither one was in sight. She thought she heard Dan's voice from far away, but she wasn't sure: the sound was lost in the wind and the screaming of the mob. Well, Tom was the one she wanted now.

He was standing by himself in front of the ruins of the staff recreation hall. Like a miracle, she thought, seeing him suddenly appear out of the chaos that way. How peaceful he looks, too. Probably he's been drifting around in all this craziness for hour after hour without even noticing what's going on.

"Tom?" she called.

He sauntered toward her. He seemed in no hurry at all. Looking beyond him, Elszabet saw a couple of figures sprawled on a pile of scattered timbers as though they were asleep. One was April. The other seemed to be the red-haired scratcher who had killed the cult leader on the steps of the bus. They lay motionless, not even stirring.

It seemed to Elszabet that she and Tom were the only two

people on the grounds of the Center just now. A sphere of silence appeared to surround them.

"It's Miss Elszabet," Tom said. He was smiling in a weird exalted way. "I was hoping I'd find you, Elszabet. Do you know what's been happening? This is the time I told you would come. When the Crossing begins to happen. As the Kusereen intended for us, all along."

"What did you do to Ed Ferguson?"

Still the strange smile. "I helped him make the Crossing."

"You killed him, is that what you're saying?"

"Hey! Hey, you sound angry!"

"You killed Ed Ferguson? Answer me, Tom."

"Killed? No. I guided him so that he would be able to drop his body. That's all I did. And then I sent him to Sapiil."

Elszabet felt a chill spreading along her arms and legs.

"And April?" she said. "You guided her the same way?"

"The fat woman, you mean? Yes, she's gone up there too, just a minute or two ago. And the Indian man. And Stidge there, when he tried to kill me. And I've sent a lot of others, all morning long."

She stared, not believing, not wanting to believe. "You killed all those people? My God . . . Nick, April, who else? Tell me, Tom, how many of my patients have you killed so far?"

"Killed?" He shook his head. "You keep saying killed. No. No, I haven't killed anybody. I've just been sending them, that's all."

"Sending them," Elszabet repeated in a flat voice.

"Sending them, yes. This is the day of the Crossing. At first I needed four helpers to do it. And then two. But now the power is very strong in me."

Elszabet's throat was dry and tight. There was a terrible pressure in her chest, a kind of silent shout fighting to escape. Ferguson, she thought. April. Nick Double Rainbow. All dead. And probably most of the others too. Her patients. Everyone she had tried to help. What had he done to them? Where were they now? She had never known such a crushing feeling of helplessness, of emptiness.

Quietly she said, "You've got to stop, Tom."

He looked amazed. "Stop? How can I stop? What are you talking about, Elszabet?"

"You can't do any more Crossings, Tom. That's all, you just can't. I forbid you. I won't let you. Do you understand what I'm saying? I'm responsible for these people—for all the patients here—"

He appeared not to comprehend. "But don't you want them to be happy, Elszabet? For the first time in their lives, *happy*?" That strange ecstatic smile, still. "How can I stop? It's what I was put on Earth to do."

"To kill people?"

"To heal people," Tom said. "Same as you. I never killed anyone, not even Stidge. The fat woman, she's happy now. And Ed. And the Indian. And Stidge, him too. And you . . . I can make you happy, right now." He leaned close to her and his smile grew even more intense. "I'll send you now, Elszabet. Okay? Okay? That's what you want, isn't it? Will you let me send you now?"

"Keep away."

"Don't say that. Here. Give me your hand, Elszabet. I'll send you to the Green World. I know that's where you want to be. I know that's where you could be happy. Not here. There's nothing for you here. The Green World, Elszabet."

He reached for her. She gasped and pulled back from him.

"Why are you afraid? It's the Time of the Crossing. I want so much to send you. Because . . . because . . ." He hesitated, fumbling for words, looking down at his feet. Color blazed in his cheeks. She saw tears beginning to glisten in his eyes. "I wouldn't hurt you." His voice was thick and hesitant. "Not you. Not ever. I wouldn't hurt anyone, but especially not you. I . . ." He faltered. "I love you, Elszabet. Let me send you. Please?"

"But I don't want—" she started to say, and broke off in midsentence as a powerful wave of dizziness and numbness swept over her. She struggled for breath. Something had happened. His words, his tears, the wind, the rain, everything all at once came rushing in on her, sweeping her away. She felt herself swaying, the way so many times she had swayed when an earthquake went rumbling through the ground beneath her, that old familiar sensation of sudden astonishing motion, the world slipping loose from its moorings.

A great abyss was opening before her, and Tom was inviting her to jump. She caught her breath and stared bewilderedly at him, appalled and tempted, and appalled at how tempted she was.

"Please?" he said again.

There was a roaring in her ears. Make the Crossing? Drop the body? Let him do to her what he had done to Ferguson, to April, to Nick? Give him her hand, let him do his trick, topple at his feet, lie here dead and smiling in the mud?

No. No. No. No.

It was crazy. All this talk of other worlds, instantaneous journeys. How could any of it be real? When Tom *sent* people, they died. He had a power, a deadly one. They died. That must be what happens to them, right? Right? She didn't want to die. That hadn't ever been what she wanted. She wanted to live, to flourish, to open, to blossom. She wanted to feel some peace in her soul, just for once in her life. But not to die. Dying wasn't any kind of answer.

And yet—and yet—what if what Tom offered wasn't death at all, but *life,* new life, a second chance?

She felt an overwhelming pull, an irresistible temptation— the Green World, that wondrous place of joy and beauty, so vivid, so real. How could it not be real? The Project

Starprobe photographs—the smile on Ed Ferguson's face—
that sense of absolute conviction and faith that Tom radiated—
  —So why not, why not, why not?
  "All right. I'm not afraid," she heard herself saying.
  "Then give me your hand. This is the time. I'll help you
make your Crossing now, Elszabet."
  She nodded. It was like something happening in a dream.
Just give him your hand, and let him send you to the Green
World. Just yield, and float upward, and go. Yes. Yes. Why
not? She thought of Ed Ferguson's smile. Could there be
any doubt? Tom had the power. The sky was breaking open,
and all barriers were down. Suddenly she felt the closeness
of that silent dark immensity that was interstellar space, just
beyond the low heavy clouds, and it was not at all terrifying. Give him your hand, Elszabet. Let him send you. Go.
Go. This poor tired world, this poor ruined place: why stay?
Everything's done for. Just say good-bye to the world and
go. Look what's happened to the Center. That was the last
sanctuary, and now it's gone too. You have no one left to
care for here any more.
  "You were so very good to me, you know," Tom was
saying. "There wasn't anyone was ever that good to me
before. You took me in, you gave me a place to stay, you
talked to me, you *listened* to me. You listened to me.
Everybody thinks I'm crazy, and that's all right, because
most people like to leave a crazy man alone. I was safer that
way. But you knew I wasn't crazy, didn't you? You know it
now. And now I'm going to give you what you want the
most. Put your hand in mine. Will you do that, Elszabet?"
  "Yes. Yes."
  She reached her hand toward his waiting hand.
  She heard someone calling her name in a peculiarly
desperate way, raggedly punching out the syllables, *El Sza
Bet, El Sza Bet*. The strange hypnotic moment was broken.
She pulled her hand back from Tom and looked around. Dan

Robinson came trotting up. He appeared exhausted, almost ready to collapse.

"Dan?" she said.

He glanced at Tom casually, without interest, almost as though he had not recognized him. To Elszabet he said in a dull toneless voice, "We should have cleared out an hour ago. There's shooting going on now. They've got guns, lasers, God knows what. They've all gone nuts since their leader was murdered."

"Dan—"

"Every way out of here is blocked. We're all going to die."

"No," she said. "There's still one way out."

"I don't understand."

She indicated Tom. "The Crossing," she said. "Tom will send us away from here. To the Green World."

Robinson stared.

"This place is done for," Elszabet said. "The Center, California, the United States, the whole world. We blew it, Dan. We got in our own way, we tripped flat on our face, we fouled our own nest. Everything's gone crazy. How long do you think it will be before they start dropping the hot dust again? Or the bombs, maybe, this time? But that's only going to happen here, on Earth. Out there everything will be different."

He was gasping. "You're serious, aren't you?"

"Absolutely serious, Dan."

"Incredible. You think you can go to some other world, just like that?"

"Ferguson did. April. Nick."

"This is completely insane."

"You can see the smiles on their faces. It's pure bliss. I know they've gone to the star worlds, Dan."

Robinson turned to Tom and studied him in astonishment. Tom was smiling, nodding, beaming.

"You actually believe this, Elszabet. He snaps his fingers, and off you go?"

"Yes."

"And even if it's true? You can just drop everything, run out on all responsibilities, skip off to your Green World? You could do that?"

"What responsibilities? The Center's been smashed, Dan. And if we stay here we're going to get killed in this riot anyway. You said so yourself two minutes ago, remember?"

He looked at her; he seemed bewildered.

"I've thought it through," she said. "Even if we could get away from this mob I don't want to stay here any more. It's all over for me here. I did my best, Dan. I tried, I honestly tried. But it's all smashed. Now I want to go away and make a second start somewhere else. Doesn't that make sense? Tom will send us to the Green World."

"Us?"

"Us, yes. You and me. We'll go there together. Here, put your hands in his. Just do it, Dan. Go on. Put your hands in his."

Robinson stepped back and thrust his hands behind him as if she had tried to pour burning oil on them. His eyes were bright. "For Christ's sake, Elszabet!"

"No. For our sakes."

"Forget all this nonsense. Look, maybe we can still escape through the forest somehow. Come with me—"

"You come with me, Dan."

Again she reached for him. He pulled farther back. He was shivering, and his skin had taken on an almost yellowish tinge.

"We don't have any more time, Elszabet. Come on. The three of us, out the back way down the rhododendron trail—"

"If that's what you want to do, Dan, you'd better go."

"Not without you."

"Don't be absurd. Go."

"I can't leave you here to die."

"I won't die. But you might, if you don't get going now. I wish you well, Dan. Maybe I'll see you again someday. On the Green World."

"Elszabet!"

"You think I'm absolutely crazy, don't you?"

He shook his head and scowled, and reached for her as if to drag her off by force into the forest. But he couldn't bring himself to touch her. His hands hovered in mid-air and halted there, as though he feared that any direct contact with her might somehow hurl the two of them careening off toward the stars. For a moment he stood frozen in silence. He opened his mouth and no words came out, only a muffled sob. He leaned close and gave her one last look, then turned and darted away between two of the shattered buildings and was lost to her sight.

"All right, then," Tom said. "Are you ready to go now, Elszabet?"

"Yes," she said. And then she said, "No. No—"

"But you were ready a moment ago."

She waved him back. The roaring in her ears had returned, even louder this time. She peered into the rainswept dimness, trying to see Dan Robinson. But he was gone. "Let me think," she said. Tom began to say something, and she gestured again, more urgently. "Let me *think*, Tom."

You actually believe this, Dan had said. *He snaps his fingers, and off you go?*

I don't know, Elszabet thought. Do I actually believe it?

And then Dan had said, *You can just drop everything, run out on all responsibilities, skip off to your Green World?*

I'm not sure, she thought. Can I do that? Can I?

Tom was watching her, saying nothing, letting her think. She stood wavering, lost in doubts.

Do I believe? Yes, she thought. Yes, because there is no real alternative. I believe because I *have* to believe.

And can I shrug off my responsibilities here and go? Yes, my responsibilities here are ended. The Center has been destroyed. My patients are gone. There's no work left here for me to do.

She scanned the distance once again for Dan Robinson. It would have been so beautiful, she thought, if he had come with her. The two of them, starting their lives over on the Green World. Learning to live again, learning to love. It would have worked, she thought. Wouldn't it? Wouldn't it? But instead he had run off into the forest. All right. It that's what he needs to do, let him do it. He doesn't understand. His Time hasn't come, not yet.

"I think you're ready now," Tom said.

Elszabet nodded. "Let's both of us go, Tom. You and me together, to the Green World. Wouldn't that be a fine thing? We'd both be crystallines together, and we'd stroll down to the Summer Palace and we could laugh and talk about this day, all the rain, the mud everywhere, the craziness all around us. Yes? Yes? What do you say? When you send me, send yourself along, too. Will you?"

Tom was silent a long time.

"I wish I could," he said at last, softly, tenderly. "You know, right now that's the one thing I want more than anything. To go to the Green World with you, Elszabet. I wish I could. I wish I could."

"Then *do* it, Tom."

"I can't go," he said. "I have to stay here. But at least I can help you. Here, give me your hands."

Once more he reached for her. She was shaking all over. But this time she didn't pull back. She was ready. She knew it was right.

"Good-bye, Elszabet. And—hey, thanks for listening to me, you know?" His voice was very gentle, and there was a note in it that was close to being mournful, but not really.

"That meant a lot to me," he said. "When I'd go to your office, you'd listen to me. Nobody ever did that, really, except Charley, some of the time, and that was different, with Charley. Charley isn't like you."

How sad, she thought. I can go and Tom, who has done all this for us, has to stay.

"Come with me," she said.

"I can't," he said. "You have to go without me. Is that all right?"

"Yes. All right."

"Now," he said.

He gripped both her hands. Elszabet drew her breath in deeply, and waited. A sense of happiness, and grace, welled up in her. She was wondrously calm and certain. She had done her best here, but now it truly was time to leave. A new life would be beginning for her on a new world. It seemed to her that she had never known such certainty before.

She felt a sudden moment of new tension, a tension she had never before experienced, a sort of suspension of the soul; and then came a release. The last thing she saw was Tom's taut stricken face, full of desperate love for her. Then the greenness rose up about her like a fountain of joyous light, and she felt herself setting forth, beginning the wondrous voyage outward.

9

It looked like a battlefield now. The rain was coming down harder than ever, and the lawns and gardens and meadows were churned into a great sea of muck, and all the buildings were smashed or burning or both. Some people were wandering about like blind men, staggering in the storm, and some were hunkered down behind the cars and buses, shooting at each other. Tom took a last look at the smiling woman lying at his feet, and walked away, still hearing Elszabet's voice saying, "Come with me," and his own, "I can't, I can't, I can't."

How could he have gone now, with the Crossing only begun?

He wondered if he were ever going to get to go at all. There were so many to send, and he was the only one with the power, wasn't he? Maybe he could teach others, somehow. But even so—there were so many who had to go. And he thought again, as he so often had before, of Moses, leading his people to the promised land and peering into it from the outside, and the Lord saying to him, I have caused thee to see it with thine eyes, but thou shalt not go over thither. Was that what was going to happen to him?

Tom looked up toward the sky, trying to pierce through the clouds to the stars. Those golden empires, waiting. Those godlike beings. Those shining cities, millions of years old.

You out there, you Kusereen who planned all this . . . is that your plan, to use me only as the instrument, the vehicle, and then leave me behind when the world ends?

He couldn't believe that was so. He didn't want to. They'd come for him right at the end. They had to, when all the others had made the Crossing. But maybe not. Maybe they'd just leave him here all by himself. How could he presume to understand the Kusereen? Well, he thought, if that's what it is, that's what it is. I'll only find out when the time comes.

Meanwhile there's work to do.

Charley came up to him, shrouded in mud.

"There you are," he said. "I didn't think I'd ever find you again."

Tom smiled. "You ready for your Crossing now, Charley?"

"You really doing it? Sending people? To the Green World and all?"

"That's right," Tom said. "I been sending them all morning. To different worlds, Green World, Nine Suns, all of them. I even sent Stidge. He pulled his spike on me, and I sent him."

Charley was staring. "You sent him, did you? Where'd he go?"

"Luiiliimeli."

"Loollymooly. Good old Loollymooly. I hope he's happy there. That goddamn Stidge. Going to live on Loollymooly." Charley laughed. He looked somewhere past Tom. He seemed to be lost for a moment in his own dreams of other worlds.

Then he focused his attention again and said in a different voice, businesslike and quick, "Okay, let's get the hell out of here, Tom."

"I can't, not yet. I got a few more things to do first—"

"Christ. Christ, Tom, what's wrong with you? Let's go find the van and start moving. Before one of these crazies takes us out. Can't you see? They're shooting at each other all over the place."

"Don't you want to make the Crossing, Charley?"

"Thanks all the same," Charley said. "That's not what I've got in mind right now."

"I'll give you the Green World for sure."

"Thanks all the same," Charley said again. And then he said something else, but Tom wasn't able to make it out. All this noise, the shouting, the drumming of the rain. The crowd came surging by again and Charley was swept away. Tom shrugged. Well, maybe it wasn't Charley's time yet. He wandered on. Around him, people were slipping and sliding and falling down everywhere. Now and then someone turned toward him with what seemed an appeal in his eyes, and Tom would touch him and send him to one of the welcoming worlds. After a while he saw another familiar face come looming up out of the confusion, a man with rough pitted skin, hard blue eyes. "Hello, Buffalo," Tom said. "How's it going?"

"Tom. Hey. That's Charley over there, isn't it?"

Tom turned. For a moment he caught a glimpse of Charley once more, trying to shove his way through seven or eight frantic people. "Yeah," Tom said. "That's Charley. I was with him before but we got separated. Look, here he comes."

Charley burst through the crowd and ran up to them, breathing hard, face shiny with rain and exertion. "Hey, Buffalo," he said, "Christ, am I glad to see you."

"Charley. Hey. Who else's around?"

"Nobody. There's none of us left but you and me. Maybe Mujer, I'm not sure. Let's go look for the van, okay? We got to get ourselves the hell away from this place."

"You bet," Buffalo said.

"And you, Tom?" Charley said. "You come with us. We'll ride away south, just like we talked about."

Tom nodded. "Maybe in a little while, a few hours."

"We're going now," Charley said. "Staying here any more is crazy."

"Then you go without me."

"For Christ's sake—"

"I got to stay a few more hours," Tom said. "People here, they need me. I can't go yet. In a little while, sure. Maybe by dark." Yes, he thought, maybe by dark. By then he would have done all that he needed to do here, and he could move along. He had made friends here and he had sent them to the stars. Now he would send some of these other people, the ones who had followed the little black man from San Diego, the taxi driver. And then he'd find Charley and Buffalo and ride off with them. He'd go somewhere else. Make other friends. Send them too. "You go find the van," Tom said. "That'll take you a little while. Later on, maybe, I'll go back there in the woods and catch up with you, okay? Okay?"

He looked through and past them and it seemed to him that he could see Elszabet over there. Smiling. Come with me, she had said. I can't, he had said. Okay. Whatever. Poor Tom. He could hardly bear to think about her. Wherever she was now. Green World, that was it. At least he had told her he loved her. At least he had managed to say that much. Come with me, that was what she had said. When he thought about that, what she had said, he felt like crying. But he couldn't allow himself that. He didn't have time to cry today. Maybe later. There was too much work to do. Walk down there where all those people were, touch them, help them to go. Elszabet glowed in his mind with the brightness of a new sun. Come with me, come with me. I can't, he had said. He shook his head.

Charley and Buffalo were still standing there, staring at him. "You really going to stay?" Charley asked.

"Only for a few more hours," he said again, very softly. "Then maybe I'll catch up with you. You go look for the van. Okay, Charley? You go look for the van."

10

It seemed to Dan Robinson that he had been running for hours: on and on in effortless strides, his heart pumping like some sort of untiring machine, his legs driving him over the sodden ground. It was the anger, he knew, that kept him going this way. He boiled with a rage so intense that he could contain it only by this blind, furious flight into the forest. Bizarre lunacy loose in the world, the Center in ruins, Elszabet gone . . . Elszabet gone . . .

Here, put your hands in his, she had said. *Just trust me and do it, Dan. Go on. Put your hands in his.*

He had no idea where he was. By now he might be at the far side of the forest, or perhaps he had just been going around in circles, crossing and recrossing his own trail. There were no landmarks here. One huge redwood looked just like the next. The sky, what little he could see of it through the tops of the giant trees, was dark now. But whether that was because evening was coming on, or simply an effect of the deepening storm, he couldn't say.

He knew he wouldn't be able to run much longer. But he was afraid to stop. If he stopped, he might have to think. And there was too much that he didn't want to think about right now.

Tom will send us to the Green World, she had said. *You and me. We'll go there together.* She had seemed so calm, so sure of herself. That was the worst of it, her calmness. He could still hear her saying, *Now I just want to go away and make a second start somewhere else. Doesn't that make sense? Tom will send us to the Green World.* She had been beyond his reach at that moment. He had come close to snapping, seeing her like that. All he could do was turn and run from her; and he had not yet stopped running.

Suddenly there was a sound in his mind like the distant roaring of the sea. Flickering shafts of green light danced in the depths of him. So there was no escape from the visions, even out here. He was still infected with the general madness.

No, he thought. Get out of my head!

Tom will send us to the Green World, she had said. *You and me.*

Robinson wondered if he might have been able to keep her from doing it, if he had stayed beside her. Tried to reason with her. Dragged her away from Tom by force, if necessary. No, damn it. He couldn't have done any of that. She had made up her mind. She had yielded completely. Maybe, he thought, it was seeing the mob smash the Center to bits that had sent her over the brink. He had wanted to take her by the shoulders and shake her. To tell her that it was suicidal craziness, giving herself over to whatever power Tom had—to put her hands in his, and fall down dead with that blissful damn smile on her face.

The sea-sound grew more intense: a surging, a crashing. The air was becoming heavy about him, a thick green blanket. He heard far-off, faint, tinkling, silvery needles of sound.

He felt the tip of his shoe snag against the exposed snaky root of a colossal redwood, and he lurched and went spinning and hurtling toward the ground. Struggling for balance, arms flailing as he skidded and stumbled, the best he could do was pull his head in and try to roll with the fall as his feet went out from under him and he landed hard on his left shoulder and hip.

For a moment he lay there, stunned, face down, arms spread wide, his cheek in a cold puddle. He made no attempt to get up. For the first time now he felt the exhaustion of his long run through the rain: chills, muscular spasms, waves of nausea. The green light grew brighter in his mind. Nothing he could do could hold back that onrushing vision. The green sky, the fleecy fog, that intricate music, those shining pavilions—

"*Get out of my head . . .*" It was a harsh, despairing sound as he pounded his fist against the rain-soaked ground.

He saw the crystalline figures moving delicately across

that flawless green landscape. The long slim bodies, the glittering faceted eyes, the slender limbs bright as mirrors. Those princes and dukes, those lords and ladies. Dan remembered how eager he had been to have his first space dream, how he had longed to have these visions flood his mind, how exciting it was when at last one had come to him. Running late at night across to Elszabet's cabin like a schoolboy to tell her all about it. Now he wanted nothing more than to be rid of it. Please, he thought. Go away. Please. *Go away* . . .

They were talking to him. Telling him their names . . . we are the Misilyne Triad, they were saying, and we are the Suminoors, and we are the Gaarinar, and we—

"*No*," he said. "I don't want to know anything about you. Whatever you are. You're phantoms, hallucinations."

We love you, they said. That eerie whispering sound echoing through his mind.

He didn't want their love. He was choking with fury, and despair.

Someone you know is among us, they said.

"I don't care," he told them sullenly, almost petulantly.

She wants to talk to you, they said.

He lay there quietly, cold, wet, numb, feeling lost. But then he heard a different sort of music, richer and deeper and warmer, and a new voice, delicate and tinkling and silvery like theirs, yet somehow less alien than the others, calling out his name across the great gulf of space. He looked up in amazement. He knew that voice. Beyond any doubt he knew that voice. So she got there after all, he told himself. He could feel the wonder blossom and grow within him. She actually got there. And that changes everything, doesn't it? He didn't dare move. Had he really heard it? Again, he thought. Please, again. And then came her voice in his mind once more. Calling to him again. Yes, he knew it was real. And at the sound of that voice he felt all resistance begin to leave him, and his anger and his fear and his sorrow dropping from him like a cast-off cloak. And he got up, wondering if there still was time to find Tom somewhere back in that madness, and began slowly to walk through the rain toward the bright green light that blazed before him in the heavens.